Three Story House

ALSO BY COURTNEY MILLER SANTO

The Roots of the Olive Tree

Three Story House

Courtney Miller Santo

An Imprint of HarperCollinsPublishers

THREE STORY HOUSE. Copyright © 2014 by Courtney Miller Santo. All rights reserved. Printed in the United States of America. No part of this book may be used or reproduced in any manner whatsoever without written permission except in the case of brief quotations embodied in critical articles and reviews. For information address HarperCollins Publishers, 195 Broadway, New York, NY 10007.

HarperCollins books may be purchased for educational, business, or sales promotional use. For information, please e-mail the Special Markets Department at SPsales@harpercollins.com.

FIRST HARPERLUXE EDITION

HarperLuxe™ is a trademark of HarperCollins Publishers

Library of Congress Cataloging-in-Publication Data is available upon request.

ISBN: 978-0-06-234429-8

14 ID/RRD 10 9 8 7 6 5 4 3 2 1

For my twenty-nine cousins who somehow manage to be the least alike and most alike of any group of people I know. Thank you for teaching me that chaos can be beautiful and that it isn't a holiday unless two dozen people show up and eat every last scoop of mashed potatoes.

Three Story House

First Story
Lizzie

1993: Old Silver Beach, Massachusetts

As the only child of an only child, Lizzie Linwood had never given much thought to cousins. Before her first summer in Massachusetts, cousins had been an abstraction, like Turkish Delight, which, after having read about it earlier that year, she'd decided must be the sort of candy that the children of royals ate. From the backseat, she grabbed a few grapes out of the container her mother had wedged between the two front seats. According to her mother's new husband, she now had dozens of first cousins and too many second cousins to count. She looked at Jim, who'd driven the overnight leg of the trip and was sleeping with his head on the window glass and his knees wedged against the dashboard. At rest he looked different, less pinched around the eyes and mouth.

"Not too many," her mother said. "Jim's family is planning on a clam bake right after we get there."

Lizzie ignored her mother and ate several more grapes. "How much longer?"

"Stop asking." Her mother readjusted her grip on the steering wheel. The car was fairly new, chosen because of its gas mileage, but it rattled on the inside so that much of what they'd said since leaving Memphis the day before had been yelled over the hum of the road.

"Is it more than an hour?" Lizzie worked her fingernail under the skin of the last of the grapes and peeled it.

"Read your book."

"What do you think they'll be like?" Of all the new relatives Jim had listed off, Lizzie had been most interested in the two cousins born improbably the same month and year as herself.

"Who?" Her mother leaned closer to the steering wheel, squinting at a road sign.

"The two," Lizzie didn't want to finish. It felt unlucky to ask about them.

"Elyse and Isobel? Everyone will be nice, like Jim."

Lizzie sighed. After almost twenty hours in the car, the backseat had begun to feel small to Lizzie. She picked up the third book of the Narnia chronicles and stretched out, putting her socked feet on the window and using her soccer ball as a pillow to get just the right reading angle. The introduction of Eustace bothered her. She'd wanted all of the books to be mostly about Lucy, but instead there were pages and pages about their priggish cousin. Letting the book fall against her chest, she looked at Jim. Those first hours in the car, he'd tried to explain his family by naming his brothers, their wives, the aunts and uncles, and the cousins, who were all connected by blood back to a woman who was too old to be alive who lived thousands of miles away in the middle of an olive grove. She didn't trust her mother's opinion about the cousins and wanted to wake Jim and ask him again about the cousins, but she couldn't quite form the right question.

It was, after all, too much, too fast. Jim had shown up after Christmas, and by the time Lizzie had finished second grade, he'd gotten married to her mother and moved them out of her grandmother's house, where they'd always lived, into a sprawling ranch house that was so new it still smelled like paint and sawdust when they moved in. It wasn't that she didn't like him. She did, but she worried that Jim would act different with family. So far, being around him made her feel like that time her class went on a field trip to see how guitars were made and her teacher kept yelling at them to keep their hands in their pockets and not touch anything. Her stepfather kept his hands in his pockets around her.

The car slowed as they left the highway. Jim cleared his throat and sat up. Lizzie closed her eyes and pretended to be asleep. She felt him looking at her and then watched under her lashes as he took her mother's hand. "It'll be wonderful," he said.

"It's been just us for so long," her mother said. "And before that it was just me and my mother."

"Family isn't about numbers."

Her stepfather kept talking, but in an adult voice kept low and indistinct. She let her eyes close on their own, the lids like weights against her eyes. In the darkness, Lizzie's mind conjured the instashark Jim had given her for her birthday a few months earlier. It had started out the size of her hand, but after three days in a plastic pool in their new backyard, the creature had grown nearly as large as Lizzie. *Instafamily.* Her eyes flew open as the car slowed for a turn and moved from the smooth asphalt of the road to a gravel driveway. Falling asleep was like time travel. An instant earlier she'd had an hour to prepare to meet them, and now she had just seconds.

"They're all out front," her mother said, tapping on the brakes to slow the car even more. "There are so many of them."

"That's not even everyone," Jim said, rolling down his window and leaning out to wave at the group of people gathered in front of the large house.

"It's enough." Her mother pulled into the driveway in front of the house and turned off the engine. Lizzie watched them get out of the car. Jim slid his arm around her mother's shoulders, and before he could introduce her, she was swallowed up by hugs and kisses from the half dozen adults who'd been waiting out front for their arrival.

Putting on her tennis shoes, Lizzie looked around at the children. Some of them were too young to walk on their own and were being held by their parents. She cracked open the far door, the one away from the chaos, and stepped out. She searched the swarm of bodies, looking for anyone who could be close to her age, worrying that being the same age wouldn't be enough to be liked by her new cousins. Jim had promised that they were excited to meet her, but Lizzie knew how adults were with children: they never understood that kids, like adults, didn't always get along. She tried to catch her mother's eye without calling out for her, and just as she closed the door, she felt a hand slide into hers.

"Come on. If we leave now, we'll get out of helping to carry stuff down to the beach."

The hand was clammy, and as she grasped it, Lizzie felt the short, jagged fingernails and the torn skin around the cuticles. A second girl wrapped her arm around Lizzie's waist.

"Stay low until we're in the clear."

As the three of them crept behind the car and then dashed for a clutch of bushes that lined the property, Lizzie tried to figure out who was who. The first girl, the one with the clammy hands, held herself with a confidence that was beyond her years. She wore red-framed glasses that kept sliding down her nose because of the heavy lenses. The other girl was rounder and softer with wide eyes and skin as perfect as a doll's.

"Run," said the girl with the glasses.

The three of them took off, and Lizzie, who'd always been fast, kept herself right at their heels. After a few moments, they slowed, looking back over their shoulders. The shorter girl, with bangs so long they fell into her eyes, offered Lizzie a sticky gumball from the pocket of her sundress and then introduced herself as Elyse. "You like gum?"

"Everyone likes gum," said the other girl, who Lizzie decided must be Isobel.

"I should have told my mom we were going," Lizzie said.

"Your mom won't care," Elyse adjusted her dress and smoothed her hair. "You're eight, right? That's how old you have to be to go to the beach without an adult."

Lizzie reached for the gumball—it tasted like marshmallows. Back home, she wasn't allowed to chew gum. She blew a large bubble and when it popped, she nodded in agreement, marveling that neither of her new cousins wore shoes. During the four- or five-block walk to the beach, Elyse and Isobel talked back and forth, finishing each other's sentences and occasionally breaking out into a rhythmic snap, clap, stomp motion and then calling out "whoomp there it is." They tried to teach Lizzie the pattern as they walked. Being with them felt familiar and gave her shivers of anticipation, like when her mother started a story with "a long time ago."

"That's the Robinsons' place. They don't like kids," Elyse said as they passed the stone façade of a house.

"Last year they called the police on my brother," Isobel said. "For shortcutting their yard."

"Grandma said Ms. Robinson's just mad cuz her husband asked for a divorce."

Where the asphalt turned to gravel, they stopped and did three rounds of the there-it-is dance, which Lizzie had figured out by then, and finished by hopping around on one foot three times in a circle before calling out "whoomp." For no reason, Lizzie giggled.

"You have to tell the guard you're local," Isobel said, waving at the man sitting on a slowly turning stool in the small gatehouse at the edge of the parking lot.

"Your mom is wicked pretty," Elyse said, drawing her long, wild hair over her face, reminding Lizzie of the crepe myrtles in Memphis and the way their bark peeled off in long dark curled strands.

"Wicked," she said under her breath, trying out the slang.

"My mom's mad that she's so pretty," Isobel said. "Said she didn't look ten years older than Uncle Jim."

"Don't be a chucklehead." Elyse flicked Isobel on the arm. "Mom also said you like soccer."

Lizzie shrugged. She loved soccer but wasn't sure how to explain that to her new cousins.

"We'll all be good at different things then," Isobel said. "I like to sing and Elyse likes to draw. You can be good at sports. We all like the color blue. That's what we have in common—oh and our birthdays and the pact we made to never cut our hair."

Elyse reached out and ran her fingers through Lizzie's tangled blond strands. "Uncle Jim says now we're like Charlie's angels. He used to call us double trouble. But he'll probably give us a new nickname now that there are three of us."

"You'll like Uncle Jim," Isobel said, picking at a scab on her elbow until it started to bleed. She put the scab itself in the pocket of her overalls. "He makes pancakes and digs moats. Everyone thinks he should move back here, but Dad says you go where the jobs are."

Lizzie listened to them but couldn't find voice enough to add to the conversation. They seemed older than her friends in Memphis. More like fourth graders. The beach, with its beauty and vastness, made her want to cry out. She felt her heart constrict and then explode in an expression of joy at the sight of the white sand in a curving crescent shape and the marine blue of the bay. A creek bordered by a rock wall divided the beach in half. Visible about ten yards from the beach was a sandbar where dozens of people in brightly colored swimsuits played.

"We're on this side," Isobel called, when Lizzie started walking the wrong way.

"They divided it so that residents get one side and out-of-towners the other." Elyse pointed: "No point in making friends with the kids on that side of the jetty. You have to be here, on the beach where everyone belongs."

As her cousin spoke, Lizzie became aware of how different the word "beach" sounded when Elyse said it.

Lizzie liked the way she talked. It reminded her of the time a girl from the middle of nowhere Mississippi had moved into her school. How that new girl had swallowed and meted out her words had been music to Lizzie.

It made her even more self-conscious about speaking, knowing that to her cousins' ears, her Southern accent would sound as foreign. Elyse waved to a group of women hovering over a beach fire and several pots that Lizzie figured would soon be the clam bake she'd been told about. "My mom is over there," she said, gesturing toward an apple-shaped woman who laughed so hard she jiggled.

Isobel unhooked the latches of her overalls and let them fall to the sand. "Watch what I can do," she called, throwing her clothes and glasses toward Elyse's mother.

Elyse sighed and picked up the scattered items, shrugging out of her sundress and dropping the pile of clothing on the edge of her mother's towel. Her hands lingered for a moment, covering her body as if she were embarrassed at her chubbiness. Lizzie shaded her eyes against the sun and watched Isobel turning perfect cartwheels in the sand. "Go on," Elyse's mother said. "They won't bite."

Isobel, looking over her shoulder, issued a challenge to Lizzie and Elyse. "Last one to the sandbar wears the seaweed."

Without thinking, Lizzie took off at full speed.

Behind her, she heard Elyse's mom talking. "There she goes now. It'll be fine."

Lizzie liked to run. Her feet plunged into the shallow water without stopping and she laughed as she kicked up water into her face, delighted to taste the salt of it. She mostly swam in chlorinated pools in Memphis. The Mississippi, muddy and full of mysterious whorls, remained off-limits. She beat her cousins by ten yards and after they'd recovered their breath, Isobel plaited a crown from lengths of seaweed and eelgrass that she pulled from the floor of the ocean and set it atop Elyse's head.

"I always wear the seaweed," Elyse said.

Lizzie put her hand over her mouth to keep the words from coming out. She was afraid they'd be the wrong words.

"Do you talk?" Isobel asked. "You haven't said one word to us. Nobody told us you didn't talk. They said you were tall for your age."

"She talks," Elyse said, turning to Lizzie.

"I don't have a bathing suit," Lizzie said, looking down to see that the cuffs of her jean shorts were damp.

"Nobody cares about that, silly," Elyse said, pulling the hem of Lizzie's oversized T-shirt and tying it into a knot at the waist. "There. Just roll your shorts up some more and you'll be fine."

From the shore, Elyse's mother waved at them and yelled at them not to go out any farther. Lizzie saw her own mother and Jim walking toward the clump of Wallaces on the beach. All of the other women were short. Lizzie watched as her mother stood apart from everyone; that was one of her tricks to appear shorter than she actually was. The Wallace men were all as handsome as Jim, with wide shoulders and full, thick hair. She blew a bubble so big that when it popped, she had to peel the gum from her nose. In the time that Jim had been with her mother, Lizzie had liked him okay. In the way that she liked her teachers. Every day he tried a different nickname with her—Sport, Chickadee, Chicken, Bunny, Elevator. She figured that was his way of trying to get comfortable. He did an Irish jig when he arrived at the jumble of beach towels and umbrellas, and Elyse's mother hugged him as if he were her own brother. She pointed out the girls and Jim called to them, "Be careful, Lollypop!" That was the name he'd settled on in the car.

"Geez," Isobel said, "You'd think we were actually in danger. This is the bay. The ocean is on the other side of the Cape. Nobody drowns here unless they can't swim."

"I can swim," Lizzie said, trying to make up for the fact that she hadn't worn her bathing suit under her clothing. "How far out can you walk?"

"Depends on the tide," Isobel said, stepping off the sandbar and walking until the water swirled around her chin. She floated on her back, her toes pointed and her arms crossed as if she were dead. Her orange hair turned a deep copper when it was wet.

"She likes people to look at her," Elyse said, sitting down on the sandbar so that the water came to her neck. She held her hair away from the waves to keep it dry and dipped her nose and mouth in the water to blow bubbles.

Lizzie dug her toes into the sand, feeling the larger rocks, and ventured a question of her own when Isobel had floated back toward them. "Y'all come here every summer?"

"Y'all," they said in unison and then started shouting it out as if it were a curse word. By the end of the summer all of them would be using "y'all" and "wicked" in the same sentence.

When Isobel started clapping like a seal and barking "y'all," Lizzie collapsed into a fit of giggles with them, forgetting entirely that she wasn't dressed to be swimming. Elyse gave up trying to keep her hair dry and Isobel spent the next hour teaching them how to make arm farts. Once or twice a younger cousin ventured their way, but they persistently ignored Elyse's mother's pleas to let the little ones play with them and drove the interlopers back with splash attacks. During one of these bombardments, Lizzie swallowed what felt like a bucketful of the salty water and coughed so hard that Elyse and Isobel had to pound on her back.

They floated for a bit after that. Lizzie was already tallying up stories to tell her friends back in Memphis about her new cousins and the beach. Mrs. Dameron, who taught the third grade always had show-and-tell the first day back, and Lizzie had started to consider the perfect item to show. It would have to be something that was unique to this beach. Lots of kids went to Destin over the break.

"Where's your other dad?" Elyse asked, and Lizzie couldn't tell whether she'd been waiting to ask the entire time they'd been together or whether the thought had just occurred to her. As she got to know her cousin better, she realized that she never planned ahead. Every action in her life was a reaction.

Isobel, as if sensing there was no answer to the question, dunked Elyse, which started a spirited round of play fighting until Elyse got sand in her eyes, which made them all stop.

"I'm not crying," she said before either one of them could accuse her.

"I don't," Lizzie said, surprised to be speaking even as the words left her mouth.

"You don't what?" Isobel asked.

"Have a dad."

"That's okay," Elyse said, pulling at the corner of her eye and trying to blink the sand out. "Lots of kids don't have dads."

"Everyone has a dad," Isobel said.

"I know," Elyse said. "I mean like my friend Susie, she doesn't have a dad. He died or something."

"I don't think mine died," Lizzie said, realizing how little her mother had told her. For most of her life, Lizzie hadn't given much thought to the identity of her father. Occasionally, faced with a daddy-daughter dance or when her friends' fathers would ferry them to one place or another, she'd remember that it was strange that she didn't have one. But it wasn't until her stepfather came along that she was forced to confront the idea that somewhere out there she had a father. Her mother tended to answer questions about her father with other questions. "What do you need a father for?" she'd ask in the same voice she used when Lizzie had been caught sneaking an extra cookie.

"Knock, knock," Isobel said.

Elyse groaned and splashed water in her cousin's direction. "She loves this sort of game. Knock-knock jokes, riddles, word puzzles."

"Fine. Try this one. It's a memory test. There's a one-story house with yellow walls, a yellow roof, yellow fridge, yellow plates—"

"I get it," Elyse said. "Everything's yellow."

Isobel continued listing the contents of the house. Lizzie knew the joke. The answer had been given away in the first sentence. She took a deep breath and swam under the water, keeping her eyes tightly shut, and closed her fist around a few errant strands of eel grass to keep her submerged. Once last year she'd asked about her father. No, that wasn't right. She hadn't asked. All the other times, that's what she'd done, started with a question: Who is? Where is? Why is? But this time, she hadn't given her mother a choice. "Tell me about my father," she'd said. What Lizzie had wanted was a description, an occupation, a location. Instead, her mother had placed her hand on Lizzie's head and smoothed her hair into a ponytail, twisting it in the back so it would hold. "You'll meet him some-day," she'd said, "and he'll love you enough to make up for not being here now." And then, as if knowing what she'd said wasn't even close to enough, she added, "You have his eyes."

Her lungs burned. She let go of the eel grass, burst-ing the surface of the water, and gasped for air. When she looked around, she saw squiggles of confetti as her body adjusted to the sudden intake of oxygen and the bright sunlight above the water.

"Girls," Elyse's mother called, walking toward them. "We're ready to eat."

"Triplins," Jim shouted after her. "Like cousins and triplets."

"I don't understand," Elyse was saying, while waving impatiently at her mother. "You never told me what color the stairs were. Isn't everything yellow?"

"There are no stairs," Lizzie said, grinning at her cousin. "It's a one-story house."

They dunked Isobel together, their laughter echoing across the surface of the bay. Lizzie knew that for third-grade show-and-tell in the fall, what she'd bring would be a bottle of bay water, a nickname for the three of them, and their own secret whoomp dance.

November 2011: Los Angeles

"You could move here," Isobel said.

"I'm not going anywhere," Lizzie said after flipping the switch that turned off the knee bender. The machine, designed to gently flex her knee after surgery, didn't make a lot of noise, but the absence of the motor's whir made every word they said sound as if it were an echo.

"But you don't live here. You really don't live anywhere." Her cousin, in mid-transition from morning gym class to afternoon run, lay down on the floor next to the pull-out couch and stretched.

"It wouldn't make sense. In a few months I could be back with the team, or playing in the European leagues, or—"

"Move into my extra bedroom and get a job teaching or coaching at one of the fine educational institutions here."

"You sound like my mother. The next thing I know you'll be sending me links to job applications and saying what a shame it is that I spent all those years getting a degree I don't use."

"The difference is you're talking to me."

"My mother and I talk."

Isobel laughed. "No pretenses needed with me. I like having you around, even if you are incapacitated." Isobel stretched her arms toward the wall and then pointed her toes, making it appear as if she were being pulled at both ends. "Besides, you need a home, and living here will give you the chance to accumulate more stuff than will fit in a duffle bag."

"I'll be around a good bit for the next few months." Lizzie needed to walk, test out how well her leg was healing. Getting up would stop the conversation from becoming about her mother. Although at least she and Isobel were in the same spot, neither one of them on friendly terms with their mothers. She massaged her knee and then maneuvered herself to the edge of the bed. Isobel, anticipating her next move, reached under the couch and pulled out the crutches. The motion set off the dancing Santa Claus on the mantle, and the canned sound of "Jingle Bell Rock" filled their half of the duplex.

The song ended and Isobel picked up the tune and continued singing as she helped Lizzie onto her crutches. At practice a few weeks earlier she'd torn her ACL and now, a few days after surgery and a month before Christmas, Lizzie found herself convalescing at her cousin's house. Such a Jane Austen way of explaining the situation, but how else to describe being propped up by half a dozen pillows on the pullout couch as a machine bent and unbent her leg to the prescribed post-surgery degree? No other word would do.

"It's the right time," Isobel sang as she let go of Lizzie's crutches.

Sighing, Lizzie started to do cautious laps around the small living room while Isobel shadowed her, anticipating any hesitations in balance. "Coaching is for people who are finished playing. I'm not finished."

"I never said you were."

There was a quality to Isobel's voice that made Lizzie reconsider their conversation. Maybe it wasn't all about getting her to think about life after soccer, maybe her cousin needed her around. Lizzie paused to rest a minute and leaned against the wall. "I'm just grumpy about all of this."

"It doesn't have to be coaching, you could stay and do something else. I'll teach you about houses." Isobel thumped her heel against the floor. "Sanded and stained these myself. You should have seen this place when I bought it. Owners had poured wax down all the drains. Wax."

"You can't escape who you are," Lizzie said. "Got your mom's looks and your dad's passions."

Isobel wiggled her ears at Lizzie. Her cousin was the perfect mix of her father and her mother. As a child, when she wasn't acting, she'd been her father's shadow—handing him hammers and using fine-grain sandpaper on intricate crown molding. She'd learned to use a jigsaw before taking the training wheels off her bike. When her career had skidded to a halt after her show ended, she put that knowledge to use by leveraging her acting money to buy dilapadated houses around Los Angeles and make them beautiful again. The bungalow Isobel lived in now was actually a duplex, with the rent from the other side covering her mortgage. But she was her mother's child too. She could be pushy and vain.

"Am I driving you tomorrow? To that soccer thing?"

"You mean the holiday party?" Lizzie had no intention of going to the hotel to spend hours decorating store-bought cookies and exchanging secret Santa gifts with her teammates, or rather, former teammates. "I've got a therapy appointment," she said.

"It's after that. You know, your coach called me to say how they especially want you to be there, and I don't mind as long as we figure out how to get out there without hitting much traffic. I heard some of the girls have endorsement deals. They do commercials and stuff, huh?"

"Nobody there will be of any use to you. All that's stuff done with the sports media guys—not an actor to be seen for miles. Besides, my being there is bad luck. If this"—Lizzie gestured to her knee—"could happen to me, it could happen to them."

"You remember that I'm no good at sympathy, right?" Isobel plaited her flat-ironed hair into a loose braid as she spoke. As beautiful as her cousin was, she had the trappings of a woman who worked at her appearance— the byproduct of being a kid who'd worn thick glasses and picked at her scabs. "I can do two things. I'll tell it to you straight or I'll take you out and we'll have a good time ignoring our problems. Which do you want?"

"I want Elyse."

Isobel adjusted her face, making her cheeks larger and widening her eyes. She spoke in a near-perfect imitation of their cousin's husky Boston-coated voice. "You're going to tell me about it and afterward I'll figure out a way to make it better, even if it means drinking for both of you."

"Be kind," Lizzie said. While Lizzie and Isobel had spent most of their twenties getting exactly what they wanted out of life, Elyse had floundered. She'd started and stopped two dozen careers. The latest misstep had been opening a bed and breakfast. In all the years she'd known Elyse, she'd never seen her cousin get out of bed with time enough to make even so much as toast. "She's the best at telling us what we should do."

"That's because she listens. You and I"—Isobel made a dramatic show of pointing to each of them—"are terrible at listening."

Lizzie smiled. "I didn't hear you. Did you say I'm amazing?"

Isobel rolled her eyes in dramatic fashion. "She does all her listening on the phone, which is easy. You can multitask. What do you want to bet that while we're droning on repeating ourselves, she's painting her nails. All she has to do is ask questions and make sympathy noises."

"Sympathy noises?"

Isobel offered several variations on the "oooh" sound.

"Your sympathy noise sounds like sex noise."

"I didn't say I was good at it."

"Listening or sex?"

Isobel responded by pulling up the corner of her T-shirt as if she intended to strip. "This coming from the girl who had to ask me if the wet spot on her boyfriend's jeans after they made out was normal."

"I was sixteen! Besides, you know how my mom and Jim are about that sort of stuff."

"I don't know any parents who aren't that way. You don't want to know how much I knew at sixteen."

As close as they were, they didn't often talk about sex. It had been established early on that Isobel had lost her virginity too early and Lizzie too late. Elyse, in typical fashion, had lost hers on prom night her senior year of high school. Lizzie's back ached from keeping her knee off the ground. She wiggled her toes. "I should walk a bit more."

Isobel tried again to talk to Lizzie about her team's Christmas party. "They're expecting you to be there," Isobel said. "Isn't your coach looking for a show of commitment? I mean if you don't go, then no matter if you're healed in time or not, won't it be a black mark against you?"

"I should, but I can't." Lizzie rested the toe of her right foot on the floor, careful to keep her knee bent. She put a little weight on her leg, feeling the shock of pain as it ebbed through her body.

Being house-bound the last few days, Lizzie had watched dozens of documentaries—on animals, historic figures, celebrities, archaeology—all the while collecting an impressive assortment of facts. Cats can bark. The king of hearts doesn't have a mustache. Women blink twice as much as men. When she was alone, she'd string them together to try to create some larger narrative out of all the smaller pieces. When she wasn't alone, she discovered her facts could be used to deflect conversations. Given what had happened to her and the uncertainty of what would happen, there were many discussions she didn't want to have. She searched her brain for a topic that would divert her cousin's attention. "The bigger question is what do we do now that we know this is our last year on earth?"

"Come on." Isobel kept her eyes on Lizzie's knee. "You can't start believing in all of that apocalypse stuff. Don't you have to believe in God first?"

"It doesn't have anything to do with God. It's the Mayans. They're the ones with the stone calendar that abruptly stops tracking time. Or maybe I should trust the new-agey folks like your mother who say there's some secret hidden planet, that will appear when Earth crosses the Milky Way."

"My mother would only think the world was ending if she had a sure way out," Isobel said, taking the bait.

She kept talking about the end of days as Lizzie hobbled into the bathroom. "Let me know if you need help," Isobel said when Lizzie shut the door.

She leaned against the sink and washed her hands. There was no reason to think she couldn't get through this injury and the rehab. Yet, why wouldn't anyone mention the Olympics? Her coach had been silent on the matter, her own mother kept talking about post-soccer careers and now her cousin had started talking around her future. If Elyse were there, she'd be on her side, telling Lizzie that there was no reason she couldn't be a hundred percent by July when they'd announce the final team roster.

Outside the door, Isobel was coming up with her own end-of-the-world theories. Twice before Lizzie had torn her ACL—once in college and once when she was much younger and had first started to play seriously. Why was this injury so much harder to face? It had come at a bad time—just before the Olympic season—and Lizzie was older now. So many of the girls at the training camp had been children—not even out of college and playing as strong as the veterans. They had young knees and had been taught the importance of finesse and strength. Lizzie closed the lid and sat for a few moments on the toilet. She liked the smallness of the room. The fact was, even if she hadn't been injured, her spot on the team wouldn't have been guaranteed. She'd been one of those players perpetually on the cusp. In for one tournament and out for another. But being at the camp a few weeks earlier had felt different. The other girls had said that to her—told her how well she played, how fast she'd gotten. It was supposed to be her year.

The tear happened during scrimmage. Unlike most Southern California mornings, that day there'd been almost no sunshine. The bit of light filtering through the heavy clouds had a greenish cast that made Lizzie think of the stacks of aquariums in pet stores. Everyone expected the clouds to blow out, but they remained even after lunch. Her teammates, louder than usual, took the field grabbing pinnies and talking smack with each other. It seemed clear from the division of teams into red and green which girls would be going to Canada for the first of their pre-Olympic tournaments and which would not. Still, they had two more weeks of camp left, and Lizzie knew from all the other years she'd been in this position that there'd be movement before the full three weeks were over.

The team's captain pulled her hair back into a ponytail, tightening it before braiding it and securing it with another elastic. She gave Lizzie a thumbs-up and then called over the girls they were playing with. "Friendly game," she said. "Ease into it."

Lizzie shook her head. The media had been portraying these athletes as girls next door for so long that they almost believed it themselves. However, each one of them had an interior wolf that emerged the moment the ball touched the grass, even at these practice games. The drive to be better than everyone else separated them from everyone else.

Lizzie liked the captain. The coach had been right to keep her on the team even though she was nearly thirty-five and had two kids. She'd been one of the heroines of the 1999 World Cup team. People tended to speak about the good the captain had done for women's soccer, but lately Lizzie had been thinking of how the woman had kept playing long past the point when everyone thought she'd have to stop. This woman had played through pregnancy and injury. It gave Lizzie hope that she had plenty of time left to play the game and afterward have the life she wanted. The only problem was she didn't know what she wanted out of her second life.

She punched her legs in excitement waiting for the game to start. One of the coaches rolled the ball in and the players fought for it. Their kicks, when they missed, stabbed into the turf, leaving behind moon-like craters. A few minutes into the game, Lizzie anticipated a sharp cut by one of the young forwards and spirited the ball from the player's foot. The opposing forward moved three or four steps toward the goal before realizing she didn't have the ball, while Lizzie swiftly booted it downfield. She felt the coach's eyes on her and then a short, quick nod of approval.

The match continued and Lizzie let herself be swallowed by the game chatter, listening to the goalie's directions and keeping her eyes as much as possible on the ball and on the young powerful forwards in green pinnies on the opposite team. When she was in a game, time moved at a different speed—not faster or slower, but she became aware of every second in a way she never could outside of the field.

Rain began to fall as the game neared its conclusion. The forward who Lizzie had embarrassed got the ball on a breakaway and crossed into the backfield. Stepping forward to challenge her, Lizzie kicked the ball out of bounds. When her foot returned to the ground, it slipped, hyperextending her knee and sending her sprawling to the ground. There was almost no pain, but the moment Lizzie tried to stand on her own, she felt a looseness in her leg and the sharp searing that accompanied the fear of realizing that her body wasn't working the way it should.

"Did you hear a pop?" her teammates asked each other as they gathered around her waiting for the trainer to come onto the field. Most of them reflexively touched their own knees. Those who'd had surgery massaged the thin scars that scalpels had sliced into the fronts of their knees and the backs of their legs. The captain got close and grabbed her hand. "It'll be a sprain," she said, and then, as if not understanding that some words weren't to be spoken, "definitely not your ACL. Not again."

Lizzie closed her eyes and lay back on the turf, letting the rain pelt her face like gravel. When she opened her eyes, it was because she'd heard Isobel's voice an octave higher than its normal tenor, asking questions of the team doctor. "If they called my emergency contact, I know it's bad," she said, letting her cousin take her hand to help her hear what she already knew, even without the MRI confirmation.

Isobel knocked on the door, her voice strained as it had been in the trainer's room a few weeks earlier. "You didn't fall down or something, did you?"

Lizzie opened the door and hopped on one foot to the bed, where she struggled to get her leg back into the knee-bending machine. "I'm not ready," she said.

Isobel locked the machine and pushed the button to start it. The hum of its mechanics filled the small living room. "Who is? All this talk about the end of the world is like a jolt, you know? And you." Her cousin used her hands to shape a ball out of the air. "It's everything."

"It was." Lizzie's mind returned to the coach's face when she'd talked with her about her injury. That woman's face, with its wrinkled, puckered mouth, was the true reason Lizzie wouldn't go to the holiday party. The coach's mouth had said all the right words, talking about how as long as Lizzie's rehab went well, she'd be among the players considered for the Olympic team, but her eyes had darkened and dismissed Lizzie with every glance.

Isobel went on talking. "I think if Elyse were here, she'd tell me that I'm bugging you so much about what's next because having you here makes me think about my own life."

"What's wrong with your life?"

Isobel reached down and tightened the laces on her shoes. "Don't make me say it."

Without meaning to, Lizzie's eyes settled on the statue her cousin kept tucked into a corner of one of the bungalow's many built-ins. Isobel had been ten when the cast of her cable show got that award. "You ever think that the world is a walled maze full of dead ends?"

"Sometimes," Isobel said, setting her wristwatch and putting her hand on the doorknob. "But I keep thinking it's like what you said earlier."

"Like what?"

"That tomorrow could be the first day of our very last year." Lizzie hadn't expressed it that way, but Isobel had somehow managed to put into words exactly what had been buzzing at the corners of her brain ever since she blew her knee out. That what she needed was for her first life to be over so she could figure out her second.

"I guess the question is what are we going to make of our very last year?"

December 2011: Los Angeles

Lizzie wished her mother would learn how to text. In the last few years, during the period that Isobel and Elyse called the cold war, texts had become her primary way of communicating with her mother, and yet her mother was terrible at it. Take these messages— more than a dozen sent one after the other and they all added up to nonsense.

> THEY say grand burn is splice
> #eYEsorE
> On TV last night . . . what should we do
> Emergency. Your closet.
> Grandmas Memphis

In the last one, her mother had typed the word "condemned" six times, with random letters capitalized.

Who does that? There was something about the sheer number of texts coupled with their insanity that made her finally want to call her mother. It wasn't that Lizzie and her mother hadn't been speaking to one another, but since her grandmother's death, the distance between them had widened from a chasm to a canyon. She steeled herself for the painful conversation. Talking with her mother was like trying to walk after her foot fell asleep—all pins and needles and awkward stumbling. As the phone rang, Lizzie figured the time difference. California was a little more than half a day behind Yekaterinburg and sometimes when Lizzie spoke to her family, she felt as if she were calling the future. While it was Wednesday night in Los Angeles, it was already Thursday morning in Russia. Early. Maybe too early to call, but as she was about to hang up the phone, her mother's voice came across the line as clear as if she were in the next room.

"It's the house," she said. "They're threatening to tear it down or auction it or—"

"The house?" Lizzie asked, thinking of all the places that were important to her mother. She knew, even as she asked, that it would be her grandmother's house, the one they'd lived in until her mother married Jim.

"Spite House."

"Condemned," Lizzie said, finally understanding her mother's frantic texts. The nickname for their family homestead wasn't one her mother often used. It came from the sign, one of those historical markers, cemented into the brick sidewalk at the base of the home's front yard. Lizzie thought of the place as her grandmother's or, on occasion, when describing it to friends, as Skinny House. The implications of "spite" had been lost to her for many years and even now, when she understood all too well how anger had a way of warping actions and turning them vindictive, she hesitated to call the house by that name. It was a name for outsiders. Lizzie had lived in the house, loved it, loved her grandmother, and she found the name wouldn't form on her lips.

"Condemned," her mother echoed.

"What happened to that couple? The ones you hired from your church to watch the place while you and Jim do this mission thing?"

"I don't know." Her mother sniffed and let out a ragged breath before continuing with her explanation. "I wouldn't even have known, but Sister Henderson e-mailed Jim to tell us it was on the news. It's awful, so awful, and they weren't kind at all—said the house was rumored to have connections to the Nazis. The Nazis!"

"Does it?" Lizzie didn't know much about her extended family. Maybe her grandfather who'd built the house had a secret history.

"Of course not. That's some rumor started by one of your grandfather's brothers because the cupola on the top looks like one of those tanks."

Lizzie, who'd spent most of her time in the house in that cupola, had a difficult time imagining the space at it would appear from the street. "I know what the house means to you, Momma."

"To you, also."

She should have recognized the trap. Her mother had been using the same emotional blackmail tools on Lizzie for as far back as she could recall. If something were important to her mother, by default it became important to Lizzie. But instead of finding a way to back out of the conversation, she plunged ahead, acknowledging what the house meant to her. "It's where my childhood lives."

"So you'll go?"

"I'm doing rehab here. It's not something you can leave."

"You could do it in Memphis. You did it before."

Lizzie sighed. Even if it were technically true, she'd planned to stay as connected to the team as she could. The last two times she'd blown out her knee, she'd rehabbed at her mother's house. The trouble with the life that Lizzie had set up was that she didn't have a home. She moved into temporary apartments depending on the team's training schedule and on which professional team she was playing for. The last decade had been one of staying in but not living in places.

Isobel came in the front door, kicked off her shoes, and curled up on the bed next to Lizzie, leaning in to hear the conversation. On the phone, her mother explained how she needed Lizzie to get to Memphis and fix what had gone wrong with the house. She talked about code enforcement and contractors and the small inheritance that her grandmother had left them when she'd died several years earlier. "Bring Isobel with you. Surely she can take a break from acting and put those skills her father taught her to good use."

"No," Lizzie said. "Isobel's too busy to come with me. I've already put her out enough."

"That house is as much yours as it is mine." Her mother took a breath and continued to wheedle, telling her that she understood how she might be angry because of her leg, but that when doors were shut, God had a way of opening new ones and that it was her obligation to walk through this one. "It has to be you."

Isobel took the phone from Lizzie's hand and put it on speaker. "Damn," she mouthed, as they listened to Lizzie's mother talk through every possible avenue of guilt.

It was if her mother knew nothing about her. This disconnect between them hurt Lizzie more than she could admit. Her earliest memories collected, like beads of dew on a spider web, around the sensation of her mother's hand on the small of her back. It had been the two of them until Lizzie was eight and she got caught up in what she had come to think of as an unprecedented season of expansion. Her stepfather brought with him not only an extensive extended family, but then in a panicked rush against her mother's biological clock and with the aid of fertility treatments, had turned out two half-brothers, Grant and Lincoln, and two half-sisters, Reagan and Kennedy. She supposed they should have been her new team, but no matter how much she loved them all, they weren't a team. She was too many years older, and she'd stubbornly held out when they'd all joined that church. Maybe when her siblings were grown, they could be a team, but for the time being there were too many differences. The barrier to camaraderie rarely acknowledged by Lizzie was that she didn't know who her biological father was or why he'd left, and until she had those answers, she couldn't commit to the blended family.

Her mother paused for breath. In the background, Lizzie heard her stepfather ask for the phone. They spoke in muffled tones to each other and after the audible sound of a door closing, her stepfather cleared his throat. "She's left the room, Lollypop."

"I can't." Lizzie looked at Isobel, who nodded and moved her hands to try to get her to say everything she thought.

"I don't think you should," he said. "You go there and you'll be digging up old history and the way things are with your mom now, the way they have been since Mellie's death." He stopped talking for several seconds as if he had to stop himself from speaking his mind. "This next year should be all about you moving forward. That house has never done anyone in your family any favors."

"It's not that bad. Grandma was happy there," Lizzie said, thinking of her rooftop sanctuary with dozens of prisms hanging in its windows. "My rehab is here and I still don't know where I'll land. They're talking about a new league after the Olympics and I should be better by then."

"I agree." Jim started to talk to her about her leg, but then in the middle of asking her about her last flex test, he changed the subject back to the house. "If it goes, you'll be okay, right? No regrets or anything."

"There are always regrets."

"I don't even think they'll tear it down. We'll be back in the States this time next year and as slow as

Memphis moves, I fully expect it to be exactly where it is now. But if it's not—"

"Then it's not," Lizzie said, watching as her cousin's eyes widened.

"Hello?" Jim's voice had a tinny peal to it. "Your mother has more to say."

"Think about it carefully," Isobel said, trying to cover the phone's speaker. "You could make it the very last thing you do for her."

"I can't do this now," Lizzie said. She grabbed the phone back and tried to hit the mute button, while Isobel listed off the reasons that she shouldn't be so hasty about saying no to her parents.

She wondered if anyone else's family was as messed up as hers. As a child, there had been long stretches during which her mother and grandmother hadn't spoken. After Lizzie's mother married Jim, the silence lasted two years. During that time, she'd taken refuge in her grandmother's house on Sunday mornings while Jim and her mother went to church. Although only eight at the time, Lizzie had refused to attend, and her parents, bless them, had readily accepted the compromise of allowing her to spend those worship hours with Grandma Mellie. Looking back on it, Lizzie understood that guilt had fueled their acquiescence. There wouldn't be an oil crisis if the powers that be could figure out how to run the world's machines on guilt. It was an endless chain reaction motivating action and reaction in families since the first mother had the first daughter. Lizzie figured that was the reason the Bible never got around to naming Eve's girls. She heard her mother call her name. Lizzie looked down at the phone in her hand, surprised to find that her mother hadn't hung up. As she moved her thumb to disconnect the call, her mother said, "I don't think she's there anymore."

"I am," Lizzie said, and before her mother could take over the conversation again, she said what Isobel had told her. "I'm not going forever. If I do this, then you can't ask me for anything else. No more guilt trips about Grandma or about not seeing my siblings enough or about church. We're done with that."

"We're a family—"

"That doesn't mean what you think it does," Lizzie said. "I'll go, and Isobel will come and we'll check out the damage and see what needs to be done, but that's as far as it goes. We'll probably hire someone and come back to California."

"That's all I was asking for," her mother said.

Lizzie kept quiet a long while, listening to the sound of her mother trying to hide the fact that she was crying. "You always ask for too much. This is the end of it. The very last time."

October 2008: Memphis

The November after Lizzie graduated from the University of Central Florida, her grandmother died. She wasn't alone in this; throughout college, teammates had training schedules and game-day line-ups disrupted by the funerals of elderly relatives. Those years were the first wave of grief. Later, when she joined the national team, a few of the women lost parents, and Lizzie saw then that the second wave of loss when it came would be more like a tsunami. But that year, when Lizzie heard her stepfather explain how her grandmother hadn't woken up, she only felt like she'd walked into water, not been swept away by it.

The images of her grandmother played on a loop in her brain. She could see her bending low to open the oven in the kitchen of her impossible house. The light streaming from the windows cast her in shadows and made her wrinkles appear as deep crevices. Even when she stood, she remained hunched—a consequence of her fear of doctors and weak bones. She did not let the collapse of her spine change how she approached the world. Compromise, as she'd often told Lizzie, was for fools who valued being popular over being true.

Lizzie's last visit had been an afterthought that had the appearance of thoughtfulness. She hadn't come home specifically to help her grandmother transition from the hospital back to her house after getting a new hip, but the timing had worked out. She needed a place to crash for the two weeks she had off between training and the next tournament; when she called her mother halfway through the drive from Florida to Memphis, her mother had thought she'd let her know about the surgery and suggested that, instead of spending her time with Jim and her siblings, she could spend it with her grandmother. Lizzie pretended to have remembered about the hip replacement and agreed that she'd drive straight to the hospital and make the arrangements needed to get Mellie back to her house and started with physical therapy. Of everyone, Lizzie had the most experience with putting the body to work after surgery.

Stepping into the hospital, Lizzie walked to her grandmother's room without anyone noticing her presence. At the floor desk, the nurse straightened up and set aside her book when she saw Lizzie approach. "We didn't expect anyone to come tonight," she'd said, leading her down a darkened hallway to Mellie's room. "Happy Halloween."

"Isn't it early?" Lizzie asked.

The nurse gestured to a plastic jack-o-lantern filled with tootsie rolls. "Given the uncertainty of everyone's time here, we try to make every day a holiday. So all of October is Halloween, and next month every day will be Thanksgiving."

"I see," Lizzie shrugged and helped herself to a candy.

"Your grandmother might be out of it—from sleep or the meds."

Walking down the hallway, she held the candy tight in her hand and let it soften before popping it into her mouth and opening the door to her grandmother's room. It closed with a soft click and as Lizzie's eyes adjusted to the low-lit room, her grandmother spoke.

"The angels said it would be my little Lizzie." Her eyes were closed.

"Are you awake?" Her grandmother's certainty about her presence in the room confused her. She didn't think she'd been told that Lizzie was coming.

"The light hurts," Mellie said, letting one eye open and then groping for the remote that adjusted the angle of her bed.

Lizzie pulled the curtain past the moon and leaned over for a hug before pulling a stool to the edge of the bed. At first, she didn't linger on her grandmother's mention of angels. It had been enough to hear strength in her voice. Her hair needed to be dyed. The gray roots were nearly as long as the colored ends. "I missed you."

"We have a lot of work to do."

"That's why I'm here. We'll take you home tomorrow and get you set up with the therapist who'll help you get used to the new hip and—"

"I'm not talking about that. I'll be fine and walking straight before you know it." Mellie leaned over, taking Lizzie's chin in her hand, as if she were a child. "You're not on the right path."

"I'm doing fine," Lizzie said, smoothing back her grandmother's hair. "Or rather I'm doing the best I can."

"But you aren't. The angels showed me how broken you were. How it started with your mother and me. I'm broken too."

"You're fixed now," Lizzie said, alarmed by the desperation in her grandmother's voice.

"But I'm not. That's why the angels let me come back, so I'd have time to fix all that I'd broken."

As her grandmother continued to talk in nonsensical ways about angels and emotional scars, Lizzie pushed the button to summon the nurse. She tried to interrupt, to stop the flow of crazy that her grandmother spouted, but each time, Mellie silenced her with a sharp rap of her knuckles on the edge of the metal bed frame. Finally, in a burst of anger, almost yelling, Lizzie said, "But you don't believe in that crap."

"Nothing like almost dying to change your mind."

"You didn't die," Lizzie said, not understanding how there could be degrees of mortality. She thought about the Sundays of her adolescence—the two of them shaking their heads at her mother's piety. "The end is what you make of it," her grandmother used to say. Lizzie had taken that to mean there was little value in believing in something other than yourself—not that she believed in even that little anymore. The nurse, smelling like cigarettes, poked her head in. Lizzie excused herself and stepped into the hall.

"Something is wrong with her."

"Her vitals are fine."

"No, I mean in the head. She's talking about angels."

Coughing, the nurse turned away for a moment. "I know I should quit, but we all need our vices. Does she seem altered? Not know what day it is or who you are?"

Lizzie understood that there was nothing the nurse could do for them at that moment. "No. In fact, if anything, she knows too much."

"Oh, that's as common as a housefly. Being under, you know, anesthetized, it does stuff to some people's brains. I wouldn't worry about it."

"But she's not who she was." Lizzie corrected herself. "I mean she never before believed in anything and for her to be talking about—"

"She's fine." The nurse looked up as a light went on in the hallway.

"You aren't listening to me. She's telling me about heaven, God, and holy angels, but it all sounds like she's out of her head."

"We should all be so lucky to be so close to our maker." The nurse gave Lizzie a hard stare, and then turned on her heel, telling her to "have a blessed day" as she strode down the hallway.

Lizzie looked up to find her own mother standing at her grandmother's door. She hadn't realized how late it had gotten. Her mother looked as if she were ready for bed, with her hair pulled into a low ponytail and not a smidge of makeup on her face. Without it, her mother had a more difficult time concealing her emotions.

She smiled at Lizzie and then, as quickly as the smile came, it faded. Her mother wrinkled her forehead. "I thought you'd come by our house before coming over here. The children were all dressed for their school Halloween party. There's so much of their childhoods you're missing."

"They missed all of mine." Even as these words formed on Lizzie's lips, she knew they were cruel. "Besides, since when do teenagers get dolled up for Halloween?"

"Preteens," her mother corrected. "That's on me and on Jim. You'll find the age doesn't matter so much later. They love you so much. Third year in a row that Reagan is going as Mia Hamm."

"That jersey must be tiny on her now," Lizzie said. She'd been too old when they were born and too often gone since then to become close to her siblings. Besides, seeing the way they adored their father often felt like pulling a scab off a wound. Not that Jim had ever made her feel less than, or as if she weren't also, his child. The resentment was something Lizzie carried into their relationship.

"And Grant went as an actual soccer ball. Blew up black and white balloons and pinned them to his shirt. He made a little soccer net with pvc pipe and strapped it on the dog."

"You got a dog?"

"Dexter. He's more like a horse. One of those grey-hounds from the racetrack across the river."

"I thought you were allergic."

"No."

"But that's why we couldn't keep that dog," Lizzie said.

"You mean Peg?"

"Peg?" Lizzie tried to remember if she'd ever known the dog's name.

"The one I hit with Mellie's car?"

"In the Datsun. But Peg wasn't her name, it's what I took to calling her when the Bishops adopted her. I can't remember what they named her, Scout, I think. No. Bear."

Her mother had been driving her to soccer practice, and the dog had run out in front of them out on Summer Avenue, which before the freeway had been the main highway between east and west Tennessee. When they looked at it together, it was clear from the heavy teats on the dog that it had puppies. They'd spent days combing the area trying to find them.

"As in leg, right peg leg?" her mother asked looking away from her and reaching for the handle of the hospital door. Her forehead creased as she tried to recall the dog. "It cost me three hundred dollars to get that stray patched up, and even then Mellie wouldn't let us keep her. Do you remember how she was back then? I saw her step on a cat's tail while it sunned itself on our porch."

"I always thought that it was you," Lizzie said. "Mellie's different now."

"Oh, I know. Everyone mellows with age." Her mother compressed her lips and ground her teeth in an expression of irritation, as if she were chewing on gristle. Lizzie had seen a picture of herself with that same look.

"No, I mean since the surgery. I don't know how to explain it. She believes in God, or at least angels." Lizzie was on the verge of saying more.

From the floor desk, the nurse offered her audible prayer. "Praise Jesus."

"Don't be that way." Her mother moved her hands in large gestures punctuated with intent. "We didn't raise you to—"

"Who's we? You and Jim? You and Mellie? You and my real father?"

"You can't bring that up too," her mother said.

"Why not? Wouldn't now be the time to tell me since you all hate me so much already? What's the secret? Is he in jail? You don't remember his name because it happened at an orgy? Tell me."

"Don't be so nasty."

"We have nothing to talk about," Lizzie said, turning her back on her mother. She walked through the hallway door, trying to slam it behind her, but the hinges prevented her from doing so, and instead of a satisfying thump, the hydraulics emitted a slow hiss as the door closed.

After that her relationship with her mother became different. Neither one acknowledged it, but they didn't talk beyond what was necessary. Most holidays Lizzie spent away from home. Any conversations they did have took place in written form or became monosyllabic. Her stepfather stepped in and translated for them, carrying messages and intentions between the two women. But at that moment, Lizzie thought the fight inconsequential. She slept at her grandmother's house, checked her out of the hospital, and drove her home in the Datsun.

Stepping from the yellow car, the smell of canned peaches tickled her nose. There were pockets of land around Memphis that had housed food manufacturers who took delivery of perishable goods from the trains chugging through town and turned out fried pies, canned fruit, and syrup by the ton. Over the years, the soil around these factories had become a dumping ground for products that perished. When the heat of the day reached deep into the earth, the smells (some fifty years old) evaporated into the air. As she looked at the steep stairs that led up to her grandmother's front door, she realized she'd need to find another way to get Mellie, who held a folded aluminum walker on her lap, into her own house.

She returned to the car, backed up, and drove over the curb. The vacant yard next door was all mud.

"Be careful," her grandmother said, bracing herself against the jostling from the uneven ground.

"We'll be fine," Lizzie said, praying that the car's tires wouldn't get stuck. She continued to press firmly on the accelerator until they arrived near the back door. She cut the engine and moved to help Mellie out.

"I'll do it myself."

"You can't," Lizzie said, trying to slide an arm around her grandmother, who'd swung her feet out of the car and was working to unfold the walker.

"Let me at least try," Mellie said, slapping away Lizzie's arm.

She stepped back and watched Mellie struggle to transfer her weight from the car to the walker. Her grandmother looked taller and as she pulled herself to a standing position, Lizzie understood the reason.

Mellie rocked her walker forward as she stumbled behind it. "See, I'm not dead yet."

Lizzie hardly heard her. The humping of her spine, which for years had kept her head tilted to the left, her eyes looking upward as if she were in a dark hole, had dissipated. She stared at her grandmother's back. The hump wasn't exactly gone, but it had shrunk in size enough that for the most part, her grandmother looked straight ahead. Her head wobbled, though, as if her neck were an infant's and not quite strong enough.

"Your back," Lizzie said, jumping ahead of Mellie to open the back door.

"It's a miracle," Mellie said. "Angels said I had to bear a few other people's burdens for a while, so they lifted mine."

"Come now," Lizzie said, opening the door for her grandmother. "You know none of us believe in miracles."

"And yet they exist."

By the time Lizzie left a few days later, Mellie had stopped using the walker, and her neck had grown strong enough to support her newly straightened spine. The doctors didn't have a good explanation for the correction. Sometimes these things happen, they said. One mentioned that the time she'd spent prone could have started the process. Another suggested the hip replacement and the removal of her limp. Lizzie said her goodbyes, her mind already on the upcoming series against Korea and her impending move to Los Angeles to play for the Sols. Nothing about that visit —except that Mellie's walk, which although it no longer had a limp, still held a hesitation, as if her grandmother didn't trust the ground not to move.—gave Lizzie any sense that her grandmother was on the verge of death.

Her stepfather explained again that they'd gone over to visit for Veteran's day and had found her in her bed. Mostly he apologized for her mother not being able to tell her. "You don't have to come for the services," he said.

Lizzie knew they expected her to come, that this offer was merely a courtesy. "I can't believe she's gone. It's a trick. She can't have died." She wanted to say more, but she found she couldn't speak over the sobs that exploded out of her chest as if her heart were trying to leap out of her body.

Her mother took the phone from Jim. "No matter what they say, there's never enough time on this earth."

"Breathe. You've got to find your breath," her stepfather said in the background.

In the end Lizzie agreed to look at flights and let them know her plans. Instead, she played three games, traveling to Richmond, Cincinnati, and Tampa before sending off an e-mail saying she'd be spending the holidays in Los Angeles with Isobel.

New Year's Eve
2011: Memphis

From the street, the façade of Spite House gave an impression of stinginess, while from the banks of the Mississippi, the rear of the house, with its sharply angled glass walls, rejected onlookers by offering only a view of their own unsettled faces. Being half as narrow as a standard house in front and three times as wide in back gave 260 Wagner Place the disturbing appearance of having been built without forethought. Already standing well above the structures around it at three stories, the proportions tricked the eye into estimations of even greater height. Every cornice bore a different embellishment. The yellow clapboard and the green trim emphasized the home's slight tilt. Preceding the arched front doors, skinny columns created a porch-like space that repeated itself on the upper levels. Heavily hooded windows contributed to the exterior menace of the house, as did the legends about the family within.

Looking up at the house, Lizzie saw for the first time how elderly neighbors might complain that the cupola had the same architectural lines as a panzer. In the back of her mind, a memory fluttered of reading books in the greenhouse-like warmth of the room with her grandmother, stopping to take sips of peach tea and count the rainbows cast by the pieces of glass her grandfather had hung before Lizzie was born.

"Looking at a place like this, you realize there's not much difference between ugly and beautiful," Isobel said, staring at the house head-on despite the blazing sun creeping toward the west.

Lizzie brought her hand to her eyes and squinted, trying to find the signs of neglect that would have prompted the city to board the lower levels with plywood and string caution tape across the porch. She picked up her cousin's observation. "They might as well be synonyms, it's another way of saying something looks different. No, what you truly want to avoid is being like everyone else or everything else around you. Ugly is beautiful because it makes you want to keep looking."

"What sort of shape do you think the glass is in?" Isobel asked, starting up the precipitous concrete steps that led to the front porch. There was no front yard to speak of—only a steep drop from the edge of the house to the street.

"There's no telling." Lizzie stopped to fiddle with the historic sign cemented into the middle of the sidewalk at street level. The bolt holding the bottom of the sign to the post had rusted away, leaving the placard to move with the wind. She took the elastic from her hair and looped it through the sign, working to secure it as best she could. Then she ran her fingers over the raised white lettering on the green background—most of the paint had rubbed off, making the sign impossible to read from any distance. Satisfied, she limped up the stairs behind her cousin.

The sound of firecrackers set off early in anticipation of the new year startled Lizzie and made Isobel yelp. The two of them moved to the porch as quickly as Lizzie's leg would allow them. She saw how battered the plywood appeared, covered in spray paint and pieces of paper matted by wind and rain. They ducked underneath the caution tape and stepped up to the front door.

In the corner of the porch, the swing rocked slowly. Lizzie took her eyes from the house and squinted into the shadows. Before she could say anything, Isobel bounded across the porch and leapt onto the swing, hugging Elyse around the neck and asking questions faster than anyone would have breath to answer.

"How can you be here?" Lizzie asked, leaning her weight against the boarded-up front door.

"I needed a break," Elyse said. She anticipated Lizzie's next question. "I didn't know I was coming. I woke up this morning and instead of getting off the blue line, I stayed on it all the way to Logan. Couldn't face spending another night at my parents' place, and so the next thing I know, I'm on a flight bound for Memphis."

"Anyone know you're here?" Isobel asked.

"You didn't have to come," Lizzie said.

Elyse stayed silent. Lizzie tore one of the notices from the plywood and read over the information—it wasn't much more than what her mother had told her. There were hearing dates that had long passed and a phone number for the code enforcement office as well as a name. T. J. Freeman. No one in the office had been able to help her the last few times she'd called. People were either on vacation or said that what she wanted couldn't be done over the phone. "You have to be here," they kept saying.

"I'm here," Lizzie said, dismayed at the sight of the peeling paint, the busted spindles on the porch railing, and the sagging underside of the overhang. Around her ankles a layer of dead leaves and other plant matter moved with the breeze coming off the river.

"We're here," Isobel echoed.

"How do you get in this place?" Elyse asked. "I'm freezing."

"This way." Lizzie motioned before stepping off the skinny porch and threading her way through the narrow path that snaked around to the rear of the house. In the early part of her childhood, it had been impossible to access the back porch without walking through the house itself. Back then it had still been sandwiched between the commercial building on the south and the warehouses on the north. When Lizzie was eight or nine, great big yellow machines had torn the warehouses apart and leveled the ground in antici-pation of a luxury hotel. Like a great many promises made to Memphis, that one hadn't been fulfilled. The empty lot that sat to the north of the property looked much as it had when Lizzie was a child. There was an identical notice tacked to the rear door. She tossed the first into the abandoned lot and watched it land next to a pile of tires. Unlike the front, the back door hadn't been barricaded, but portions of the second floor win-dows, as well as the ground level, were. With plywood covering so much of the house, it lost all familiarity to Lizzie. She gazed at the upper floors, relieved to find the glass mostly intact. There was a smattering of small holes, but the heavy glass hadn't shattered as so many modern windows would have under the pressure of a rock or a baseball.

Taking several deep breaths, Lizzie turned her back on the house and looked at the view from the bluff where the land sat sixty feet above the Mississippi River. Watching the sun creep toward Arkansas, she gave herself a pep talk. Thanks to all the years she'd spent playing soccer, at twenty-eight she had a lifetime's worth of aphorisms to draw upon in times of stress. "Work the plan," she repeated aloud several times. Isobel and Elyse rounded the corner and stepped up onto the back porch.

"You still talking to yourself?" Elyse asked.

"Positive reinforcement," Lizzie said, trying not to look too closely at the spray-painted warning against occupying the house. When she let those orange letters come into focus, the air froze in her lungs as she took it in and stabbed at her alveoli.

"They don't really mean that," Isobel said, tapping her knuckles against the wood. "It's to warn bums off and stuff."

Lizzie's eyes adjusted to the dusk and she turned back to the house, seeking out the turtle-shaped rock where the spare key would be. The rock looked as if it had never been moved. She patted its top, which had been sun warmed, and then pried it up, breaking two fingernails in the process. A single key sat underneath the rock, embedded with dirt and as cool as a lizard's belly. She raised her hands in gratitude and in a moment she had unlocked the back door and stepped inside the house.

The aroma of wet dirt and moldering books made her recoil. When her grandmother was alive, the house had smelled like cleaner and vanilla. She used her phone as a flashlight, holding it firmly in one hand and clasping the strap to her overnight bag with the other. After sitting for so long on the plane and then in the taxi, her knee felt unstable. Isobel reached out and put a hand on the small of her back to steady her. With the windows covered in plywood, not even moonlight penetrated the house. Any optimism that Lizzie had felt earlier dissipated. The back door opened into the kitchen, which was one of the largest spaces in the house. Lizzie groped her way around the perimeter, banging her head on the metal cupboard doors that had been left ajar. It didn't look as if her mother had removed much of anything from the house after her grandmother's death. Orderly rows of jelly jars filled one of the metal cupboards, and the baker's rack still held cookbooks and spices.

They should go to a hotel. That would be the sensible action. Instead, Lizzie collapsed into a kitchen chair that was covered with a sheet and had a good cry. Her cousins, knowing she needed to be alone, explored the house using their own phones as flashlights. She knew girls who didn't cry, who prided themselves on it, but not Lizzie. So many times in her childhood, she'd stepped behind a tree, or into a closet, and one memorable time into a large cardboard box that held the first grade's red rubber balls, and allowed herself a body-wracking cry. And afterward, she always found she could do what was needed. Of course, it hadn't worked very well over the last year. Even after crying, the weight of hopelessness remained ever present, better at casting a shadow than even the sun itself. She blew her nose on the sheet, using the underside to avoid the layer of dust.

"It's not how you start, it's how you finish," Lizzie said to the empty room. In response, the beaded curtain with its lotus flower pattern rustled. She listened to her cousins as they opened doors and called out to each other. In the time she'd sat, the house had become familiar to her again. She groped underneath the sink until her hands touched the gas lantern that her grandmother had kept there. Memphis was prone to storms and full of aging trees set too close to power lines.

Moving cautiously to the stove, she found the long-tipped lighter and then after a few minutes of fumbling, the lantern illuminated the house.

Walking through the curtain, Lizzie embarked on her own exploration of the house. The hallway narrowed as she walked along it so that by the time she reached the stairwell and the open space by the front door, her shoulders almost touched each opposing wall. She started at the front door in the constricted space her grandmother had often called the receiving room. Two slivers of stained glass framed the front doors. Lizzie stood at length in the warm entryway, soothed by the proximity of the horizontally laid poplar walls before allowing their seamlessness to pull her deeper into the house, past the pocket door that opened onto a tiny closet and up the stairs.

The stairs divided the narrow portion of the house from the large trapezoid-like rear rooms. The second and third floors were identical to each other. At the landing of the stairs were three doors: one opened to the front bedroom, the other to the back bedroom and the third to the bathroom. The front rooms were barely five feet wide, but they had French doors that exited onto the balconies above the porch. The bathrooms were as long as the front bedrooms and only three feet wide—they shared a wall with the front rooms. The trapezoid rooms had the same floor plan as the kitchen and featured the same tall windows running nearly the height and length of the walls that faced the river. On the third floor, the entryway to the cupola took up most of the landing.

Each door she opened made her a little angrier with her mother, who had assured her that she'd taken good care of the house before leaving nearly two years ago for Yekaterinburg. Clearly her mother had a skewed perception of caretaking. At the door to her grandmother's room, Lizzie picked up the overnight bag she'd left on the landing and entered. Her phone buzzed a warning of a low battery as Lizzie opened the wardrobe in her grandmother's room and searched it for linens. It seemed as if every spare sheet in the house had been used to cover furniture. There were several wool blankets and what appeared to be a wedding dress sealed inside a cloth covering. Behind her, the pewter urn on the mantle reflected the moonlight streaming into the room at eye level above the plywood boards.

Picking up her phone, she started to search out the nearest hotel, but she didn't even get to the point where she could call before the battery died. What she ought to do is find her cousins and work out a plan. But the thought of all that would have to be done with the house overwhelmed her. It was too much to take in. At least they had a place to sleep. *Count your many blessings,* Lizzie thought, bouncing on the bed and listening to its springs groan in protest. Her leg throbbed. She didn't plan on being in Memphis long enough to find a permanent therapist, but the doctor and the trainer had insisted she follow a demanding schedule of therapy and rehabilitation. One day into her travel, and she'd already let the exercises slide.

Life had a way of being a son of a bitch. The dampness of the room left her with clammy skin and again the earthy smell tickled her nose. At least it was warm, especially for being nearly January. Why had her mother left so much of her grandmother's stuff in the house? The thought of all that would have to be done exhausted her. Without intending to, she slept.

The fireworks woke her. They flared above the river and ignited into patterns of light with such ferocity that the panes of glass shook. A sheet she recognized as having been on a table in the hallway covered her, and the lantern was gone. She stretched and walked to the windows. Placing her hand against one of two rock-sized holes, she looked out and saw that Isobel and Elyse had wrapped themselves in blankets and were sitting at the edge of the bluff watching the celebration. She must have been asleep for hours and wondered what her cousins had done with themselves and why they hadn't woken her.

Outside, it wasn't as cold or as deserted as she expected. A rowdy group of young people had set lawn chairs in the vacant lot next to the house. They waved to her and offered best wishes on the start of a new year. Lizzie returned their greetings and then faced the river, sitting down next to Elyse and putting her head on her cousin's shoulder. "We brought you food," Elyse said, sliding over a Styrofoam container.

Lizzie opened it and then closed it without looking at the contents. Without discussing it, she understood that it had been decided that they'd stay in the house that night. The wind blew sporadically, carrying hot ashes one moment and murmurs of awe from the crowd in the park below the next. She stared at the flat gray water until a mirror image of the explosions in the sky appeared in the river. She felt like that—as if she were a blurry reflection of herself. Her eyes drifted to the bulky brace wrapped around her right leg. Before the fireworks concluded in a bombardment of color and sound, headlights illuminated the asphalt lot adjacent to the river park. Determined to beat the traffic, eager fathers hurried children into cars and gunned their engines in a bid to be the first to leave. Her own father, or rather stepfather, mocked such pragmatism.

He preferred to wait for the park to clear, wrapping the children in blankets and naming the few stars visible against the wash of city lights.

He'd use those waiting moments to teach his children to tell time by drawing an imaginary clock around the position of the big dipper. "The stars are proof that we're never standing still," he'd tell them. Scratching an itch on the back of her calf, Lizzie wondered why they'd never watched the fireworks from the bluff before. She supposed it was her mother's doing. Most everything that didn't make sense to Lizzie could be traced back to her mother.

The vacant-lot revelers called to them as they tromped off the land, blowing noisemakers and swigging the last of their alcohol. One last firework, launched well past the finale, exploded behind them and the sound of it pressed in on Lizzie like all the losses from the previous year.

As if sensing her thoughts, Isobel raised an invisible glass. Elyse followed, then Lizzie. "To our very last year," Lizzie said.

"To the Triplins," Isobel offered.

Elyse ducked her head and then cleared her throat. "May the most we wish for in the coming year be the least that we get."

January 2012: Memphis

Lizzie unplugged her phone and put it inside the medicine cabinet in the bathroom. What was it they said about insanity? Repeating the same action and expecting different results? She knew what her trainer and her coach had told her before she left Los Angeles, and yet she'd still expected them to tell her what she'd wanted to hear this time around. The fact was, they didn't know her. Neither one of them had been there the first two times she busted her ACL. *A year.* It hadn't taken her but six months to get back on the field the first time. Lizzie knew there were other messages about other problems on that phone, and yet she couldn't bring herself to listen to them. She closed the mirrored front, leaving it fogged from her shower, and maneuvered down the narrow steps and then the equally small hallway that led from the base of the stairs to the kitchen, careful to keep her knee from straining.

Here it was a week into their occupation of Spite House, and none of the women had made any move to leave. The first few days had been rough, but instead of decamping to a hotel, they hooked a generator to the circuit box, turned the water on with the curb key, and claimed rooms. The guy at the hardware store warned them against the generator as a permanent solution, but he'd sold them an inverter that gave them enough juice to power the refrigerator, a few lights, and when it got really cold a space heater. Using a permanent marker, Isobel scrawled lists of what each room needed on yellowed wallpaper. She called contractors and talked about electrical updates and plumbing issues of homes built in the Jazz Age. In the mornings, Lizzie often found Elyse making her way through the house with a pad of sticky notes, tagging every item of potential value to check it against similar antiques online. Nothing about these actions appeared temporary to Lizzie.

Her body ached from the rehab and conditioning she'd put herself through that morning. She eased into a chair next to Elyse, who wore three shirts and was paging through one of Lizzie's grandmother's ancient cookbooks.

"Found these for you," Elyse said, pushing over several dusty shoe boxes. "They were in the wardrobe in my bedroom."

"Grandma always did like to hide stuff. You can't open a closet or a drawer or even dust under the bed without unearthing some container stuffed with bits of her life."

The back door opened, letting the chill of the January air into the sun-warmed kitchen. "We've got to get the power back on. That generator is ridiculous. I have to drive to the gas station every day to fill the damn thing." Isobel dusted her hands against her jeans. She had dried leaves in her hair. "You get in touch with code enforcement yet?"

"Can't find my phone," Lizzie lied. She opened a tan box marked "Halloween."

"So, you haven't talked to your mother? Or code enforcement?"

"I will." Lizzie tried not to be defensive, to expect Isobel of all people to understand how hard it was to call her mother and have a conversation—about money, expectations and failures.

Isobel looked as if she were about to say more, but instead she mentioned cleaning up and disappeared upstairs.

"She's not going to let you slide much longer," Elyse said.

Lizzie let her fingers sift through the contents of the box, which contained dozens of letters and handfuls of photographs from three or four different decades. "What about you?"

"I'm a free spirit," Elyse said, dog-earing a page in the cookbook. "Nobody cares if I disappear for weeks, or even months. Besides, it's a place I could see myself staying."

"Honestly?" Before Lizzie could push her cousin further on the idea, she glimpsed several Polaroids of her mother with feathered hair. Lizzie turned the box upside down and let its contents spill onto the floor. She'd seen a photograph like that once before—it was from the year her mother was pregnant with her.

Isobel reappeared with a towel wrapped around her. "I found your phone. Forty-two text messages and seventeen missed calls."

Lizzie ignored her. Among the pictures she clutched was one of her mother taken when she must have been six or seven months pregnant.

"What are we going to do about this?" Isobel asked, putting an emphasis on the word "we" that made Lizzie think there was about to be an intervention.

"Why do we have to do anything?" Lizzie moved her thumb over her mother's face and studied the photograph for clues about what had been happening in her life that year. Who had she spent time with? What had she been like?

"What if we wake up tomorrow and they're bulldozing the place on top of us?" Isobel brought her hands together, as if the house had collapsed in on itself.

"That won't happen," Lizzie said. In the photograph, a man a little older than her mother stood to the side. He had heavy eyebrows and splotchy skin. She couldn't tell if he was with her mother or just in the background. "Last time I talked to that secretary over there, she said to wait for them to call me."

Isobel handed Elyse the phone. Looking up, Lizzie saw that they were reading her messages. "You can't ignore your family," Elyse began before changing topics. "And what about your leg? When does your trainer want you back in Los Angeles?"

Lizzie didn't want to talk about her knee. During their last phone conversation, her trainer had kept talking about where Lizzie should be instead of where she was. The fact that he wouldn't talk about the Olympics and cautioned her about expecting too much from her body worried her. "What about you? Why is it that you left Boston?"

"I'm on vacation," Elyse said, looking at the photograph in Lizzie's hand. "That your mother?"

"We're not getting anywhere with this," Isobel said.

Elyse had taken the picture from Lizzie. "I bet this house is full of stuff from your mom."

Lizzie looked around the kitchen. The walls were lined with handwritten notes from her grandmother and mementos from her mother's childhood. She thought about the other rooms in the house and the sheer amount of miscellany hidden in its nooks. The most success she'd ever had in rehab had been with her first therapist, Phil. He'd believed in her in a way no one ever else had. She thought about what her mother would owe her if she rescued the house. "I've been thinking about staying," Lizzie decided. "I mean for a while. For as long as it takes."

"To fix the house?" Isobel asked.

Lizzie didn't meet her eyes. She wasn't thinking only about the house.

"You can't do this stuff on your own. Hell, I can't even do some of it. We're talking wiring at the very least, and I wouldn't be surprised if the plumbing is compromised." Isobel looked at Elyse, who passed her the photograph.

"I'll hire someone."

"You'll be lonely," Isobel said and then nudged Elyse as if to give her a line prompt.

"It has to be her idea."

Lizzie reluctantly set the photographs aside. She'd been right to suspect her cousins of intervening. They talked over her, as if she weren't in the room.

Isobel rubbed Lizzie's back in slow circles. "But she won't. You know that."

"You have to ask us," Elyse said.

Lizzie shook her head. She couldn't ask them. It was too much, even for almost sisters.

"Wonder if your mother still has that T-shirt." Elyse had a sense of when to press people and when to give them a break. "My dad talks about being at that game all the time, says the AC was out and that it must have been a hundred degrees in the arena."

Lizzie took the photo back, staring at her mother's green Celtics' shirt and started to ask Elyse when she needed to go back to work, but instead of answering, Elyse again brought up her rehab plans.

"I could do it here. I've done it before." And then before she could lose her nerve, she asked about Elyse's timeline. "How long could you stay?"

Elyse looked away from her. "A day, a week, a month. I paid extra for one of those open-ended tickets."

Isobel caught Lizzie's eye and then shrugged; there was a sense in everything Elyse had told them about her visit that she was holding back. Before she lost her nerve, Lizzie asked Isobel about staying. "Don't you have to get back to auditions and your property and such?"

"I don't have to do anything. If you asked me to stay, I could," Isobel said, stepping back from the two of them and running her fingers over the frames of the doors and the windows. "I can rent out my half of the duplex if we stick around here a while. That'll give me some walking-around money."

"Your trust fund all tapped out?" Lizzie teased. They'd always given Isobel a hard time about the money she'd earned from the show. Mostly because the sums, at least when they were children, had been staggering. They pictured rooms full of gold coins with Scrooge McDuck swimming through them. "It's all tied up in real estate," Isobel said, her voice flattening.

"I like this house," Elyse interrupted. "It's a little bit pissed off, like all of us."

"You don't have to stay," Lizzie said, her mind already considering how much she needed them to. "The more I'm here, the more I feel like I can't leave."

"Come on," Elyse said. "You can barely move around with your knee."

Isobel, channeling their childhood, moved her index fingers in circles to indicate how crazy Lizzie was acting. "How are you going to fix a place when you can't tell me the difference between a Phillips and a flathead."

"What is she talking about?" Lizzie said to Elyse.

"Are you asking us to stay?" Isobel asked.

"I'm asking," Lizzie finally said.

"Then it's settled." Elyse picked up Lizzie's phone and scrolled through the contacts until she found the number for Lizzie's parents in Russia. She pressed call and handed over the phone. Lizzie listened to the metallic ping of the ring and began a mental list of who she'd have to call next. Before her mother picked up, Lizzie put her hand over the receiver.

"I'm glad you're here," she said to her cousins, who stood by the large windows looking over the bluff. She stretched out her leg on the empty chair next to her. Isobel blew her hot breath on the glass panes in the door, and Elyse reached over and traced out three figures connected at the hands, like a chain of paper dolls.

When code enforcement finally caught up with them, Lizzie, in between conditioning and therapy appointments, had put on one of her grandmother's cocktail dresses and had a fox stole, complete with leathery paws and glass button eyes, draped around her shoulders. Her cousins had offered to run errands while she sorted through the items that the three of them had cleared out from several of the house's wardrobes. Clothing, hat boxes, shoes, and the like were piled on the kitchen floor. A deep pounding at the front door startled her. Although the noise demanded her immediate attention, her leg had stiffened while she'd been on the floor and getting up proved a challenge.

Commands were shouted through the door. She couldn't make out but a few words: police, unlawful. "I'm coming," she called, as she leaned against the narrow hallway and limped toward the entrance. The wood of the front door groaned. Frantic to get to it before they could burst inside, Lizzie took a step on her right leg, and it buckled under her. She scooted toward the door, reaching to unlock and open it. When the door swung inward, she still sat on the floor. The fox had slid down her shoulder so that the tail tickled her collarbone.

The men looked over her head and yelled more agitated words.

"Why are you here? Who are you?" one of the officers shouted.

Lizzie backed away in surprise. The man had appeared by her side as if by teleportation. He crouched next to her. The shoulders of his uniform shirt were too wide.

"I live here," Lizzie said. She struggled to stand. Another officer, this one large and imposing, held his arm out. When she reached for him, he grasped her by the wrist, pulling her to her feet in one quick motion. She swayed, unsteady and unsure who was in charge.

"Who are you? Do you have identification?" the small officer asked again. He reached out and put his hand on Lizzie's shoulder. The fox fell to the floor without her moving to pick it up. With his other hand he pointed at her purse, which was hung on the banister post at the base of the staircase. She realized they were the same height. "Is that yours?"

Her knee wavered as if someone had kicked the back of it, and she felt the color drain from her face. The officer steadied her. A black man in a shiny suit pushed his way into the house. He had a clipboard and radiated authority.

"This is my grandmother's house. It was," Lizzie corrected herself. "I mean my mother owns it now."

"You're in violation," the man in the suit said. He moved his hand across his clean-shaven head and looked down at his papers. "Didn't you see the notices? This house is set to be sold at auction at the end of February."

"I don't know." Lizzie didn't want to lie, but she wasn't ready to admit to having ignored the signs until she knew how much trouble she was in. "I tried calling about the power and stuff, but nobody ever calls back."

"Our records show the certified letters we sent to the property owner were returned. Do you know anything about that?" The man rocked on his heels and made notes in block letters. He looked to be in his early thirties and had high cheekbones and full lips. Looking at him, she thought that despite his hard edge, he could be generous.

He'd realized she was staring at him, and she felt the blush of embarrassment. "No. I mean my parents are out of the country and I—"

"But you're the current homeowner's representative?"

"I don't understand," Lizzie said. She wanted to fill up the space between them with words. To explain to the man in the suit and the police officers about all the work that they'd already done on the house, to prove to them that the place shouldn't have been condemned at all. She thought that if she could walk the men through the house, have them feel its odd sturdiness and read Isobel's wall lists, they'd clap her on the back and tell her what a good job she'd done and what a fine daughter she was.

"Miss. Miss. Are you all right? Are you in an altered state?" The smaller officer had picked up the fox and was trying to settle it back onto her shoulders.

The man in the suit smelled improbably like the beach. He pushed past them, motioning for the larger officer to follow him. "She's fine. Get her identification."

"I don't know about this, T. J.," the larger man said, eyeing the narrow staircase. He turned to Lizzie. "You don't have any dogs, do you?"

The man in the suit compressed his lips into a thin line. Lizzie realized that his had been the signature on the paperwork tacked to the front door. *T. J. Freeman, Code Enforcement.* "Fine. You talk to the girl and Slim Jims here can come upstairs. None of this is code. None of it. These old houses drive me crazy. Built on a wing and a prayer with secondhand wood."

The two officers shrugged and switched places, the smaller one rolling his eyes as he followed T. J. up the stairs. Lizzie wondered what he was looking for. She grabbed her purse and motioned for the larger man to follow her, walking sideways down the hall so he wouldn't feel crushed by the narrow space.

"Did your grandmother pass away recently?" the officer asked, surveying the open trunk, photo albums, and old greeting cards scattered next to the piles of clothing.

"No," Lizzie said, digging through her purse for her wallet and extracting her identification. She gave him the license and tried to explain how her parents—or rather her mother, stepfather, and four younger half-siblings, were in Russia. "It's a church thing," she said finally, knowing how inadequate it sounded. "He's in charge of the mission work they do over there."

"To each their own," the officer said. "Did you want to call someone?"

Lizzie raised her head up and looked at him. "Who?"

"Your contractor? Your lawyer? Your priest? I mean, with a house like this . . ." he trailed off.

"My grandfather built it," Lizzie said, feeling a flush of anger at the dismissal of her and the house.

"You think about it," the officer said, taking the driver's license she held out to him. He looked down at the plastic card. "Florida, huh? You're a long way from home."

"It isn't home," Lizzie said. "It's where I sometimes stay."

"Don't go anywhere. Not that you look like a runner," he said, explaining that he was going to go to his car and run her information.

She took her phone from her purse and texted her cousins. Elyse sent back a frowning face, and Isobel assured her they were on their way. In the few moments she had to herself, she navigated to the city's code enforcement website and tried to figure out how much trouble she'd gotten herself into.

The oversized cop thumped back into the house, waving Lizzie's license in front of him as he walked through the beaded curtain. "You're clean. No warrants, no arrests."

Unlike that of his partner, his uniform fit well. "Will that help?" she asked.

"Standard procedure in situations like this"—he gestured toward the ceiling, indicating where, she presumed, his partner and the enforcement officer were cataloging violations—"is to cite you and escort you off the property."

Lizzie didn't listen closely to the rest of what he had to say. She put her head in her hands and held her breath in a vain attempt to hold back the tears. Her knee twitched with pain. The larger officer put his hand on her arm. His palm felt rough and calloused against her skin.

The laughter of the other men echoed above them. He stepped away from her. "It's not so bad as you think."

The back door opened, and a rush of wind blew dead leaves and small clumps of dirt over the threshold. Isobel threw out her arms, and said, "I'm here. Elyse is in the car calling some lawyer she knows in Boston."

"It's hopeless," Lizzie said.

"Nonsense." Isobel shrugged out of her coat and took off her sunglasses. She appeared oblivious to the officer, who hadn't stopped smiling since her cousin entered the house. If Lizzie were a gambler, she'd bet that he'd seen every episode of her cousin's show. Like most child actors, Isobel was often recognized but not identified. People tended to think she was someone they knew in school—a familiar face from their childhood. And in a way she was, especially for anyone close to her age. From the time Isobel was eleven until she was twenty, she'd played Gracie Belle Wait on *Wait for It*—one of the first attempts by a cable network at a sitcom.

She turned toward the officer. "What can we do to fix this?"

He looked over his shoulder and then in a low voice said, "Play dumb and flirt a little. Code enforcement spends their days dealing with slumlords and squatters. Pretty women like you ought to be able to change T. J.'s mind."

The tinkle of the beaded curtain announced the arrival of the other men. Lizzie watched her cousin transform into someone else. She pulled her shoulders back and lowered her chin, striking a pose that made her breasts seem larger. The officers snuck quick glances at her chest and, as if to encourage them, Isobel leaned toward them as they spoke. Lizzie saw that by closing the space between them, her cousin had made the men seem like old friends. She lowered her voice when she introduced herself; instead of shaking hands, she ran her hand down each man's arm and then gripped his outstretched hand in both of hers.

By the end of the visit, T. J. Freeman had explained their options—which consisted of paying a $500 fine for contempt and asking Judge Hootley, who ran the court where their case would be heard, for an appeal of the court's decision to auction the property. As he spoke, T. J. kept wiping his shaved head with his hand and then drying it on his front-button shirt. Unlike the other men, he didn't look at Isobel. Whenever Lizzie glanced at him, she found he was already looking at her. Before he left, he pressed his card into Lizzie's hand, urging her to call him if they ran into any further problems.

Elyse came in the back door. "I saw them leave," she said, before looking at Lizzie. "What in the hell are you wearing?"

Lizzie pulled self-consciously at the satin dress, getting a scent of mothballs as she did so. "It's too much to explain. We got lucky, though."

"I didn't even notice the fox," Isobel said, reaching for the shrug, which had been dropped on the table and then hugged it to her chest before responding to Lizzie's earlier comment. "That's because he liked you."

"Hardly," Lizzie said, pulling her hair out of its ponytail. "You're the one they kept their eyes on."

"She's right," Elyse said. "You've got a vulnerability right now that's working for you. In fact, I've never seen it in you before. You've always been so damn self-sufficient that a man can't fathom how he fits into your life."

"So, the way to find a man is to fall on your ass in front of him?"

"Not all men, some men. Men like T. J. are providers by nature. You've mostly dated takers." Too often, Elyse's assessment of the cousins proved uncomfortably accurate.

"Let's not talk about it." Lizzie gathered the memorabilia she'd been absorbed in earlier that day, dumping the whole lot of clothing into the give-away pile. Isobel helped, stacking photographs into tidy piles.

"Your grandmother was a hottie," Elyse said, thumbing through several postage-stamp-sized pictures. "She's got that thing where you don't want to look away."

"Charisma," Lizzie said, putting the last of the pictures back in the trunk.

Isobel buttoned the fox around her shoulders. "Can I keep this?"

Lizzie nodded. "I was planning to dump all this stuff at Goodwill."

"Let me ask you something." Isobel leaned close. "What's the plan here? If I learned anything today, it's that we need to be serious with this. Do we have enough money in your grandmother's trust to hire someone to work on this place?"

Elyse interrupted. "What do your parents have to say about this mess? I mean, it really is their mess when it comes right down to it."

"What Mellie left should be enough—especially if I have the two of you helping with the stuff we can do. But when the money's gone, it's gone. You know how my parents are about debt."

"They still think credit cards are the sign of Satan?" Isobel asked.

"They're not that bad. I can't ask them for money—not after all the sacrifices they've already made so I could play." One of the guilt trips that Lizzie's mother often laid on her was what it had cost the family to support her in soccer. They'd added it up one time and it totalled nearly fifty thousand dollars when they took into account fees and travel. "And I had this idea that if I do this, then my mother will finally owe me something."

"They really sold their house and used that money to pay for this mission?" Elyse asked.

"Called of God is called of God," Lizzie said, echoing what her mother always said. "I don't have any money either, I mean not really. They don't pay you to play soccer—at least not anymore."

"Let me at least pay rent," Isobel said.

"I've been thinking about getting a job," Elyse said. "I could use the distraction."

Lizzie argued with Isobel. "We talked about this. Doing what you're doing—taking charge of the stuff I don't know about is enough. When we really get into the fixing stuff, then you'll have to earn your keep—you know, look over the shoulder of whoever I hire to do this stuff and make sure he's not cheating us."

"You got someone in mind?" Isobel backed down, and Elyse followed her lead.

She nodded. In the last conversation she'd had with her parents, her mother had suggested a man she went to high school with who'd worked on the house over the years for Grandma Mellie. He worked cheap and he knew the house, which Lizzie guessed was what they needed. "Enough about money. It's fine. Or rather, it'll be fine."

"You've got to stop saying that," Elyse said, touching Lizzie lightly on the head. "If I could change one thing about this world, it would be the need for everyone to hide their panic."

On the third floor, in the ceiling above the landing, there was a metal pull that concealed the stairs to the cupola. Since arriving in the house, Lizzie had tried in vain to get the stairs to pull down. With their first meeting with the contractor scheduled for the next day, getting into the cupola and then out onto the roof felt like a mandate. Isobel took the rope from Elyse and tied it to the brass ring. Lizzie stepped back, wondering at her cousin's confidence.

"If we all put our weight on it, the stairs will have to come unstuck," Isobel said, grabbing the rope at a point near the top. The others copied her and on the count of three, they pulled down sharply and lifted up their feet.

The stairs popped and then slid out with excruciating slowness. They made Elyse go first since she put up a fuss about climbing the backless stairs. Isobel followed, carrying a broom. Lizzie had tried to warn them about how small the space was, but when she finally made it up the stairs, she found Elyse marveling that by stretching her arms, she could touch all sides of the cupola. Behind them, a second room expanded the area beyond the telephone-booth-like space that the stairs opened into. The larger room had a barn door on rollers and window seats. There were a few cast-off items littering the floor, including a smaller replica of Spite House that, if she remembered correctly, had once been a mailbox. The prisms that were so much a part of Lizzie's childhood remained in place. Isobel pushed through both rooms, spilling out onto the roof with the relief of someone who didn't like small spaces.

"Did I hear you on the phone with that inspector last night?" Elyse asked, stepping out behind her onto the roof.

Lizzie shrugged. He'd called officially a few days earlier to help her file the paperwork to get the utilities turned on and to get their property removed from the auction listing. The conversation had surprised her by feeling familiar and by the end of it, he'd given her his cell number and she'd called, at first to ask about garbage pick up, but mostly to hear his voice.

"I told you he liked you," Isobel said, turning and looking back at the cupola, holding her hands out in a frame and then walking around the structure. "Flat roofs are so much trouble. You need an angle, something for all of this crap to roll off of."

"When will anything not be trouble?" Lizzie asked, her good foot kicking at the muck of decomposing leaves that lined the outer edges of the roof.

"Don't you want gloves?" Elyse offered a pair to Lizzie before working the handle of the broomstick under the layer of debris on the easternmost corner of the roof and watching as several beetles crawled away after having their soft bellies exposed.

Lizzie grabbed a handful of leaves and threw them over the side of the house, wiping her hands on her jeans before putting on the gloves.

"What's the story with this house anyway?" Elyse asked when the debris was mostly cleared.

"My grandfather's brother gave him a piece of land that he thought useless. And instead of letting it go fallow, he built this house."

"No romance? No illicit activity? Places like this always have a bit of scandal attached to them." Elyse took a handkerchief from her pocket and wiped her hands. "It smells strange."

"That's the scent of a storm. Winter rains clean off the dirt in preparation for spring," Lizzie said, echoing a phrase of her grandmother's. She stood the broom against the cupola and turned toward the horizon, watching dark clouds roll across the sky from Arkansas. The broom fell with a clatter that made them jump.

"Rain's back," Isobel said. "I guess the storm is moving faster than predicted."

"This wasn't the end of the storm, it was a break," Lizzie said, picking up the broom and sweeping furiously at the edges of the flat roof.

"Do you get tornados out here?" Elyse asked, using the edge of her dustpan to clear acorns piled against the roofline.

"Who's to say? People around here believe that the bluffs keep tornados from hitting Memphis, but a few years ago we had one take out part of the mall, so you never know." A wet drop stung Lizzie's cheek. It was followed by the long boom of thunder rolling across the sky.

"Too much uncertainty for me. I'm beginning to feel like this end of days stuff is something I should take seriously," Elyse said. She'd always been more worried about natural disasters than most people were. It had something to do with never having lived in a place where natural disasters happened. Both Lizzie and Isobel had spent much of their lives living on fault lines—the San Andreas and the New Madrid.

"We haven't even talked about earthquakes. The last one reversed the direction of the river and rang the Liberty Bell all the way up in Pennsylvania."

Isobel continued to stand too close to the edge of the roof. "Stop scaring her."

Elyse pulled up the hood on her sweatshirt as protection against the increasing rain. "So, this whole place could fall? Collapse the sixty feet down to Front Street?"

"You worry too much. There would be signs. Nothing happens unexpectedly. The trick is to know what you're looking at," Lizzie said.

"I'm never sure what any two things add up to," Elyse said.

"Come on, we can watch the storm from the cupola." Lizzie covered her head with her arms. She held the door open for them and they settled onto the window seats that had been built along three of the walls. Sometimes the rain fell so heavily that they couldn't make out the river, and other times piercing lightning exploded in the sky. All the while, Lizzie talked about what she knew of Spite House's history.

"Is that a leak?" Elyse asked, pointing to a thin line of water running along the inside of the glass. Each of the windows was divided into a dozen rectangles, and the glass in each portion held slight imperfections.

"It could be condensation," Isobel said. She showed her cousins the imperfections. "All of this was hand blown." She touched the few panes of bull's-eye glass. The slight outward bowing of the glass was where the glassblower had separated the melted glass from his wand.

"It's pretty," Elyse said, pointing out two more on her side of the cupola, "like someone started to form a bubble and it froze in mid-blow."

"You never see it anymore. Most builders considered it imperfect, and when they cut the glass, they put these in out-of-the-way places, like barns or back rooms," said Isobel.

Lizzie placed her palm flat against one of the rectangles until the outline of her hand appeared. "I didn't think you'd remember so much about houses. Your father stopped taking you out on jobs with him when you started the show, right?"

"Memory is a funny business." Isobel stood on the window bench to better inspect the ceiling. "So this house sits at the very southern end of what would have been your family's land?"

In answer, Lizzie blew on the window and then in the spreading of fog traced a rough sketch of the property lines. The warehouses to the north of the house had all been torn down, and the rail yard that had been to the south of the property had been developed into the kind of homes NBA stars and Cybill Shepherd lived in. She explained how her grandfather had worked out a way to build a house that mimicked the shape of the river. "See, the skinny part of the house is like the thin trickle of the start of the river, and then it explodes outward as it reaches the edge of the bluffs—like the delta."

"And they called it Spite House because he built it just to show it could be done?" Isobel asked, running her fingers along the roofline to try to locate the source of the water.

"Yes and no," Lizzie said.

"What about the story out front, on the marker?"

"Ooooh," Elyse said, her eyes widening. "What it says about unmentionables being hidden from prying eyes makes me think there's so much more to the story."

Lizzie hated the simplistic nature of the story on the historical marker. The sign explained that there were two kinds of spite houses. The first were made out of spite—that is to piss somebody else off. And this house had supposedly been built because it was the only land their grandfather was given. The other reason was particularly Southern. There'd been a tradition during the 1800s of hiding away disgraced relatives (the knocked-up, the financially ruined, the sexually confused) in smaller houses on large estates. After emancipation, estate owners discovered they had an excess of smaller structures.

Lizzie shrugged, blew again on the glass, and drew a heart. "I don't know much about that part of the story. Grandpa Roger died long before I was born. Mama didn't even know him that well. She was eight or so when he had his heart attack while working up at the brewery. They paid him to watch the place at night."

Lightning struck the protective rod on the office building next door, and the windows shook in their frames. Elyse jumped as if she'd been bitten, pointing and yelling, but her words were lost in another bromide.

"You're such a scaredy-cat," Isobel said.

"There's another leak," Elyse said, "and now my pants are wet."

The two of them started arguing as if they were sisters rather than cousins. They'd been like this when they were children. The tension made Lizzie nervous. Looking for a distraction, she took up the broom and nudged the ceiling, seeking the source of the leak. The handle landed in a soft spot near the center of the room, and without thinking, she pushed against the give of the tile. In one rushing motion, the center of the ceiling split and water rained down on the three of them.

When the screaming stopped, the laughter started. Lizzie had gotten the worst of it. Because the water had soaked her, bits of the drywall and insulation stuck to nearly every part of her body. Her feet sloshed in her sneakers as she tried to step over the rubble. Elyse had managed to stay mostly dry by jumping down the ladder to the third-floor landing. She lay sprawled on her back, like a pill bug turned over, laughing so hard that her stomach jiggled. Just past where the ceiling had opened up, Isobel stood, her hands still raised to protect herself and spewing out a long string of swear words that were as nonsensical as they were loud.

In the noise of the collapse, Lizzie couldn't make out what her cousin had been saying, but now that it had stopped, she heard the tail end of Isobel's tirade. "Holy hell and dammit all for fucksake stop."

"Yes," Lizzie said, reaching for the broom handle that stuck up from the rubble like a flagpole. It took a minute to wrench it free and then another minute for her to decide where to start sweeping.

It took the better part of the day to mop the water from the space and clean up the bits of drywall, roofing tile, and insulation that littered the cupola floor. Because Lizzie couldn't stand for long periods of time, Isobel had taken away her broom and given her a screwdriver, telling her to pull the hinges off the window seats and set the cushions to dry in the empty front rooms.

To their surprise, neatly stacked inside each seat were dozens of wooden cigar boxes. Lizzie didn't remember them being there when she'd spent time at the house regularly. But that in and of itself wasn't remarkable. Although Mellie's house had been stuffed, she'd constantly moved her keepsakes around. Once they got a tarp strung across the hole and Isobel was satisfied that they'd cleaned up most of what they could in preparation for the contractor, they carried the boxes to the kitchen table.

There were only a few items remaining from their last sorting project, when they'd emptied the wardrobes. Elyse had a pile of items in the corner that she felt they could sell online, and Lizzie had taken the mementos she wanted to keep to her room. "I feel like that girl who learns the spell to make soup but doesn't know how to stop it," Lizzie said as she set her stack of boxes on the table.

"Time," Isobel said. "Your grandmother spent decades putting her stamp on this house. Don't tell me you expect to undo that in a matter of weeks."

"I don't feel like I'm learning anything."

"Patience," Isobel said.

"I guess old Grandpa Roger smoked cigars, " Elyse said, opening a wood box with a white owl on the lid and passing a handful of black-and-white photographs with scalloped edges to Lizzie. A girl in eyelet lace stood in front of the remains of a building that appeared to have been flattened. The wing of an airplane stuck up from the wreckage. Flipping it over, she saw that someone had written "Melanie L., 1944."

"None of these are of any use," Lizzie said as she opened a few of the cigar boxes and rapidly flipped through handfuls of photographs. "I need stuff from the eighties."

Lizzie found a few more photos that showed various angles of the downed plane and puzzled over the wreckage and her grandmother's presence in it. In the background, she recognized several buildings from the Crosstown area of Memphis.

Isobel examined the photographs as Lizzie set them down. "What was your grandma's maiden name?"

"Linwood," Lizzie said.

"I thought that was her married name," Elyse said. She carefully stacked the square photographs and then asked if she could have them. "There's a mystery here and a hint of tragedy."

"It's not a book," Isobel said.

"Still." Elyse closed her eyes and for a moment looked as sad as Lizzie had ever seen her. "There's so much you don't know about people."

"They're yours," Lizzie said before shutting the lid of each box and scowling. "Do you know my mom never had any photo albums of her childhood in our house once she married Jim? I didn't even know these existed."

"Everyone values different items," Isobel said. "My dad carts all of his high school swimming trophies to every house he's ever lived in, but I've never seen a graduation picture."

"Useless," Lizzie said, gathering up the last of the boxes without opening them. She'd wanted the pictures they'd found to have value. At that point, she couldn't see how anything about her grandmother's life would tell her what she needed to know about her mother's pregnancy. She kept searching the house hoping for anwers about her father, but instead, every clue affirmed how little she knew about her family. She'd come back to the boxes later, when she had the patience for her grandmother's secrets.

Benny, the contractor, didn't believe in knocking. This is what he said to Lizzie the next morning when he walked into the house unannounced and surprised her in the kitchen. She had her back to the narrow hallway and had been doing her prescribed leg-strengthening exercises. Although she hadn't admitted it to anyone, her knee didn't feel like it should. There was a resistance when she tried to straighten it that had never been there in her previous recoveries. She had an appointment with Phil, her old therapist, for the first part of February. In the few weeks she'd been in Memphis, she'd tried the rehab specialist suggested by the team, but it hadn't felt like a good fit, and she'd missed more appointments than she should have. Although she was careful to follow the regimen prescribed by the team, she found that she couldn't make herself actually see the therapist. The woman who worked with her kept telling her how poorly she was doing and using words like "realistic." Phil had been there for her through her other two surgeries and what she knew about him was that he believed in her healing.

"Biggest flood we ever had was in winter," the contractor said by way of greeting. "Course we been in a drought situation ever since last summer. Not that you'd know it looking at what the Lord blessed us with today."

Lizzie tightened the belt of her robe and took his extended hand as he introduced himself. She wished Isobel hadn't scheduled some interview with the local paper about her temporary stay in Memphis. That was the girl's mother in her, seeking publicity at the least opportune times. She would have dealt with Benny (and his handshake, which had turned into a high five) with much more ease. Afterward, Lizzie shook her stinging hand, thinking that she couldn't remember the last time she'd engaged in such an adolescent gesture.

"I didn't expect you so early," she said, forcing her eyes to his so as not to stare at the birthmark covering his neck. It was a deep purple and looked for all the world like a pair of hands trying to choke him. His eyebrows were so thick they looked false, like something you'd buy at Halloween to dress up as the mad professor.

"Isobel left me a message, said you girls had made a big ole mess yesterday. A roof collapse? I have to say I was worried you girls might not hire me, but now I can prove what I can do."

Lizzie felt her face redden and knew she wouldn't admit her fault in the matter. "Upstairs," she said and motioned for him to follow her. His eyes lingered on the stacks of cigar boxes.

She apologized for the mess and directed him to the top floor.

"Those boxes down there look old," Benny said as Lizzie tugged and heaved at the rope attached to the stairs.

"The water must have made the wood swell," she said, breathing harder than she had anticipated as she tried again to pull down the stairs.

"I'd tell you to put your weight into it, but you haven't got any," Benny said, reaching for the rope. He gave two short tugs, like warm-up pitches, and then put enough force into the third pull that he was left swinging on the rope when the stairs popped free. He gave one last jerk and the stairs came down with an audible groan.

"Grandma Mellie liked to say that wood likes to remind you it was a living thing once," Lizzie said.

"She was a great old lady. We got to be friends after your mama moved out." Benny looked away from her.

"It's true. Wood has a way of talking to you when you work on it—with the groaning and the squeaks."

Lizzie realized that Benny was close in age to her mother, which made him younger than she'd expected—closer to fifty-five than seventy. He had the weathered skin of someone who'd spent most of his life outdoors. Isobel's daddy was like that. Lizzie's stepfather was the youngest of the Wallace brothers, and no matter what happened, he would always look the part because he hadn't ever lost the little-boy fullness in his face. Benny started up the stairs.

"You may want to leave them open for the time being—give the place some air and let the wood dry out a bit," he said and then winked at her.

Lizzie turned away as he climbed the stairs, realizing she couldn't follow without shoes. Not wanting to go all the way to her room, she ducked inside Elyse's room, which had been Lizzie's mother's room. It was one of the smaller rooms that shared a wall with the bathroom and opened up by way of French doors to the front of the house. Lizzie hadn't spent much time in the space, but looking around, she was surprised at the sparseness of the room. In her youth, Elyse had been a clutterbug—arranging mementos like Laffy Taffy wrappers and trinkets purchased with arcade tickets—on every flat surface of their grandparents' summer home. The only clue that she lived there was a small notebook on her bed. Picking it up, Lizzie thumbed through it. She heard Benny call out to his crew, who she assumed were outside, and only took the time to glance at a few pages. She hadn't written much in it. Mostly it looked like passwords to her e-mail accounts. Grabbing a pair of sneakers, she shoved her feet into them, thankful that she and her cousins also shared the same shoe size.

"What's the damage?" Lizzie called as she emerged into the cupola.

Benny didn't respond. He was tossing chunks of the ceiling to the two men below, watching as they raced their wheelbarrows in an attempt to catch the shingles and pieces of wet drywall. His laugh sounded like a smoker trying to clear his throat. "Man, I could do this all day," he said, turning toward Lizzie and waving at his men to join them on the roof.

"Even in this rain?" she asked. She was a little angry that he'd been so presumptuous as to bring workers with him. "You're pretty sure you got the job, huh?"

He shook his head as if the topic weren't worth discussing. "This is a drizzle and as long as you've got money to pay, then I've got time to work. Y'all got enough money? Can't say as your grandma ever had any; that was why your mama was so unhappy here."

Lizzie pulled her shoulders together and stepped back from him so she'd appear taller. "Isobel said that's what you're here to do. Give us an estimate."

"Oh, we will," Benny said. "But it seems to me the most pressing concern is the hole in your roof, and that wasn't something me and Isobel discussed over the phone. That is what we call a change order and it's what kills any budget." He gestured to the sagging roof on the cupola. "Looks like another twelve hundred."

Lizzie didn't want to think about money. "Write up an estimate, and then we'll come to an agreement."

Benny continued talking as if he hadn't heard her. "The last time I worked on South Bluffs, the lady of the house kept changing her mind. I retiled the kitchen four times, and don't even get me started on the painting. Took me six weeks and fourteen colors to get one she could stand. I do love rich women."

"We're not rich," Lizzie said.

Benny licked his lips. They were chapped, suggesting it was a habit rather than a come-on. "Didn't that cousin of yours use to be famous? And you were in the Olympics or something?"

"Or something," Lizzie said. She walked to the cupola to inspect the damage.

Benny returned to the work. "People like that always got money."

Lizzie's eyes turned to the damage to the cupola. The hole itself wasn't as large as it had felt the day before—it was about the size of an open umbrella. She heard the clatter of Benny's men as they entered the cupola awkwardly, trying to bring up a small ladder. Lizzie tried to help them maneuver the space, concerned about the panes of glass. The thought of breaking the irreplaceable terrified her.

Benny mocked them for a few minutes, then, growing visibly impatient, he told them to get some rope and hoist it up from outside. Not sure of what she should be doing, Lizzie joined Benny at the end of the roof. They stared at the Mississippi in silence. It was a light brown color—reminding Lizzie of rinsing off after playing on a muddy field. The river was wider than it had been when she'd first arrived. She mentioned this, and Benny told her that the Big Muddy expanded and contracted into the flooding fields along the Arkansas side.

"I didn't play in the Olympics," she said.

"Neither did I," Benny said, offering a half-smile.

"Guess we're the same then," Lizzie said.

"More than you know," Benny said. His workers shouted at him and tossed up a length of rope, which he caught with the ease of a former athlete. Lizzie wondered what his sport had been—baseball or lacrosse, she thought, looking at his broad shoulders. In a moment, the roof was busy with the men's activities. Lizzie continued to stand at the edge of the house. Benny shouted to her from his position at the edge of the roof. "You know I've got kids that play soccer."

"It's a good sport," Lizzie said. "You don't have to be one particular build to play. You gotta know how to run and how to listen."

"They're not any good." He held the rope with one hand and tucked his hair behind his ears. It was longer than that of most men she knew. Some of the South American players Lizzie had known had kept their hair that long. She thought it odd for a Southern man. Granted, she hadn't been back in nearly a decade, but it looked out of place. "Don't get me wrong, I mean they do okay, but they're not phenomenal, like you were. Your grandma used to talk about you like you was Atalanta."

Lizzie shrugged. It embarrassed her to hear that other people had talked about her, even if it was praise. She certainly wasn't worth the comparison to mythology's fastest runner. With the brace on her leg as a constant reminder of what she couldn't do, discussing soccer was like drinking water in front of a desert hiker.

"They're always looking for coaches in the church leagues," Benny said.

"Maybe," Lizzie said. She hadn't ever wanted to coach—not that she'd ever even tried. Unlike most of the girls she'd played with growing up, she hadn't given a serious thought to much. Soccer kept her from getting serious about her life. Just the other day, she'd steered T. J. clear of the coaching subject when he brought up the need for one at his sister's school. Her only goal was to prove her coach wrong and be ready before the Olympic team roster was announced.

"No, no, no, no, no," Benny said, as the ladder slid from his grasp. Swear words in both Spanish and English echoed around them. After a heated exchange, Lizzie understood that one of the men below had stepped on a snake and inadvertently tugged on the wrong part of the rope, pulling the ladder out of Benny's hand.

"You afraid of snakes?" Benny asked, directing his men to send the ladder back up. "I don't like snakes."

"Snakes aren't any trouble at all," Lizzie said, still thinking about her injury. "Tendons, those will undo even the strongest."

February 2012: Memphis

When Lizzie's physical therapist had told her he'd opened his own office, she'd pictured a light-filled space with wood floors and private spa-like rooms for individual consultations. Aesthetics were how those who treated elite athletes differentiated themselves. The last time she'd visited his office, he'd been part of a vast complex attached to the hospital and she'd told herself that this new practice, one located near the trendiest part of Memphis, was sure to be a step up. She continued to tell herself this as she parked in the base-ment garage of the office building and took the musty-smelling elevator to the fifth floor.

She almost turned around when she stepped off the elevator and saw the vinyl lettering that differentiated Tremain's Target Therapy and Rehabilitation in Suite

508 from Lara's Paralegal Service in 506. Instead, she thought of the way her temporary therapist—the one suggested by her coach—compressed her lips into a straight line when she talked about wanting to be able to start playing by April at the latest.

The intake girl sighed heavily when Lizzie entered the gray and pink waiting room. She was several months pregnant, and the top of her scrubs rose up and exposed her belly when she reached for Lizzie's insurance card. After glancing at it, she told Lizzie to go on through to the patient area. "He'll find you. All he's done today is yip and yap about you coming in."

The space, about the size of a high school gymnasium, was carpeted. The white Nautilus machines were scuffed and grimy from heavy use, and rips to the leather tops of the treatment tables had been repaired with duct tape. None of this was as off-putting to Lizzie as the people she saw working on their rehabilitation. Not one person was under the age of sixty. When he'd worked at the larger office, they'd had a wide variety of patients and Phil had always worked with the athletes. That had been his specialty.

She cast her eyes to the right and watched a small woman with thinning white hair strain to push the hip abductor machine even a quarter of an inch. Her therapist, a heavyset black man wearing blue scrubs coached her in his unusually high voice. "Come on Ms. Lorraine, come on. I know you wanna beat Ms. Priscilla. I think she'll be giving up her walker any day now."

"Competition works whether you're young or old," Phil said, sliding up behind Lizzie and clasping her shoulder. "My heavens you've grown up."

"I'm not any taller, just older." She leaned down to hug Phil, who was one of the few short men she knew who wasn't self-conscious about his height.

He put his hand on the small of her back and walked her to a training table in the farthest corner of the room. "I know it isn't fancy, but I wanted to do it right, you know. Without loans and cosigners and—"

"It's fine." Lizzie dropped her eyes to the rubber-banded folders he held tucked under his left arm. She wanted to know what the doctors and the other therapists had said about her recovery. "What do you think?"

"Go ahead and lay back," Phil said, as he rolled the sleeves of his coat up. He ran his fingers along the side of her knee, pressing gently and then feeling it as if he were blind and reading Braille. Under his touch, she relaxed. This had been why she'd wanted to see him—his hands had a way of radiating healing just in the way they touched. He set her knee down and then took out his tape measure and goniometer and took her through the paces every other specialist had put her through to figure her range of motion.

Phil told her to sit up. "I gather you haven't been hearing what you want to."

"They have other agendas," Lizzie said, thinking of the dozens of other players who fell under the umbrella of the national team. "Everyone's risk averse these days. Besides, you know me. You know my knee."

"Have they talked to you about scar tissue?" Phil rubbed the knuckles of his ring finger and then spun his wedding band around. "There's a slight resistance and you're at 120 degrees when I'd thought you'd be closer to 125—"

"It's not. I mean I've never had that issue before."

"And you're ready to work?"

"Yes." Lizzie sat up. "Is that a yes to all of it?"

"It's more of a wait and see," Phil said, taking out a sheet of paper and walking her through the second eight weeks of her rehabilitation. A morning session followed by weights and interval training on the bike and then after lunch another therapy session.

"At least I get Sundays off," she said, folding the paper into thirds and tucking it into her pocket. "What do you get out of it?"

"You'll be good for business," he said, handing her a length of PVC pipe and explaining how to roll it against the back of her knee to break up any scar tissue. "I'll have you jogging in a month and then it's just a hop and a skip, literally, away from the pitch."

He took her through all of the exercises she needed to do in between appointments and then walked her through the conditioning portion of her rehabilitation. By the time they were finished, the rest of the patients had cleared out. The other physical therapists had settled into their offices in the back of the space, and the assistant put on headphones and wiped down the machines, cleaning in a rhythm that only she heard.

Sitting on the bike, Lizzie looked around the room and decided it was better to be in a place that looked like people had to work hard. She pushed herself faster even though she was supposed to be cooling off. If she had any chance of getting back on the team, she had to become so good that they couldn't ignore her.

Sunday mornings were quiet at Spite House. Lizzie allowed herself to stay in bed after sunrise and on those days, lying in the bed that had been her grandmother's, she let herself imagine the life she'd have after soccer. She imagined a satisfied life—one lived in a sunlit house with a husband who looked younger than he was and studious children who ran cross-country and played instruments. It was a lot to ask of the world, but the thought got her through the monotony of her present life. When she heard her cousins stir, she collected the newspaper and brewed coffee. After nearly a month and a half of living together, Lizzie knew to set aside the comics for Elyse and the real estate section for Isobel.

When they were awake enough to talk, they discussed the past. Elyse became a natural storyteller, recounting the demise of her ill-themed bed and breakfast, The Boston Cream, or her disastrous engagement at nineteen to a German pastry chef. "You wouldn't believe the sex jokes," she said and Lizzie didn't know if she were talking about the chef or the inn. There was little doubt that Elyse embellished her failures, but at least (and Lizzie envied her for this) she enjoyed them. Isobel tried to tell stories in which she failed, but in the end, there was always triumph. She bought a house in which chickens were kept indoors that turned out to have marble flooring under the soiled carpet. There was the time she and her father had to pay to have asbestos siding removed and discovered that the ugly cement tiles had been hiding striking stained glass windows. Lizzie talked about the incremental successes and failures that marked her time in rehab.

A knock on the front door interrupted their reminiscing. After a long pause, the bell rang twice. The cousins looked at each other and, although they'd done nothing wrong, they felt as if they'd been found out. At times, living in Spite House offered the same insulation from the outside world as a fortress. Lizzie offered to get rid of the salesman or Jehovah's Witness or whoever the uninvited party might be. With her rehab, she counted every step she took as one that got her closer to being whole. She opened the door, letting light into the confined space of the entryway. T. J., whom they had not seen since he threatened to evict them from their own house, stood with his hand raised as if to knock again. After speaking with him so often on the phone, the intimacy of seeing him in person was almost too much for Lizzie. "I took you for the sort of man who spends his Sundays in church," she said.

"My sister is the one who's big on church," he said, giving her a look that made her wish she were wearing something other than sweatpants. "But I have been known to sing in the choir."

"I thought so." Seeing him made her wish she'd done more to follow up on their case. "Are we in trouble?"

He held out a manila envelope. "Is that coffee I smell?"

"Subtlety isn't your strong suit." Lizzie stepped aside and invited him into the house. As they walked toward the kitchen, she opened the envelope and slid out the paperwork from the code enforcement office. They had stopped the auction process and issued a temporary occupancy permit for the house, which gave them the legal right to stay.

T. J. reintroduced himself to Isobel and Elyse and then helped himself to a cup of coffee. He stood slightly behind Lizzie and watched her look over the papers. "It's not bad," he said. "It looks worse than it is and you'll have until June."

Isobel reached over and took the paperwork from Lizzie. "We'll need far longer than June."

"There's a renewal option," T. J. said, blowing on his coffee and then taking a sip.

"It's like you started speaking French," Elyse said.

"How's this?" Isobel said. "We can get Benny to do real work now. Stuff that will make a difference, like the wiring."

"That's worthy of a celebration," Elyse said.

Isobel folded the paperwork into a square and put it in her pocket. She looked at T. J. and narrowed her eyes. "Why do this in person? Seems like the sort of news that goes through the postal service."

"I thought if we talked in person, I might convince you to go on that date I keep asking about," T. J. said, setting his cup on the table, and looking at Lizzie. "You know it took me all weekend to get up the nerve to knock on that door? I drove by on Friday and couldn't even get out of the car. On Saturday I made it up to the top of the stairs before I turned around."

"Date," Lizzie echoed.

In a rush, as if he'd prepared a speech, T. J. began to apologize for his behavior when they first met and told Lizzie that afterward he felt bad, like he'd kicked a puppy. He kept seeing her in the hallway dressed up in her grandmother's clothing and how, instead of looking vulnerable, she looked determined. "The difference between the possible and the impossible is a person's determination," he said as if it were a closing statement.

Elyse laughed. "Are you asking her out?"

"Of course he is," Isobel said. "And I'm sure she'd love to, wouldn't you?"

Lizzie had lost track of the conversation, but without knowing why, the no that had started to form on her lips changed to a yes when she looked into T. J.'s eyes. They agreed to brunch the following Sunday, and then he left with their coffee mug, one of Elyse's cranberry-orange muffins, and Lizzie's interest.

As February closed in on March, Lizzie watched Benny from the safety of the house. She brought boxes of Grandma Mellie's possessions into the kitchen and sorted through the crap. From what Lizzie observed,

Benny didn't work. He supervised. In the empty lot next to the house, which he referred to as the staging area, he'd parked a half-size recreational vehicle and plastered a vinyl sign to its side that read LaRusso Construction. Each morning he arrived with four or five day laborers in the back of his orange truck, gave them directions in Spanish so rudimentary that Lizzie wondered if he'd learned it from watching *Sesame Street*, and then shut himself inside the RV. He'd come out at lunch to check on the progress and then again before quitting time.

Isobel didn't like him. When she was home, she shadowed his workers, pointing out their flaws directly to them. More than once she stormed over to Benny's camper-cum-office to complain, and afterward he'd meekly asked Lizzie to help Isobel be a little less hands-on. Elyse, on the other hand, had let her interest in Benny and his stories develop into a near obsession. It was if she were cataloging his life. To what purpose, Lizzie couldn't fathom. It wasn't sexual and it wasn't fatherly. If it weren't so improbable, she'd say they'd become friends.

The last Thursday of the month, as Benny was giving his day's report, Elyse arrived home with a small bag of groceries and announced her intention of trying to use the cast-iron waffle maker. "Breakfast for dinner," she said and then greeted Benny with a kiss on the cheek. He spoke in low whispers to Elyse, who covered her mouth like a schoolgirl to laugh. The giggling unnerved Lizzie. She clapped Benny on the back and told him to go home before his workers demanded overtime.

Elyse sighed watching Benny leave. She opened the fridge and talked about the recipes she'd been finding tucked away inside Grandma Mellie's kitchen. "Time stopped around here," she said, taking out a can of lard. The effort Elyse put into food puzzled Lizzie, who saw meals merely as fuel for what her body needed to accomplish on any given day; and then there was Isobel, who after so many years living among skinny women, saw food as a necessary evil. Yet, of all of them, Elyse was the most comfortable with herself. She was sexy without being sleazy and nice without being a pushover. She was a little bit fat, but it wasn't what you noticed about her. Only after you'd been around her a while did you see that her pants were too tight and her arms doughy.

"The chef at the bar thinks Mellie's cookbooks could be valuable," Elyse said, closing the refrigerator. "I'm going to take her the Memphis ones tomorrow so she can look at them."

"How can you spend your time doing something like that?" asked Lizzie. Within a week of announcing her intention to get a job, Elyse had been hired as the afternoon bartender at a popular restaurant. She worked the lunch shift and then right up to dinner. She and the chef who showed up in the afternoons to oversee prep had become friendly. "It can't be what you want to be doing. I keep thinking about Mellie and how little choice she had. And look at us, the world is our oyster."

"You do what you can," Elyse said. "The two of you don't get it, you know? You're living your childhood dreams, and my dreams are more complicated than growing up to be the thing I wanted to be as a kid."

"There can't be any money in it," Lizzie said.

"You've never met afternoon drinkers," Elyse said, pulling a wooden spoon from the drawer. "There's a lot of shame and hush money involved."

"I've got to sit," Lizzie said, massaging the back of her knee.

"Still don't understand how you can spend six hours a day working out."

"Rehab is different from exercise."

"If you say so." Elyse put her finger to her mouth and looked upward in consideration. "Are you hungry now or can you wait? These waffles will be best right out of the pan."

"Isobel said she'd be out later than usual, something about having a conference call with her agent and some production company guy. We should wait."

"I'll make a few test ones and then we can fire it up again when she rolls in."

Lizzie watched her cousin crack eggs like chefs did on television, effortlessly with one hand. "You know, people think everything is better now, but it's not. Feel this." Elyse passed her the cast-iron waffle pan, which felt greasy to Lizzie. It weighed as much as a small car.

When she was cooking, her cousin exuded calmness. It was only in between activities that restlessness overcame Elyse. There was a girlishness about her, or even more than that, a childlike approach to the world around her—as if she still believed that puppy dogs and rainbows could brighten anyone's day. Here they were all still who they'd been as children. Elyse had always been chubby, but in an adorable way, and she'd been saved from ridicule then as now by her perfectly creamy skin and her girlish charm. She was the sort of woman men wanted to protect and women felt unthreatened by. Lizzie hadn't exactly given much thought to her appearance as a child. Some people would have called her a tomboy, but it wasn't so much that she disliked feminine traits as that she didn't have time for them. They hadn't known Isobel would be beautiful. What she had going for her, what she'd always had going for her were perfect proportions and dimples. Casting directors love dimpled children.

"What is it that you want? I mean, what are your dreams?" Lizzie asked. "I know what they used to be, but now that we're all grown up, I can't figure out what you want."

"The recipe calls for melted shortening, but you know what? I think I'm going to try using that bacon fat left over from this morning instead. Doesn't that sound yummy?"

"Not going to talk about it, huh?" Lizzie said. She didn't remember her grandmother ever making waffles with that particular pan, but she did remember that whenever the milk soured, Mellie used the curdled dairy to make what she had called dinner waffles. "Are you using sour milk?"

"That's the other recipe." Elyse passed over the large note card she was holding.

Lizzie stared at her grandmother's handwriting that noted simply "Breakfast Sour Waffles." It wasn't at all what she remembered. It looked like a version of her own handwriting when she was a teenager. Large circular loops—so that the *f*'s looked like *b*'s. The black ink had lightened to a milky brown over the years.

1 teaspoon salt
2 cups flour
1 teaspoon baking powder

2 eggs
3 tablespoons melted shortening
1½ cups sour milk

Use fork to stir salt, flour, and baking powder to-gether. Combine egg yolks, shortening, and sour milk. Stir with same fork. Beat egg whites in sepa-rate bowl with whisk until stiff. Set aside. Pour the wet ingredients into the dry and mix until batter is smooth. Fold in the stiffly beaten whites of eggs. Bake on hot irons. Six waffles.

Her cousin reached over and flipped the card in Lizzie's hand. "I'm doing those. I like a little sugar in my waffles. Only difference is you add a bit of sugar, use regular milk and wait to add the shortening, or in my case bacon fat, after you mix the wet and the dry."

Lizzie's stomach growled. "I guess I am hungry."

"We can always eat the test batch," Elyse said and winked as she used a whisk to stiffen the egg whites.

"There's a hand mixer somewhere," Lizzie said, moving to get up from the table.

Elyse waved her down. "I'm doing this the old-fashioned way."

She set the whites down and turned on the porta-ble propane burner they'd gotten at one of those giant camping stores.

"You want this back?" Lizzie pushed the cast-iron pan toward her cousin.

She picked it up and settled the base over the open flame and then set the waffle-patterned plates in place. "I'm going to let it get hot first."

"You should get a pot holder." Lizzie couldn't see how the mesh wire handles wouldn't be too hot to touch in a moment.

"It'll be all right." Elyse folded the egg whites into the batter and then dumped a large ladle of the batter onto the plates. Steam rose up into the air and condensed on the windows. Batter ran down the sides of the waffle maker, puffing as it came into contact with the hot iron.

A sweet, yeasty cake smell filled the kitchen. "You could always open a waffle house," Lizzie said.

Elyse flipped the pan and then scraped off the drippings with her fingernail and popped them into her mouth. "If I did, I'd be as big as the moon and then no one would ever love me."

"What?"

"I don't want to talk about it." The setting sun lit up all the flyaways in her cousin's hair and made her seem even more like a child.

"You should." Lizzie wondered if the thing bothering her cousin was the failure of the bed and breakfast or something larger.

Elyse opened the pan and pried out the waffle. "I'm fine," Elyse said, and although she didn't stamp her foot, her tone gave that impression. "My sister's getting married. BFD."

Although Elyse would never admit this, she disliked her little sister, Daphne, for being the favorite. This was understood between the cousins. Just as it was understood that Lizzie hated her mother for holding onto the truth about her real father, and Isobel didn't speak to her mother because she wasn't sorry about having left her father.

"That's not such a big deal," Lizzie said. "It isn't like biblical times when the older sisters had to get married first."

"I don't like weddings," Elyse said, taking a break from cooking to pour a large glass of white wine.

"I guess Pinot Grigio does go with everything," Lizzie said, tapping her fingers on the table. "There's something you're not saying."

Elyse finished the glass and poured a second, mumbling an answer in between.

Lizzie snapped her fingers. "Who is Daphne marrying?"

Elyse tore up bits of a waffle and dipped them in syrup. She wiped her mouth with the back of her hand. "Landon."

"Landon? Landon? The guy with only one arm?" Lizzie asked. Landon was the boy her cousin had had a crush on all through high school. He'd been born with some genetic condition and didn't have the lower half of his right arm. There came a point every summer when Isobel and Lizzie had to put a moratorium on any mention of Landon.

"It's not that I care," Elyse said before Lizzie could say more. "I had to adjust my expectations, you know? I mean there are things that you never dream of happening and then when they do—"

"You adjust," Lizzie finished.

Elyse didn't look at Lizzie. She made waffles until the batter was gone and then set a plate in front of Lizzie and put the rest in the oven to stay warm. "I lied to my mom, you know."

"That's a first."

"Told her that I thought you might kill yourself. That's the excuse I gave her to make it okay for me to be here while she and Daphne plan that wedding."

Lizzie wanted to be upset, but instead she laughed. "I guess that's as good an excuse for running away as any. She didn't believe you, did she?"

"She didn't even listen to me." Elyse looked at her fingernails and cleaned out the waffle residue.

"Moms never do."

Elyse fixed a plate and settled next to Lizzie at the table. She held still long enough for Lizzie to see the sadness settle on her. Her shoulders dropped, and she blinked often enough that Lizzie suspected she was afraid of crying. She clearly wasn't able to admit how deep her sadness was because her sister was marrying the man Elyse had always thought was hers. When life doesn't go the way you expect it to, you make strange choices. They ate until their plates were shiny with syrup and butter.

As they were doing the dishes, Isobel came into the house, all smiles. She took up Elyse's nearly empty wine glass and proposed a toast. Lizzie and Elyse fumbled around trying to find a glass to raise.

"I can't wait any longer," Isobel said. "I'm going to be back on television."

"Holy hell," Elyse said, clinking the whisk she'd grabbed to her cousin's glass. "How'd you manage that all the way out here?"

"Congratulations," Lizzie said, feeling her stomach constrict at the thought of Isobel's leaving them. She and Elyse would never be able to finish the house on their own.

Isobel talked about the offer, which was to be part of an hour-long "where are they now" type special on child stars of the nineties. A film crew would show up at Spite House for a few days and film Isobel working in the house. "I've even decided to try to do a little local theater, you know, so they can see that I'm still working on my craft."

"What does that even mean?" Elyse asked.

If anyone else had asked Isobel that question, she'd have turned cold. Arched one eyebrow and offered a half-smile as if responding would merely expose the asker to more embarrassment. Instead, Lizzie laid a hand on Isobel's arm as if to tell her all that she and Elyse had talked about earlier—Landon and the disappointment of not even knowing what dream it was that you were waiting to come true.

"I don't want to settle for one of those small lives—filled with jobs that pay for cookie-cutter houses in suburban neighborhoods where children are sent to good schools and I can't help but feel like it's all over." Isobel paused for breath and then took a long drink of wine. "I keep looking for a new start, but the past looms so large—as if the shadow of what I'd already done is enough to keep anything new from happening."

Without a word, Elyse got up, removed the remaining waffles from the oven where they'd been kept warm and fixed Isobel a plate.

March 2012 : Memphis

By the time the dogwoods bloomed in early March, Lizzie had a job. The dwindling balance in her grandmother's trust and the mounting costs of the renovation pushed her into calling T. J.'s sister, who needed help with an afterschool program her nonprofit organization ran. In less than an hour, Rosa May had hired Lizzie and put her to work.

"Walk with me," Rosa May said, motioning for Lizzie to follow her down a dim hallway Ignoring the grinding in her knee, she tried to keep pace with her.

"You must be a runner," Lizzie said, struggling to match Rosa May's stride.

She slowed. "I'm sorry. T. J. said you'd only now started to make real progress with therapy. I damaged my Achilles a few years back. It was murder to come back from."

"Murder's about right." For the last month, she and Phil had worked six hours a day on strengthening and conditioning exercises. Although he remained optimistic, her leg wasn't back to normal, but it was stronger. "If all goes well this week, I can start jogging again."

"Bet you're tired of that damn stationary," Rosa May said.

"Just the seat. No way a woman would ever design something so tortuous as a bicycle seat."

A girl approached them. "Miss Freeman," she said, and then dropped her voice too low for Lizzie to hear. Rosa May put up her hand indicating to Lizzie that she'd be right back and escorted the girl back to a classroom. Returning, she explained that the girls were divided by age and that they spent ninety minutes on homework and then ninety minutes on extracurricular activities. "This group has been playing basketball, but I'm tired of basketball. I can only use five at a time and it isn't easy for all the girls—the ones who are shorter or struggle physically. It's no good for them."

Rosa May's voice had a musical quality that made Lizzie think of choirs. She talked about why she'd started the program and the risk the girls were at for teen pregnancy. "I know what you're going to ask: How do we know who's at risk?"

Lizzie hesitated, thinking Rosa May would answer her own question, but the pause in the conversation became uncomfortably long and finally Lizzie ventured, "All of them?"

"That's right," Rosa May said, pausing at a closed door. " The reason T. J. had you call me is that what I want, what I've wanted from the beginning, is a way to get these girls active. Not to be blunt, but I want to exhaust them, leave them with not enough time or energy to get into trouble."

"Active," Lizzie echoed, looking at her knee. She needed that too.

"Can you coach girls who hate running?"

"We'll find out," Lizzie said.

"Let's say you can because I need you." Rosa May opened the door with a flourish. Inside were two dozen girls all looking glumly at textbooks or scratching in composition notebooks with chewed- up pens. "Meet your team."

A week later, the question of whether she could coach still echoed in Lizzie's mind. For the first three days of her new job, it rained. This meant that after homework had been completed, she was forced to stay with the girls in a portable classroom where they watched soccer games on tape, talked about the rules of soccer, and engaged in team-building and confidence-boosting activities (which were worksheets dropped off by a harried Rosa May). On the fourth day the rain ceased, but after walking the grassy field next to the community center where the outreach program was housed, she deemed it too wet to play. On the fifth day, the girls set fire to a trashcan of crumpled paper.

They'd been working on goal setting and Lizzie had made the mistake of crumpling a piece of paper and using her left knee, juggling it in the air several times before letting it fall and then kicking it into the wastebasket as if it were a ball. The girls erupted into hoots and calls for her to do it again. When she refused, they tried on their own to mimic her motions. Most of them weren't any good, but a few of them managed to juggle their pieces of paper more than once. Neela, who had short, flat-ironed hair that stuck out from her head like cedar shingles, particularly impressed Lizzie. But she'd lost control and she'd had to raise her voice and demand that the girls pick up their missed shots and return to goal setting. It had seemed such a simple exercise. What is your goal for today? What is your goal for tomorrow? Lizzie had been thinking about her goals and was erasing what she'd written down as her goal for a year from now when she smelled the smoke.

She looked up. Two girls in the back were smirking at her, and the rest of the class had their heads bent toward their papers. The two in the back were already pregnant. They weren't far enough along to show, but they'd made a point of telling her on the first day. Well, one of them made the point of telling her. Sonja had waist-length black hair and wore hoop earrings that were nearly larger than her face. The other girl, Drayden, didn't speak, but she made faces that were the equivalent of texting abbreviations—WTF and LOL seemed to be her favorites.

"My papa thinks I should play soccer," Sonja had said, winding her long hair around her hand. "But Drayden and I can't do that sort of physical stuff now, well, you know."

"I'm pretty sure you can," Lizzie had said, putting her hand on the girl's lower back and escorting her to a seat. There'd been women on the national team who played right up until they gave birth. Kelly had been four months pregnant during one of the World Cup games. She didn't share this with the girls: she'd always worked harder at their age for coaches who held themselves apart.

Neela, her favorite, told her about the fire. "There's smoke," she'd said, turning her head away from the side of the room where the fire had been lit. The flames had started to catch when she said this. Lizzie steadied her knee and walked quickly toward the fire. She picked up the basket with both hands and dropped it in the classroom sink just before its plastic bottom melted. She turned on the water and ashes floated up around her face. She rubbed at it and then turned to face the girls.

Drayden covered her mouth and then doubled over in laughter, pointing at Lizzie. *LMFAO*, Lizzie thought. Then Sonja curled her lips in a smile, and said in an attention-drawing voice, "You've got a little something right here." She moved her hand to indicate that the little something covered Lizzie's entire face.

In the bathroom, she saw that the ashes from the fire had left charcoal smudges all across her cheeks and forehead. The girls had too much energy. Lizzie had been too tired at their age to think about setting fires or talking back to her teachers. The thought again occurred to her that she wasn't at all qualified to be responsible for so many lives. What were her skills? What did other women who left soccer do with their lives? A few of them got married and started having kids right away—having put that part of their life on hold earlier. Some of them, the starters from that first year when women's soccer captured the nation's attention, brought their little girls to practices or demonstration games. These mothers made Lizzie wary. She couldn't decide whether they were teaching their children about who their mother used to be or what the children were expected to become.

There was a knock on the door and Rosa May entered. "They giving you a hard time?"

Lizzie wiped the last of the charcoal from her face and shook her head.

"I can't have you quitting on me already. Those girls have already run off our basketball coach—they've got me out there and I can't even dribble. Besides, it'll look bad on our grant renewal if there's no consistency." Rosa May smoothed her eyebrows with her index finger. She kept her hair short and wore large earrings and pantsuits. She spoke the girls' language in a way that Lizzie did not. Growing up in Memphis, Lizzie was familiar with the divide—people like Lizzie lived out east. These at-risk girls didn't live in any one place in particular, but they tended to keep to a certain neighborhood—Orange Mound, Glenview, Hollywood. They moved from apartment complex to apartment complex as relatives were evicted for not paying rent, or an uncle whose name was on the lease went to prison, or great-grandmothers died and none of the relatives could agree on who would live in a house that was too ramshackle to be worth selling. She wasn't sure which of these neighborhoods T. J. and his family had lived in, but it hadn't been east.

"They'll be getting restless," Rosa May said by way of a prompt.

"To hell with field conditions. I'm taking them outside," Lizzie said, thinking that after the recent rainstorm, there'd be precious little that would catch fire. "It's wet, but maybe a little mud will do them good."

"Feel free to hose them off afterward," Rosa May said.

"Oh, I wouldn't," Lizzie said before realizing that Rosa May had been joking.

The descent into silence when she returned to the room told Lizzie that the girls had been talking about her. None of the girls looked ready to practice; most of them had remembered to wear tennis shoes, but of course they were all untied with their laces dragging on the floor. She put two fingers in her mouth and let out a piercing whistle that had most of the girls covering their ears. "We're going outside," Lizzie said. "Lace up."

They grumbled. Outright refusal erupted with several girls flopping themselves down onto the grass the moment they stepped outside the community center's double doors. Lizzie set the ground rules. They were going to run drills. Everyone was to participate. If someone didn't participate, they'd run the drill until everyone did. A few of the girls lying on the grass got up. Sonja, Drayden, and the heaviest girl, Coraline, didn't. Lizzie put them through their first drill, which basically involved jumping. They drew an imaginary circle around themselves and then she had them jump from the center of the circle to points on the invisible circle as if it were a clock.

Lizzie did it with them, knowing she needed to strengthen her legs.

"Get up, Sonja," one of the girls yelled after the third time Lizzie drilled them. The weather was cool and Lizzie felt they could do this until their time together ended without a water break. She'd promised them a water break once everyone did the drill.

Sonja rolled onto her back, the laces on her shoes still defiantly untied. "She can't make us do this. She ain't got power."

This was the way they talked to each other, dropping articles and deliberately taking up colloquial speech patterns. If Rosa May were out here, she'd move toward Sonja in a way that said she was going to beat the crap out of her if she didn't get up. The difference was that they'd laugh at Lizzie if she tried that.

But Lizzie had been a part of all sorts of teams. She'd been a thirteen-year-old girl and she remembered the insecurities, coupled with the dawning realization that adults truly couldn't force you to do anything. What Lizzie knew that these girls didn't was that a coach's ability to manage egos was as important as her ability at a particular sport. She considered what she knew about Sonja and Drayden. The other holdout, Coraline, hadn't gotten up from the ground and as Lizzie tried to work out a way to manage Sonja, she knelt next to the larger girl and explained in a low voice that if she wasn't comfortable hopping from one point to another, she could step. Coraline looked at her sideways and without acknowledging their exchange, lumbered to her feet.

"Again," Lizzie called, explaining that the numbers would be out of order this time.

"Y'all are idiots," Sonja said, looking at her nails. Drayden covered her mouth and snickered. LOL, thought Lizzie.

"Three o'clock," Lizzie called, and then before they had time to think about what Sonja said, "Five o'clock"

Drayden was one of the taller girls; thinking she was the right size for playing goalie, Lizzie called out to

Whitney, who was also tall. "Look at Whitney's reach. She's going to make a fine goalie. I don't think anyone can jump higher."

A few of the girls straightened their backs and put enough spring in their next jumps that they nearly fell over. "Six o'clock," Lizzie called.

From behind her, Lizzie heard Rosa May's rich voice. "You don't think Drayden's taller? I thought she'd be a natural at goalie."

God bless that woman, Lizzie thought. Drayden sat up, knitting together her eyebrows and pursing her lips. *There it was,* Lizzie thought, WTF *or maybe more accurately "the fuck you talking about."* That was how Lizzie would have said it if she were one of these girls, if she were Rosa May and had grown up in Orange Mound.

Instead, she kept up the pace of the drills, and called, "Round Four." More than one girl told Drayden to get up off her butt. "We'll go odds forward and then evens backward."

With the grace of a puma, Drayden rose to her feet, stretching up to her full height, which Lizzie would have guessed was close to six feet.

Coraline, who was huffing and out of breath, pushed herself and actually hopped during the first two numbers. Lizzie smiled and continued calling out even numbers. Drayden made a point of not waiting until Lizzie called a number, but jumped to her own rhythm and finished about thirty seconds ahead of the other girls.

The next round, nearly all the girls shouted at Sonja to get up and join them, but it wasn't until Drayden nudged her with her foot that Sonja rose. A collective murmuring of thanks rippled through the girls, and Lizzie called out the numbers on the imaginary clock at a rapid pace.

Lizzie told the girls to go get some water and meet her back there in five minutes. She warned any girl who was late that she'd have to run an extra lap for every second she was late. "I think I'll work with them outside from now on. Rain or shine," Lizzie said to Rosa May.

"You ever going to let it get around that you used to be something more than nothing in the soccer world?"

"These kids don't care about that," Lizzie said.

"Maybe not," Rosa May said, "but they might start caring about it."

The truth was that Lizzie didn't want to talk about it because it made her feel like a failure. She stammered some statistic to Rosa May about how much more successful girls who played sports were. The way Rosa May's face pinched up made Lizzie think she already had a familiarity with that subject. She wasn't going to let the issue of Lizzie's semi-celebrity status go.

"Maybe we should talk about why you're keeping my brother at arm's length." Rosa May didn't appear to ever shy away from tough subjects. "He's not showy with his affection, but he likes you and I don't think the occassional brunch is what he's looking for."

"How can I get in a relationship? I could be gone in a few months if the renovation and kneehab goes the way it's supposed to."

"Not being the right time is the worst excuse for not starting something up. You're ending it before it even begins."

Not knowing what to say, Lizzie changed the subject. "It's hard to believe they're already pregnant," Lizzie said.

Rosa May arched her eyebrows. "Who told you that?"

Lizzie started to explain and then realized that Dray and Sonja had wanted an excuse to get them out of practice and thought that claiming to be knocked up would do it. Rosa May laughed and then stepped back as the girls returned before their five minutes were up. Lizzie stretched her knee a bit before walking with them around the perimeter of the community center's field. "Are you sure you should do that?" Sonja asked her, falling in step with Lizzie. "I Googled you."

She looked at the girl's profile. "As long as I don't land on it funny or somebody doesn't slide tackle me I'll be all right. It's a wonder you aren't worried about yourself, considering your condition."

Sonja blinked and then turned away for a moment. "That leg of yours why you're not playing anymore?"

Lizzie nodded.

"I thought so."

Lizzie turned away from her and shouted at the girls to pick up the pace. She yelled at the ones still jogging.

"When you're done healing, will they let you come back?" another girl asked.

Lizzie shook her head, trying to think of the girl's name. It was an odd one, with an apostrophe in the middle—like a contraction. La'shondra, maybe. After the third lap, five of the girls started walking. "We'll need to work on conditioning," she said, urging on the walkers. When they finished the run, it was nearly time for the girls to head home. A few of them had parents or older siblings idling cars in the parking lot. Most of them lived within walking distance of the community center.

She started to explain to them about how they could put together a club team to play when she was interrupted. "I didn't come here to play soccer," the girl said. "They told us they was going to teach us how to get into college and stuff."

"We'll do that too," Lizzie said, thinking about how she could integrate academic work and study habits into soccer. "But I want to keep you out of trouble. That's what'll prevent you from going to college. And the only way I ever kept myself out of trouble was exhaustion. After soccer practice, I was too tired to fight."

They nodded, and Lizzie saw that she could win them over. Rosa May, who had continued to watch, walked over and indicated that she'd like to talk to Lizzie. Waving goodbye to the girls, Lizzie felt the familiar throbbing in her knee; she limped over to a wall and leaned against it. As she'd suspected, Rosa May had not forgotten about her earlier intentions.

"I think you should give a motivational speech to all the girls, even those not in the soccer track. We might be able to get some press out of it."

The need for water attacked Lizzie's throat. "Excuse me," she said and made for the water fountain. Rosa May followed her in her sensible pumps. Memphis had the best water—she'd missed that when she traveled. In most cities the tap water either smelled like sulfur or tasted like feet.

She wiped her mouth with her sleeve and offered up her cousin as a bargaining chip. "I could get her to speak to the girls. Isobel does all sorts of motivational speeches."

Rosa May nodded and then turned back to her office. "You don't get the difference between the two of you, but you will. You will."

Near the end of March, Lizzie stood in the kitchen listening to Isobel with half an ear. She was thinking about the girls and whether or not they were ready to play another team. So far, she'd had them scrimmaging with each other. Which, although instructive, wasn't improving their playing skills. They were too timid with each other—they needed to learn to play with their elbows up. Outside, a large yellow machine that Benny had hired for some unspecified purpose groaned and whined, sounding very much to Lizzie like a brass section warming up. She covered her ears and rolled her eyes at Isobel.

"He'll have to shut that down pretty soon," she said. In preparation for the television crew that was coming to film Isobel for a segment of *Where Are They Now?*, she'd put her hair in Velcro rollers as large as toilet-paper tubes. She had also slathered on a home facial remedy of olive oil, honey, and avocados. It was hard to look at her without giggling.

"Of course," Lizzie said, turning down the corners of her mouth in an attempt to avoid laughing at her cousin. Isobel had only just told them that this was the opportunity she'd been talking about over waffles. She'd been afraid of jinxing it before contracts had been signed.

"What room do you think they should film in? I told them to get exterior shots of the house for their b-roll. I think it'll make for an interesting story—my agent said they were particularly excited when they heard I wasn't living in Cali anymore."

"The cupola is the only place that isn't torn all to bits," Lizzie said, wiping at a few breadcrumbs on the counter. All around her the insides of the house lay exposed, the wires and ductwork reminding her of the roots of the many houseplants she'd repotted over the years as they outgrew their containers.

"Or maybe on the edge of the yard, with the river in the background."

"I thought you said they wanted to film you working on the house."

"Oh, they will, but mostly I'll talk about my new project."

Lizzie wiped again at the crumbs, which seemed to be moving. "What new project?"

"Nothing too specific, I'll tell them about wanting to form my own company that promotes films, but not just any films, ones that feature women prominently."

"Since when?" Lizzie asked, walking to the table to pick up her glasses where she'd set them earlier.

She knew that Isobel had flirted with feminism over the years—blaming the paucity of roles for her on patriarchy, but most of the time, she talked about the house. For most of March, Isobel had spent her time on the second floor stripping the front room of its wallpaper and then the rest of the month peeling the layers of paint from the doors and molding that trimmed the floor and ceiling. She'd even ordered a specialty iron, which when placed on the wood essentially melted the paint to a consistency that enabled Isobel to wipe it away with a rag. Lizzie bent down and looked closely at the crumbs on the counter. They *were* moving.

"There are plenty of people who'll pay for ideas. There's this Peter Taylor story where he talks about the Memphis Demimonde."

"Yeah. But that's a story written by a man." Lizzie didn't read much, but she was vaguely familiar with the story—having had one of her English teachers rave about it and then take them on a field trip to the Old Forest, where the story was set. Mostly she kept looking at the crumbs that had turned out to be tiny yellow ants.

"Demimonde." Isobel pronounced the word as the French would have. "Isn't that a great name for the company? And besides, the story is about women."

"Doesn't it mean whores?" Lizzie asked Isobel. "Do you see this?" She followed the tiny yellow ants from the countertop to the cupboard below the sink and hesitated before opening the door.

"Looks like ants," Isobel said, leaving the table to stand next to Lizzie. "Translated from the French, it means half the world. It's the idea that there's a whole half of the world living contrary to what is expected of them."

"Just like us," Lizzie said. The thought didn't make her happy. She squished several ants with her thumb. "I'll get Benny to use that spray stuff and squirt it around."

"I'd call somebody," Isobel said, reaching around Lizzie and opening the cupboard. The trail of ants led to a small hole at the base of the hot water pipe. Isobel's phone beeped, and she gestured that it was time to remove the facial mask. Taking a paper towel, Lizzie wiped away as many of the ants as she could and then sprayed the area with bleach before going outside to find Benny.

As usual, their contractor was in his RV, which remained parked on the vacant lot next to the house. She banged on the door and waited a full five minutes for him to step outside. Lizzie had never been invited into his office space, and she suspected that she'd find it resembled a bedroom more closely than an office. Benny looked at her with half-closed eyes, then stretched and scratched his stomach before asking her what she wanted. His lackadaisical attitude infuriated Lizzie. "What's the caterpillar for?" she asked, gesturing to the large backhoe sitting on the small patch of grass between their property and the trolley tracks.

"Landscape," Benny said, gesturing to the backyard. "I had to bring in more topsoil. Yours had been all but washed away, and I thought we'd give Isobel some sod for her big day."

She wondered how much he knew about their lives. "We've got ants," she said. "Little yellow ones that seem to be living under the sink. Grandma had a guy that used to do all the pest stuff, but—"

"Of course I can take care of it," Benny said, reaching behind him into his trailer and rummaging around until he pulled out a canister of pump-and-spray pesticide. He looked at her and then smiled as if he'd remembered who she was. "I had my kid look you up on the Internet. You're as close to an Olympian as I've ever met, and I don't know why you're wasting your time out there in North Memphis coaching those ghetto kids."

"Benny," Lizzie said.

He paused before putting a hand on her shoulder in an almost paternal gesture. "I grew up there. Didn't used to be that, but it is now and you can't tell me it isn't."

"I'm not an Olympian," she said, hoping he'd stop before he vocalized the racism she suspected he was capable of. "We've been over this."

He nodded and banged the can of pesticide against his leg. "Almost is good enough for us," he said and moved toward the house.

Lizzie watched him walk away. He must have grown up when the neighborhoods up there were in transition from white to black. She turned her back to the house and watched the backhoe scrape the yard down to the sandstone that made up the bluffs. It took minutes for the machine to finish stripping the small yard of its grass. Benny's men then moved in and started spreading topsoil that had been dumped in a large pile in the vacant lot. They transferred it to wheelbarrows and rolled it over. One man stood at the far corner of the yard and watered the soil as they spread it. As much as she disliked Benny, she had to admit that the outside of the house was much improved.

She left the men to their work and walked around to the front porch. Benny had wanted to change the color of the house, but Lizzie had been adamant about its remaining the same color it had always been. Who would recognize the house if it weren't obnoxiously yellow? Lizzie thought that the house ought to own its identity and that trying to hide behind some paler shade of butter yellow or—heaven forbid—cream would make the house look even more strange. Behind her the rumbling of a large truck caught her attention. Turning, she realized that the film crew had arrived.

"We made good time," a man in denim shorts called to Lizzie. "That airport of yours is tiny. I think we were the only ones coming in with bags."

He continued talking, but Lizzie waved at them and then hurried inside the house, calling for Isobel. She'd hoped to be gone when the actual filming happened, but now she'd been caught in the house and there were too many things to take care of before she could head over to the community center. Isobel yelled back to her from upstairs, but Lizzie couldn't make out what had been said. She assumed it was something along the lines of she'd be right there. She squeezed down the impossibly narrow hallway and moved through the beaded curtain without parting it.

Benny stood in the kitchen in front of the open sink cupboard, staring at a line of ants that marched like the veins of a leaf all along the countertop before splitting into separate destinations. "I think I screwed up," he said. "These are the kind of ants you have to bait."

Lizzie brushed past him and grabbed the bottle of bleach, spraying all around the counter. The ants appeared unaffected by the toxin and were slowed only the tiniest amount by the water.

"It's poison, isn't it?" Lizzie asked, pointing to the large container he still held in his hand.

"Yeah. It's just that some ants die right away because they only have one queen, but others—" He scratched his head. The birthmark along his neck deepened to a reddish purple.

"Others," Lizzie prompted.

"They scatter," he gestured at the procession of ants marching along the kitchen, "and if these are pharaoh ants well, it's going to take a bit to get them out of your hair."

The continued commotion of the camera crew distracted Lizzie. She left Benny in the kitchen, thinking it was pretty obvious why two women had left him. She called again for Isobel and then, putting on the same conciliatory smile she used when she shook opposing players' hands, she opened the door.

The man in the denim shorts now had a camera on his shoulder, although from the loose way he held it, Lizzie didn't think he was filming. "This is some fuckin' house," he said.

"Isobel's upstairs," Lizzie offered by way of greeting.

A smaller man whom she hadn't seen before stepped onto the porch and extended his hand toward her. She gripped it, surprised at its softness. The men she knew possessed calloused hands. "Lizzie, right?"

She nodded and he continued, moving from shaking her hand to placing his on the side of her arm, as if they were the same height.

"We were hoping to talk with you a bit about Isobel, you know, get some perspective on what she's really like and maybe we can talk about the Olympics. If you have anything to say about Hope, Abby, or what is it you call Shannon? Boxxy? Everyone says they have a shot at the gold this year."

Lizzie stepped closer to the man, who had a very large head. The shadow of his nose gave the impression of a mustache, which would have been his only manly attribute. He held his ground, which was perilously close to the top step of the porch. "I don't talk about that," she said.

Isobel appeared as if out of the wind, stepping next to Lizzie and embracing the small man. "Craig," she said. "Nobody told me you'd actually be onsite." The curlers had given her hair twice its normal volume, and it was pinned up in some way that made Lizzie think of the women in Peter Taylor's stories. Looking at the thick smear of concealer on Isobel's face and the shadowing around her cheekbones, Lizzie realized how little makeup her cousin had been wearing while in Memphis.

"I was asking your cousin about what you're like in the South. I'd expected to find a regular Southern belle and here you are all turned into Cinderella." He lifted her hands, which showed the signs of her work upstairs, for inspection. In addition to the few nicks, her knuckles were scraped up and a fresh Band-Aid covered her thumb. "What'll I find under here?" Craig asked, teasing the edge of the adhesive with his manicured fingernail.

"Proof that I can do more than act," Isobel said in what Lizzie knew was her television voice. Like any normal child, she'd bragged to all of her friends about having a cousin on *Wait for It,* but the actual process of watching the show had been difficult. The girl Isobel played on television was like somebody in *Invasion of the Body Snatchers.* Little Gracie Belle looked exactly like Isobel, but she spoke in a much more affected manner and moved her face in ways she'd never seen in her cousin's expressions. Through the veil of the screen, it came across as endearing, but here in Spite House in front of this little man, Lizzie was less charmed than she was frightened.

As quickly as they'd appeared, Isobel's visitors had been ushered off the porch and upstairs to the cupola.

Over her shoulder, with that expansive smile still plastered on her face, Isobel said through gritted teeth, "For Pete's sake, agree to talk to them. And tell them how down-to-earth I am. Just like a real girl."

"I can't. I've got a date," Lizzie said to her cousin's retreating back.

Elyse arrived home in a whirlwind of activity. "Did I miss them?" she called as she came around the back of the house. "I lost track of time at the bar, and if I missed them—"

"They're here," Lizzie said from her spot on their newly sodded backyard. After surveying the house, Craig had sent one of his men to the nearest home improvement store for two Adirondack chairs. Then he'd told Benny's crew to rip out the row of azalea bushes blocking the view to the river. The chairs were carefully positioned so that when the camera framed them, the Mighty Mississippi remained visible.

"This is nice," Elyse said, sinking into one of the chairs. "Do we get to keep these?"

"Benny's pissed," Lizzie said, bending her knee several times to keep her leg from growing too stiff. "He left early after I screamed at him about the ant problem."

"We have ants?"

"Don't open any cupboards."

"I guess we'll order pizza then."

"Not for me. Rosa May's having me over for dinner."

"T. J. going to be there?"

Lizzie shrugged. She wasn't sure what to do with T. J. She knew he wanted their relationship to be something more, but she couldn't explain how scared she was to take that step. Instead, she hung out at his sister's house and played Madden football when he came over. They talked about the house—endlessly discussing the particulars of the code violations and the requirements they needed to meet to stay in the house. The truth was, she'd jumped at the opportunity for this dinner to get away from Isobel's cameras.

Elyse tilted her neck back to stare at the roof. "That's them up there?"

Isobel stood with her back to them, her hair tucked under the back of her shirt to keep it from blowing. The man in the denim shorts was winding up the cord to the camera, and Craig pointed out various items to his helpers. From this distance, Lizzie thought they looked like dolls. Action figures moving in stiff spurts. "I've got to go," she said, putting her feet on the ground. "They were supposed to talk with me, but now that you're here maybe I can get out of it."

"Don't you want to be on television?"

"It's not that fun," Lizzie said.

"Oh, that's right. I guess when you played—" Elyse trailed off, looking at Lizzie's knee and then obviously not looking at her knee.

"Isobel's up to something," Lizzie said, breaking their rule about talking about each other.

"She's always up to something. Behind her laid-back, sleep-'til-noon attitude is a woman who would take over the world if she could."

"I mean it."

"What makes you say that?" Elyse twirled her hair around her finger, leaving little ringlets at the edges.

"The way she's been so coy about this crew coming and all that business about none of it being that big of a deal." Lizzie continued, listing off her other concerns, including the fact that the producer Craig knew far too much about them. She tried to explain the bad taste she had in her mouth, but it felt too silly to say aloud. "They're friends," Lizzie said of Craig and Isobel, "but he's far too interested in us for that to be all there is to it."

"You're jumping to conclusions." Elyse had a habit of always thinking the best about people. "Being around all those gossipy teenagers has turned you paranoid."

"Maybe," Lizzie said.

"Definitely," Elyse said, offering her hand to help Lizzie up. "You're going to be late."

"You should put some lipstick on. For the cameras," Lizzie said, pulling up the hem of her T-shirt and rubbing at her mouth. At some point during the long day, Isobel had pulled her aside and put a dash of mascara on her eyes and forced her to smack her lips on a napkin. She'd changed a few minutes earlier into her workout clothing. "Isobel says to tell them she's a real girl. As normal as you or me or—"

"So she wants us to lie?" Elyse grinned. How was it she was still so much like the little girl that Lizzie had first met that day at the beach? "Because if that's normal"—she gestured to the roof—"then the rest of us are crazy."

April 2012: Memphis

Because it was April Fool's Day, Lizzie didn't believe Benny when he told her about the hidden door. With the outside of the house nearly complete, the crew had started work on the interior—specifically the electrical. The house still had the original knob and tube wiring, which meant they'd been forced to install an entirely new electrical system. At least when it was all over, they'd have overhead lights and enough outlets to power all of their modern conveniences. In the time the Triplins had lived in the house, they'd each learned what they could plug in where without blowing a fuse. There'd been so little that ran on electricity when her grandfather built the house.

Since moving into Spite House, Lizzie had become more interested in the lives of her grandparents. Why had Mellie married a man who was so much older than her? And how come it took them so long to have children? And why just the one? When Benny came into the kitchen to tell her about the hidden room, she'd been underneath one of the kitchen cupboards trying to flush out the last of the ants. She'd barely listened to him, thinking that there'd been no end to the jokes and puns Isobel and Elyse had come up with once they found out that the pests invading their kitchen in Memphis were indeed pharaoh ants. For a solid week, they'd taken turns walking like an Egyptian. Benny's poison hadn't killed any ants; spraying had divided the colony and the ants had multiplied. Either way, following Isobel's television interview, Lizzie had taken everything out of the kitchen cupboards and sealed the jars and cans in plastic bags or Tupperware. She'd had Benny pull out the fridge so she could see behind it and she'd baited the entire kitchen. Elyse and Isobel ganged up on her one night, telling her she ought to call the pest service, but she felt certain that getting rid of the ants was something she ought to be able to do on her own.

After a particularly long pause in Benny's explanation, she backed out of the cupboard and straightened up, pleased that her knee hadn't stiffened in the few minutes she'd been on the floor.

"Do you?" Benny asked.

"Do I what?"

"Wanna see what's in there before we start working back there?"

"Let's go," Lizzie said, taking a few steps, trying to convince herself that her leg was improving. The last few appointments had been a disappointment to Lizzie. After getting the go-ahead to jog, she'd made little progress on her flexation, and although she didn't like to admit it, there was a tightness in her knee that seemed to be growing.

"What are you smiling for?" the electrician asked as Lizzie and Benny crawled past him in the narrow low-ceilinged closet space off the receiving room.

"All of it," Lizzie said. The electrician, Elton, had been a delightful addition around the house. He had an enormous yellow-white mustache and called all the women "dahrling" in a drawl that was distinctly not Memphis. Isobel was almost smitten with him and excited because once the wiring was done, they'd finally be able to patch the plaster on the third floor and paint. That would allow them to move on to the second-floor renovations. Benny liked him too, which made all of their lives easier. The last few days, instead of day laborers, Benny had showed up with two coffees. If you didn't know better, you'd think he was working for Elton who, before becoming an electrician, had been a stage manager for a few big-name bands. The cachet seemed to impress Benny enough to at the very least have him feign a work ethic.

As they neared the back of the closet, Benny shone a flashlight ahead of them. "There's a whole bunch of them boxes," Benny said. "Like the ones you pulled out of the cupola."

"Why wouldn't my grandmother or my mother have ever mentioned the door?" she asked Benny.

"This is one strange house," Elton muttered, focused on the fuse box.

"You don't know the half of it," Benny said, sitting cross-legged and reaching across Lizzie to push at the wall. "I know it's here someplace."

The cigar boxes, moved into Lizzie's bedroom for safekeeping, hadn't been touched in months. At first, they'd each take a box at night and sort through its contents, throwing away receipts and sorting the photographs by decades. But sometime during February they'd fallen out of the habit. The randomness of the contents depressed Lizzie. In one box they'd find photographs from Grandma Mellie's childhood and ticket stubs from the early 1980s. In another, they'd find two dozen buttons, coupons clipped from stores that no longer existed, and a pair of rusty nail clippers. It reminded her of the time capsules that Andy Warhol had left behind. She heard they opened up one of them and found dirty underwear. At least she hadn't experienced that particular horror. Benny continued to push against different parts of the wall.

"I bumped up against it with my tool belt when I was tracing down a wire for Elton," Benny said, gesturing to a small hole in the wall where he'd sawed through the paneling and the plaster behind it.

Lizzie looked at the hole and eyed Benny, making an educated guess as to where the secret press would be that opened the hidden door. She brushed her fingers against the wall and then pushed firmly. The wood paneling opened with an audible pop and the smell of mildew drifted out. "I've got it," she said to Benny, reaching for his flashlight.

He sneezed three quick times, not once covering his mouth, and then crawled back toward Elton, who was humming to himself. The rise and fall of his voice was too muddled to be understood. The boxes were similar, but unlike the ones they'd found in the window seats, these were dust covered. They hadn't been disturbed in a great many years. She opened the first one she touched, which featured a picture of a man in green pants with the word "Cremo" above his head. Inside she found a stack of what appeared to be index cards, but they weren't like the ones you could buy at an office supply store. The unlined, cream rectangles had a single hole punched on the bottom, and as she held them, they felt smaller than the cards she was more familiar with. She grabbed a small stack and rifled through them. Each had a number on the front, and the back contained writing and sometimes a photograph or ticket stub adhered with a yellowing piece of tape.

She stuffed the handful of cards into her apron pocket and then crawled out of the space. Benny slouched in the hallway outside the closet listening to Elton talk about Isaac Hayes. "He was bigger than you'd think," Elton said, taking out a fuse and then putting it back. They looked up as Lizzie dusted herself off. "Bring the rest of the boxes to the kitchen."

Benny groaned and popped his knees before crawling back into the room.

Elton's mustache twitched. "Your problems aren't as bad as they seem," he said.

"Benny's not a problem," Lizzie said, taking the weight off her bad knee out of habit.

"I mean with the electrical." Benny nodded at the panel. "I'll install an updated system next to this one and then when we're ready, I'll switch the power from one box to the other."

"How long?"

"Depends," Elton said, stepping away from the panel and running his hands along the walls.

Lizzie's face colored watching Elton caress the walls. It had been months since she'd been touched as intimately as that plaster. Rosa May had kept urging her to give her brother another chance at a date, but Lizzie couldn't find the energy in herself to care about T. J. and the house. She told Rosa May that once the house passed inspection, she might give him a try. But now when she thought about it, all she felt was the overwhelming sense of dread. She pictured his clipboard and felt failure settle around her like a heavy winter coat.

Benny emerged from the space carrying at least ten of the cigar boxes. In the light of the hallway, Lizzie could see that different years had been written on the sides of many of the boxes. The ballpoint ink had faded on most of them, and what was left behind looked more like chicken scratch. She reached for the top box, which had a date of 1982, three years before she was born. As she touched its lid, Benny let out a horrifically loud sneeze that sounded like a jet engine, and the boxes fell to the ground, the individual cards scattering and falling around them like snowflakes.

"Shit," Elton said.

Benny dropped to his knees, frantically gathering cards and mashing them into stacks.

"Stop it," Lizzie said, reaching out for Benny's arm. "I can do it. I'm not even sure what they are or whether they're worth keeping."

"You two look like you spilled gold dust." Elton took a card that had landed on his shoulder. "Whatcha got here anyway?" He shook the card, labeled 359 on the back and read the front to them: "Momma says Santa's coming. She's lying."

Lizzie took the card from Elton and looked at it in the hazy light of the foyer. While they'd been in the room, a spring storm had gathered over the area and it was nearly as dark as it was during twilight. She squinted at the handwriting, turning it sideways and then running her finger over the lettering.

"I'll get you an overhead light wired in here," Elton said, looking up at the ceiling, "and enough volts to run air if you ever decide to put it in."

"It's my mother's handwriting," Lizzie said. It had been years since she'd seen her mother's script. Everything but birthday cards and checks was done electronically. Her mother had unusually loopy handwriting—it reminded her of a teenage girl and although she dotted her *i*'s, it wouldn't have seemed out of place for her to replace the dot with a smiley face or heart.

Benny read a few of the cards in his hands and touched the photographs and other mementos taped to the sides. "I guess it is a diary of some sort."

Lizzie picked up a cigar box, finally connecting the years on the boxes to the cards. "One day for one card." She picked up half a dozen cards and quickly looked at the fronts and backs. None of them marked the year. A thousand cards lay scattered around them, and Lizzie realized it would be nearly impossible to put them back in order.

"What a funny way to keep track of your life."

"Grandma Mellie was a librarian," Lizzie said, realizing at last why the cards seemed familiar to her. "My mom's funny about a lot of stuff. She alphabetizes the breakfast cereal and color codes our towels. Growing up my color was powder blue—same as my eyes."

Elton raised his bushy eyebrows, which were more gold than his mustache. "All our mamas are strange in one way or another."

"I suppose so," Lizzie said, her voice catching in a way that surprised her.

Benny looked at her out of the corner of his eye. He was still gathering the cards and returning them to the boxes. A few had remained in ordered stacks of twenty or so cards, but most were scattered and out of sequence.

She sank to the floor and started to help him, hoping that he and Elton would ignore the fact that she was in the middle of a breakdown. Gathering up a stack, she placed it inside a cigar box and then groped around for another one.

"There, there," Elton said, patting her back. She opened her mouth and small mewing sounds escaped.

Benny rubbed at the birthmark on his neck. The tips of his ears were red. When he spoke, his words ran together. "I'm sure it won't be that hard to get them back in order. And look, you've got all them other boxes, which are intact."

"I shouldn't read this," Lizzie said. "It's private."

"Ah, now, well," Elton said, scratching his head.

"If she didn't want them read, she would have destroyed them," Benny offered. "I always thought your mother was an honest woman. You know, not all girls were like that in high school They had the tendency to think two or three boyfriends ahead. But when your mother talked to you, that was it. She was the type of gal who fell in love with one man at a time." He moved back toward the secret compartment and after a moment, started listing off the years that were still there. "Looks like it goes as far back as 1970."

"She would have been ten," Lizzie said, trying to remember what she'd been interested in at that age.

The skies opened up, releasing a sudden flood of water. It streamed down the windows of the receiving room and pounded insistently against the house. She wiped at her eyes with the edges of her T-shirt and finished gathering the cards. Benny walked past her, carefully carrying two cigar boxes. She gestured toward the stairs. "Could you put them in my room?"

"I bet there are other secret spaces in this house," Elton said, stopping his work on the electrical panel to hand her a box. "I've seen this before. People who like to hide things find lots of spaces in houses to conceal their secrets. You'd be surprised how many spots there are that no one thinks to look—closets, under the stairs, false cupboards. I wired a bookcase once that turned out to be a door."

Lizzie looked at the date etched on the box. Her heart beat twice out of sequence. She rubbed her thumb across it and then turned it toward Elton. "What does that say?"

He squinted down at the box, his mustache twitching. "1985."

"Huh," Lizzie said, opening the box quickly. That was the year she was born. If there were any information about who her biological father was, it would be in that box. Inside were a clutch of cards in sequence starting with 158 and going to 170, the day she was born.

On the last card, her mother had written, "Elizabeth Grace born at 2:25 P.M. at Baptist Memorial Hospital." Attached to the card with the same yellowing tape was her hospital birth picture, which she'd never seen before.

"That you?" Elton asked, peering over her shoulder.

"I guess so," Lizzie said. She flipped through the few other cards, which seemed to be about the pregnancy and the heat.

"Cute baby. My wife says that babies always look like their fathers the first six months. What do you think? Take after your dad there?"

"I don't know," Lizzie said, staring at the cards remaining on the floor.

Benny paused at the bottom of the stairs. "They're all up there for you. Maybe your mom can help you sort them all out. Crazy system she had."

Lizzie picked up a cluster of cards from the floor and looked at them. The years were mixed up. If there were clues as to who her father was, it would take her quite some time to put them all back in order. She could ask her mother about them, but that would mean taking the first step to thaw the ice between them. Right now they only spoke, or rather e-mailed, about the costs and timeline associated with the renovation. Lizzie wasn't yet ready to give, even a few degrees. How long had it been since she'd given up finding her biological dad? It seemed like since Jim and her mother had their own children. She didn't know if she'd stopped wondering or had just accepted that a stepfather was as good as it would get for her. And here were the tools she needed to uncover who her mother had been when she got pregnant with Lizzie and who her father was. She looked up at Benny and Elton, who she realized were waiting to see if she would be all right before going back to work.

"Thank you," she said. "Thank you." She hugged them both around the neck before taking the remaining cards to her room to begin her search.

It was Rosa May who finally called the Triplins out on the absence of men in their lives. They were watching Lizzie's team scrimmage one of the stronger church leagues. The cousins looked out of place on the sidelines—Isobel in her enormous sunglasses and Elyse, her hair tied in two low ponytails that made her seem much younger. Rosa May had brought her family to the scrimmage. Her husband, who she'd met at college, watched their three small children run around the back lot imitating the play on the field. Rosa May's voice had the same inflections as T. J.'s and as she chatted with her, Lizzie kept glancing at T. J., who sat in one of those sideline chairs with the brim of his cap pulled low over his eyes. Lizzie paced the sidelines, stopping most often in front of her cousins, who lounged on a blanket.

"Switch," Lizzie yelled to her girls, trying to get them to move the ball to the opposite side of the field. "We're wide open over here. Wide open."

Rosa May kept pace with her, chatting about the girls and their progress. As they paused next to the cousins, introductions were made. Elyse barely glanced up from her phone to shake Rosa May's hand.

"You've got good genes in your family," Rosa May said.

"We're not actually related," Lizzie said, reflexively.

"Could have fooled me. You girls look alike. Pretty."

"Pretty isn't alike," Isobel said, putting down the notebook she'd been writing in.

"My momma always said it was a mistake for pretty girls not to have their kids when they're young. That's the only way to stay pretty."

"I know," Elyse said, at the same time that Lizzie and Isobel protested how much time they had left before they had to worry about their biological clocks and how their looks were tied more to working out than popping kids out before they hit thirty.

"How old are you girls anyway?" Rosa May asked.

"The truth?" Isobel asked.

"We'll be twenty-eight by the end of next month," Elyse said.

Lizzie called her right middy, Coraline, over to throw in an out-of-bounds ball and stood on her toes so the girl wouldn't lift her feet off the ground. She patted her on the back as she jogged onto the grass. She'd lost at least ten pounds since that first week, but more important, she could run the length of the field without getting winded.

Isobel dropped her voice and continued speaking with Rosa May while Elyse returned to tapping out messages on her phone. Lizzie didn't hear much of what they said, but once in a while, she felt them looking at her.

"I know you aren't talking about me," she said as the first half wound down and the girls on both teams began to drag their feet, mindlessly passing to one another. She heard Sonja's father let out a stream of Spanish that embodied urgency and direction. Then, out of the backfield, she saw Sonja streak by, stealing the ball from one of her own players, and dribble it toward the opposing goal.

The parents, who had been mostly uninterested, got to their feet. The opposing coach yelled at the goalie to challenge Sonja, who expertly slid around the girl by moving the ball to her left and then kicking it into the net as the referee blew the whistle signaling the end of the first half.

Drayden, who had in fact turned out to be a fine goalie, ran out of her net and lifted Sonja off the ground. Lizzie herded them together and tried to offer as much coaching advice as she could before they were called back to play. Mostly she urged them to drink water and maintain focus. "Wait, wait," she called as the girls jogged back out onto the field. "Before you can be winners, you have to believe that you are worth it. Go out there and instead of being aggressive, be brave."

The girls looked at her as if she'd spoken another language, but she heard them, under their breaths, telling themselves to be brave.

Rosa May slapped her on the back. "That is why I hired you," she said. "Your cousin tells me that both of you are looking for the sort of man who doesn't care who you were, just who you are."

"I'm not looking right now," Lizzie said.

"Every single woman I know is looking," Rosa May said and then, anticipating Lizzie's objection, continued, "even if she tells me it's not the right time."

"I'm not lonely enough and I don't know where I'll be after this," Lizzie said, looking back at her cousins. "Tell her we don't need a man."

"Speak for yourself," Elyse said, finishing sending a text.

"I'm holding out for the right one," Isobel said. "You know any right men, Rosa May?"

"I know plenty of men but right's a whole other matter. I married the one I did find."

They laughed and looked at Rosa May's husband, who raised his hand in a friendly wave before picking up his son and swinging him around. When Elyse bent her head toward her phone again, Isobel snaked her hand out as quick as a viper and snatched it from her. "Hot romance?" she asked.

Elyse shrieked and grabbed for the phone.

Isobel read from the screen, putting air quotes around the words typed in text language.

"I'm so excited?"

";"

"Talk 2nite?"

Elyse continued howling in protest.

"Geez," Isobel said, "you gotta give the guy a chance to respond. How do you expect him to get a text in edgewise? And what the hell is asterisk, backslash, oh, backslash, asterisk?"

"Cheerleader," Lizzie said, thinking of the texts she used to exchange with her teammates while they were on long bus rides to and from games. She watched her cousin scroll through Elyse's texts.

"Ah, here we go, one from him 'Texting one-handed is hard.'"

"Whoa," Rosa May said.

Elyse pushed Isobel's chair over in a burst of strength and snatched her phone back.

"That girl is up to something," Rosa May said, watching Isobel chase Elyse across the field.

"Coach, coach," Sonja said.

Lizzie looked up and realized the referee had called her team for a handball inside the goal box and was trying to explain to the girls how to set up for a penalty shot. They hadn't practiced this particular turn of events, and the team milled about kicking at the grass with their cleats. Drayden paced in the box like a cougar about to pounce. "What you mean she gets to kick it right at me?" she shouted at her team and then at the referee.

The referee walked over and tried to explain what would happen, but Drayden continued to escalate her complaints, stepping close to the college-aged girl, as if she'd challenged her authority.

"Whitney, Whitney," Lizzie said, trying to catch the sideline player's attention. "You're in goal. Get out there now before—"

A commotion erupted on the field and Lizzie realized too late that Drayden had shoved the referee, who was only a few years older than the players themselves.

As the other team's players pulled the referee to her feet, she took a red card from her pocket and held it up to the crowd. Lizzie saw Drayden clench her fists and take another step toward the referee. Coraline stepped in between the two of them and began yelling at Drayden to "back down, back down."

In a flash, Lizzie dashed onto the field and pulled Drayden to the sidelines, apologizing to the referee and yelling at Whitney to get her butt in the goal. The opposing player took the penalty shot, which arced high and left, floating in over the tips of Whitney's fingers.

"I could've stopped that," Drayden said, kicking at the ground and at Lizzie's ankles.

"You don't know what you could've done because you're not playing," Lizzie said, ignoring the menace on Drayden's face.

"So?"

"You let someone else determine your fate. The only way you should come off that field is if you're injured." Lizzie pounded on her leg with her fist. "That's what you can't control."

Drayden started to speak, but Lizzie cut her off. "Shut up."

Rosa May started to walk over toward them, but Lizzie waved her off. She wanted to see how the other girls would react. They'd been listening with rapt attention to the exchange and when Lizzie dismissed Drayden, she turned toward her teammates on the sidelines, who opened their arms to her, offering encouraging words. "It's okay." "We've got this." "We love ya, Dray." Lizzie turned away from her girls and smiled. One of a coach's greatest tricks in forging a team was to create a common enemy.

Near the end of the second half, Rosa May returned to Lizzie's elbow. They watched the church team, which was made up of mostly white girls in sponsored uniforms. Their ponytails bounced high on the crowns of their heads. "You know in every other country, soccer is a sport for the poor kids. It doesn't take much equipment—basically a ball and an empty space."

Lizzie shrugged. "Doesn't much matter. That's what's great about soccer—it's an equalizer. You can be good if you're big or if you're small. Some girls bring precision and others bring passion. That's why I love the game. It plays to everyone's strengths. Hard to do that in basketball."

The whistle sounded. "Tie game," the ref said, congratulating each team before walking off the field. Out of the corner of her eye, Lizzie saw Dray move toward the ref. Rosa May tensed and the other coach, who'd been walking toward them, turned, ready to intervene if necessary.

"Wait," Lizzie said, more to herself than to those around her. "Give her the chance."

When she got within striking distance, Dray dropped her head like a dog losing a challenge and mumbled an apology to the referee, who smiled and clapped Dray on the back.

"How about that," Rosa May said.

Lizzie let the girls drift toward their families and rides home. She reminded them about practice and then turned back to her own family. Elyse and Isobel were still squabbling over the phone, with Isobel threatening to write every word Elyse uttered into a screenplay and Elyse claiming that one in ten people in the world had psychopathic tendencies and that she felt quite strongly that Isobel was one of those ten percent. It made Lizzie laugh to see how much like sisters the three of them had become. The last few months had been the longest they'd ever been together.

Rosa May gathered her family and after helping to strap her children into their car seats, she turned toward Lizzie. "Call my brother."

"Nah," Lizzie said. "I've got too much going on."

"No, that's just it. You don't have enough going on. Besides, it's like you told the girls with that pep talk of yours: you gotta be brave if you want to win at life. Calling him, that's the brave act."

In the car, Isobel decided she wasn't speaking to Elyse. "She's up to something," she told Lizzie as they loaded the balls and other practice gear into the back of Grandma Mellie's old yellow Datsun, which served as the main transportation for all of them.

"I can hear you," Elyse said from inside the car. "It's not like this thing is soundproof."

Isobel pushed her sunglasses up off her face. "You should ask her why she's texting Landon."

They got into the car and Lizzie started the engine and then just as quickly turned it off. The trouble with Elyse had always been that she thought she was smarter than everyone else. One of the reasons she dressed the way she did and kept her hair in that girlish style was so that she had the advantage on other people. She liked to be underestimated.

"What's going on?" Elyse crossed her arms. "We should get home."

Isobel, who'd taken the backseat, leaned forward and shook out her hair in a single flamboyant motion. "We've got nothing but time."

"Really?!" Elyse said.

Lizzie tried not to laugh.

"We all know that's your line from the cop show that got cancelled after three episodes," Elyse said, putting her own sunglasses on and then pulling them off in mimicry of her cousin. "There's a flipping gif of it floating around the Internet, where you take the glasses off and put them back on again in an endless loop."

Isobel adopted a serious pose, her eyebrows knit together in false injury. She held it for a moment before smiling. "You two are impossible."

They laughed together for several minutes before Lizzie finally started the car. They'd find out sooner or later what Elyse was up to. Because even if she hadn't realized it, Isobel had spoken the truth. What they'd done by abandoning their other lives and coming to Memphis was give themselves time.

"You've got to give yourself time," Phil said, watching Lizzie jog on the treadmill.

"My leg feels good. I feel ready," Lizzie said, reaching for the buttons that would propel the machine faster and steeper.

"I say when you're ready," Phil said, swatting her hand away.

"Now that I'm out there with the girls, I want so badly to play. Biking and jogging and balancing on rubber balls isn't even close to the same feeling. How can I get my body ready if I can't even play a pick-up game with high schoolers?"

"Patience," he said, running his hand over his recently buzzed hair. He insisted on keeping it in the same style he'd had since serving in the military. Gray hair was never meant to be in a flattop. The old people didn't like Phil because he talked in a soft voice that none of them could hear when he worked with them on their strengthening exercises.

"But I've got full movement," Lizzie said, switching her walk to a march to show him how well her knee was doing.

"You've got to have strength too," he said, tapping her knees to stop any bounce in her step.

The receptionist called Phil to the front. He left Lizzie to walk for a few more minutes to warm up. "Look," he said, backing away, "today might be the day I tell you that your knee is as good as new, but I won't know until I put you through the paces. So let me do it. Okay?"

Lizzie nodded.

"You don't look very happy, girlie," the man on the treadmill next to her said. "What'd he say to you? Bad news?"

Lizzie tapped the arrow on the treadmill, sending her speed up one-tenth of a mile. She smiled at the old man next to her.

He took it as encouragement. "I got a new set of knees, and I told the therapist that I'm going to run a marathon with them."

"Is that so?" Lizzie asked, thinking how short older people were. The man barely came up to her shoulder.

"What?" he said.

Lizzie swallowed and spoke as loud as she could. "I don't doubt that you will."

The man gave her a wink and then pushed his speed button twice.

What Lizzie wanted most was to be told that she could play soccer again. The surgeon had warned her against it. He said that if her knee blew a fourth time, they might not be able to fix it. She'd known girls who'd come back from their fourth or even fifth surgery and maybe they didn't play at the national level, but they played professionally. Not that being paid to play was even an option anymore unless you wanted to go to Europe. The problem with the surgery before this last one, Lizzie decided, had been the cadaver tendon. It had seemed like the perfect fix when the surgeon suggested she consider using someone else's tendon instead of crafting one from parts of her own body. In the end, she'd had only a year of use with that tendon before it had blown. When she thought about it, Lizzie kept hearing the captain's voice ringing out over the practice field asking about her ACL.

The treadmill slowed and Lizzie stopped moving, letting the last rotation of the machine push her off the back end of it. She strained her eyes over the heads of the elderly in the room, trying to find Phil. Now that she'd warmed up her leg, he'd manipulate it to see if she'd regained full mobility.

"Good luck, sweetheart," the older man called as she walked toward reception. She peered through the small glass window separating the exercise room from the waiting area. Phil was deep in conversation with what appeared to be the parents of a teenage girl who had a cast up to her hip and headphones big enough that they obscured most of her head. She considered interrupting but instead fished her phone out of her pocket and situated herself on Phil's examination table. The tables weren't even screened off from each other; two tables down, a woman in her mid-sixties pounded her fist against the bench in pain and protest at the bend her therapist was putting into her knee.

She read over the text messages she'd been exchanging with T. J. about their second date. Lizzie had made it with a sense of celebration in mind. She felt sure that Phil would give her the go-ahead to play, which meant she could talk to the coach about maybe working out with the team. Tentatively, she flexed the thigh muscles in her left leg and then her right. So much muscle mass had been lost in the past year. One leg was literally twice the size of the other, and there was an uncomfortable stiffness when she bent her knee. There was only so much conditioning could overcome.

She picked up the piece of plastic pipe that Phil used to massage the back of her leg where they'd taken out part of her hamstring. Last week, he'd expressed concern that the small lump of scar tissue he'd noticed on earlier visits seemed to be increasing in size. He'd given her the length of pipe and told her to do it at least three times a day. It felt like walking on marbles, but she'd been doing it. He kept bringing up the possibility of surgery, but she resisted. "Sorry, so sorry," Phil called as he crossed the room to Lizzie. "Young girl broke her leg in three places playing roller derby. Roller derby at fourteen! Can you imagine? Anyway, I wanted to talk with them before the cast came off so we'd have some sort of plan."

Lizzie lay flat on her back as Phil continued to talk about the girl. She kept her good leg flat, while he bent and twisted her right leg, occasionally interrupting his story to ask her to bend or flex or stretch as he took measurements. When he was done, he put a warm towel over her knee and told her to sit still. "I need to look at your chart," he said.

He returned and leaned over the table. "It isn't what you want to hear."

"But it's better, right?"

"I'm still concerned about the grinding noise and the fact that you can't straighten your knee."

Lizzie looked away from him. "Today's just a bad day. I've been massaging it."

"This is a whole different area. You can't get to it with massage. I think we're looking at scar tissue, maybe a cyclops lesion."

Over the next thirty minutes, she learned more than she ever thought she would about the body's reaction to being cut. It turns out that scar tissue is made up of the same material as the tissue it replaces, but an abundance of collagen means it's knitted together in a way that makes it inflexible. Some people never get scar tissue and others, especially those who've been immobile, had painful buildups of the material that interfered with motion. "This is what I get," she said.

"I know you're opposed to more surgery, so let's see what happens if you keep working, massaging the area as you increase the muscles around it."

"Can I play?"

"With due caution, yes."

At home, she gathered her cousins around her and told them in a burst not only about her leg, but in an attempt to leave them with some good news, about T. J. Isobel hugged her and told her it was about time she took that code inspector for a test drive. Elyse's face changed for a moment when she heard. It hardened in a way that made her look much older. Seeing this version of her cousin's face made Lizzie think that not having a dream of her own had taken its toll on her.

"I've got to be eating or cooking to talk," Elyse said. She opened the refrigerator and pulled out a pile of ingredients.

Isobel eyed it with suspicion. "What's that going to become? Please tell me you aren't actually going to use that heavy cream for anything."

"Stop worrying about your weight for once," Lizzie said.

"It pays the bills," Isobel said, moving her hand along her body as if she were displaying wares.

"Not right now it doesn't," Elyse said.

"Whoa," Lizzie said. She wasn't prepared for the shift in the emotion.

"See, that's frank talk. We need more of it. Because if there are people I don't have to be careful with, it should be the two of you." Elyse lined up celery, carrots, and onions and began chopping. "I can maybe see how you can act and not eat, but there's no way you can write a script and not eat. Your brain needs food."

"Are you crying?" Lizzie asked Elyse, still shocked at how coldly she'd spoken to Isobel.

"It's the onions."

Isobel stood up and walked to the counter. She put her arms around Elyse. "If I stand next to you, can I claim it's the onions too?"

"You can say what you need to," Elyse said, waving the knife in Isobel's direction. "Crying is cathartic and whether you're crying out of relief or joy, I'd say what we all need is a good cry and a bowl of soup."

"What are you two crying about anyway?" Lizzie asked, and even as she said it a sob rose up in her throat and made the words come out muddled.

"I don't cry," Isobel said. "I mean, sure I get teary eyed watching movies on the plane, or listening to any torch song on the radio. What I don't do is cry over my own life."

"You're fooling yourself," Elyse said. "All those little tears stand in for the big ones you don't have time for."

In a moment the three of them were crying—each one only vaguely aware of what the other two were crying about.

"Isn't there some superstition about getting tears into the soup pot?" Isobel finally asked, sniffling and wiping her eyes and nose on the edge of her shirt.

Elyse dumped the vegetables into the Dutch oven and added a splash of oil. Then she blew her nose on a paper towel and dried her eyes. "I think it has to do with salt. A salty soup means the cook is in love."

"That pot is definitely going to have too much salt in it," Isobel said.

"You should find a way to move on with your life," Lizzie said.

"I'm not ready for that. I can't even talk about it," Elyse said. "All I know for sure is that I can't be in Boston right now. My sister keeps calling and asking me about being a bridesmaid and wants to know what I think about flowers and appetizers. But I can't do any of it. So I'm here because, as my parents are so fond of saying, the only way to forget your own problems is to get involved in helping someone else overcome theirs."

By the time the soup was ready, the women had cried themselves out. When she heard T. J.'s knock on the back door, Lizzie thought about how the beauty of a rainstorm was that it made the whole world a little bit cleaner and occasionally gave way for a brief moment to a rainbow.

Second Story

Elyse

May 2012: Memphis

As etiquette demanded, the invitation arrived exactly eight weeks before the wedding date. It had remained unopened for the last twenty hours—doing a better job than caffeine at keeping Elyse awake and agitated. She ran her fingers around the edge of the textured paper and over the indentations made by the nib of the calligrapher's pen. Because her little sister still lived with their parents, the return address was that of Elyse's childhood home in Boston. The last time she'd been home, snow had covered the ground, dampening the boisterousness typical of her family's gatherings. She weighed the envelope in her hand, glad at its heft. Lord knows people have been undone by something as insubstantial as an e-mail, but Elyse needed her problems, especially this particular difficulty, to carry weight.

"My sister is marrying the man I love," she said to the window.

The indistinct chatter of Benny and his crew answered her. She listened to the house, hoping for some acknowledgment of what she'd said. The usual hum of her cousins getting ready for the day and the creaks and groans of an old house greeted her. No single sound rose above another, which was how it should be. She took a deep breath.

"The man I love is going to spend the rest of his life with my sister."

A small brown bird landed on the sill of her open window and ruffled its feathers. It wasn't enough. Her admission still held an omission. That version of the problem put the blame on Landon. But wasn't it his fault? She'd loved him since she'd known how to fall in love. And that business he'd said at Christmas dinner when they announced their engagement—the bit from Plato about how the gods divided the soul into two halves, leaving people to spend their lives searching for the missing part to make them whole. He said he didn't know where he'd heard the story. Elyse knew. After reading the *Symposium* in a classics course, she'd heavily highlighted Aristophanes' speech and then deliberately left the book in Landon's car. How could he not know? Right up in the front of the book she'd written *Property of Elyse Wallace.*

The bird turned its head and dipped its beak down as if urging her to go further. She tightened her grip on the wedding invitation. A warble escaped the bird's throat and it nodded at her again before alighting and flying toward the river.

"I love my sister's fiancé," she said.

From below the house, voices rose quickly, followed by a deep clanging sound. She said it again, louder and then with a quick flip of the wrist, she sent the card sailing out the window.

After a good cry, she padded down the stairs in her bunny slippers and walked through the beaded curtain without first moving it aside. Neither of her cousins raised their heads from their phones as she took a seat at the table. Lizzie had pushed her cereal bowl to the side of the table and, based on the rapid finger typing, Elyse guessed she was texting with T. J. before he left for work. Isobel, still in her workout clothes, had positioned her chair directly underneath the ceiling fan. Judging by the way she gripped her phone, her thumb hovering over the screen, she'd spent the last five minutes refreshing her e-mail. Since filming the television special last month, Isobel hadn't gone three minutes without checking for an airdate for the project.

"You realize it's like six in the morning in Los Angeles, right," Elyse said.

Isobel looked at her as if she'd been caught picking her nose. She set her phone down and busied her hands holding her hair off her neck. "I forget," she said.

"They'll get in touch," Elyse said and then asked if she could eat some of Isobel's cereal.

"It's so sticky," Isobel said, pulling her shirt away from her chest. "Besides, I thought you didn't eat hippie food."

"Too hot to eat anything better," Elyse said, lifting the box of organic something or other crunch off the table. The wedding invitation, its ink smudged and slightly damp, leaned against a half-gallon of soy milk. One of the workers must have found it and brought it in. Elyse swallowed and turned away from the table.

"This isn't hot. This is just the summer preheating. Wait until August, then it's like standing inside an oven with a damp towel around your head," Lizzie said, glancing up from her phone at Elyse. "What's going on? You never eat healthy."

Elyse pinched the fat on the side of her stomach. "I've been thinking I ought to start."

"That stuff's not low-cal," Isobel said. "It's just good for you. They only buy grain from small farmers and the ingredients are designed to work together to give you energy and vitamins and—"

"Let me guess," Elyse said, "sunshine."

"It's full of fiber. Guaranteed to make you fart rainbows," Lizzie said, the corners of her mouth twitching.

Isobel laughed, sounding like an angry goose. Lizzie giggled and Elyse, because crying could be mistaken for laughter, joined in until they heard the men outside mutter about crazy girls.

Elyse wiped her eyes with the back of her hand and glanced at the envelope on the table. "Seriously, what's the best way to lose weight?"

"Eat less, move more," Lizzie said, flexing her arms.

"Depends," Isobel said, fanning herself.

"On what?" Elyse asked.

"How much you want to lose and how quickly. Some of the actresses I know decide they want to drop ten pounds and choose to eat one thing—like grapefruit or carrots and then they chew nicotine gum to curb their hunger."

"That's terrible advice," Lizzie said. "You don't need to lose weight anyway. You're beautiful."

"I'm not looking for compliments," Elyse said. Since exiting adolescence, neither of her cousins had struggled with their appearance. Tall and athletic Lizzie never looked as if she carried any fat on her. Her body had the sort of purposeful beauty people admired in Michelangelo's sculptures. Isobel's attractiveness lay in her face—oversized eyes, all the more alluring because they were so closely spaced, framed by wild auburn hair. Arresting. That was the word used to describe her when she appeared occasionally on the pages of those garish tabloids. Of course she was too thin, but all actresses were too thin. Isobel didn't have any of Lizzie's muscle tone, but that would have drawn attention from her face, and the whole point of Isobel's attractiveness was her face.

"You've got your boobs working for you," Isobel said. "Men get tunnel vision when they see a good rack. And you, my dear, have a great rack."

"The day is wasting," Lizzie said, looking at the time on her phone and then at Elyse. "What do you have planned for the day?"

Elyse shrugged and grabbed a handful of cereal from the box. She decided to forgo milk as it would mean acknowledging the wedding invitation. "I'm off today and it's too damn hot to consider any kind of cooking," she said. She couldn't admit the truth, which was that from the moment that invitation had arrived, she'd spent every waking second plotting. She played out all the scenarios in her mind trying to find the best way to stop the wedding and get Landon for herself.

"Yeah, the girls are in finals and can't practice," Lizzie said, setting aside her phone and glancing at Isobel with more directness than the observation deserved. "I don't know what to do with myself."

Elyse doubted that her cousin didn't know what to do. Lizzie kept a running list of things to do—not only what she had to do, but what she could do. There were lists of books to read, albums to listen to, places to visit, people to write letters to. When she was younger, she'd kept these lists, organized by category, in a spiral notebook, but now they were all on her phone. Turns out there was an app for her cousin's obsessive list making. If Lizzie had five minutes of spare time, she'd find an activity to fill it. Lately most of her extra time had been spent trying to put that diary of her mother's back in order.

As if waiting for a cue, Isobel agreed, noting that her day was wide open as well. "We should do something together to celebrate our birthday month. I never see you."

"We live together. I see you every day," Elyse said, feeling as if she were in the middle of a scripted sales pitch—at any moment her cousins would lead her to the inevitable conclusion that she needed a $1,200 vacuum or a new set of Japanese knives. She figured it had to do with the invitation. They were worried about her.

Lizzie suggested going to the Metal Museum and then to lunch. "You always liked the small stuff—the miniatures over the murals. There wasn't ever anything worth seeing when I lived here and now there are as many museums as churches."

"Not even close," Elyse said, thinking of the number of churches she'd seen in her aimless walking around the city on days when she couldn't stand the sight of her cousins or herself. Seems all it took in Memphis to start a church was to hang a sign on your front door and convince your friends that you knew the word of God better than the man or woman at the last pulpit they'd been to.

"Then it's settled," Isobel said, stripping off her shirt and heading upstairs. "I need a cold shower if I'm ever going to stop sweating. Leave in an hour?"

"Better not let Benny see you in that sports bra," Elyse said. "He'll have a heart attack trying to get enough blood to his—"

"Don't be crass," Lizzie said, twisting her high ponytail into a bun and securing it with the rubber band that had held the morning paper closed. She set her phone on the table face side down. "There's mail for you. Must have gotten dropped on the way into the house yesterday. Benny found it in the monkey grass."

"Right," Elyse said, picking up the invitation and examining it as if she'd never seen it before. "It's got your name on it too, and Isobel's for that matter."

"It's not for us."

"She should have sent three invitations. I mean, as it is, sending it this way means that none of us can bring a date. No T. J., no fling of the month for Isobel."

"That's not news. Your mother told you it was going to be a small wedding. Family only. Besides, you make a much better date than T. J., and Isobel won't be with that bartender much longer—you know she only likes the beginning of a relationship."

"Don't we all?" Elyse said, even as she thought that what she was most familiar with was the end of other people's relationships.

"Open it," Lizzie said.

"I thought maybe it wouldn't happen," Elyse said, pushing back from the table.

"You want a list of all the stuff I didn't think would happen?" Lizzie asked, tapping the floor with her right foot. She took the envelope from Elyse's hand and ripped it open before handing it back to her.

"Knowing you, there's a list of all that stuff somewhere."

"Nobody ever needs to keep tabs on their failures. All the stuff that doesn't happen gets written in that part of your brain that never forgets."

Elyse slipped her finger inside the envelope and edged out the invitation. Lizzie was right. The brain filed its grievances against life and stored them, waiting for another situation to come up to compare it against. She had to leave her failures alone—playing what-if games never made anyone happy. *What if*, she thought and pulled the thick packet of invitation components from the envelope.

"Looks like Mom and Dad got Daphne the invitations she wanted despite the fact that they're crazy expensive. When they started all of this, there was a budget." Elyse let the envelope fall to the floor.

Lizzie reached down and picked it up. "Maybe they're saving elsewhere, you know, because it's a small ceremony?"

"Nope. Daddy assured his little girl that she could have whatever she wanted. Besides it's only small because there's this church tucked away on a side street by our house that has room for seventy-six people. Daphne's wanted to get married there since I showed it to her when we were kids and liked to make believe we were saints."

"Sounds lovely," Lizzie said, describing a similar chapel she'd seen in Florida. Elyse half-listened while she separated the parts of the invitation, dropping bits of tissue paper on the floor as she flipped through the pieces. Lizzie continued to reach down and pick them up.

"If you'd wait a minute, I'll pick them up all at once," Elyse said, letting out a short breath. "Frickin A." Her hands had stopped moving when she reached the photograph of Landon and Daphne. She held the photo back and pushed the other papers into Lizzie's hands. "We should room together. The hotel information and stuff is there."

"Or we could stay at Gram's house," Lizzie said.

Her cousin continued to talk and, without thinking about it, Elyse put her thumb over her sister's face and considered what it would be like to be in that photo. It had been taken at their grandparents' beach house, the one where they'd all spent summers over the years. Landon and her sister stood on the beach, wrapped around each other in a way that made it look like he had both arms. He was too tall for Daphne. Hell, he was too tall for Elyse too, but what did that matter to people in love? They were barefoot. Behind them, the surf lapped at a heart someone had drawn in the sand. Their jeans matched and both wore flowing white shirts. Instead of facing the camera, they stared at each other. Landon's lovely jaw line was in profile. He had what Elyse had always thought of as a King Arthur jaw—strong and square. When he'd first been able to grow a full beard, she'd talked him into shaving it into a thin line that traced the architecture of his face.

"We're not walking to that museum, are we?" Isobel asked as she thumped down the hallway in an impossibly high pair of wedges.

Lizzie shook her head, fanning herself with the invitation. "Too far in this heat. We got little cousin's wedding invitation though."

"Can't wait," Isobel said, holding the beads of the curtain carefully to the side before passing through them.

"You guys coming? Going to fly out to Boston and everything?" Elyse asked, looking up from the photograph.

"Wouldn't miss it for the world," Lizzie said. "You going to get dressed so we can go out and celebrate our birthdays?"

Elyse looked at her bunny slippers and then back to the photo, not able to stop herself from staring at the picture and considering what her life would have been like if she were marrying Landon. Isobel stepped behind her and peered over her shoulder.

"I always thought you were the better-looking sister," she said, taking up the photograph.

Elyse swallowed the bile that rose in her throat. "She favors our mother—one of the reasons she's the darling of the family. Mom loves her because they're alike. Dad loves her because he loves Mom."

Lizzie started to speak, but Isobel interrupted her and held the picture up, her thumb covering most of Landon. "Can you believe Sissy Daphne is all grown up and getting married?"

Elyse forced herself to look at the photo again. Daphne had the body of an adult, but her face held the same wide-open expression of a child. Elyse remembered that feeling—the way time opened up in front of you and the pull of the adult-run world with its obligations and expectations seemed as distant as the first snowfall of the season.

"I wish we were closer. There's such a vast chasm between twenty-seven and twenty-two," Elyse said.

"Twenty-eight," Lizzie said, twisting her lips into a rueful smile.

Isobel returned the photograph. "It gets better. My brothers didn't speak to each other for, like, five years, but then they got married and had kids and I'm the one they don't speak to. Sometimes it takes that long to work through what happened to you as a kid."

"Nothing happened to you," Lizzie said. "You have to give it time. Distance narrows with age—at least that's what my parents are always saying."

Isobel exchanged a quick look with Elyse and shrugged. At the very beginning of getting to know Lizzie, she'd planted her flag in the territory of hardship childhood, and she never let anyone else even get a foot in. Mention how much you hated your parents and she was right there to remind you that at least you knew who your parents were. Complain about a sibling, and she'd bring up that her mother and stepfather had the nerve to prove they were sleeping together by bringing her half-siblings into the world when she was a teenager.

"Are we going to do this?" Isobel asked, pushing Elyse toward the hallway. "Put on something other than shorts. It doesn't hurt to look a little fancy now and then. Besides, I know this guy who works at the bar that overlooks the river and you're exactly his type."

Elyse left the room as Isobel continued to talk about the chef she'd met a few days earlier. She kicked off her bunny slippers at the landing to the second floor. They'd finally finished the work on the third floor last week. Although tiny, the bathroom now had a shower and gleaming white porcelain tile. She'd moved her things from the small room on the second floor to the small room on the third floor. The newness of the flooring and the paint made what few possessions she had look used up. She sat on the twin bed, which still needed a frame, and took another look at the photograph. Bending it in half, she separated her sister from Landon and then ran her fingernail down the crease until the photo lay flat. She slipped it into the frame of the oval mirror she'd hung on the back of the bedroom door. Landon's face looked back at her while her sister pointed that wide-open smile toward an infinite reflection of itself. Lizzie had said to give it time, but she didn't have time. She had eight weeks to find a way to separate the two of them.

In an effort to distract herself from the agony of her sister's wedding (and to lose a little weight), Elyse had agreed to serve as an assistant coach for Lizzie's soccer team. The farther the Olympics slipped from her cousin's grasp, the more tightly she held onto her dream. The day before, Elyse had overheard Lizzie on the phone with someone from the team—a friend or maybe the trainer—and they hadn't told Lizzie what she wanted to hear.

As they drove, Lizzie kept up a steady stream of chatter about the girls she coached and what she knew of their families. "You can do them so much good," she said.

"I don't know." Elyse unzipped and then rezipped her recently purchased athletic jacket. "I'm not exactly qualified to coach soccer."

"But you can be the good cop," Lizzie said. "Besides, it's like Rosa May is always telling me. These girls have a way of making you exactly what they need."

"And what is that?"

"A backup."

Elyse made a stab at confronting her cousin about her plans. "For if you leave?"

"I'm not leaving yet."

"But you might?" Elyse knew she was being disingenuous, letting her cousin think that she'd still be here after the wedding, but she couldn't risk sharing her plans. She understood that trying to stop her sister's wedding with the idea that she and Landon would ride off into the sunset together was a little like telling someone you were abducted by aliens.

"We all might." Lizzie pulled into the turning lane. She seemed to be considering adding to her response. Or maybe not. Elyse tended to read too much into people's actions. "I keep thinking about that wedding invitation and how fancy they've gotten. How much do you think it costs to get that gold-embossed lettering and then seal the whole thing with wax?"

"A shitload," Elyse said. Lizzie was acting for all the world as if this conversation she were having about the wedding and the invitations were normal, but Elyse couldn't shake the feeling that she was up to something.

She continued to talk about weddings as they neared the school. "Did your sister do the postmark thing?"

"Huh?"

"You know, send it off to Bridal Veil, Oregon, or Loving, Texas, and get them to do the postmark?"

Elyse shook her head, and as Lizzie looked for a parking spot, she explained that a bride could for some nominal fee send all the invitations to some other post office in a better-named place and instead of being postmarked Memphis or Boston, the envelopes got a special stamp and an appropriate postmark. "People do it for valentines too, and secret admirers. Although I'm not sure those exist anymore. How can you keep who you are a secret these days with Facebook and Twitter and Google?" Lizzie squeezed the Datsun into a spot and put her hand to her heart and then mock collapsed back into her seat. "Curse you, technology."

Elyse couldn't keep herself from smiling. "Surely somewhere in America there are still second-graders slipping anonymous valentines into shoebox mailboxes."

Lizzie cleared her throat. "You're okay aren't you?" she asked with a timidity that signaled an acknowledgment that the subjects they'd danced around were difficult.

"I'm fine," Elyse said.

The reflexive response didn't satisfy her. "You've been so angry lately. Letting little things like that picture—"

"I'm not angry." She fumbled with her door.

"I'm good with body language. You know that. And right now, yours says you're angry as hell and maybe a little bit sad."

"I'm tired," she said, finally opening the door.

"You're not the only one."

Elyse hesitated, realizing that her cousin hadn't been picking up on her own insecurities but had been wanting to confess her own secrets. "What's going on?"

"I've got to have another surgery."

"Shit," Elyse said.

"Scar tissue." Lizzie rubbed the top of her knee.

"When?"

Lizzie opened her own door and stepped out into the summer heat. "After the wedding."

"What does it mean for your plans?" Elyse couldn't bring herself to say Olympics.

"It isn't good. I think."

Elyse didn't let her cousin stop talking. "You think what?"

"That I never had a chance. One of the girls told me last week that the coach is already set on the team and plans to make the announcement early—at the end of this month."

"But she might not?"

"She doesn't have to until July, but nobody thinks she's going to wait and nobody thinks I should keep pushing myself to try to be ready."

"And now surgery," Elyse said, a wave of shame creeping up her neck. She'd been so consumed by her problems.

"I'll need help then. That's where you come in."

"Or Isobel could help," Elyse said, and then realizing that what she'd said could give away her own secrets, she amended the statement. "I mean I'm happy to. But, you know, Isobel's been there before for you after surgery, so she knows what to expect."

"We're late." Lizzie put her arm around Elyse and they walked to the field, which looked like more dirt than grass. She hugged her. "You ready?"

Elyse wiped at the sweat on her forehead, glad her cousin hadn't followed up with any more questions. "Bring it on."

"Take these," Lizzie pushed the keys to the car into Elyse's hand. "T. J.'s picking me up afterward and he can bring me home."

Elyse smiled. It gave her hope that Lizzie had found someone like T. J. She put the keys into her purse.

"You coming, coach?"

Elyse looked up to see a tall girl with heavy eyeliner waving at them. Lizzie waved back.

"How does she play in that?"

"At least I convinced her to stop wearing foundation."

"What does a sixteen-year-old girl need foundation for? That's the only time in your life when your skin looks as good as airbrushed."

"Boys," Lizzie said.

"Boys," Elyse echoed.

Lizzie leaned in close. "You'll be fine," she whispered. For a moment, Elyse wavered, thinking she should come clean with her cousin, but she knew she'd hold her accountable, lead her toward the moral choice, the decision that might make her miserable in the short run but that would at least open the door to future happiness.

"I will," she said and followed Lizzie as she took off in a slow run.

By the end of practice, Elyse's ponytail had come undone and her bangs were plastered to her face. The new jacket, which had looked so crisp in the store, lay abandoned by the chain-link fence. She'd gulped down all of her water and had resorted to putting her mouth dangerously close to a spigot on the side of the community center to quench her thirst. Driving home, Elyse made promises she wouldn't keep. At a red light, she pulled her phone from her purse and dialed her sister. It rang until the next light and then before the voicemail could make demands of Elyse, she hung up the phone, dropping it back into her tote. As she neared Spite House, which was tucked away at the very edge of downtown, her eyes lingered on the small storefronts that populated South Main Street—the only bright spot in the city's failed attempt at urban renewal. A bunch of balloons tied to a sandwich board caught her eye. *Post Perfect* the sign read in bright pink letters. Without fully considering her motives, she pulled into a parking spot and walked toward the store.

A bell rang as she entered.

"My first real customer," the woman behind the counter said.

Elyse nodded at the girl, who continued talking.

"I mean you can't count my mom or sorority sisters, they were coming because it's the right thing to do, but here you are. In off the street as they say. What caught your eye? The window display? Those are all my own designs, but I have more traditional stuff, you know fancy pens and invitations you can custom order."

"The balloons," Elyse said faintly, gesturing outside. She wondered how the girl could talk so much without pausing for air. She must be a swimmer—the only explanation for her lung capacity. "What kind of store is this?"

"Oh," the girl said, finally drawing a deep breath.

Elyse waited for her to finish.

The girl recovered herself and put on a bright smile. "Stationery. I sell customizable sets and original designs. I know, I know," the girl put her hand up. "My dad already said it was like opening a store that sells records or heaven forbid eight-tracks, which he says are like old cassette tapes, but then I asked him what those are and he shook his head. Of course I convinced him it would be a good investment. I feel like we're hungry for nostalgia and that people writing real letters is going to be fashionable—"

From the depths of her tote, Elyse's phone began ringing. The girl continued talking and in desperation, Elyse grabbed up the phone without looking at who was calling, hoping that the girl would let her be.

"Seeester," Daphne said, drawing out the word as they had as children, mimicking some since forgotten television star with a heavy accent.

Elyse was unprepared to speak with Daphne. The store had given her the idea that she could write her confessions in a letter. She looked at the storeowner, who fidgeted from the effort at keeping quiet for Elyse's phone call.

"Are you there?" Her sister's voice sounded like their mother's.

"I'm here. I'm here," Elyse said.

"Mom and I've been shopping all day and my phone must have died—I didn't even realize it until Landon called Mom's phone trying to find out why I wasn't answering mine. So that's why I'm—"

Her mother's voice, sounding far away, interrupted Daphne. "Tell her I still need her measurements for the bridesmaid dresses."

"She can hear you—she's on speaker phone," Daphne said, holding back a giggle. Their mother's inability to understand technology had always been a running joke. In high school, she'd broken their first DVD player by putting in both discs of the special edition *Gone with the Wind* box set she'd gotten for Christmas. When it jammed, she pulled the tray out, breaking it off and then sliding both discs back into the machine. The clerk at the electronics store hadn't honored their warranty.

"I need to know your bust size. Have you gotten any larger since we last saw you?"

Elyse didn't understand why her mother had insisted on making the dresses. She hadn't sewed since the girls were in grade school. The wedding was making her regress. "I haven't changed," Elyse said and then under her breath she added, "not one bit."

"Still, send me the measurements," her mother said. "You know how you have a tendency to get bigger without you noticing. And I wish you'd consider a breast reduction. Your grandmother had hers done and her back has been a thousand percent better."

"I'll send them," Elyse said, desperate to end the conversation.

"Soooooooo," Daphne said. "What did you think? I picked out the gold embossing myself. Wicked nice, huh?"

The noise of her mother's car blinker sounded extraordinarily loud to Elyse. "They're nice. Quite lovely."

"I'm so glad you think so. Daddy was the one who fought for the bells and whistles. You should have seen him in the boutique. He had the clerk chasing down examples from her storeroom. I tried to be practical and go with a basic invitation, but he insisted on calligraphy, embossed lettering. The whole kit and caboodle."

"It shows," Elyse said, trying to head off the discussion from veering into questions about the photograph. "Everyone's coming. I've got Lizzie setting up hotel rooms, although we might stay with Gram, and she's figuring out flights right now."

Daphne squealed. " Can you believe I'm actually getting married? I can't wait to hang out with everyone now that we're all grown up. I told Landon I'd need at least three nights out with the girls—one for you and the cousins, one for my college friends, and one for my high school girls. We're gonna party!"

"Yes," Elyse said, not sure if she were agreeing to the night out or acknowledging that her sister had spoken. She looked at the girl behind the counter, who held up several styles of note cards and mouthed "my designs" to Elyse.

"Wait until you see the wedding dress. I wish you lived here. At the bridal shop for the fitting, there was a whole roomful of brides with their sisters and their mothers and their aunts. And everyone kept remarking on how strange it must be when I told them I was getting married before my older sister."

"It's not that unusual," Elyse said, her voice becoming strained even as she tried to sound flip. "This isn't an Austen novel or, heaven forbid, the Bible. No one is going to make Landon marry me and then wait another seven years for you."

The girl behind the counter wasn't even pretending not to eavesdrop. She thumbed through a few more of her personal note cards and pulled out one with a red and orange design on the front.

"Oh, sweetie," her mother said. "You'll find someone. We've got to get you back home where the eligible bachelors are."

"The right someone," Daphne added. "I'm sending you a photo of the dress fitting so you'll feel like you were there. Love ya!"

Elyse didn't say goodbye. A few seconds later her phone buzzed and a picture of her sister in a wedding dress appeared on the screen with the text, "Yay! Me!"

"She's pretty," the girl behind the counter said.

"My sister," Elyse said.

"I don't suppose she needs—"

"Already sent."

"Of course, of course. I however have found you the perfect statement card," she fanned out several of the red and orange cards. "Red is definitely your color. These are one-of-a-kind—like little pieces of art, handmade by *moi* and for you today only twenty percent off on account of our grand opening sale."

"Grand opening," Elyse echoed, bringing out her wallet.

"Do you want them personalized? I can add your name. It's very popular. Or even your sorority. Were you in a sorority? I'm Chi Omega. I think it'll add to the handcrafted sentiment of stationery. Make it personalized—that's what Daddy told me. If this is going to work, I needed to personalize all of it."

"No," Elyse said handing over her credit card. "These are fine the way they are. Right now what I need most is a little anonymity."

"Ahhh." The girl boxed the cards and leaned across the counter. "You must have something up your sleeve. Besides, life's better with a little mystery, especially if it's handwritten."

June 2012: Memphis

Few women know how to fall out of love. Elyse didn't. In truth, she didn't know much of anything about love except that it mattered in that same soul-crushing way that God used to matter to whole populations of people. She lifted the hair from the back of her neck and waved it, trying to dry the sweat that ran down her back. How did people think in this heat? In Boston, June was light breezes and sunshine, but in Memphis it smelled like sweat and sour garbage. Maybe she'd feel differently if Spite House had proper air conditioning. Glancing at the inefficient window unit, she cursed and then curled her body around the letter she was writing as if concealing test answers. She carefully printed Landon's name in block lettering, looking up after each letter to be sure no one had snuck up on her. She was supposed to be by herself in the house, but everyone's schedule was too erratic for guaranteed aloneness.

She continued writing and eyeing the back door—her ears attuned for footfalls or the bumping of a tire against the curb. During one of these furtive glances, she caught sight of the top of Benny's head through the glass of the back door. Before he could see her, she turned the red and orange note card face down and crumpled several pieces of notebook paper with scribbling on them. Then, as he raised his hand to knock, she opened the door, hoping he wouldn't want to come in. A blast of heat and the sweat dripping from his nose nearly wilted her resolve not to invite him in, but glancing behind her at the atlas open on the table, she merely greeted him, waiting for him to explain what it was he needed.

"Ma'am," Benny said, looking past her. He was searching, Elyse thought, for someone with authority—either Lizzie, who paid him, or even Isobel, who'd improbably become like a boss to him. He swallowed, stepped back, and took off his hat. She'd never seen the top of his head before and watching him run his fingers along the edge of his baseball cap as if he were looking for a way to tear it open, she saw that the hair near the crown of his head was noticeably thin. The spot on his neck seemed more purple than usual.

"They're not here," she said to preempt his question and hurry him along. She felt the sweat trickle down the back of her knee. How on earth could Southerners be so slow to get at what they needed in the face of such heat?

Benny cleared his throat. "Have they seen it?"

"Seen what?" Elyse let her impatience show by keeping the screen door shut between them.

He took a yellow piece of paper from his back pocket and unfolded it. "We missed the deadline to renew our TOP."

Elyse blinked at him several times. The acronym didn't mean much to her.

"Temporary occupation permit." He put the hat back on and gestured at the house. "So you can stay here during the work."

She cracked the screen door and extracted the permit from Benny's hand. He had unusually long fingers for a man—and they appeared to be more delicate that one would anticipate based on how he made his living. Of course, if Isobel were here, she'd joke that Benny's version of working with his hands meant hiring someone else's hands to do the actual labor. She read over the yellow paper, taking note of the court date, and then refolded it, shoving it deep into the wide pocket of her wrap skirt before raising her eyes to his. "Is this bad?"

He took a handkerchief from his back pocket, shoved the brim of his hat up, and wiped his forehead. "I—uh. I'm not—"

The sweat pooled at the small of her back. She locked her knees—giving them no chance to buckle as the heat enveloped her. "I'll tell them," she said, starting to push the door closed. In the distance, she thought she heard rubber brush against concrete.

Benny nudged the screen door open with his elbow and stuck his foot inside the door before she could fully close it. "I need to look at that panel," he said, "to see if it's ready for the HVAC guys who are coming in tomorrow."

Elyse stepped back. He smelled like sawdust and gasoline. With his baseball cap back on, his most prominent feature was his large roman nose, so straight and solid. "So, that's actually happening? It'll be a relief to have central air."

"You looked a little peaked. Is the window unit not working?" Without waiting for an answer, he walked to the air conditioner in the corner of the room and made a few adjustments. The air stirred her papers on the kitchen table. "That ought to be better for you," he said before exiting into the hall.

Elyse stared after him, watching the beaded curtain rustle where he'd walked through. Sitting at the table, she put her hand firmly on the card she'd been writing and let the noticeably cooler air wash over her. She read over what she'd been writing. Would her gambit work? Of course she shouldn't be doing it, but her hand, as if it held its own free will, sealed the note, deliberately unsigned, and addressed the matching envelope to Landon in her disguised handwriting.

Benny called to her from the hallway. "The lights may go out."

She replaced the cards in their original box and tucked the one for Landon into her skirt pocket. Standing at the stove, she turned on the gas and lit the bundle of crumpled paper on fire, watching it burn a moment before tossing it in the sink. It had taken her six pages to figure out what she'd wanted to write—trying to be coy and interesting was more work than she'd imagined. Leaving the ashes in the sink, she entered the hall and stood next to Benny at the new electrical box Elton had installed a few months earlier.

"The current isn't quite right," Benny said, flipping the switches in order, checking the power to different parts of the house. The lights went out in the hallway where they stood, and he turned to her. "I promise I'll fix this," he said.

She stepped back. It had seemed to her that he spoke directly about her problems, the ones she was running from. "Fix what?" she asked.

"The permit, the electric, all of it." He leaned his head against the wall, forgetting to flip the switch to bring the hall lights back up and looked at her through half-closed eyes.

Elyse saw that he was drunk. "You should go home."

"Don't fire me," he said.

"We wouldn't," she said, realizing as the words left her mouth how automatic they sounded. "Besides, I would have thought that T. J. would have told Lizzie about the TOP."

"It's not the boy's fault—he's not in Hoot's court all that often."

"Whose fault is it?"

Benny looked as if he couldn't draw a full breath. "It wasn't on purpose. I had it, and I thought I'd give it to Lizzie after I took care of it. I mean, I'm the one who understands this house and all of the secrets the old girl is keeping."

"I know you do," Elyse said, taking another step away from him, but at the same time wanting to lean past him and flip the circuit breaker to bring up the overhead lights.

The rattle of keys in the back door quickened Elyse's heart.

"Who's home?" Isobel asked, parting the beaded curtain and clomping along the hallway. "I've got good news. The very best sort."

With one quick motion, Elyse reached around Benny and flipped the switch, flooding the hallway with light.

Isobel threw her arm up against the sudden brightness, which gave Elyse the opportunity to grab Benny's arm and drag him toward the front door. She felt protective, knowing that if Isobel discovered he was drunk, she'd fire him on the spot and find some way to oversee the project herself. And the last thing any of them needed was Isobel in charge. Besides, she thought, it was in Lizzie's best interests if Benny stayed on the project as long as possible, even if he had screwed up on the permit.

"Is he feeling all right?" Isobel asked, after watching Elyse shove Benny out the front door.

"No," Elyse said, fishing the paper out. "He feels guilty because Lizzie has to go through another one of those ridiculous court hearings to get permission to live in her family's own house."

As if on cue, Lizzie stepped through the beaded curtain. "You left the back door open," she said to them. "That's the sort of carelessness that explains our utility bills."

"I wanted the fresh air," Isobel said. "I can still smell that poison you keep laying down to try to kill all the ants in that kitchen. It tickles my nose."

"It's odorless," Lizzie said, returning to the kitchen.

"Not to the ants," Isobel said. She lowered her voice and turned toward Elyse. "You going to tell her about the permit?"

Elyse shrugged. Isobel had never been able to stomach conflict. In her mind, Elyse held a perfect picture of her cousin as a child, holding her hands over her ears in response to any discipline administered by any adult. Or maybe that had been in her television show. Sometimes, the two bled together in her memory, the television version of Isobel, with her scripted problems and solutions, becoming the cousin she played with at the beach.

Instead of telling Lizzie the bad news, Elyse palmed the yellow paper and passed it to her as if she were tipping a concierge.

Lizzie looked at it without comment, pulled her cell phone from her pocket and sent a short text message. While she was typing, Isobel returned to the kitchen and Elyse followed her.

"They're getting serious, you know," she said, nodding toward Lizzie.

"Who?" Elyse asked.

"That code officer, the one with the shaved head."

"We're not serious," Lizzie said, setting her phone aside and tapping a rhythm out on the table. "We're friends."

"That's what everyone says these days," Elyse said.

"Everyone I know isn't dating and then one day out of the blue they're engaged—telling me how it was like *When Harry Met Sally*."

"He hasn't slept over," Lizzie said as if that were a distinction that mattered.

Isobel fluffed and then smoothed her hair so that, rather than parting it in the middle, she slanted it to one side so a part of her hair covered her eyebrow and forehead. "They're going to broadcast the special at the end of August."

"Congratulations," Elyse said, wondering if she should comment on the length of time between now and when it would be shown.

Lizzie clapped her hands together. "This is exactly what you need."

"I haven't seen it, but my agent said they ended up making me the tease."

"The tease?" Elyse asked.

"You know, the interesting story that you watch the whole show for. Stay tuned and all that nonsense."

Lizzie brought her hand to her mouth as if it were a microphone. "You'll never believe what America's sweetheart has gotten herself into way down South. Coming up after the break a hunka, hunka burning house."

Isobel giggled. "More like Spite House rock."

"Her current living situation has her singing 'Don't be tool'," Elyse added.

A sharp rap at the door startled the women. Lizzie jumped to open the door and greeted T. J. with a hug. Isobel let out a whistle and nudged Elyse with her elbow. "I told you they were getting serious."

Lizzie buried her face in T. J.'s shoulder and her neck, visible because of the high ponytail she kept her hair swept up in, turned a splotchy red. She murmured something that sounded like, "Shut up, you guys." T. J. rubbed her back. He appeared taller and younger than Elyse had remembered. He had the look of many men his age, with his head shaved and impressive muscle tone that spoke more about his discipline than genetics. He had lovely eyes, though. They were dark brown, like aged wood, and soft at the edges.

Lizzie passed him the yellow paper. "It isn't right, is it?"

"It's unusual," he said, working to smooth a crease from the paper.

"How unusual?" Lizzie said, putting all her weight on her good leg.

"I don't understand where this scrutiny is coming from," he said.

"I know," Lizzie said, and Elyse got the feeling that the two of them had discussed the situation before. To her left, Elyse felt Isobel's agitation at the situation. Her cousin had the ability to give off heat when she was angry or upset. She looked at her, wondering when Isobel had become so invested in Spite House. Her direction of Benny and the construction had become over the last few months a real job. She raised an eyebrow at her cousin, who shook her head and continued listening to T. J., who was relating a worst-case scenario for them.

"They might tell you to get out, there are still the issues with the electrical, the plumbing, and I'm not sure the insulation's up to code, and Lord help you if you find asbestos or lead paint. The ventilation in the—"

"There's nothing inhabitable about this place," Isobel said, half rising from her chair.

T. J.'s eyes widened. Elyse put her hand on her cousin's arm. "Isobel's upset because she's gotten invested in the changes to the house. Benny can be—"

"Unpredictable," Lizzie said, and again Elyse had the feeling that T. J. knew much more about them than they knew about him.

"I don't think this is coming from Judge Hootley," T. J. said, his fingers running along the signatures at the bottom of the paper. "Or if it is, he isn't particularly interested in this case. My guess is that it's being pushed at a higher level."

Lizzie nodded at him, as if telling him to divulge what he knew. "Let's go for a walk," he said, drawing Lizzie closer to him. "It'll be easier to clarify if I can show you what I mean."

The four of them slipped out the back door, and Elyse listened to T. J. explain how code violations typically worked. Most of his job consisted of working with new construction or renovation. The idea was to have those doing the work get the permits and then pass inspection. Most of the time they did. It was all very informal. On a few of those jobs, he'd get word that if possible he was to let the little stuff slide. He walked them to the edge of their property and then glanced back. "You understand this isn't stuff that will make or break a house. But I have leeway, so if the guy is a jerk to me, I may look real close at exact measurements, or have little tolerance for variations, but if the guy's a good dude, treats his crew right, takes us out to lunch once in a while, then I'm nice to him. And the thing is, sometimes I don't make that call on who to be nice to."

Elyse suspected that the world worked this way. She guessed Isobel did as well, judging by the way she nodded along to T. J.'s explanations. Lizzie looked stricken and although Elyse couldn't be sure, she might be limping again. They stopped walking at the property line. T. J. gestured to the large empty lot that sat to the north of Spite House. "If I had to say, it's this."

"Dirt?" Lizzie asked.

"You've got to see the big picture," Isobel said. "What do they want to put here? A restaurant? An office tower? A—"

"A little bit of everything. Hotel, condos, office space, retail. You name it, the plans call for it."

"We'd heard something about a hotel," Lizzie said. "Back when Grandma was still alive. They tore down the warehouses and then there was the recession and"—she gestured toward the lumpy mounds of dirt and weeds—"nothing happened."

"Guess nothing got bigger while they were waiting," Isobel said.

"It seems to me that problems never get smaller." Elyse watched as her cousin leaned against T. J. Lizzie wore shorts and for the first time that she could remember since arriving in Memphis, she got a good look at her cousin's legs. She hadn't been limping. The change in her gait seemed to be a result of the difference between her two legs. They were both pale, but one was twice the size of the other and the muscles rippled under the skin. The damaged one, her right leg, looked childlike. Not so much withered as undeveloped.

232 · COURTNEY MILLER SANTO

"My guess is that when they expanded the project, they decided they needed more land and if you look around—" T. J. trailed off.

It was obvious to everyone that Spite House and the sliver of land it stood on could be useful to those developing the property next door. The two parcels looked like they belonged together—as if they were pieces of a jigsaw puzzle waiting to be joined.

"Who signed the paper?" Isobel asked. She paced along the perimeter of the property as if marking the boundaries.

"She's done this before," T. J. said to Lizzie. The two shared a smile that spoke of other conversations.

"Not in a long time," Isobel said, "but you don't forget that the world runs on favors. The guy who signed the permit probably owes the mayor or the developer, and maybe this judge of yours wants somebody to owe him. Who's it going to hurt to enforce the law and make sure some dead woman's house meets all the requirements for occupancy?"

T. J. nodded. "It's a lot easier to take a property by paperwork than it is to take it by eminent domain. They got in trouble with trying to do that a few years back. Lots of court costs."

Elyse didn't understand the conversation. They continued to talk around her, walking the property and discussing contingencies of what would happen at the hearing the next week and what they needed to prepare. It seemed to be happening a world away from the muggy June evening. She turned her back to the river and looked at the house. The bubble of glass windows, like a funhouse mirror, distorted their reflections. Elyse's reflection, because she was closest, loomed large and the others, moving about the property, were watery images of colors that bled into one another.

The house had called them there. Elyse was sure of it. The place was practically alive, and there was something in the way that its façade failed to accurately represent its oddness that reminded her of all her favorite drinkers at the bar. She watched the reflections of her cousins and T. J. morph into large and small versions of themselves. To Elyse, their worries were irrational. She knew it would all work out. This house had to have been built for more than spite.

From behind her, Lizzie approached, the shape of her reflection growing more solid the closer she got. "They speak the same language," she said, kicking the dirt with her strong leg. Behind them, T. J. and Isobel talked with large gestures and voices punctuated with intent.

"What do you know about your grandfather?" Elyse asked.

"What does anyone know about their grandparents?"

Elyse guessed that was true. She was among the lucky few who'd known not only her grandparents, but her great-grandparents well. Hell, last she heard, her father's great-grandmother was still alive on some olive farm in California. The women were as distant to her as they were legendary in the family.

"I'm curious about how he built the house," she said.

Lizzie glanced at her sideways and turned as if she had a secret to share. Elyse knew the look from countless times of listening to people talk at the bar. The trick to hearing the secret was to appear uninterested. People wanted everyone to think they were the center of their world, and holding back often made them desperate enough to open up. She held her breath, not sure if silence would work on her cousin.

"There might be some of his papers mixed in with the stuff we pulled out of the window seats in the cupola," Lizzie said.

That wasn't her secret. Elyse held still, not even acknowledging that her cousin had spoken.

"Seems like this house is full of papers. Trouble is making sense of them. Sometimes I feel like the person writing has to know they're writing for someone else. If you're only writing for yourself, none of it makes any sense. It's like a person trying to prove the existence of aliens or that we're all part of some computer simulation."

Elyse searched her mind to try to put together the pieces of what her cousin was telling her.

"Like all those note cards of your mom's?"

Lizzie kicked at the ground some more, knocking away gumballs from the neighbor's sweet gum tree. "There's an answer in them, but I can't put them back in order and—"

Elyse let her cousin take in a few deep breaths. She wrapped her arms around Lizzie and urged her to let the air out. "Still wish your mother would come out with it, huh?"

Her cousin shook her head and then pounded her fists against her legs. In the reflection of the window, Elyse saw T. J. pick up his head and look at them, and then look away. Isobel started to walk toward them and then, when she was several strides in front of him, T. J. followed.

"We sort of thought she would have by now," Elyse said, still rubbing her cousin's back. "It can't be that important. Trust me when I tell you it won't change anything."

Gently squeezing Lizzie's hands, which were long and elegant, Elyse worked to keep her voice even. Those on the edge often took offense at even the slightest inflection on a word. It was normal for Lizzie to want to know who her father had been, or who he was, but in the end it wouldn't do her any good. Chances were her mother had a logical reason for keeping the information from her. It might be incest, or abuse, or that the guy was a bad man. But she couldn't tell her cousin that. She couldn't explain to her that not knowing was better than a truth so awful that it changed who you were. And now with DNA and genetics, it seemed that people put too much stock in heredity.

In a moment, Isobel had wrapped her arms around them. "It's been a long day," she said.

"Such a long day," T. J. echoed and somehow embraced all three of them. They stood in the yard a long while. Elyse listened to everyone's heartbeats, noting how the rhythms seemed to echo one another. Lizzie opened her mouth and did this funny breathing pattern that took the place of sobs. She and Isobel withdrew, leaving T. J. to comfort Lizzie.

"Was that about the house?" Isobel asked as they entered the back door.

"About her father," Elyse said.

"Family," Isobel said, opening the refrigerator.

Elyse slipped her hands in her pockets and felt the thick envelope, thinking about her own family and all the tears she'd shed over them.

Before moving to make dinner, she stood a long while in the kitchen, facing her altered reflection in the heavy window glass. The sky and the river stretched beyond the glass taking on what Elyse thought must be their true form. It was only the reflection of Elyse that smeared and folded in on itself in the old glass. The next day she mailed the envelope to the postmaster in Lovejoy, Georgia. Maybe if she got outright rejected, that would help her to fall out of love.

March 1999: Memphis

During spring break just before she turned four-teen, Elyse and her family took a road trip to visit her father's brother in Memphis. For most of the trip, Elyse hadn't understood why they were in Memphis. Of course there'd been the stated reason, which was the birth of her twin cousins a few weeks earlier and the understood reason—that her father and Uncle Jim were more like twins themselves than brothers. But that year, there was an urgency to the trip that Elyse didn't understand until it had ended and she and her sister were back in the car, drowsy from the medicine their mother had given them to help them sleep on the long car ride home.

Mostly Elyse had been bored on the trip. Her younger sister, Daphne, was close in age to Lizzie's younger brothers and the three of them quickly became the best of friends—with Daphne acting as a Wendy to their Lost Boys. The plan had been for Lizzie and Elyse to pair up and leave the adults to their visiting and holding of babies, but Lizzie didn't have time for Elyse. Soccer ate up nearly every waking moment, and it wasn't until nearly the last day of their trip that she and Lizzie got to spend any real time together.

The families drove downtown and took an aerial tram to a riverfront park that boasted a scale replica of the Mississippi and, according to Lizzie, steep grassy hills that were perfect for sliding down. The adults pushed strollers filled with sleepy babies, a picnic lunch, and squares of cardboard. "For the hills," Lizzie had whispered, sliding them into the bottom of the strollers when the parents weren't looking. The park fascinated Elyse—every step was the equivalent of a mile. She walked the length of the river to the place it ended in a pool meant to represent the Gulf of Mexico and then raced back again to where she and Lizzie had left the parents at their meandering stroller pace.

Her little sister and the boys had taken off their shoes and were walking in the river. Lizzie reached underneath the stroller and snagged the cardboard, telling the parents they were going to do some sliding. They walked up the steep hill, which sat adjacent to an outdoor amphitheater, and Elyse tried to engage Lizzie in conversation about boys, about Isobel, about her parents, but all she wanted to talk about was soccer. A few months later, America would watch their women defeat the Chinese in the World Cup finals held in California and would fall hopelessly in love with the game. But this was before anyone knew about Mia's goals and Brandi's sports bra and especially the crazy rule that allowed games to be decided by what essentially amounted to a roll of the dice. What Elyse did remember of their conversation was her annoyance that Lizzie kept asking her how close she lived to the stadium where the Patriots played and if she was going to buy tickets to see the preliminary games. She also remembered thinking that the Lizzie of Memphis was a different creature than Lizzie at the beach.

At the top of the hill, they realized that her little sister, Daphne, shoeless and breathless, had tagged along with them.

"Are you ready?" Lizzie's voice cracked when it got loud.

Elyse looked down the hill, which appeared twice as steep as it had from its base.

"Let me go first," Daphne said, pulling at Elyse's square of cardboard.

"No, it's mine," Elyse said. "Get your own." Out of the corner of her eye, she saw Lizzie take a running start at the hill. She felt the deep urge of competition in the pit of her stomach and for the first time since meeting Lizzie when they were all eight, Elyse felt she had to prove her worth. Maybe it was because they had always felt so inadequate compared to Isobel that it never occurred to them to measure themselves against each other, or it could have been that Lizzie's star seemed that much brighter because they were on her home turf. Either way, Elyse wanted to beat Lizzie to the bottom of the hill like she'd never wanted anything in her life. Without thinking, she shoved her sister, tearing the cardboard out of her hands and then ran as fast as she could before leaping onto the square and sliding down the hill. She heard a cry behind her and thought how tired she was of everyone babying her little sister. It was time she grew up.

The ride down was exhilarating. She'd gotten a good start, a quick start, and in a moment she flew by Lizzie going so fast that instead of stopping at the base of the hill, she glided as if on snow onto the concrete and into the portion of the Mississippi meant to represent Vicksburg. She laughed out of victory and out of the thrill of the race ending unexpectedly in a splash. Standing up, she brushed the grass from her legs and arms and looked around to see who'd watched her performance. Aunt Annie and her mother stood clustered around the strollers, their hands over their mouths. At the base of the hill, Lizzie sat, cradling Daphne in her arms, as Uncle Jim and Elyse's father rushed to her.

"She fell, she fell," Elyse heard her mother saying.

"It wasn't that bad, it can't be that bad. It was a tumble, just a tumble. The boys take those all the time," Aunt Annie said, patting her mother's arm.

"Oh, God," her mother said.

A look flashed across Aunt Annie's face that conveyed an inner struggle and then before anyone understood what she was doing, she sank to her knees and started pleading with God to let Daphne be unhurt. Elyse's family was technically Catholic, but they'd had the sort of casual religious upbringing that had left her with only the briefest of familiarities with such prostrations. She'd never in all her time on Earth seen an adult pray outside of a church.

Elyse's mother didn't notice, but everyone else, even the few passersby who'd stopped to watch, echoed Aunt Annie's "amen" at the end of her words. For Elyse's part, she listened to her sister's cries. She'd come to know which sounds she made when she was playing it up for her parents and which sounds she made when she was scared. Her hurt cry sounded like a kitten—more mewing than yowling.

"It wasn't my fault," Elyse started to say, knowing even as she spoke that she shouldn't be defending herself. But she couldn't help it. She wanted someone else to take the blame. It made her feel too awful to take responsibility for her carelessness.

"There, there," she heard Uncle Jim say.

Daphne let out a few soft cries and a hiccup.

Her father took Daphne from Lizzie and ran his hands across all the parts of her sister that could be broken. His hands seemed to double in size as they passed over Daphne's head and arms and gently tested joints. At last, he stood her up. "I think she's hurt her ankle. A sprain."

The women murmured to each other, and Elyse's little brothers, Daphne's Lost Boys, ran toward her, relating to each other the awesomeness of the fall. The day was, of course, over. The mothers packed up everyone, and the fathers took turns giving Daphne piggyback rides to the tram so she wouldn't have to walk.

Lizzie, who the parents seemed to feel was some sort of hero, didn't even talk about what had happened. Instead, sitting on the tram, in the back away from the family, she whispered a plan into Elyse's ear. As the group exited the tram, Lizzie spoke as if she were offering a favor. "Why don't Elyse and I walk over and visit

Grandma Mellie? I'm sure she could use the company and then you can have adult time while the kids nap."

"Oh no," Elyse's mother said.

Uncle Jim cut her off. His light blue eyes twitched and it felt to Elyse like he was on their side. "That's a fine idea."

The two adults looked at each other and, for the first time, Elyse thought that her mother might not be so fond of Uncle Jim. Elyse dropped her chin to her chest, convinced that she was in for an afternoon of reprimand. The adults lowered their voices to talk about the proposition. And Lizzie, who seemed to always get what she wanted, at least for all those years she played soccer, barely waited for the yes to come before grabbing Elyse by the arm and taking off as if she'd heard a starter pistol.

"Why are you always running?" Elyse asked, trying to keep up and to catch her breath.

"Why not?" Lizzie responded, undoing her hair from its ponytail and letting it stream out behind her. It was even blonder than Elyse remembered from previous summers.

"Well then, at least tell me where we're going," she said, settling into a pace that allowed her to talk and race. They ran out of the parking garage and instead of waiting for the walk sign to show up indicating it was safe to cross, they sprinted across four lanes of traffic, trying to beat the cars honking at them for jaywalking.

"Away. I couldn't take them anymore. Any of them," Lizzie said. "Did you see my mother? Why has she got to be so ridiculous?"

Elyse couldn't hide the surprise on her face. She'd felt the whole visit that Lizzie had gotten a life better than a fairy tale. Instead of an evil stepmother, she'd gotten Uncle Jim, who as far as stepfathers went, was pretty awesome. They had enough money and everyone was beautiful. Elyse still had enough fat on her stomach and arms to be pinchable. Her cousin was tall and looked nearly insect-like in the way you could see how the muscle attached to her bones.

Lizzie must have thought she meant the trouble with her sister. "Not Daphne. She's fine. A brave little girl and I love your family. It's my mother," Lizzie screamed as if it would take too much from her to explain the whole of the situation.

"I get it," Elyse said, thinking how much her own mother irritated her.

Lizzie stopped running and put her hand to her side. "A stitch."

They walked, turning down several streets and then once again without warning, Lizzie sprinted away, leaving Elyse to do her best to catch up. Finally, as she

246 • COURTNEY MILLER SANTO

closed the distance between them and was on the verge of passing her cousin, Lizzie slowed. *I'm winning, I'm winning,* Elyse thought before stopping short at the strange sight of Spite House.

"That can't be real," Elyse said, taking in the thin columns and odd windows that fronted the house. Back then it had been painted canary yellow and in the late afternoon light it appeared to glow.

"That's Grandma Mellie's house," Lizzie said, smiling and racing up the steep stairs for one last sprint.

The house hadn't yet settled into neglect and the yard looked well tended, although shaded by the office complex on one side. An atypical mailbox fronted the property. It looked like a replica of the house itself, or as if a dollhouse had been put on a post with a red flag stuck on the side of it. There was a sign, the kind where the letters were burned into the wood, that read "Spite House" hanging down from the top of the porch.

"Does your grandmother know we're coming over?" Elyse asked as Lizzie bounded up the steps toward the front door.

"She's never surprised by company—it's sort of her thing, you'll see. She'll have cookies and lemonade and—"

The door opened before Lizzie could finish her sentence. "Girls," said an old woman whose back hunched in such a way that her chin rested on her shoulder so that she looked up at them sideways—as if her neck muscles had ceased to work.

Elyse averted her eyes and tried to not think the word that had instantly sprang into her head: *hunchback.*

Lizzie bent down and wrapped her grandmother in a sideways hug. She appeared to be almost twice as tall as her grandmother. "I've got cousin Elyse with me," she said.

"They didn't tell you I was crookback, did they?" Grandma Mellie asked, as if she were commenting on the weather. Her voice was high and sweet, like a cardinal. Elyse followed her cousin's lead and offered a hug, pressing her cheek to the old woman's. She was so much older than either of Elyse's grandmothers.

Walking down the dim hallway, she followed the sound of Lizzie's footsteps toward a beaded curtain in the back of the house. She sucked in her breath as the walls narrowed around her and threw up her arms against the unexpected light from the floor-to-ceiling windows. She blinked, trying to erase the bursts of yellow and orange in her vision and find Lizzie.

"I told you treats," Lizzie said, holding up the largest chocolate chip cookie Elyse had ever seen.

"I've got lemonade too," Grandma Mellie said as she entered the kitchen.

"You're the best," Lizzie said, halfway through the enormous cookie.

"Had enough of your mother for today, did you?" she asked, settling into a rocking chair in the corner of the kitchen.

"Always," Lizzie said, glancing at Elyse to see whether or not she could be trusted.

"I raised her, but I'll be the first to tell you how impossible she is."

The deformity of her spine was less noticeable in the chair. Elyse remembered her manners. "Thank you," she said and then because they were in the South, she added, "Ma'am."

"Oh no, none of that," Grandma Mellie said. "I don't go in for that sort of business anymore. My father made sure I used the word 'sir' after every sentence. The day I left his home is the day I stopped all of that nonsense."

Lizzie started eating a second cookie. "Mom still makes me call her 'ma'am,' at least in public."

"Your mother didn't used to have such ideas about what was proper, but then she had you and I suppose she's still bending over backward trying to make up for the impropriety of that." Grandma Mellie turned away from the girls and whistled a bit of song and what sounded like bird calls to Elyse.

"Oh," Elyse said.

"She speaks her mind," Lizzie said, nodding toward Grandma Mellie and holding back the sort of smile Elyse had only ever seen on grown-ups.

"She belongs in this house," Elyse said. From the moment they'd stepped into this strange world, Elyse had been captivated by the house. The oddness of its shape and the peculiarity of Mellie made it instantly a bastion of myth and legend and, if Elyse had to guess, romance.

"My mom hates this house," Lizzie said. "I'm going to live in it someday just to spite her."

From the corner of the kitchen, Grandma Mellie let out a chattering sound, like the engine of a car trying to turn over, which Elyse soon realized was laughter. Lizzie joined in and Elyse felt like an outsider. She excused herself to find a bathroom and left the two of them wiping away tears of laughter and telling each other stories about Lizzie's mother.

She left the bathroom and felt herself pulled farther upstairs—toward the roof. Along the walls, the framed photographs alternated between pictures of Lizzie and photos of Lizzie's mother. They appeared to be placed so that a portrait of Lizzie at age two appeared next to one of her mother at the same age. The line of smiling girls who looked nothing alike was bookended by wedding-day pictures of what must have been Grandma Mellie and her husband.

Sound traveled in strange ways in the house. She reached the top floor and opened the door that allowed access to the one large room that took up much of the third story. All of the furniture had been pushed to walls, and a pair of roller skates sat in the center of the room. Elyse crossed to them, wishing she'd learned how to skate. She'd only ever been to one rink—for a friend's birthday when she was six or seven, and she hadn't been brave enough to let go of the rails and try to skate. The floor of this upper room with its wide planks and dark stain looked exactly like that rink. She picked up the skates, thinking she'd take them to Lizzie, who might know a trick or two for moving around on eight wheels. She was about to leave the room when the sound of Lizzie's voice—more child-like than it had been all day—carried up through a vent. She picked up the skates and walked to the opening.

"You have to talk to her. It's not fair. None of it is and now with the new babies, it's all gotten so much worse. You should see the way they fawn over each other. Happily ever after."

Elyse froze and although she knew she shouldn't, she moved closer to the vent, and her heart fluttered at the thought that the wavering in her cousin's voice meant that her life wasn't as perfect as it seemed. She couldn't hear Grandma Mellie's response. What she understood from the tone of the response was that Lizzie wasn't being coddled.

"I won't do it. I won't join their stupid church. Just because Mom found God and tricked Jim into believing it doesn't mean I have to have anything to do with them. I'm still a good person." Lizzie sniffled.

"God loves you," Grandma Mellie said. Elyse guessed from the other noises in the room that she'd left the rocking chair and moved closer to Lizzie. "I probably should have taken your mother to church, given her the traditions and ceremony she's craved her whole life, but after your grandfather died, all of it seemed pointless—an exercise for those who needed other people to see their faith."

"It's all so silly. They got baptized. Dunked under the water and everything and when Mom came out of the water, she smiled at Jim and all I could look at was her dumb pregnant belly."

"You're too emotional over this to get any answers," Grandma Mellie said. "Try some leverage."

"Leverage?"

Elyse pressed her ear to the vent and plugged her other one, concentrating on their voices.

"Tell her you'll give in on the church stuff if she'll tell you about your father."

Elyse gasped and dropped the roller skates. She'd never heard an adult speak this way—with malice and also to give such direction to a kid. Elyse could have spent all day dreaming up ways to get back at her mother and her sister and never come up with such a tactic. She felt ill and at the same time reckless. She bent to retrieve the skates. *How hard could it be anyway,* she thought and instead of slinging them over her shoulder and going downstairs, she loosened the laces.

They were too big for her. She looked around the room, took two small balls of yarn from a basket and placed them in the toes of the shoes. Lacing the boots as tight as she could and using the wall, she got unsteadily to her feet. Holding her arms wide out to the side, she shuffled her feet, surprised that the motion propelled her forward. She made a tentative lap around the room before trying to get more momentum by pushing down and out with her feet. "Oh," she cried, comforted by the sound of her voice. She started to coach herself through it, using familiar phrases, like "you can do this," and "just a little bit faster." Pretty soon, she was moving at a decent clip and the conversation with herself had become like the chatter of an audience at a baseball game. She didn't even notice when Lizzie opened the door.

Her cousin stepped into her path, and shouted, "Boo." Elyse looked up when she heard the noise, but she was moving too fast to stop and wasn't skilled enough yet on the skates to avoid a collision. She screamed and threw up her arms as if she were crashing into a solid object. Lizzie, laughing, flung her arm out and Elyse went over and around it in a perfect front flip landing safely on her feet, or rather on her wheels, with her cousin's steadying hand on her back.

Lizzie didn't confide her secrets and insecurities to Elyse. Instead they spent the afternoon trading turns with the skates. The competitiveness she'd felt earlier in the visit melted away, and she found herself worrying that Lizzie was pushing herself too hard and putting too many eggs in the idea that her escape would come through soccer. By the time the sun started to set and the cicadas took up their dusky song, Elyse had learned how to skate forward and backward and could even do small jumps over a footstool they'd placed in the middle of the floor.

Her parents drove twenty-two hours straight on the return to Boston—with her father driving the entire leg telling Elyse's mother to stay awake and keep him company. Daphne, with an ice pack on her ankle, slept from sunset to sunrise. Elyse pretended to sleep. She listened to her parents talk about their jobs—they both taught at the same middle school Elyse would graduate from that year—their summer plans, bills that needed paying, items around the house that needed fixing, and their children.

Her preferences were for other people's problems and while her parents were too steady to have their own problems, she'd discovered by listening that they shared Elyse's preference. Like her, they listened for the telling change in other adults' tones that indicated conflict. Some of the adults yelled, while others dropped their voices, but the words, no matter the volume, all sounded to Elyse as if they were being strangled. Overhearing these disagreements, these secret accusations, sent a thrill of delight down her spine. Years later, the few times she got high, she'd experienced a similar rapture.

On that drive home, she didn't learn anything she hadn't heard one of the dozen other times she'd eavesdropped on her parents, but finally close to two in the morning her father had shaken her mother awake again, wanting to talk about Uncle Jim.

He didn't understand his brother's sudden conversion, and he talked about their religion with contempt, calling it a Ponzi scheme. "Adult baptism. I've never heard of anything so stupid. We've already been baptized, christened like good Catholics when we were infants. I don't know what sins he's trying to wash away. Becoming Mormon of all things—it's practically like joining a cult."

"I like that Lizzie," her mother said, clearly trying to change the subject. "She's a good child, and I wish that Elyse could be more like her."

"Lizzie's the only one with enough sense not to get involved in it, and she's just a child."

Elyse's ears burned listening to her parents discuss her so candidly. "Don't be too hard on our Elyse. She's not showy. She's like an iceberg—keeps most of herself hidden."

"I'm afraid she's too selfish. Look at what happened with Daphne."

"Nothing happened. She fell. Children fall."

"She pushed her."

"Don't make her into a villain." Elyse loved her father fiercely for standing up for her. Maybe she had pushed her sister, but she hadn't meant to.

"I guess. But afterward, it was Lizzie who tried to make it better and it should have been Elyse."

"Lizzie was there," her father said, changing lanes.

They didn't speak for several minutes and then in a voice that sounded as if it were coming from far away, her mother asked her father if he knew who Lizzie's father was.

Her father grunted. "I have my suspicions," he said. "Jim tells me it's none of his business."

"I'll bet he doesn't even know. Tell me. Would you marry someone who kept that sort of information from you? Would you?" her mother had said, fiddling with the radio.

"Lower your voice," her father said.

"If I were her, I'd be more concerned about marrying a man who was so much younger than me. I'd be afraid my husband would leave me. At least they were able to get fertility treatments to have that last set of kids."

"I'll never leave you," her father said.

"No one's going to take well to this new religion. Did you see her? The way she knelt down and prayed over that little fall Daphne took?"

Her father grunted. "I don't think we should criticize prayer, it feels dangerous."

"Fine," her mother said, settling on a radio station playing Billy Joel.

The two of them were silent for a while, and then the chorus of the song started and they sang along. Elyse fell asleep, wishing her parents had kept talking about Uncle Jim and Aunt Annie.

June 2012: Memphis

The court date had been set for the last day of June in the late afternoon. Elyse didn't go to the hearing to find out whether or not they'd have to move out of Spite House. What could she possibly contribute? She spent the day looking for more of Grandma Mellie's recipe cards. For almost a week now, she'd been trying to find the woman's recipe for chocolate chip cookies. How had she made hers crunchy on the outside but chewy on the inside? Over the last few months, she'd found cards slid into cookbooks, taped to the underside of pans, and on the inside of cupboards. Lizzie had found one or two in the pile of note cards that were her mother's diary—copied in her own mother's handwriting from some lost source.

What surprised her most about Lizzie's relationship with her family was how she failed to see how romantic it was. Thinking about being the sort of woman who kept secrets from her family gave Elyse chills. When she was alone in Spite House, she often pretended it was her house, making up elaborate backstories about how she'd come to live in such an extraordinary place. She had one reccurring fantasy of being a Cinderella sort of character who becomes caretaker to her overly large stepmother and stepsister. Her revenge comes when the sister gets stuck trying to wedge herself through the impossibly small front door of Spite House.

She looked at the clock every twenty minutes, surprised to find herself waiting for them to come home or to text her the news about the hearing. She hadn't realized before that she'd come to care so much about the outcome. As dinnertime neared, she poured herself a glass of wine and texted the cousins. Looking around the kitchen, her eyes fell on the pile of cards Lizzie had been trying to sort. Why Aunt Annie had put her diary together like this puzzled Elyse. Most people kept a diary knowing full well someone else would eventually read it. Why else write anything down? The cards were spread across the table and stacked in various piles. Some of the papers were smudged and beginning to look dirty from being handled so often, while others were as white and crisp as hotel sheets.

She thumbed through the stacks. The one that had been handled the most contained cards having to do with Aunt Annie's pregnancy. Most of that year was in order, and flipping through the cards was like watching a time-lapse video of pregnancy. *Test positive. Feel great. Threw up. Still throwing up. Morning sickness lasts all day. Pants don't fit. Skirts don't fit. Underwear doesn't fit. Lots of energy. Baby kicked. Baby has hiccups.* A small part of her began to think about what her life could be like in the next year if everything worked out. Maybe she'd be having a baby before thirty after all. Maybe not. But maybe. If Landon didn't work out, then she could always have a baby on her own, throw caution and other people's idea of what she should do with her life to the wind.

That had been why the thing that Lizzie had said about it being their very last year had rung so deep in her. If it were, then she didn't have the life she'd always wanted, she had a life full of other people's problems, when what she wanted were her own problems. *Some say the world will end in fire. Some say in ice.* Elyse couldn't abide her world ending in ice—in a culmination of all that she'd left undone in the world, unsaid. Sighing, she looked at the corners of the cards, where Lizzie had shown her the numbering system Aunt

Annie used and then decoded it. A number represented each day of the year. How much work had it been to untangle this mess? It made Elyse's head hurt to think about it.

She looked at a few of the other stacks. They were white, untouched, and, judging by the subjects on them, Elyse guessed that they'd come through the mix-up and remained in pretty much their original order. Lizzie hadn't told them what she was looking for, but it had been pretty clear that her objective was to figure out who her father was. She wanted clues, or even evidence that would point her to the man who gave her half her DNA. The unsorted cards remained in a pile in the center. This jumble of paper reminded Elyse of a fact she'd learned as a child practicing magic tricks: each time a deck of cards was shuffled, it created an arrangement that had never been seen before. There were more possible arrangements of a deck of cards than there were stars in the sky. Then, of course, she'd offer a deck of cards and urge them to shuffle it. Find an arrangement that works for you, she'd tell them.

Looking at the scattering of cards on the table, Elyse imagined different ways they could be arranged and what it would tell them about Lizzie's mother. What would happen if Lizzie got it wrong, if she put the

134th day of 1981 into the pile with the cards from 1972? Would the arrangement of her life change? The notes were so cryptic—take the one with the notation "swan boats." Elyse hadn't even realized they had those in any other place but Boston's public gardens. But Aunt Annie hadn't ever been to Boston before she met Uncle Jim, had she?

Everyone has their love story—and none of them are easy. Imagine two people so different and so far apart falling in love? She wasn't even sure how the two of them had met, only that they had. Something about a business trip that Uncle Jim took for FedEx. Elyse ran her fingers over the paper, thinking of the cards she'd sent to Landon and the fake e-mail address she'd set up waiting for a response. Cards with postmarks from places that evoked lovers, cards that urged Landon not to turn marriage into the practical choice, but to try for love. True love. "I'm someone you know," she'd written in the last letter. "Someone who knows you well enough to tell you that marrying Daphne is a mistake."

That last one might have taken it too far. She finished her glass of wine and poured another before sitting down at the table. She checked her phone. No texts, but it was nearly five o'clock and they could still be in the courtroom, which probably didn't allow phones.

She squinted at the cards on the table—moving them in and out of focus.

Elyse had always loved Landon. When she'd lost her virginity on prom night to Jeff Lee, she'd closed her eyes and pictured Landon's eyes. All during her impetuous engagement to the German pastry chef, when he'd ask her about children (The man had wanted at least a dozen in some fantasy of being von Trapp himself.), she'd said no children, not ever. And it wasn't true. She'd always seen herself as a mother—but to Landon's children. Waiting for other people's stories to work out—Lizzie's and Isobel's just brought to mind the first time she'd met Landon, the moment she counted as her beginning.

His family had moved into their neighborhood when Elyse was ten. Any older and she'd never have developed a friendship with him—the next year she'd become acutely aware of boys and the ways that their attentions made her fizz up inside, like a shaken can of soda. She liked the attention. But she'd met Landon before the fizzing, so they remained friends. There was no television in Elyse's house. Her parents had heard someone tell them to kill their television, and they'd actually complied. There were photos in an album of her parents with long hair and her dad with a mustache that was too long at the ends standing by a television they'd dropped out of the window of their two-story apartment. Her mother would look at that photo and shake her head. "We should have sold it," she'd say. And if her father was in the room, he'd always reply, "But that would be passing the evil along to someone else."

In her mind, she and Landon stood barefoot in the sunroom eating sugar and butter sandwiches. Her parents also didn't believe in Hostess products. Why were they barefoot? It had been raining, and there had been some issue with their shoes being too wet to come inside. He'd run his fingers along her bookshelf and pulled out the X volume of the encyclopedia. "I've never seen one of these," he'd said, fanning the book open until it landed on xenophobia.

"An encyclopedia?" she said.

"No."

"A book?" At this suggestion, he alternated raising one eyebrow and then the other at her until she collapsed into a fit of giggling.

From above her, he dropped the slender volume onto her chest. "Just an X volume. The ones we have at home are grouped with Y and Z."

She rolled onto her stomach and paged through the book, licking her fingers to get more traction on the slippery pages. That afternoon, they practically memorized the entries, reading back and forth to each other. *Xebec, xeres, xenon.* This trading of x words was a habit they'd continued into their adult lives. Sometimes when he broke up with a girl, he'd call her and offer a one-word explanation: "Xanthippe." As if one word could cover the breadth of falling in and out of love. Of course they dated other people. More often than not, it was Elyse who had a serious relationship. In high school it had been Jeff, a football player who gave her a kitten for her birthday, even though she was allergic. In college it had been Josh, a short boy with an overly large head and a sweet voice. He'd been the driving force behind Smooth Sounds, the men's a cappella choir. She remembered his serenading her, snapping his fingers and singing new arrangements of songs his parents had grown up falling in love to.

But always, in her heart, there had been her love for Landon. She never wanted to act on it until it was the right time because she knew that when they fell in love it would be forever. Then last December, Landon had shown up at their house on Christmas Eve and in front of the entire family, knelt down and asked her sister to marry him. Elyse hadn't even known they were dating. She thought the fact that Landon hadn't told her held some deeper meaning, but she couldn't be sure. The truth was, and she had a difficult time admitting this, she hadn't known she'd planned on marrying Landon, at least not consciously, until she'd seen him propose to her sister, and just like that, plans she hadn't known she made evaporated into the air and she felt as if her soul were trying to claw itself out from inside her flesh. She'd left Boston feeling less as if she were running away and more as if she were running toward something.

She picked up a handful of cards and instead of reading the notes on the cards and looking at the numbers in the corners, she tried sorting them based on what looked like it belonged together. Stack, stack, stack. Placing the cards quickly into piles, she kept her mind on the problem of Landon. The wedding was only a few weeks away, and she would have to face him. She'd have to face her sister and, worst of all, she'd have to stand up there as one of the bridesmaids and offer her support.

Happily ever after. Elyse knew in her brain that those words were useless. They were more than nonsense, they were dangerous. She could be practical with other people. With herself. What? She was still waiting for her happy ending. In the movies, in books, and especially in pop songs, the men always ended up with the women who loved them most. Honestly, she thought that her sister loved the idea of Landon more than Landon himself. What did they know of each other?

Her phone chirped. Looking down she saw that her cousins were on their way home. "News," the text said. Not good or bad, but just news. Her thumb moved to the e-mail icon, and she checked for any messages in the account *marrymeinstead@gmail.com*. It remained empty. It was too needy, too obvious. What was her proof? Why should Landon choose her over Daphne?

Before Elyse had left for grad school and Landon for his Teach for America assignment, they had spent the summer together. Both were living with their parents, and neither had a real job. Instead, they volunteered at a Boys and Girls Club day camp and on their days off, she'd ride on the back of his motorcycle to her grandparents' beach house. He'd worked for nearly two years to modify the motorcycle to allow him to ride—switching the controls to the left and working out the stability issues with his prosthetic. Elyse liked the freedom the bike gave him. That might have been their summer to fall in love, but he was at the very end of a relationship with his college sweetheart. Landon made a perfect boyfriend. His girls were usually the president of the student body or the head of the debate club. High achievers were attracted to him because he was smart and laid back. They liked that he only had one arm—it made them feel like they were better people. Lacey, the girl he'd dated throughout most of college, had political aspirations. Teach for America had been her idea for Landon, although it suited him perfectly. She'd planned on working in Washington, DC, for one of the local congressmen at the same time he'd be teaching in a low-income school in the city.

A week before Elyse and Landon were to leave on their last day off together, they ignored the weather report predicting an afternoon storm and rode out to the beach anyway. The day was like most days they spent there—they had lunch with her grandparents, built sandcastles with some of the younger cousins who were still spending their summer there, and played pinochle with Elyse's parents before heading back to Boston. Daphne, who was sixteen that year and coming into her beauty, had begged Landon to take her around the block on his bike before they left for home. He'd done it and when he came back, he held the helmet out to Elyse and everyone had tried to get them to stay, citing the storm. They hadn't listened.

For most of the trip, the weather cooperated beautifully, but about thirty minutes before they reached their neighborhood, the skies opened up and poured down on them. She was never sure how it happened, but Landon pulled off into a secluded park, studded with trees. He slowed the bike to a stop and pulled a yellow bloom off one of the low-hanging trees. The color was so vibrant that it glowed in the shaded light of the storm. They talked about how they hoped their new lives would go—Elyse defending her decision to pursue her master's in hospitality and Landon talking about how he expected his Teach For America assignment with middle school children to go. They complained, as always, about their families and the expectations they were failing to live up to.

By the time they took shelter in a wooden pavilion designed for family reunions and weddings, they were drenched. She undid her hair from its ponytail and tried to wring it out. The damp fabric of her T-shirt clung to her nipples. She blushed. He shrugged out of his jacket and set it on the edge of the railing. When he leaned forward, Elyse could see the sharp bones of his shoulders through the thin fabric of his shirt.

He'd gone through a chunky, awkward phase before he'd had his growth spurt, and because of that, he was one of those men who didn't know how handsome he was. During college, he'd grown a beard to hide his baby cheeks. Elyse thought about how soft it would be if she kissed him and then about how it would feel to have him rub his face against her skin.

After their initial burst of conversation, each found they didn't know what to say, so instead they stared out at the sky and watched the lightning jump from cloud to cloud. He had his back to her and the translucence of his shirt felt like an invitation. She loved everything about him, even the prosthetic arm that looked real until you noticed it never moved. She put her hand on the small of his back, and then pressed herself against him.

"I don't know how to be with you, like this," he said without looking at her. "Xystus."

"Xystus," she repeated, looking over his shoulder at the thin strips of wood that made up the interior of the gazebo. How was it that they'd come to a place that the two of them had a name for?

He turned and it was exactly like she'd imagined. The look he gave her reminded her of the reflection of two mirrors—endlessly bouncing the light from one space to the next. He swept her up in his arms and kissed her softly at first and then with more urgency. "You're everything to me," he said. "You always have been and you always will be."

"I love you," she said. They kissed each other more and his hands wandered over her body, making her feel weak-kneed. The air smelled as if they were at the base of a waterfall—crisp and wet, and there was the same loud roar in the air. His hands worked at the clasp on her bra. She slid her fingers inside the waistband of his pants as he pushed up her shirt and kissed her nipples.

They fumbled with each other in a way that made her think of the first times she'd slept with a man. She became conscious of the stiffness of his prosthetic. Landon spread his hand across her chest, rubbing her nipples with his thumb and pinky. The base of his palm was calloused and the roughness felt good against her skin.

"Yes," she said as he teased at her neck with quick bites.

She reached for the buckle on his pants and was glad when it came open quickly. She pressed her palm against his jeans, feeling how hard and long he was. "I can't believe we're doing this."

He took his hand from her chest and pushed at the top of his pants. With his hand gone, she felt the cold chill of the day on her. She pulled his face to her breasts and leaned back. She thought of all the ways in which her life could change, now that they were together. He was sliding off her pants, his tongue working its way down her stomach when shouts of children echoed around the pavilion. The rain had stopped. They hastily covered themselves, not looking at each other as a group of boys, no older than ten, appeared on the sidewalk as if out of nowhere. All of them were on bicycles. One of them broke away from the pack and rode through a large pool of standing water that had gathered at the back edge of the pavilion. The others followed, and in a moment the boys were covered with mud, and she and Landon quickly pulled their riding gear back on and walked toward his motorcycle. Elyse held her wet T-shirt away from her body and reached for Landon's hand. She fumbled around a bit before realizing she'd grabbed his prosthetic. Looking at him, in hopes of sharing a joke, she found that he wouldn't meet her gaze

When Landon dropped her off at her house, she invited him in. He shook his head, not even taking off his helmet before riding away. She assumed that he felt guilty because of Lacey. The day before she left for grad school, she drove over to his house in the middle of the night and snuck into his bedroom. It wasn't what she'd intended to do, but when she tried the back door and found it unlocked, she couldn't help herself. She slipped into his bed and they finished what they'd started in the gazebo. Never once speaking about what might come next.

Elyse wasn't sure what she expected. What happened was that he moved to Washington and taught in a middle school there for two years. They resumed writing pithy e-mails to each other and life moved on. She dated. She quit the hospitality program and switched to urban anthropology. He and Lacey broke up, and he spent two years in Uruguay teaching English and then a little more than a year before, when Elyse was in the middle of a messy relationship and trying to make her bed and breakfast be something more than a failure, Landon had gotten a job teaching at the same middle school as Elyse's parents and started spending time with everyone in her family, including Daphne. What a screwed-up concept time was in the end. You could spend hours, weeks, months with a person and none of it mattered if it wasn't the right hour at the right time. When had he and Daphne fallen in love? During family dinners that Elyse hadn't attended because of a water leak, or during Saturday barbecues when she was busy dealing with bed bugs? She didn't know and she didn't want to know. What she wanted she couldn't have.

The door opened and Isobel swept in. "It was a disaster," she said and collapsed into one of the chairs pulled up to the table.

"Do we have to leave?"

"We're not leaving," Lizzie said, standing in the doorway.

"They can't make us move," Isobel said, "but they're making us test for lead, asbestos, and a dozen other potentially dangerous chemicals."

"Sounds expensive," Elyse said, tapping the edges of the cards she'd sorted so they stood up in straight columns."

"It is," Lizzie said, sighing. "And if they do find anything toxic, removal is going to kill the budget."

"At least the ants are dead," Elyse offered.

"Put out a fire and find out there's an earthquake," Lizzie said.

"I don't want to talk about it," Isobel said.

"Agreed," Lizzie said, coming up behind Elyse's shoulder. "Solve any mysteries for me?"

Elyse shrugged and checked the e-mail on her phone again. Lizzie picked up a few of the cards from one of the stacks. She shuffled through them and then quickly put several of them in order before reaching for more from the same stack.

"How'd you do this?"

"Do what?" Elyse asked, considering another glass of wine. She turned her phone off, tired of being disappointed by the lack of a response. If her phone were off, it would take her longer to check that damn account and maybe she could break the habit.

"These all seem like they're from the same year. It's a whole series of entries about working at the law firm. Do you know that's what my mom did after she got out of college? I guess she'd intended to be a lawyer before she got pregnant."

"When was that?" Isobel asked.

"I don't know. She doesn't talk about that stuff."

"You'll have to talk to her about the house," Isobel said, "so you might as well bring up the law firm. Maybe she'll give you enough information to make some headway on this mess."

"I still don't understand how you did this," Lizzie said.

Elyse squinted her eyes at her cousin. "You have to look at the handwriting. The color of the ink, the size of the letters."

"I guess," Lizzie said, trying to compare the handwriting from two of the stacks.

"You might not have the gift," Elyse said. "You're too organized. It's like—"

"Right," Isobel said. "Like that experiment that shows the different ways kids and adults think. If you give people a picture of a monkey, an orange, and a banana, the adults always put the orange and the banana together. But kids—"

"Kids and some of us creative types," Elyse said, taking back control of the conversation, "will always sort the monkey with the banana."

Lizzie shook her head, trying to understand Elyse's sorting method. Elyse, feeling brash, puffed out her cheeks and pretended to be a monkey eating a banana. Her mind was on Landon and those words he'd said all those years ago. In her heart, she believed he'd e-mail her secret account. She was convinced he was settling for Daphne and that if he knew how she truly felt, they could be together.

July 2012: Massachusetts

The bones of Spite House were covered with asbestos. After testing the ceilings and opening up the walls, the inspectors determined that the vermiculite insulation needed to be removed. The city required the cousins to be out of the house for all of this. And so in mid-July, Elyse found herself not only packing to leave for her sister's wedding but going early. Her grandmother had invited the Triplins to spend the week before the wedding at the beach house, which would leave Benny enough time to oversee the abatement crew and give the cousins a chance for a real vacation.

Not that Elyse's mother saw it that way. "What have you been doing this whole time?" she'd asked during a phone call earlier that week. She'd gone on complaining about having to do all of the wedding chores herself and how much they'd expected and wanted Elyse to be involved. Elyse zipped her suitcase and set it on the floor with a thump. She should cut her mother some slack. For the first time in her twenty-eight years, she hadn't done what her mother had wanted her to. The nagging was her mother's way of expressing disappointment and covering her confusion. The unspoken question remained: "Why did you leave?"

Through the vents, Elyse heard Isobel muttering complaints about trying to fit every piece of clothing she wanted to take into a carry-on. Lizzie went up and down the steps moving items from one room to another in a last-minute effort to prevent heirlooms from having to be thrown away. She'd developed an irrational fear that the removal process would contaminate them. Benny followed her, his tread on the steps slower. While it was Benny's fault that Lizzie was currently in a panic, she'd been on edge every day since the hearing.

Elyse slid her laptop into her oversized purse. She waited until Lizzie was in between trips up and down the stairs and then slipped into the bathroom next to her room. *Now.* She pulled the light on, closed the lid to the toilet, locked the door, and sat down, taking her phone from her pocket. There'd finally been a response to the secret e-mail address. *About damn time,* she thought, the memory of the five anonymous love letters she'd sent burning in her consciousness. His response totaled three words:

who are you

How many times had she read it now? A hundred? Two hundred? No punctuation, no capitalization and no context. The carelessness of that made her think the response had to be from Landon. Her sister, like her parents, was a stickler for grammar. Daphne carried a red permanent marker in her purse and if she saw a sign that had grammatical errors, she'd vandalize it with the correct usage—complete with little copy editor's marks. So, no, these three words were without a doubt Landon's. It could be worse, she thought. It could have been *leave me alone.* But it also could have been better. The larger question now was how to respond. She had to believe that any response was a good response. If he truly loved her sister, he wouldn't have time for such nonsense as secret admirers. Would he?

Her response had come to her last night in the middle of her dreams, which had been filled with bricks. Brick walls, brick paths, brick buildings.

I'm nobody! Who are you?
Are you nobody, too?
Then there's a pair of us—don't tell!
They'd banish us, you know.

It wasn't a love poem. Emily Dickinson didn't go in for those, but the stanza somehow expressed exactly what Elyse needed it to. She and Landon were a pair and if it worked out, then there'd be certain banishment. Before slipping into the bathroom, she'd studied the agenda her mother had sent. It listed everyone's whereabouts and duties beginning two days before the wedding and ending the day after. She picked a time that Landon would be free of obligations and suggested a place to meet. The where was what she'd agonized over all morning. She wanted it to be a place that was special to them, but she didn't want it to be obvious that it was her. Why? At the same time that part of her mind figured it was guilt, another part thought about what it would feel like to be rejected again. So, no. Not until he actually arrived at the location would he know for certain who he was meeting. She typed in the GPS coordinates of the gazebo where they'd kissed. Knowing him, he'd plug the coordinates into his phone, put in his ear buds and let the direction lady tell him where to go. She flushed the toilet in case her cousins were paying attention to her actions and then sent the message.

For the next twelve hours, Elyse was never alone. The cousins picked up a rental car and drove straight from the airport to the beach house, arriving late in the evening. Their grandparents had already tucked in for the night, but Gram had left sandwiches on the counter and a few extra sets of keys to the house with a note telling them to come and go as they pleased. Elyse ate a turkey sandwich and listened to Isobel and Lizzie reminisce about summers spent at the house.

"You're quiet," Lizzie said, poking Elyse in the ribs.

"Too quiet," Isobel said. "You aren't still mooning about the wedding, are you?"

Elyse shook her head.

Lizzie patted her arm. "You'll be okay once they get married. You'll see how it all floats out the window when you're ready to let go."

"I guess," Elyse said. She didn't understand why her cousins were so interested in her reaction to the wedding. It made her nervous and suspicious. She shouldn't have told them her fears about Daphne marrying Landon, but she'd confessed to them when it had seemed as likely that they wouldn't get married as that they would.

"Let's go swimming," Isobel said.

"We can count the stars," Lizzie said, unzipping her bag and pulling her swimsuit out.

Elyse fought the instinct to stay and pore over her sister's and Landon's social media profiles for clues as to how they were handling the stress of wedding planning. She jumped up. "Race you," she said, heading out the door in the clothing she'd worn on the plane.

Isobel followed and Lizzie, after starting and abandoning an argument about bathing suits, called out a challenge: "First one in the water wins."

"Last one wears the seaweed," Elyse shouted back, determined for once not to be last.

They hit the beach at almost the exact same time, but on the sand, Elyse's run slowed to a trot as she peeled off her clothing. She was out of breath but still determined to beat Isobel to the water. Isobel did cartwheels the length of the sand, while Lizzie ran directly into the water, slowing only to shrug off her hoodie.

She arrived last, but nobody noticed. The water was cold and then it wasn't. Isobel floated on her back with her magnificent red hair waving around her and glowing in a bit of moonlight that was streaming onto the beach. Lizzie, weighed down by her wet clothing, bobbed like a buoy. Elyse splashed them both and soon a full water battle erupted. It was as if in the ocean they'd shed their adult selves and become the children they'd been when they first met.

Elyse thought about the bay—how she'd previously wanted more from this stretch of beach—bigger waves, steeper drop-offs and even riptides. But as the women wrestled in the water, dunking and splashing each other, she realized that she'd underestimated the benefit of calm water. They played until they were too tired to move and then they followed Isobel's lead and floated on their backs, spreading their legs wide and touching their toes together so that, as they moved, their feet created a contracting and expanding star.

"I see the W," Isobel said. "Which one is that again?"

Without her glasses, the stars were a blur to Elyse.

"Cassiopeia," Lizzie said. "And look, you can see her daughter tonight, Andromeda."

"I didn't realize the two were related," Elyse said, considering what she knew of the Greeks.

"Jim pointed it out to me one time," Lizzie said. It puzzled Elyse that her cousin had never taken to calling her stepfather by anything other than his first name. "And it stuck with me, like how I know 'sequoia' is the only word with all the vowels. Bits of trivia taking up space in my brain."

"I wish I could remember their story," Isobel said. "It's something about how Cassiopeia boasted about Andromeda's beauty and it got her killed."

"Moms and daughters never get along," Elyse said.

"Don't do that," Lizzie said.

"She has her own galaxy," Isobel said. Her education had been so different from either Lizzie's or Elyse's. She'd had a private tutor throughout high school so that she could focus on acting. Elyse remembered her parents questioning the choice, saying the tutors they hired spent too much time on ancient society and not enough on math.

"Who?" Elyse asked.

"Andromeda," Isobel said. "I remember it because of the boasting. Reminded me too much of my own mother at the time."

"All daughters should be so lucky," Lizzie said before diving under the water like a dolphin and swimming for shore. Isobel followed while Elyse squinted her eyes at the night sky trying to make the irregular "W" of Cassiopeia take form so she could find the hazy spot it pointed to and see Andromeda's galaxy.

A few days before the wedding, the Triplins returned from the airport, having collected Elyse and Isobel's great-great-grandmother, Anna, who because of her age was something of a celebrity. Elyse didn't often remember that she was related to the oldest person in the world, but it did give her an occasional notoriety at parties or interminable meet and greets. Anna had become an easy answer to the question, "What's unique about you?" Everybody else's great-great-grandparents were so long buried that their descendants didn't even know their names. Elyse conjured Anna when it was convenient for her; the matriarch sometimes came up in conversations with her parents, who still felt some connection to her.

Elyse pushed down on the gas pedal, glad for the distraction of moving from one place to the other. For the first time since arriving in Boston, she'd have to face Daphne. There was one version of reality in her head, where if Landon only knew how she felt about him, he'd realize that her sister was just a placeholder. The situation kept reminding her of how angry she'd been at the part in *Little Women* where Jo chose to marry the professor instead of Laurie. And that might have been okay, except that Laurie had turned around and married Jo's little sister, Amy. Of course, her grown-up self understood that if she tried to explain any of this out loud, what she felt would sound less like true love and more like obsession.

In the backseat of the car, Isobel and Lizzie made small talk about California and olives with Anna. She half listened as her cousins discussed what they wanted from their own lives should they live to be half as old as Anna. The meeting with Landon was set for the next day. She tried to stop thinking about how Jo should have just said yes to Laurie in the first place and let herself, for one moment, imagine what the rendezvous would be like. She pictured him walking through the park to the gazebo, his face brightening with the memory of the time they waited out the thunderstorm.

Elyse's phone chirped from the depths of her purse. She would have ignored it, but Isobel, who sat in the passenger seat, reached into the oversized bag and fished around until she pulled it out.

"It's your mom," she said, looking at the face of the phone.

Elyse panicked at the thought of her phone being in someone else's hands. Her heart raced as she considered whether or not she'd logged out of her secret e-mail account before dropping her phone back into her purse at the airport. She nodded to Isobel, indicating that she'd take the call.

"Ma, what do you want?" she asked clipping off the ends of the words. She hated to be so short with her mother, but she knew that if she didn't force her to get to the point, she'd be listening to her ramble on about a dozen wedding problems, told a dozen different ways.

"Making sure you collected Anna without trouble. Your sister tells me we should have sent her and Landon out there, and I'm beginning to think she's right."

As she listened, Elyse moved right, out of the carpool lane, and sped up in order to pass a caravan of SUVs that doggedly obeyed the speed limit. "She's not right about everything—just because she's getting married."

Her mother sucked in her breath. "Your sister is causing me enough grief. You can't possibly understand this, but the thing you don't want to do is tell a bride no. Elyse Eloise Wallace, I don't have the patience to deal with your attitude."

"Who can say anything without an attitude? You're either happy or bored or sad. All of it's attitude."

"Put me on speaker."

Instead Elyse hung up the phone and pushed the button that turned it off, planning to explain the abrupt end to the call as loss of battery. She drove faster, wishing they'd rented a sports car or at least some vehicle with more than four cylinders. Speed had a way of outrunning the feeling of misery that had settled into her chest since hearing about her sister's engagement. What she truly needed was twelve cylinders—that would give her enough power to outrun the bad thing she was planning to do.

Her sister sat on the porch swing with one leg curled under her and the other gently pushing off the ground to keep the steady rocking motion of the swing going. Lizzie helped Anna up the slope of the driveway while Isobel carried Anna's two suitcases. The luggage had to have been purchased in the late sixties. It was hard sided and made of a pebbled plastic material. In addition to the suitcases, Anna had a powder-blue rounded cosmetics case that rattled when Elyse grabbed it off the backseat of the car. Daphne waved to them energetically and then held up a finger indicating she'd be a minute and returned to her phone, which she held cradled to her ear.

Elyse took the moment to appraise her sister, hoping for some sign that would make her feel better about the meeting with Landon. From head to toe, her sister looked perfect. Her hair was a light brown that with the help of a hairdresser became a rich caramel color with a white blond streak near the front that looked as natural as the striations in sandstone. At that moment her hair was rolled up into some sort of donut-shaped bun but she still looked more pulled together than Elyse ever had. She had wide-set light brown eyes that were framed with lashes so thick they didn't need mascara. If she had one flaw it was perhaps her nose, which had been broken during a volleyball match and never quite healed right. Sometimes Daphne complained about it, but Elyse figured that without it, her face would be too smooth. It needed an irregularity to stand out. Her best feature, however, was her oversized mouth, which made people think at once of horses and of generosity and loud laughter.

At twenty-two, she had a perfect body. It didn't look like it needed work to be thin, and her flesh had the gentle give of youth to it. Standing next to her, Isobel appeared as if she worked too hard at being pretty and Lizzie not hard enough. Whereas moments before if you'd have asked Elyse about her cousins, she would have gushed about their attractiveness. She guessed that was the difference. Her cousins were good looking, but her sister was beautiful. Where did that leave Elyse? On a good day, she felt like she was passable, but on a bad day—and there had been so many in the last few months—she felt like the troll underneath the bridge letting the billy goats prance by her.

Just before she would have crossed the line into rude, Daphne hung up the phone and exhaled an apology and explanation about a last-minute wedding snafu with the chairs. She ushered Anna onto the swing with her and took both her hands in hers, going on and on about what an honor it was to have her at the wedding.

Elyse took the opportunity to slip into the house without having to speak with her sister. The cousins followed, talking about how happy her sister looked and how much fun weddings turned out to be.

"There you are," Elyse's mother said, telling Isobel that her father was in the kitchen and sending Lizzie upstairs with Anna's luggage. "I expected you ages ago. What is this nonsense about you girls continuing to stay out at the beach house instead of the hotel?"

"We thought it would be easier. Our stuff's already there," Elyse said, following her mother through the kitchen where Isobel and her family were filling miniature bottles with olive oil. Wedding favors, she guessed. Probably as some tribute to Anna.

"It's not easier. We've only got three days until the wedding. I'll need you here tomorrow and no arguments. You can stay there tonight and bring back your stuff first thing in the morning. We still haven't had you try on the bridesmaid's dress, and I'm afraid it's going to pucker in all the wrong places. For now, you can help me with the centerpieces," her mother said, handing Elyse a pair of garden shears and a basket before pointing her toward the rose bushes. "Only cut the pink ones."

"How many?"

"All of them," her mother said, turning away from the bushes before Elyse could make her first cut. The roses were her mother's pride. She'd never before cut them, preferring to watch them from the kitchen table as they moved from bud to bloom and then she'd deadhead them gently with her own hands and collect the petals to make rosewater that she gave away anytime she needed a hostess or housewarming gift.

From the rose bushes, Elyse had a clear view of the kitchen. She saw her mother move about as if she were directing a play—repositioning and appropriating people as they came through the doors. By the time she finished with the centerpieces, the day had escaped. Her cousins had wandered off with different visiting family members for dinner with promises to meet at the beach house that next morning before moving their stuff to the hotel, which would be closer to the wedding festivities.

It worried Elyse that her time was being accounted for. She needed several hours tomorrow to make the rendezvous work. She left the centerpieces on the patio table and moved into the house, opening the refrigerator in search of a snack. Most of the racks had been removed to make room for the cake, which stood five layers tall. It surprised her to find how much of the work of the wedding her parents were doing themselves. The figurines of the bridegroom and bride were already in place. They were exact effigies, even down to missing the lower part of Landon's left arm.

Elyse shut the refrigerator door at the sound of footsteps padding into the kitchen.

"It's perfect, isn't it?" Daphne asked.

"Where'd Mom hide all the snacks?" Elyse asked. When they were alone together, the pretense of sisterly closeness evaporated. Without an audience, they didn't know how to be with each other.

"I was worried that they wouldn't get it right—cut off the right arm instead of the left. And then Mom said it was in bad taste. Landon wanted us to get"— her sister's voice faded as she walked into the pantry and reemerged with an oversized candy bar and cheese crackers—"these monster figurines. Cute monsters, you know?"

"Of course," Elyse said, reaching for the chocolate bar. It was her favorite, the one with toffee and nuts. "The summer we were twelve, we made up an entire line of monsters—drew their pictures and made trading cards of sorts."

Daphne smiled at her choice. "I love that Landon has always been a part of our family. He was like an older brother to me back then. The two of you were inseparable for so long."

"Inseparable," Elyse echoed.

"But Dad, of all people, said no monsters. He went on and on about how it wasn't a party it was a wedding and that we should have proper figurines that look like little versions of ourselves. So I told them to cut off the arm and he almost said no to that, but then Landon laughed."

"Dad's like that." Elyse ate her chocolate bar, breaking off a piece and handing it to her sister. "Intractable when you least expect it."

"He told me I was too young to get married, but because it was Landon, he wasn't worried. Something about having had Landon grow up with you that made him more like family. Can you imagine?"

Elyse folded the aluminum foil from the candy into increasingly smaller squares. She wasn't sure what she was supposed to imagine—her father's hesitation at his youngest child getting married, or how being married to Landon made everything all right. "I think they're afraid you'll break his heart," Elyse said.

Daphne took her sister's observation as a compliment and blushed. "He's good for me. And I think good for the family. Like the son he never had."

"Who says Dad ever wanted sons?" Elyse asked.

"Of course he did. He just said he never did so I wouldn't feel bad about being a girl."

Elyse hadn't thought her sister capable of understanding such truths. When they were still living at home, they'd found a box of their father's childhood memories stored in the attic. On the box, which had once held bottles of rum, their father had written in careful script *For my son.* Inside were his letterman's jacket, a stash of baseball cards with a rubber band around them, a baseball glove, several Superman comic books, and a handful of paperback books—*Lord of the Flies, A Separate Peace,* and *The Godfather.* Each of them had taken a book and started reading. When their father had seen Elyse curled up in the sunroom devouring his boyhood copy of *Lord of the Flies,* he hadn't mentioned it directly, but over the course of that year, various items from the box appeared on each of their beds, which was why to this day Elyse carried a thumb-worn Lenny Dykstra card in her wallet.

"Do you still have the stuff he gave you?" Elyse asked. Judging by the look on her sister's face, her thoughts were on the wedding or on Landon, and Elyse wasn't sure she could talk rationally about the nuptials with her sister. If she changed the topic, she could leave Daphne with the impression that the two of them were as they'd always been, which is like two people who share a background but are too different to truly understand each other.

"I sold a few of the baseball cards. They weren't in mint condition, but we got enough money to pay for our plane tickets."

294 COURTNEY MILLER SANTO

"You sold Dad's cards?" Elyse's voice rose and echoed back to her in the cave-like kitchen. She realized how accustomed she'd grown to Spite House with its narrow spaces and sound-absorbing windows.

"We're not all sentimental," Daphne said, picking up Elyse's trash and refastening the lid of the box of crackers. "I like my birds in the hand."

"Sentimental is better than selfish," Elyse said, knowing that her voice had taken on a hard edge that contained all the resentment she'd ever felt toward her sister.

"Oh, come off it," Daphne said. "It was Dad's suggestion. If your cards were worth any money, he'd tell you to sell them too."

"I've got a long drive," Elyse said. Her hands were balled into fists, and she imagined that that if she didn't leave the kitchen first, she'd open the refrigerator and put all her frustration at the unfairness of life into a helpless cake, and then she'd never be able to explain herself.

"You're not leaving," Daphne said. "I thought we could do a sisters' slumber party. I mean, it's been so strange with you in Memphis these last months. My whole life it has been you and Landon and now you've disappeared on us."

"Later," Elyse said, still walking out the door. She took the keys to the spare vehicle—the one her parents had kept long after their children had grown up. Sometimes she didn't know if her sister was oblivious or willfully ignorant. She'd overheard her once telling her friends that she never fought with her family. Which on the face of it was true. She never allowed anyone to fight with her.

The truck was blocked in, but instead of going inside and figuring out whose sedan was parked behind her, she angled the truck and reversed across the lawn, realizing only as she backed off the curb that it had rained earlier. She glanced at the tire marks she'd left in the soft grass and then peeled away, embracing the sense of satisfaction she felt at seeing those dark gashes from the tires in her parents' perfectly manicured lawn. Whether her sister wanted it or not, conflict was headed her way.

It was past midnight when Elyse pulled off onto the private road that led to her grandparents' beach house. In addition to their vehicles, the rental car was parked along the curb. Before going into the house, Elyse pulled her purse into her lap and searched it for her phone. It wasn't there. She turned on the overhead light in the car and looked again. Still no phone. Her heart started to pound and in a rush, she dumped out the contents of her bag onto the seat next to her.

It wasn't there. She reviewed the day, trying to figure out when she last remembered using it and frantic at the thought that her sister or her mother or anyone would find it and snoop. She let herself into the house quietly. Picking up her grandparents' landline, she dialed her own number, realizing as the phone clicked through to voicemail that she'd deliberately turned her phone off. Her mind wandered to all of the worst-case scenarios. She worried that she'd be found out. She worried that Landon had e-mailed her and she'd missed it. Taking several deep breaths, she looked around the kitchen, leaving her shoes at the back door. The floor was grainy against her feet. There was no getting the sand out of the house. Her mother complained for weeks after coming back from the beach house about there was sand everywhere. Elyse liked the feel of the granules against her feet. It gave her movements purpose.

There was nothing to be done. Nothing. She should sleep. Climbing the stairs to the attic, which had been converted years ago into a dorm-like sleeping space, she forced herself to think positive thoughts. She knew the odds were that the phone was inconspicuously at her mother's house—sitting on a table in the backyard or on the counter next to the refrigerator. Her cousins were asleep in their cots—Lizzie's long legs dangling off the end of hers and Isobel curled into a ball like a cat.

Elyse stripped to her underwear and fell onto her cot. Her eyes had adjusted to the darkness—the room's only light came from a small dormer window at the north end of the house. She rolled over and something clattered to the ground. She leaned over the edge of the cot and looked around until she saw her phone with a sticky note attached to the face. Relief flooded her mind—she tore the note off, glancing at her cousins' explanation of finding her phone in the rental car. It was still off. She turned it on, holding her hand over the speaker so the noises of the phone coming to life wouldn't awaken her cousins. It looked as if it had been left alone. There were no new messages from Landon. She fell asleep with the phone clutched to her chest, dreaming of being kissed.

In honor of it being their last day at the house, Grandpa Matthew had made pancakes. He stood in the kitchen surrounded by flour and eggshells, grinning at the chastising his wife was giving him over the mess. Her cousins were seated around the table with half-finished plates pushed away as if they couldn't stomach any more food. Improbably, they were dressed and looked as if they'd been up since dawn. Elyse checked the clock. It was not even eight. She had plenty of time to fix herself up before she had to leave for her meeting.

She grabbed the counter, her knees shaking at the thought of what she was about to do. "You can go back to bed, pumpkin," her grandfather said. "Your ma told me today was a relaxing day. She wanted everyone in shipshape form for the day before the wedding."

"The day before the wedding," Gram echoed. "Sometimes I don't understand that woman. When Matthew and I got married, we walked to the justice of the peace and then had a little reception at my mother's house."

"And my mother never did forgive me for telling her I got married after the fact," Grandpa Matthew said.

"Your mother was a crazy woman."

"Not as crazy as Anna," Grandpa said, leaning over and sprinkling a bit of flour on his wife.

Lizzie looked up from the table. "They've been like that all morning."

Isobel nodded. "You should hear the things they told us about Anna."

Elyse took several pancakes from her grandfather and sat down at the table. She wasn't paying close attention to what was happening around her. Each time she tried to concentrate on her grandparents or her cousins, her mind drifted to imagine one of three scenarios that would happen in a few hours. He would see it was her and confess his love for her. He would see it was her and leave. He wouldn't come at all.

"What do you say?"

Elyse swallowed and realized after the silence left in the air that the question had been directed at her.

"To what?"

"Going canoeing." Lizzie smoothed her hair away from her face and plaited it into a single braid that reached halfway down her back.

"We'll be back in time for that girls' night out your sister has planned."

Elyse massaged her temples. "I've got a headache. Probably best if I stick around here."

"It'll be better if you come along," Lizzie said, clearing her plate and helping their grandmother wipe up the mess their grandfather had made.

"So much better," Isobel said, taking Elyse's plate with her to the counter.

Her eye twitched and her stomach heaved. They didn't know how right they were. It would be better for everyone if she abandoned her foolishness and spent the morning on the water watching the herons and hoping to sight a dolphin. But she also knew herself. If she didn't see this through, she'd always wonder what might have been. And wasn't it much worse to break up a couple after they were married? Not that they would break up, but if they did, doing so two days before the vows would be so much less destructive. "I can't," Elyse said, not looking anyone in the eye.

The sunshine irritated Elyse. The glare on the window of her parents' beater truck never let up the whole drive to the rendezvous spot. She had sunglasses, but they weren't prescription and when she put them on instead of her regular glasses, the glare dissipated, but so did the road and the cars opposite her. It wasn't safe. Instead, she fiddled with the visor until it settled into an awkward angle that cut most of the sunlight out of her eyes. She'd driven too fast. As she approached the turn-off for the park, she glanced at her phone—she was twenty minutes ahead of schedule.

The park was well shaded, which made her feel safer and less exposed than she had when she was on the road. She parked away from the gazebo, preferring to walk to it as they had during that day in the storm when they hadn't been able to see straight and so had made a run for the covered building across the great lawn of the park—only realizing when they arrived that there was a parking lot behind the structure.

They'd painted the wood since she'd been there last. Instead of a creamy off-white, the structure was green— they'd left the interior roof alone and it remained a lightly stained wood—almost blond in color. She sat on a bench along an inner wall of the structure and looked at the woods that ringed the park. The squirrels were fat—obese, really, and were probably a sign that there were too many people here. In the distance she heard children screaming. Funny how the sound of happy children could at first sound like anguish. Each time she heard an engine, her throat constricted and her stomach turned over. She was sure he'd be riding his motorcycle. It had a distinct purr that she'd recognize before it came into view.

She counted to 500 forward and then backward. In the letters she'd confessed her love, stating and restating the reasons he didn't belong with Daphne. All the words she wrote were directed toward trying to convince him that this anonymous woman knew him best and therefore must love him the most. She was in love with him enough for both of them, but she hoped it was mutual. The wooden steps of the gazebo creaked. Elyse said her ABCs before moving—not wanting her eagerness to show. She pulled at her skirt. She took a deep breath and then turned around.

Isobel and Lizzie stood inside the entrance to the gazebo.

"What are you—?" Elyse didn't finish her thought. She needed to get them out of there before Landon showed up. Her cheeks colored and then she leaned over the side of the gazebo and threw up. "You have to leave," she said, wiping her mouth with the back of her hand.

"He's not coming," Lizzie said, walking slowly toward Elyse.

Elyse backed away. "What are you talking about? You don't know why I'm here." Even as she spoke, she understood that her cousins knew exactly what she was planning. Her back touched the railing and her knees buckled, leaving her sprawled on the wooden floor that matched the ceiling. She'd sat in gum.

"Oh, honey," Isobel said.

"No, no, no, no, no," Elyse moaned, dropping her head into her hands. "You can't know why I'm here."

Lizzie reached down and picked Elyse up as if she were a child. "Come on," she said.

Isobel put her hand on Elyse's back. "It'll be okay. It'll be fine. Just think of this as an intervention."

"I don't need an intervention," Elyse said, thinking she ought to be standing on her own two feet. She struggled a bit, but her cousin was so much stronger than her.

"You can't do this," Isobel said.

Elyse stopped fighting, and Lizzie set her down. They didn't touch her, but they walked behind her—essentially herding Elyse toward their car. Once she was in the front seat, Isobel buckled her in and asked for the keys to the truck. "I'll follow you."

Lizzie slid into the driver's seat; her hands shook. "I wasn't sure about this," she said. "I'm still not sure."

Elyse reached for the door.

Lizzie started the car, not even bothering to look behind her as she put the car into reverse. "It's so messed up. What were you thinking? It's not like we're teenagers. What did you think would happen?"

"He loves me," Elyse said, knowing even as she spoke how pathetic she sounded.

"It doesn't matter," Lizzie said.

"It has to." Elyse threw open the car door and moved to get out, forgetting entirely that she'd been buckled into the seat. As she struggled to unlatch herself, a car leaned on its horn and Lizzie slammed on the brakes. The canoe, which was tied precariously to the top of the car, made terrifying squeals and groans as it strained against its ropes.

"What's wrong with you?" Lizzie flipped off the car she'd almost backed into and then let out a guttural scream that sounded to Elyse like a war cry.

The seatbelt unlatched. "I'm staying here," Elyse said, knowing that in the end she wouldn't get out of the car.

"You're acting like a crazy person," Lizzie said.

In the face of her cousin's fury, Elyse tried logic. "What if he comes? I can't let my sister marry someone who doesn't truly love her."

"You realize you're the problem. None of this would be happening if you hadn't started stalking him with those ridiculous letters. And he's not coming. We e-mailed him yesterday from your phone. Told him it was off. Are you even sure it's him? What if it was your sister pretending to be him?"

Lizzie's outburst answered so many of the questions that raced through Elyse's mind. They sat silently in the car for a moment, each of them breathing as if they'd finished running for their lives. She supposed she could still stop the wedding—go and find Landon and her sister and tell them what she felt. The thought of it seemed like too much work and as she considered being honest, not just to Landon, but also to her sister, the heat of shame crept up her back. She reached for the open door and closed it.

After they'd been on the road several minutes, Lizzie cleared her throat. "I get it. The second time I blew out my knee, I thought I might kill myself. Not in that dramatic *Heathers* teen suicide way, but real. You know? I used to go for long drives and I'd stop the car on bridges that spanned freeways or lakes or railroad tracks and what I did was think about all the choices I'd made and how they'd all been the wrong ones. Then I'd stand as close to the edge and dare myself to take that last step. Finally I tried to talk to someone, a therapist, and it was all bullshit."

Elyse reached for her cousin's hand.

"He'd listen to me and then offer platitudes—say crap like even your failures have value or you learn the most from your regrets. And it's all useless. Sometimes you make the wrong decision and it sets you back years or screws you up in ways you can't foresee. You know this. You have to know this."

Lizzie paused, lifting up the corner of her T-shirt to wipe at her face. "Isobel wasn't sure we should do this—get involved, but I know we did right by you. Right up until this morning, I didn't think you'd go through with it. And maybe you can't see it now, or maybe you'll never see it. But it was right."

The sun was still too bright and the road curved in nauseating ways. The trees that lined the highway cast their shadows on the asphalt and created almost a checkerboard pattern of light and dark. Elyse closed her eyes against the sick that rose in her stomach, trying to block the harsh variations of light.

A motorcycle passed them in the opposite lane. Elyse whipped her head around, listening to its engine and trying to remember the sound of Landon's bike.

She caught a glimpse of the rider's silver helmet and the back of his fringed jacket.

"That's not him," Lizzie said. "Too old, wrong jacket."

"He would have come," Elyse said, as her cousin reached to turn the radio on. "It would have changed everything."

"Not for the better," Lizzie said.

Elyse turned the air conditioning vents away from her and rolled down the window. She stuck her arm outside and let the air push against it. Who was to say what would be better? Lizzie left the main highway and made several turns. The trees thickened and the pavement turned to gravel. Just as Elyse thought to ask where they were going, the road ahead of them dead-ended at a boat dock.

"We're really going canoeing?"

Isobel had parked her truck off the road, hidden among the trees. She walked forward and started to untie the boats from the top of the car. "I was afraid you'd gotten lost," she said.

"We almost did," Lizzie said, shutting the car off and stepping out to help with the boat. "Get the oars and the life jackets, will you?" she said to Elyse.

Elyse's eyes shifted to her legs. She wasn't dressed for boating. She wore a thin cotton sundress and flip-flops. Stepping out of the car, she shaded her eyes against the sun's reflection off the water. The lake—or rather pond—was as still as glass. It mirrored the surrounding trees and small houses perfectly.

"It's bigger than it looks. Opens up into a river that's shaded all the way down. Or at least that's what it said on the Internet," Lizzie said. Elyse only half listened. The water spoke to her and without thinking about making a decision, she ran down the dock, dodging past her cousins, who nearly dropped the canoe, and did a cannonball into the water. Screaming as loud as she could and as long as she could until the water entered her mouth, tasting like fish and grass. When her head broke the surface, she saw that her cousins had set the canoe down and were laughing and clapping. Elyse knew that they'd spend the day on the water not talking about Landon, Daphne, or the wedding and they'd only go to the wedding if Lizzie and Isobel believed that Elyse would be okay. At that moment, she wasn't sure she would be, but at the edges of her brain, she felt buoyant, like a cork. All her extra fat was keeping her afloat and it would continue to keep her afloat throughout the difficulty of seeing her sister married to the man Elyse had always loved.

Daphne and Landon were married without incident and the day after the wedding, the Triplins found themselves at the airport once again with Anna, whose flight left at about the same time as theirs. Elyse's shoulders and face had burned something terrible during the day they'd spent in the canoe, and her skin had started to peel that morning. She'd felt it slough off in the shower and now, waiting in line to be ushered through security, she couldn't keep herself from using her nails to peel long strands of skin from her shoulders.

The line was incredibly long, and Elyse had begun to worry about how well Anna would hold up. She appeared fine, not even leaning on Lizzie, although her cousin's arm was around her in case she did falter. A security employee tapped Elyse on the shoulder, and she winced. "We can take you through the pilots' line," she said, indicating Anna. "That's not a woman who should be standing."

"I'm older than I look," Anna said, handing her license over for inspection. The security officer waved his blue light over her California license to make sure the document wasn't fraudulent and then did a double take at the birthday. "You don't drive, do you?"

"I passed the test," Anna said, smiling at the man's discomfort. She patted his arm. "Don't worry, I only drive in Kidron, and even then I only make right turns."

Even though their gates were in different parts of the airport, the Triplins waited with Anna. Once they'd seated her in the chairs, she'd started to tell them stories—one after the other about her childhood, about her trip to Australia to try to find her real mother, about a turtle. There seemed to be no pattern to her stories, and the only connection between the events was Anna herself. Gratitude for her great-great-grandmother overwhelmed Elyse. It didn't seem possible that life could be so long or so chock-full of so many stories. Her cousins' body language indicated that they were less compelled by Anna's stories. Isobel had her phone out and was typing an e-mail—she responded to Anna with an occasional "uh-huh," or an "isn't that right?" Lizzie appeared to listen to Anna, but her face kept a skeptical expression—as if someone had just given her a million dollars and she was examining the gift for any attached strings.

Anna paused to drink some of the water Lizzie offered.

"Are you going to live forever?" Elyse asked.

"I've stopped thinking about it," Anna said. A dribble of water escaped the bottle and fell onto her shirt. "I wake up every day excited to consider what comes next. For me, for my grandchildren and great-grandchildren, and the lot of you. What is it you are?"

"Great great grandchildren, I think," Elyse said

"Who even knows what forever is," Lizzie said. "I mean one hundred seventeen years sort of seems like forever."

"At least until you're that old," Anna said, laughing so hard that she doubled over.

Lizzie laughed, and Isobel set aside her phone to ask what was so funny.

"I wish we really were related," Lizzie said. "They say it's all in the genes and I wouldn't mind living to see what changes over a hundred years."

"Blood matters far less than you think," Anna said. "Besides, you are all my Elizabeths."

"No, that's just me," Lizzie said. "Although I never use my full name. My mom said she named me after the queens of England before she even met my stepdad and found out it was a family name."

"Is that so?" Anna asked, in a tone that hinted at all the knowledge she had that the Triplins couldn't possibly appreciate.

"But I'm honored, I mean, if you associate the name with your daughter," Lizzie said.

Elyse listened as her cousin continued to fumble around trying to find the right words to lessen the sting of what she'd said. A few years earlier, Anna's daughter had drowned after following her husband into the Sacramento River.

Nearing tears, Lizzie finally got more words out. "I'm sorry. I didn't mean to say that. From what Grandpa Matthew and Jim say, Bets was an extraordinary woman. She died trying to save her husband."

"She died because she was tired of living," Anna said, her mouth compressing into a thin line.

"I'm sorry," Lizzie said again, her voice cracking. "I don't even know who my father is, and sometimes I say the wrong thing because my family is such a mystery to me."

"No matter, no matter," Anna said. "Not that any of you realize this, but you're all named Elizabeth. Same name, different forms. There's only a handful of names and most of them are from the Bible. We used to have to read it in school. There wasn't much else and now whether you believe in it or not, you ought to at least know where your name comes from."

Elyse said their names aloud, sounding out the vowels and trying to make them sound alike. She didn't hear it.

"I hear it," Lizzie said.

Elyse thought she was eager to make up for her earlier gaffe.

"Doesn't matter, they're all the same. Just like Anna is Hannah. So, now I've given you a gift, makes you even more like triplets, huh?"

"You don't think our parents did it on purpose?" Isobel asked. "I mean did they know they were naming us after Elizabeth? After each other?"

"Must have been an accident," Lizzie said. "Not like we share the same blood."

"There's no accidents in this world," Anna said. "You, my dear, were always meant to be in this family. Isn't that what we take away from weddings? The ability to create relations in ways other than by blood?"

Elyse turned away at the mention of the wedding. She couldn't stand to listen to any small talk about how lovely the bride had been, or how happy the couple had seemed. The wedding had felt like a funeral and instead of facing her grief and starting the mourning process, she pretended it hadn't happened. During the whole ceremony, she'd focused her attention on the fact that the bridesmaid dress fit her perfectly despite her mother's concerns. At this point she was still so raw that make-believe was the only salve for the stabbing pain inside of her. It wasn't fair that such intense pain didn't leave behind any evidence.

Anna stretched out her hand and patted Elyse's knee as if trying to draw her back into the conversation. "Just remember how very long life can be and how very unexpected."

The counter attendants called for passengers who needed assistance to board the plane. Anna shouldered her purse and stood, as steady as anyone. Elyse was embarrassed to think that when she'd first arrived, she'd thought the woman would need a wheelchair. There were whispers around them as Anna bid each of the Triplins goodbye. It appeared that Anna's notoriety had traveled from the security line to the gate. The flight attendant held out her hand to Anna, telling her that they'd upgraded her to first class, but only if she promised to tell them what it had been like to be born into a world without airplanes. Anna smiled as if such indulgences were commonplace.

August 2012: Memphis

Two events conspired to keep the Triplins from falling into their old patterns when they returned to Memphis. The first had to do with Spite House and the second with Isobel. Benny met them, hat again in hand, on the front porch. Looking around, Elyse saw that the yard, which had been the only finished part of the house, now looked as if a prehistoric gopher had burrowed through it. As had been the case since the work on the house had moved indoors, it was Isobel who strode to meet Benny. Lizzie and Elyse hung back, each wincing at every word that came out of Benny's mouth—especially "no plumbing," which caused Lizzie to sit down on her suitcase and put her head in her hands.

"There's no money," Lizzie said to Elyse. "I used all Grandma Mellie had left after the initial bid on the asbestos."

Hearing the fear and desperation in her cousin's voice snapped Elyse out of the pity party she'd been throwing since tossing rice at her sister and Landon as they ran to his motorcycle and literally rode off into the sunset. She knelt in front of her cousin, taking her hands as if they were praying together. "It's going to be fine. You don't even know how bad the problems are, and I'm sure your parents can come up with a few thousand more to cover this last bit of work."

Benny walked by them, his chin tucked into his chest, his birthmark purple next to his reddened neck. "See ya tomorrow," he said.

Isobel stepped off the porch and told them to hurry up out of the heat.

"Is it bad?" Lizzie asked. "Tell me how bad it is."

"Not in this heat," Isobel said.

They trudged inside the house, which for the first time all summer offered relief from the heat. As part of the asbestos removal, they'd had new insulation installed and sealed the gaps that had been letting the hot air run through the house as if it were a slatted fence. Lizzie took her hair down; it fell so that it half hid her face.

"She's worried about money," Elyse said. Of the three of them, Isobel was the only one without money problems. She hoped that by putting it out in front, her cousin would volunteer to help out, seeing as how they'd all been living there rent-free for the better part of seven months.

"Don't be," Isobel said as she bent over her carry-on bag and searched its numerous zippered pockets. "I think I've got that about figured out." She pulled her phone out of the last one she searched and tapped a few buttons before handing it to Lizzie. "I got this a few days ago, but I wanted to sit on it, you know. Think about it."

"What is it?" Elyse asked, trying to read over her cousin's shoulder.

"An offer to do a show," Isobel said.

"About Spite House?" Lizzie asked, moving her fingers to enlarge the type on the e-mail and then passing it to Elyse.

She half listened to them, reading through the e-mail from Isobel's agent. Although the *Where Are They Now?* special hadn't yet aired, the reaction to Isobel's segment had generated enough excitement for the producer to want to film a sizzle reel of Isobel at Spite House. Isobel explained to them that the idea was to capture highlights of a potential reality show to entice networks to pay for a pilot or even green-light an entire show.

"The money they'll pay us to let them use the house will cover the rest of the repairs," Isobel said, her voice rising with excitement. "But it could also lead to so much more."

Elyse, having lost so much more, immediately thought how dangerous it could be to want something too much. "Don't get ahead of yourself," she said, handing back the phone. "There's no mention of future projects, and you still haven't told us what Benny said about the house."

"Like I said, the fees should cover it," her voice lowered almost as if she were a child admitting a mistake. "There's no plumbing. It'll take most of the month to fix it."

"No plumbing?" Elyse asked, trying to think how that was possible.

"Pipes were in bad shape and emptying into the front yard instead of the sewer."

"Where are we going to live?" Lizzie asked. "That's going to cost something on top of the repairs."

Isobel coughed and looked away from them. "If we don't live here, we'll violate the terms of the TPO. The second one was set up with a default clause. That is, if we move out of the house for any reason, it will be considered to be abandonment. If we leave now, coming on the heels of having been gone for the wedding, then . . . ."

Nobody seemed to know what to say. Elyse had never planned on coming back to Spite House and now she had no other place to go. She wondered what her cousins were thinking. Lizzie broke the silence by picking up her suitcase and walking into the house. "You don't have to stay," she said. "I'll make it work—shower at the community center and what not."

Isobel turned to Elyse. "Are you going to stay? I wasn't sure you were even before all of this." She lifted her arm to indicate the house. "Did we do the right thing?"

"I don't know yet," Elyse said, not knowing which question she was answering.

"Lizzie isn't doing well," Isobel said.

"Are any of us?" Elyse walked past her into the house, leaving her suitcase on the front porch where Benny had carried it.

"I'm grand," Isobel called after her, laughing.

The sound of her cousin's amusement had the effect of lightening Elyse's step, and for the first time in as long as she could remember, she felt like it all might turn out in the end.

When Landon called Elyse, she was at the hospital with Lizzie. The day before the United States played Japan in the final match of the Olympics, Lizzie had arthroscopic surgery to remove a stubborn bit of scar tissue near her hamstring. The cousins had joined her for the procedure and Elyse, against her cousin's wishes, had promised to keep her family informed of her progress by sending them texts as the surgery progressed.

"She'll be fine after this?" Isobel asked the surgeon.

"Hard to say," the woman had said, looking over their heads at a nurse and then motioning that she needed her. "I imagine so, as long as she's mobile."

"We've been over this," Isobel said, carrying a large box in both her arms. "She'll be in therapy twice a day if needed."

Elyse took the box, which contained more of Lizzie's mother's journal entries. "I know we've been over it. There are to be no more stunts of self-pity."

"It wasn't self-pity," Lizzie protested as her cousin set the box next to her bed. "Grief. I was grieving."

"Same difference," Isobel said, turning on the television and surfing for the soccer match.

"Not even close," Lizzie said.

"The farther you get from grief, the more you realize it's always selfish." Elyse, hearing her phone buzz, silenced it, afraid she'd get reprimanded by the nurse. She looked at the number and then excused herself, finding her way to the smoking area outside the building.

She dialed her voicemail and listened to the message at least a dozen times, not even caring about the cigarette smoke she inhaled. He said their flight had them stopping in Memphis, and they'd changed to a later connection. "I wanted to talk to you about the letters. Expect us around lunchtime," he'd said. *Us.* Why hadn't her sister been the one to call? The thought that Daphne might know what Elyse had been planning turned her stomach to ice. It clenched. Why had they changed their stopover? Why had he lied about it? It had to be deliberate—planes, especially those from London, flew direct to Boston or, at worst, had a stopover in Atlanta. No one but FedEx had layovers in Memphis anymore.

She considered lying to her cousins to try to get home to meet him. But, no. They were as much a part of this now as she was. The glass walls of the hospital reflected her worst self. Her wild hair hung in a sad ponytail. Red blotches from the heat covered her face. Without considering the consequences or the long-ago pact made with the cousins, Elyse dug through her purse and pulled out a pair of scissors she'd used to cut coupons. Holding her ponytail out from the side of her head, she cut it off, watching it fall on the concrete patio.

"Holy hell," said a man smoking a cigar.

She pulled out the elastic and made random cuts until she was crying so hard she couldn't see her reflection.

Isobel waved to her through the windows and then walked around to the door "Lizzie's waiting for you."

"I'm not going."

"Are you crying?" Isobel squeezed past the cigar smoker and around two sisters sharing a cigarette. "She's not in any danger."

Embarrassment flooded Elyse. She kicked at the piles of hair on the cement, trying to move them out of sight. "It isn't that."

Her cousin looked first at Elyse's head and then at the ground. "The heat get to you?" she asked.

"Something like that," Elyse said, sniffling and then wiping her nose with her T-shirt. She held her phone out to Isobel. "He left a message."

Isobel's face remained passive as she listened to Landon's call. "You should see her before she goes into surgery, and maybe when you're done, you should bring Daphne and him up to see her. The whole procedure only takes an hour or so."

Gratitude overwhelmed Elyse. She couldn't have taken being told not to see him. "Definitely." She reached out for the keys Isobel held out to her and then linked arms and walked through the hospital to wish Lizzie good luck.

They arrived before lunch. Elyse watched her sister get out of the cab and immediately lift her long hair off her neck as the humidity hit her. Elyse scratched at her bare neck. Before she left the hospital, Isobel had done her best to clean up the mess she'd made of her hair, giving her an asymmetrical bob and side-sweeping her bangs. Somehow, even though it was choppy, it made her face appear thinner. Or maybe she'd finally lost weight. She couldn't remember the last time she'd been on a scale. Before the wedding maybe. Turning away from the window before Landon could exit the taxi, she pressed her ear to the door and listened for their steps on the porch.

She needed to find a way to speak to Landon alone. Who knew what he'd told Daphne? It had to be a good sign that they'd decided to come to Memphis in the first place. She heard them speak softly to each other before one of them rang the doorbell. She counted to thirty before opening the door.

"I don't think I've ever been here before," Daphne said, leaning in for a shoulders-only hug. "I mean I've heard Lizzie talk about it and you too. But seeing it." Her sister shook her head and then ran her fingers along the doorframe.

They were tan with sunburned cheeks. Landon's nose had peeled, leaving behind pink skin. "Catch a sunny day in London?" she asked.

"They have beaches not too far from there," Landon said and then offered an awkward hug. He held her away from him for a moment and then play-fully hit her on the chin. "Who ever thought you'd be my sister?"

"Sister-in-law," Elyse said. She ushered them inside and explained Lizzie and Isobel's whereabouts. "I'll take you up there when she's out of surgery."

"I can't imagine going through that," Daphne said. Landon looked at his arm and then looked away. He had a new prosthetic and stood taller than she remembered. "She's not going to be able to keep playing, huh?"

"Everyone's optimistic," Elyse said. She didn't vol-unteer her own observation, which was that Lizzie needed an excuse not to have to play anymore.

They started the tour of the house in the cupola. Her sister marveled at the prisms and the rainbows they cast. "It's exactly like *Pollyanna*." She sighed and sat down on the window seat with her feet pulled up under her. "I totally understand why you abandoned Boston for the chance to live here."

"It has its charms," Elyse said. How much she'd hated that book. That stupid glad game. Her sister had lived her entire life as an embodiment of looking on the bright side. By the time they reached the kitchen, it was clear to Elyse that Landon hadn't spoken to Daphne about the notes she'd sent him before the wed-ding. Instead of relief, she felt disappointment.

"I have to use the ladies' room," Daphne said, rising and kissing Landon on the cheek.

"The water's not on yet," Elyse said. Typically when the cousins had this problem, they'd use the portable toilet that Benny had put on the corner of the vacant lot, but she saw in this dilemma an opportunity to be alone with Landon. She dug through her purse and held out the keys to the Datsun along with a few bills. "There's a gas station on the corner. Maybe pick up a few cold drinks?"

Her sister kissed Landon goodbye. Elyse walked out the back door to the edge of the bluff and looked out at the Mississippi. She waited, knowing he'd follow. Landon cleared his throat and when she turned toward him, he extended his left arm as if they would shake hands. She ignored it and walked to the Adirondack chairs that had been left behind by Isobel's production crew. "Sit," she said. "I don't know how long we'll have. We'll hear the car when she comes back. It has a squeaky belt you can hear a mile away."

"It's a nice view of the river." He glanced at her, taking in her haircut, and then continued to speak as if nothing had changed. "Daphne talks about Memphis sometimes, but never this house."

"She's never been." Elyse thought about trying to explain how it had been Lizzie's grandmother's house and how her family hadn't had much to do with the woman, but she didn't want to waste what time they had talking about what didn't matter to them.

Although she'd changed her clothes when she got home from the hospital—putting on a green top that highlighted her cleavage and made her eyes look less brown—she hadn't been able to brush away all of the bits of hair that had fallen down her back. She scratched at her shoulder blade and then rubbed at it through the thin cotton of the shirt. A trolley whistled half a mile down the tracks. They turned their heads toward the sound and watched it motor toward them. Although there weren't any stops along the south bluffs, the trolley slowed as it approached their yard. A child leaned out the window and waved to them. Elyse nodded to where the bushes had been. "Used to be more privacy out here."

"Do we need any more of that?" Landon asked.

"Privacy is different from secrecy," Elyse said. This wasn't a conversation she wanted to have with Landon, but she understood its necessity. She looked again at his new prosthetic. He'd never found one that he felt comfortable with—switching from the purely cosmetic, which looked like a mannequin's hand, to one with limited movement that he controlled with his own body. This new arm was unlike any she'd ever seen. Instead of flesh-colored plastic, it had been painted to look like an x-ray of his arm—or what it would look like if his arm were still intact—and the robotic hand looked to be straight out of a science fiction movie.

He saw her looking at his prosthetic. "Daphne picked London for our honeymoon so I could get fitted for this. I was on the waitlist for two years." He winced and then touched a few spots on the arm. The robotic hand closed into a fist and gave her a thumbs up. "I'm still figuring it out."

"Me too," Elyse said, glancing back toward the street and wondering how long they had. How long would they need to talk about falling in love with the wrong person? "I could make you happy."

"I already am." He started to say more, but another trolley rolled by. Unlike the last car, this one was filled with tourists—they looked to be on a sponsored trip with several of them wearing gold sunglasses in cheap imitation of Elvis. The driver pulled the whistle and slowed as it approached the house. People leaned out of windows to take pictures of Spite House. They wouldn't turn out well. The glass made the house nearly impossible to shoot from the back—mostly what people would see when they scrolled through their pictures were watery reflections of themselves.

"Why are you here?" Elyse said, swinging her feet around the side of the chair and sitting up. She needed to face him.

"Daphne—"

"I've heard a lot about my sister since you got here. But that isn't why you came over here, is it? To tell me what my sister thinks. Because I'm not sure that's any of my business."

"You're right." He mirrored her posture and looked toward the house. "Don't you feel watched up here? Like you're on display?"

"Sometimes." When Elyse imagined her life with Landon, their children had his eyes. They were brown, but with tiny flecks of gold near the pupil. She thought of those flecks as bits of his soul peering out into the world, like sunlight breaking through the clouds. Her chest tightened and then inside of her she felt a collapse and the coming heat of tears.

"I should have told you," he said. "I lied to myself about us because it was easier and because what happened between me and your sister felt different. Almost like it wasn't happening to me, but to some better version of myself."

"It doesn't matter," Elyse said. She swallowed, thankful that he hadn't brought up her blunder of asking him to meet.

"It does." He blinked and Elyse saw that he too was close to crying. "Because you were right about me. I'd thought for a long time that we would have our moment. You know? When we were both in the right place, then we'd find each other. It's why girls kept breaking up with me. I wouldn't commit because I'd already committed to you."

Elyse took a deep breath and held it. There was nothing about his posture or in the words he'd said earlier that had prepared her for this. "We'd talked about it," she said, softly. "That day in the gazebo. Do you remember? So when you responded to my love letters, all of that came back up—"

But Landon had kept talking, clearly wanting to get out his prepared speech. He talked over her, and afterward Elyse was never sure he'd heard her—not that it mattered. "But then I saw your sister. I mean really saw her and it was like a flood washing away all the dams and locks and canals that I'd been down when I thought I'd been in love before. Love is so much bigger than waiting for the time to be right. I mean, didn't you ever think, Elyse, that if we were waiting for the right time that something was wrong?"

"No." Elyse let out her breath.

During his speech, Landon's gaze had jumped around the yard, focusing on the back of the house, the corner of Elyse's chair, and the trolley tracks. But when she didn't agree with him, his eyes landed on her as if pulled by an unseen force. They looked at each other a long time.

"You'll find it. You will. Maybe." Landon dropped his gaze to his hands. The prosthetic unclenched. "The thing is, with her I don't feel like I'm missing out on anything."

"Of course you don't," Elyse said, realizing that the collapse in her chest wasn't out of not being loved, but anger because he'd found what he wanted. "What were you going to say? Got a diagnosis for me?"

"I don't have to say it," Landon lowered his head. "You know all this is because you're as afraid of commitment as I used to be."

"Is that why we never talked about that night after the xystus?"

"Xystus." He grinned.

"I like you better with a beard." Elyse wasn't afraid of commitment. All those other men had been as real to her as dolls. She'd spent her love life rehearsing for the one true thing and it had gone and found that with someone else.

"You like the idea of me better than me."

"That's just what you tell yourself to make all of this okay."

"I have my own idea of you too." Landon shook his head. "That's all we ever would have been to each other—nostalgic ideas."

"What is it about her?"

"She hasn't got any faults." Before Elyse could point out a few, Landon corrected himself. "I mean, to me. I keep trying to find what I don't like about her, and there isn't anything. She even understands what you did and even why you had to do it. She's on your side and maybe if you'd talk to her about what you're feeling, you can be more like sisters. You can't know how much she wants that."

"I didn't think you'd told her."

"We're married," he said.

"We're sisters." She thought again about how her sister had been with her as they toured the house. It hadn't been like old times, but it hadn't been awkward either.

Landon closed his eyes. "You aren't though. She can't be what Isobel and Lizzie are to you, and that keeps you two from really being close."

"My parents did that when they played favorites."

"Let it go," Landon said. "You realize that believing that, believing that you are less, is going to keep you from ever being loved."

"We're through, aren't we?" Elyse stood.

"Are we?" Landon looked up at her, searching for confirmation. "You could come back to Boston for Thanksgiving."

She scratched at her right shoulder blade again. "I can't."

"You won't," Landon said.

"I'm not ready. But I promise that when I do come back, I'll be ready for you to be my brother-in-law." A flock of birds flew up into the sky, leaving their power line perches simultaneously at some unheard signal. The squeak of Mellie's Datsun echoed in the wake of their flapping wings. Elyse started for the house, but he called her back.

"Wait, I have another trick." He touched the prosthetic near his elbow and extended his hand. Awkwardly, she slid hers into the outstretched Teflon-like attachment and they shook hands. "It's a deal." He grinned, looking as young as he had the day they first met.

To celebrate the *Where Are They Now?* episode, the Triplins held a viewing party. Everyone had been warned beforehand about the plumbing issue. (There was always the port-a-potty.) As the airdate for the show had grown closer, Isobel had become increasingly energetic. Elyse heard her late at night moving around on the third floor, making phone calls to friends on the West Coast who were still up because of the time difference and because of their lifestyles.

Now she was waiting for Isobel to come out of the flower shop. They'd been running errands the entire day in an attempt to make Spite House appear less like a construction zone and more like a home. Lizzie hadn't wanted to have people over, but Isobel insisted, saying it would be bad luck to watch it anywhere but where it had been filmed. Through the window of the shop, Elyse could see Isobel making oversized gestures with her hands at the clerk. It looked as though she were telling a story—most likely about Spite House. Since learning that the house itself might be part of the pitch for the series the network wanted, Isobel had started to exaggerate their living conditions when she spoke of it to strangers. She angled the air conditioning so that it blew onto the backseat, where they had a dozen trays and boxes of premade food for their guests.

"I got snapdragons," Isobel said, settling bunches of flowers into the backseat. "Greenery too. She threw that in for no cost because it was all about to turn yellow."

"Hope it doesn't turn before tonight," Elyse said.

"Don't be such a pessimist. If it does, it does. It was free anyway and I can always cut a bunch of stuff from that lot next door. It looks like a jungle. T. J. told Lizzie we ought to get a cat to hunt the snakes and rats that are probably running through it."

"Or let the snakes eat the rats," Elyse said, pulling away from the curb.

Her cousin shuddered and then struggled to fasten her seatbelt. "I hate snakes."

"Since when? I remember you catching striped garters at the beach and sticking them in Lizzie's Keds because it was the only thing she was afraid of."

Isobel started to disagree with Elyse and then stopped. "Wait, you're right. I'm not afraid of snakes."

"You're crazy," Elyse said, stopping at a red light and taking the opportunity to study her cousin. She'd lost weight in the last few weeks, and there were dark circles under her eyes that couldn't be erased even with Isobel's skilled touch with foundation.

"Sometimes I think I am crazy," she said. "Green light."

Elyse stepped on the gas pedal too fast and nearly rear-ended the car in front of them. The man leaned out his window to flip them off.

"No, I mean it," Isobel said. "I do this all the time. For some role I have to pretend that I'm afraid of snakes or that I don't like beets. And then it's like I've repro-grammed my brain so I come to believe stuff that's not true. I love beets."

"Maybe you're a good actress," Elyse said, worried that she'd insulted her cousin.

"If I were a good actress, I'd be working."

"That's not true. Look at all the talented people who don't work anymore. When was the last time you saw Meg Ryan in a movie?"

"She pissed people off with that affair. Can't be a sweetheart if you cheat on your husband. Plus she's old."

"Okay, bad example. But you know what I mean." Elyse pulled to the back of Spite House and killed the car's engine. "Besides, you've got this show. Isn't it going to change everything?"

Isobel reached for the flowers in the backseat. "It has to, but I think I want it too much. One of the women I worked with on *Wait for It* used to talk about how you had to go about getting a role much the way you try to catch a cat. You ever try to catch a house cat?"

Elyse shook her head, juggling several boxes of food.

"You want to hold a cat? You have to sneak up on it. Walk around the room and pretend to dust. You've got to come at it sideways, putting on airs the whole time as if you've got no interest in the cat. That's how you catch them."

"What exactly are you coming sideways at?" Elyse asked. She closed the car door with her rear end and followed her cousin into the house.

"I'll tell you when this is all over, but only if I get it."

Lizzie stood in the middle of the kitchen with a kerchief tied around her head and wadded-up newspaper around her ankles. "Do you see it?" she asked as they entered.

"Don't tell me you've gone crazy too," Elyse said, jerking her thumb at Isobel. "This one here seems to have had feral cats instead of house cats when she was a kid."

"The windows," Lizzie said. "Cleaned from top to bottom. Inside and out."

The light in the kitchen held a different quality than it had previously. It bent in unexpected ways, and when it bounced off reflective surfaces, there was a sparkle to it that hadn't been there before.

"It's too bright," Isobel said, squinting. "Like stepping outside a movie theater to find it's still daylight."

"Let your eyes adjust," Lizzie said. "This is how it used to be when I was small and we stayed here. There's something in the windows—lead or irregularities. I can't remember which. It twists the light all around as it passes through. I guess it didn't work with all the dust."

"Are we ready?" Isobel asked, moving toward the partitioned hallway.

"Mostly," Lizzie said, reaching to help Elyse stow the food in the refrigerator.

"I wish I could have cooked," Elyse said, taking out a frozen plastic box of eclairs. "Your grandmother has a recipe for rumaki that I'm dying to try."

The only room large enough for the crowd coming to view the television special was Isobel's room. The third floor, unlike the rest of the house, was finished. Elyse thought about how much work it had taken to refinish the floors. Isobel had done a beautiful job on the finishing details of the room. She was nearly done with the second floor. Then, if there was time and money enough, she'd redo the kitchen. They'd used the kitchen as their gathering place, but with the windows, there was no place for a television that didn't glare.

"We've got it," Elyse said, waving Isobel through the curtain.

Before Elyse could start a conversation with Lizzie, T. J. showed up on the back steps. He knocked softly and apologized for being early. They put him to work and as they'd finished their preparations, the bulk of the guests arrived. Elyse was the last to go upstairs.

In all, there were a dozen people gathered to cheer Isobel on during the premiere of the show. Benny had brought one of his daughters along and she sat giggling with two of Lizzie's soccer players, who'd come with T. J.'s sister. The room was warm, but the sticky heat reminded Elyse of baking bread with her mother when she was a little girl. She hoped Isobel had the same feeling of warmth from the crowd.

"Are you ready?" Isobel asked, her thumb hovering over the volume button on the remote. The room quieted with expectation as the commercials moved from products to hype for the network's own television programs.

Typical of the format, the first few minutes showed teasers on all three celebrities who would be featured in the episode. In the early moments of the show, stills of Isobel as she had been as a child on the show drew shouts of recognition from the crowd and giggling from the girls, who couldn't believe that the woman in front of them had ever worn braces or high-waisted jeans. Isobel shot them all down with a calculated look that set the tone. Rosa May couldn't put down her phone during the entire show. She kept tweeting and reading messages about the show, handing her phone to those around her for their silent reactions to the tweets.

338 · COURTNEY MILLER SANTO

Elyse had started by watching Isobel to gauge her reaction to the show, but it was pretty clear that every millisecond she was the focus of the camera was a moment of pure joy for her. Trying to catch Lizzie's eye, she got up from the beanbag she'd been sitting in and walked behind the guests. They were all rapt, waiting for Isobel's segment.

Finally the program went to the last commercial break after teasing the final segment, which would feature Isobel exclusively. "There might be some footage of you two," Isobel said to the television.

"Us?" Lizzie asked. "Why?"

Isobel didn't answer. "I dunno."

The cousins knew that Isobel had already seen the show. Her agent had sent it over via FedEx a few weeks earlier. Isobel had locked herself in her room and watched it obsessively for several hours, then she destroyed the disc—telling the cousins that she wanted their raw reactions to the show when it aired.

The segment lasted eight minutes. It was twice as long as they'd spent on any other celebrity, including the busty teen star who kept running into and over people in her series of increasingly expensive automobiles. They talked mostly to Isobel, following her around the house in a way that made her seem like she was in charge of the renovations and of fixing her cousins. The air was still and silent every moment they were on the television. Occasionally, Elyse looked at Lizzie and they exchanged furtive looks that indicated their outrage. The last shot of the program was of Spite House, a long shot as the camera moved away, held by a man walking backward down the porch steps and down the steep stairs to the street. It lingered on the beat-up historical sign.

"It doesn't look as bad as all that now," Rosa May said.

Elyse sensed that she was trying to gauge the mood of the room, which had shifted. People were gathering their belongings and murmuring about how they had to get back home.

"I don't understand why they said all that stuff about me," Lizzie said. "I'm not even limping in those shots. That one they showed, where it looked like I fell. My foot was asleep. Besides, do you know how many women didn't make that team? The game's changing and not everyone's positioned right. What they want is less power and more finesse."

The block of time spent on Isobel had felt more like a teaser for another television show. One in which Isobel moved to the honky-tonk South with her good ol' boy relatives and tried to save her grandmother's house. The fact that Mellie wasn't her actual grandmother

didn't matter. What mattered was that this grandmother had come from slave-owning folk. That was a
fact that Elyse hadn't known. In truth, she didn't know
anything about Lizzie's side of the family except what
she allowed herself to romanticize.

Elyse had come off okay. They made her out to be
more Yankee than she was in real life, but they showed
her weighing herself and tugging at a pair of pants that
were too tight (she promised herself she'd find them
and throw them out immediately). The whole time
they'd talked about how the failure of the bed and
breakfast (who had given them the awful shot of her
painting the sign?) was the latest in a long string of failures, and then lingered on her ringless left hand.

"They're certainly not subtle," Elyse said.

"I'm not sure I get what the show is supposed to be
about," T. J. said.

Benny, with his hand on his daughter's back, took
his hat off. "At least they didn't go into the incest stuff
about your grandmother marrying her uncle."

"Incest," Lizzie said.

"How did they get all that information?" Elyse
asked.

Isobel waved off their questions. "It won't be like
that in the show. That's just hype to get people to
watch. You'll see."

T. J. hugged Lizzie and whispered a few things in her ear. Elyse was pretty sure he was trying to convince her to stay at his place that night. Since the wedding, Lizzie had just as often stayed with T. J. as at Spite House, explaining her need for a shower and a working bathroom.

"Kisses," Isobel said to the departing guests. Her cheeks were flushed as if she had a fever.

Not knowing what else to do, Elyse cleaned.

Lizzie slumped to the floor. "Did he say incest?"

The moment after she'd seen the last guest to the door, Isobel had declared the night a success and flung herself across the bed, where she remained, avoiding eye contact with her cousins. "What did you think? Did you love it?" Isobel asked.

"Did you hear him?" Lizzie asked.

Elyse took the greenery, which had indeed turned yellow, from the vases. "I'm sure he didn't mean incest, incest."

"Benny's full of crap," Isobel said. "Did you like the show?"

"Of course," Elyse lied. She opened the window and tossed the greenery out into the yard, figuring they were as likely to compost out there as at the bottom of a garbage can. She left the purple snapdragons to stand alone in their containers.

Her cousin had a way of not seeing what she didn't want to. Elyse didn't have enough energy to say what she thought so instead she cleaned around her cousins, keeping a close eye on Lizzie, who'd pulled out her cell phone and appeared to be calling her parents. Isobel, oblivious to the unfolding drama, kept chattering about the program and occasionally reading texts people she knew were sending her. Finally, as Elyse grouped the vases on her cousin's dresser, Isobel finished with her dissection of the show and its possible outcomes. She sat up and crossed her legs in what Elyse thought looked like a yoga pose.

Lizzie let out a long sigh. "Answer the fucking phone." She hung up and dialed the same number again.

"Enough about me. I'm sick of me. I'm sick of the show. If I never say one more word about myself, I'll be happy." Isobel patted her king-sized bed, inviting them to join her. "We can all sleep together tonight and pretend we're giggling school girls."

"Not now," Elyse said, trying to get her attention and direct it toward Lizzie.

"Of course it's an emergency," she said in response to whoever had answered the phone. "Wake her up."

Isobel raised her eyebrows. Elyse joined her on the bed and drew her knees up to her chest.

"Incest?" Lizzie screamed into the phone. "You never bothered to mention the incest."

"We should go downstairs," Elyse said.

"Stay right there. You have to listen to what she's saying." Lizzie put the phone on speaker and dropped it into an empty glass to amplify the sound of Aunt Annie's voice, thin and reedy, bouncing around the room.

"It wasn't incest exactly. Roger was her uncle. He and her daddy were brothers."

"She married her uncle?" Lizzie leaned forward and pounded on the floor.

"Half-uncle, really," Aunt Annie said.

"Who else knows this? Does Jim know?"

"Of course. It used to be common knowledge. I mean when I was growing up." Aunt Annie's voice quieted, and although Elyse expected her to share her own pain over it, she didn't.

"There's got to be more to it than that," Isobel said. "I mean, did he force her to marry him? Or did her father force her?"

"It's not my story, it's my mother's."

"You have to explain this," Isobel said.

Aunt Annie was quiet a long while. Elyse suspected she was trying to find some way out of telling Lizzie this truth. In the distance, Elyse heard the call of a bird.

Tika, tika, tika-swee, swee, swee-chay, chay, chay. She could hear in its cadence the rhythms of starting a car. She motioned Lizzie to join them on the bed. Then, reaching for her hand, she held it as Aunt Annie told them the story. Isobel took her other hand and they waited, listening to the birdsong and Lizzie's mother crying. For the first time in Elyse's life the drama of romantic decisions made her ill instead of elated.

Third Story
Isobel

September 2012: Memphis

S liding on oversized sunglasses, Isobel checked her reflection in the rearview mirror and then stepped from the car. Since her episode of *Where Are They Now?* had aired, she'd taken particular care with her appearance—wanting to look like she belonged, but also needing people to look twice. In Memphis, that meant shades even when it was overcast, a fresh manicure, and lace. Southern women loved a little frill. Each time she went out it felt like a test. *Had people seen the show? Did they recognize her? Did they want to see more of her?* Her years in the business had taught her that what mattered most was attention. She entered the home improvement store and set her purse in the cart. To be a working actress meant the public had to react viscerally to you—it didn't matter if it was good or bad. The best celebrities evoked the holy trinity of emotions—love, hate, and envy.

Waiting to be noticed, she observed the other shoppers through her glasses. The overwhelming feeling coming from them was one of purpose. These women with lists, these men with broken bits of plumbing, were like determined ants marching from hill to crumb. What they needed was a reason to look up from their busyness. She crossed in front of a young couple striding toward the refrigerators and cut in line at the paint counter. Murmurs of irritation rose behind her. She felt the people in the store turn their attention away from their tasks. The first time she'd felt that lift from having people's attention was at an audition for a grape juice commercial. She'd been seven and how she'd explained it to her mother was to say she felt like she'd jumped into the air and never landed.

The paint clerk had a sleeve of tattoos. At her approach, he'd crossed his arms showing a small circle of ink-free flesh around his elbow.

"Can you tell me—" she began, dropping her voice to a whisper so he'd have to lean in to hear her.

"There's a line," he said, remaining an arm's length from where she leaned against the counter.

"I didn't realize," she lied.

He stepped forward to take a scrap of fabric that an older woman held out to him. Isobel glanced behind her at the line and sighed before moving to the displays of paint samples and fingering the various shades of yellow offered by Ralph Lauren. She eavesdropped on the conversations around her, trying to will someone in the store to recognize her and start the whispered trail that would prove her relevance. She didn't even want paint. Benny needed industrial-strength solvent to pull the glue off the tiles he'd uncovered underneath the linoleum in the kitchen, and she'd volunteered to go to the store. Standing at the array of vibrant colors, Isobel thought about the kitchen and how much nicer it would look if it were painted a soft butter color with enough gold undertones to deepen as the light changed in the room. Moving on to the other displays, she pocketed samples labeled *Goldfinch, Cornbread, Sweet Chamomile,* and *Beeswax.* Just as she reached for *Butter Cookie,* a woman holding a toddler in a smocked linen jumper caught her eye and then smiled. Isobel took off her sunglasses.

"Are you—?" the woman said, stepping closer. "The Waits, right? No, *Wait for It.*"

Isobel nodded.

"Oh, I loved that show. I had the biggest crush on the guy who played your brother. What was his name?"

Isobel said his name. The guy had gone on to a successful career as a comedic actor—playing the straight man in gross-out buddy comedies. They hadn't been close and hadn't kept in touch. He'd been one of those actors who looked young. Already old enough to drink when he landed the role of her fourteen-year-old brother and by the time the show ended, he'd married, divorced, and fathered two children. She assured the woman he was as nice in person as he appeared on the screen. "He taught me how to drive," she said because it was true and because it would endear her to this stranger.

The woman looked at the paint sample in Isobel's hand. "I heard you have a new show. Something about fixing up a house?"

"No, that was one special. One of those shows where you satisfy people's curiosities as to how the famous turn out in the end." Before she could finish her thought, she felt the presence of another person at her elbow. Turning, she saw an older man holding out a pen and green paint sample he'd taken from the display. She asked his name and signed it. In less time than it took for her to write *Love, Isobel,* people surrounded her, each of them wanting her to do the same. She wrote out autographs until the crowd thinned to a handful of people who clutched already signed paint samples talking about who she used to be. Chatting with the stragglers, she searched their eyes and their body language for some sense of adoration or, at the very least, envy.

One of Isobel's worst flaws was her impatience. Taping the show earlier that year had seemed to her like an omen—an indication that the next part of her life was about to start. Despite having aired weeks ago, she had no clear sense of what would come of it. The thought that nothing would happen, that she'd go back to clutching at any role to make sure people didn't forget her, terrified her. What calmed that fear was being recognized. As cheap and shallow as that was, it remained true.

She posed for one last picture, listening to the noise around her. The purposeful hum of activity had been replaced by a buzz as shoppers stopped other people to ask who that woman was, or a few people called their parents or their sisters to tell the story of who they'd seen while they were shopping for a new light fixture. Satisfied, Isobel put her glasses back on and prepared to leave the store. It wouldn't look right to actually do her shopping after being recognized.

"Don't you need something?" the tattooed man from behind the paint counter asked. He'd come out from his work station and stood closer to her than any of the autograph seekers had. "You've chased off all my customers and now there's no line for you to cut."

"I wasn't cutting," she said. "I didn't see the line."

"You seem to be the sort of person who never sees the line."

Despite the tattoos and the blue apron, he was an attractive man. She guessed they were about the same age although he'd seen much more sun than she had, so his skin had a weathered quality. That, along with his height and calloused hands, gave him the appearance of a man who'd be good in a crisis. He wore several rings, but not a wedding band.

"I never seem like the sort of person I am," Isobel said, pushing her sunglasses off her face and onto the top of her head.

"Who are you?" the man asked. His nametag said Tom H.

She thought about her father. What would he say to such a person? She'd have to ask for something more than help finding the perfect butter yellow. Her mind clicked through the possible projects she needed to finish at Spite House. She'd had Benny start on the kitchen, even though she wasn't quite finished with the second floor. There was so much to be done—at this point mostly cosmetic, but that's what she'd helped her father with. Buried deep inside her brain were the words she needed to surprise Tom H.

"What do you have that will remove mastic without damaging a mosaic made up of glass, porcelain, marble, and slate tiles? I already tried heat, so don't suggest that. I also need some replacement tiles because some fool took out part of the border when they put a new door on the back porch, but I doubt you carry what we need. It has a strange color palette. We should talk about the grout too."

Tom stepped back. "I thought you were after paint."

"Mostly I was cutting in line, as you said, to try to find out whether you can match the color of the grout I'm trying to replace." She smiled as she dug around in her purse for the bit of grout Benny had given her after he scraped it from the tiles and put it into a Tupperware bowl. She hadn't thought she'd need it today, but it was pleasant to surprise people once in a while.

"We could do that," he said, reaching for the plastic bowl. "I'm sorry. Did you say your name?"

She looked at him, wondering if he really didn't know who she was—*Wait for It* had been ubiquitous for nearly a decade, and rare was the individual who'd never heard of her or who didn't recognize her once she'd been identified by fans. He met her gaze with his dark brown eyes. Shifting his weight from one foot to the other, he peeled the lid from the container.

"I'm Isobel. I used to be on television," she said.

"It's nice to meet you, Isobel-who-used-to-be-on-television," he said. "Now, how much square footage are you trying to cover with this grout? What else do you need? It seems like quite the project you've undertaken."

They spent the rest of the morning working out a plan to update the kitchen at Spite House. Without thinking about Lizzie and the way her eyes pinched when Isobel spent money, she filled her basket. Mostly she talked with Tom about Spite House, which he was vaguely familiar with and then at some point, when they'd gathered what she needed, they moved past discussing the renovation and onto their own lives. When Tom wasn't mixing paint or cutting wood for do-it-yourselfers, he played in a band, which at once thrilled and worried Isobel. She wanted someone who was happy with his life and not looking for something more. In the past, if she heard the word "aspiring" attached to a man's career, she moved in the other direction. Aspiring had become synonymous with wanting to use Isobel as a stepping stone.

"I'll help you load all this stuff," Tom said as they neared the checkout lane. "I don't know if you'll need help unloading it."

"I suppose I could always use an extra pair of hands." She looked at her overflowing cart and thought about how neither Lizzie nor her family were in a position to pay for an extensive update to the kitchen. What Lizzie had money for was to repaint the walls and clean up the tile underneath the linoleum. People thought Isobel had more money than she did—everyone underestimated the cost of living in L.A. and not working. And living there for more than a decade had made a serious dent in her savings. Still, she could swing the stuff in the basket without too much trouble. There was a sharp beep each time the clerk ran an item across the scanner. She needed this in her life. Having a real project, one where she could tear the place up and start over, kept her from thinking about what she wasn't doing with her career. What she'd done in the upstairs portion of the house had been cosmetic, but the kitchen held true opportunity for change.

Tom had continued talking as she deliberated, excited about the possibility of seeing Spite House. "Memphis is full of these sorts of gems," he said. "I should take you to Graceland Too."

"Too?" Isobel asked as she handed her card to the cashier.

Tom flashed his employee card and the cashier rang in a discount on the items. "The guy who owns it, Paul, painted it blue, and it makes you think of the songs and the movies." He continued talking and then broke out singing a few lines of "Blue Suede Shoes."

The warmth in his voice struck Isobel as an invitation. They walked through the automatic doors and into the parking lot. "That song'll be stuck in my head all day now," Isobel said, as they puzzled a way to fit all that she'd purchased into Grandma Mellie's Datsun.

"I guess you didn't plan on buying all these supplies," Tom said.

"I rarely plan on anything." She pushed at the passenger seat to try to get it to lie flat.

"Why don't we put this stuff in my truck and I'll follow you over there."

"It really isn't any trouble?" she asked. A breeze lifted her skirt and she became aware of the fact that what was happening between them was more than good customer service.

"It's my day off and I'm wide open. I was handling the paint counter for my buddy, Will. His dogs set off his burglar alarm again, and his neighbors get pissy about the sound if it goes on too long."

"And I'm guessing he came back around the same time you started helping me."

Tom smiled and closed her trunk. "Come on, I'm parked around the corner."

As Isobel was waiting at the stoplight to cross Main Street, a monarch butterfly landed on her windshield. She looked at it and then adjusted her rearview mirror to make sure Tom's truck had remained behind her. He appeared to be singing along to whatever music played in his car. She glanced back, surprised to find the butterfly in place. It stayed with her, flattening its wings against the glass, until she pulled up in front of Spite House. Before she could step out of the car, Tom had jumped from his truck and opened the driver's side door for her. Out of habit she moved to put on her sunglasses, but then stopped. She wanted Tom to know when she was looking at him.

Benny stepped out of the house and walked down the stairs to meet them. Gauging by the speed with which he appeared, he'd been watching for her. "I didn't know you'd be gone so long," he said. His eyes looked runny and yellow at the edges.

"My fault," Tom said, extending his hand. "You must be Benny. Isobel told me about all the work you've put into this place. This house is extraordinary. I mean I've seen it from the riverside before—you know, all that glass, but I never realized the front was so skinny or the plot so small."

"That's Tom," Isobel said, confident that she didn't need more of an explanation. He patted her shoulder as if he agreed.

"Give me a tour?" Tom asked Benny. They grabbed as much as they could carry and walked up the stairs, into the house, and down the narrow hallway, setting the supplies on the kitchen floor.

"I'll make tea," Isobel said, sending Tom and Benny off on their walk through the house. She put the kettle on and set out the mugs and then examined the kitchen, trying to see if the changes she wanted could be made.

They hadn't planned on pulling up the linoleum, but last week, Benny had used the kitchen floor as a work surface while soldering. The result had been a dozen dime-shaped holes burned into the laminate. He and his crew had pulled the linoleum up, intent on replacing it, but when Isobel saw the original flooring, she'd insisted they try to restore it instead. Bits of felt lining and mastic marred the overall beauty of the floor, but it still wowed Isobel, even though she'd been looking at it for a solid week.

For one, she'd never seen its like. They'd uncovered dozens of wonderful floors in all the houses she'd done with her father—and there had been close to fifty, counting those before she started acting and those renovated during the years he spent with her in Southern

California—but none of them were like this one. The original flooring resembled a mosaic—shards of a dozen different types of broken tiles scattered in what appeared to be a random pattern. Except that the more Isobel stared at it, the less random it appeared.

Getting down on her knees, she ran her fingers over the tiles clustered near the center of the floor, scraping away at some of the mastic with her fingernail. The colors of the tile faded in intensity as they radiated out from the center of the room. Putting her face to the floor, she squinted and looked across the floor. The tile appeared almost to have an ombré effect. She couldn't discern the pattern of the center design. The remnants of the linoleum obscured it, and the image was also too large to view up close.

The teakettle whistled. She looked up to find Benny and Tom watching her as she crawled around. Standing next to Tom, Benny looked wan. The blotchy redness that normally covered his cheeks had disappeared and instead of making him look sober, it made him look ill. Her overriding impression of Benny over the last few months had been of a man who looked like he belonged in Spite House, but now he had the look of a valet handed the keys to a car he wasn't sure how to drive.

Tom clapped Benny on the shoulder, and he turned even paler. "This is some fucking house."

Isobel nodded, realizing only as Tom spoke how much she'd come to love Spite House. Her phone rang, and as the men poured themselves tea and continued to talk about what had been done on the house and what could be done, she pulled her phone from her purse and glanced at its face. It was her agent, who she hadn't heard from since the day after the *Where Are They Now?* episode aired. Her thumb hovered over the accept button. Wanting something too much could be dangerous.

"You okay?" Benny asked.

Isobel declined the call and then looked up at him and Tom. "I'm fine," she said. "Just fine."

It had taken the better part of a week, but with a bit of elbow grease and the solvent Tom had suggested, Isobel had restored the original kitchen floor to near-pristine condition. The grout needed to be redone and she hadn't yet found replacements for the few missing tiles around the edges of the room where entryways had been altered over the years. But even in its unfinished state, the floor was magnificent, especially in midmorning. She ran her socked feet over the tiles and glanced back at her computer. The pattern she'd been trying to figure out had turned out to be a lotus. It was Lizzie who'd first seen it. She pointed at the similarity in the flower shape on the beaded curtain to the one in the tiles. The floor lotus, after it had been cleaned, was a brilliant yellow color. The tiles radiating out from it gradually lightened to an almost clear milky glass.

Isobel looked at her watch and closed her computer. The production crew was nearly two hours overdue. Isobel's natural impatience often meant she came off as brusque. She knew this, and yet she couldn't stop herself from being upset. Part of her lamented the lost time. There was so much left to do in the kitchen and with two hours, she could have been removing the metal cabinetry, which was the next item on her list. Instead, she'd been listlessly searching the Internet for tiles similar to those around the edges of the room. Taking up her sketch pad, she once again drew possible configurations for the kitchen. The western wall of windows limited her options, as did the slanted walls. When she'd first arrived, Lizzie had described the house as being shaped like a thermometer, but that wasn't quite right. The sketch on her paper looked more like a child's plastic sand shovel—long skinny handle with a trapezoid at the end. She heard the echo of a car door slam.

Finally. Isobel stood and forced herself to unclench her fists. Walking down the long hallway, she worked to compose herself, to put an authentic smile on her face—or at least what these Hollywood folks would take as genuine. She stepped out onto the front porch and raised her hand in a greeting to the three people clustered around the rented SUV. The producer, Craig, had never been someone she'd liked, but because Hollywood worked the way it did, he'd never suspected how forced her apparent liking for him was. It made her uncomfortable to have him back in the house, especially after he'd misconstrued so much of what she'd shared with him about her cousins for the *Where Are They Now?* show.

He looked up at the porch and waved to her, his booming voice echoing across the vast space between the curb and the front of the house. "There she is. Isobel Wallace. America's Tweenheart."

Isobel winced at the nickname, which over the years had been made ugly by the snark of tabloid headlines—especially during that time when she'd been dating Hollywood men. "You're late," she said.

"Come on now. You can't hold that against us," he said crossing the narrow sidewalk with short choppy steps. His heavily muscled body worked against him—the inner thighs of his suit pants were worn shiny from rubbing against each other.

She stepped down toward him, fighting the urge to be bitchy because they were late and he'd insulted her. "I won't." She forced the smile back onto her face.

"I'll hold you against me then," Craig said, enveloping her in a hug that she hadn't been prepared for. It took her breath away.

"You look different," Isobel said when he let her go. Then quickly, so he wouldn't be insulted, she added, "Have you lost weight? Or maybe it has to do with confidence? You seem like a man grown into himself."

He kept his arm around her. She felt the metallic coolness of his wedding ring tap against her arm. "I am thinner."

The other people he'd brought hovered behind him. She wondered what had happened in the intervening months to change Craig so markedly. It didn't take much—often finding a bit of power or having an affair brought out a new cockiness in people.

"I'm Isobel," she said, extending her hand to the small, thin woman who cowered behind Craig. To the older bearded man next to her, she said, "Jake, it's good to see you again. I thought the camera work on the special was exquisitely done." The woman introduced herself as Kitty and indicated that she'd be handling the sound, lighting, and such until the full crew arrived, and then she'd be field producing. Wanting to alter the tone of the conversation, Isobel took a deep breath. "I was worried about you guys."

"Bags took forever coming off the fucking puddle jumper we had to take from Atlanta," Craig said, taking a pack of gum from his front shirt pocket and slapping it against his palm as if it held cigarettes. "Flew right over Memphis and then had to get on another plane to fly back."

She took the stick of gum he offered. "Makes you wish they'd given you a parachute."

"Or a private jet." He turned toward Jake and shooed him toward the vehicle where they'd left the equipment on the sidewalk.

"Maybe if I can make you some money, that'll change," Isobel said, looking over the producer's head to see what equipment they'd brought with them. Three wasn't a large crew.

Craig continued to talk while the woman hovered somewhere in between Jake and Craig. "The numbers were good. Real good and if this goes the way I think"—he rubbed his hands together—"it might just be private next time. Think of it. The two of us in one of those executive Cessnas."

"I don't know if I'll go back to Cali," she said.

"Right, then. We'll get all of that figured out," he said, walking around the porch and inspecting the exterior of the entryway. He cracked his knuckles repeatedly and then took out a small notebook and, with a pencil no longer than his pinky, he started making notes.

Jake closed up the SUV and waved Kitty over to help him with the equipment. She was a petite woman who had the androgynous frame of a teenager waiting on puberty. Jake had the look of a man who'd been filming other people's lives too long. He wore belted jean shorts and sported a beard that whorled and matted like steel wool. Isobel figured he'd shave it before too long. Even in September, Memphis was unbearably hot. It wasn't the heat but the stickiness that made facial hair impractical. As if reading her thoughts, he scratched at his beard and sighed.

"You aren't filming today, are you?" she asked, slipping past Craig, who'd become fascinated by the windows on the front porch. Over the years, she'd learned it was better to have the cameraman like you than not.

Jake grunted, but before he could speak, Kitty, who'd loaded herself up with equipment that weighed more than she did, popped up. "Oh, my gosh. I've wanted to meet you forever. We're not filming *you* today. Just the house, and Jake wants to make sure he has enough lights or rather the right type of lights. The grip is coming later, but still that's my job today to take light readings. Of course, we'll have to come back and do them all throughout the day."

She continued talking even as she moved toward Isobel, arms extended in a gesture of embrace despite the equipment on her shoulders. Isobel bent down and hugged the woman, offering appropriate responses to her running commentary. "Hmmm . . . I see . . . Of course."

"She's a talker," Jake said.

Kitty appeared not to hear him. She talked on, adding details about the last show she'd worked on and how she'd never been on location, as she trailed Isobel back up to the house and set some of the equipment on the porch.

In the face of such relentless enthusiasm, Isobel's energy escaped her. She hadn't slept well in weeks. At night instead of counting sheep to fall asleep, she counted possible outcomes of this production, of Tom, of Lizzie, of Elyse. Her brain hadn't worked so hard since learning how to solve for X when she studied algebra.

Craig had let himself inside Spite House, leaving the door ajar. "What a house," Kitty said, craning her neck to peer at the small balconies that extended from each of the floors. "Is that a room? On top of the house?"

"Cupola. It's an Italian feature, dates back a couple hundred years," Jake said, setting the rest of the equipment on the porch. "I worked on a few projects with Vila. Got to know my way around architecture. It was in the middle of being repaired when we were here last time."

"You should see the kitchen," she said, opening the door for them. "I mean the whole house is under construction, but the kitchen is my mess."

Craig appeared on the stairs, his girth making the rise seem even more precarious. Isobel nodded before continuing to explain the layout of the house to Kitty.

"What did we film when we were here last?" Craig asked, leaning against the banister in a way that made it groan out a complaint.

"I'm not sure that's secure," she said, gesturing for the producer to move back. The special had been filmed in the spring, and all of the women had been shot on the porch or in the backyard with the Mississippi River behind them. "They did lots with the house—really played it up."

"I'm picturing a floor plan in the opening of your reality show. This place is impossible. It's like something out of a set designer's nightmare. Who built it?"

"Lizzie's grandfather."

"Lizzie? I thought it was your grandfather."

"We're step-cousins, although close as any family. She doesn't even know who her father is."

Craig narrowed his eyes. "She's the soccer star, right?"

Isobel felt as if she'd stumbled. It'd been too long since she'd been around cunning people. Memphis was a town without guile, but sharks like Craig, assholes from Los Angeles, were dangerous. Here he was pretending not to know what he ought to. She realized that she'd given him too much information and tried to move past it. "We've got blueprints of the house if that would help with the graphics."

He made more notes in his book. "Nah. I've got it." He told Jake and Kitty what he needed and instructed Isobel to relax until they'd been through the house.

"Have at it," she said. "There's nobody here but me."

Kitty turned and pressed her cheek to Isobel's as if bidding her farewell. "I love this place," she said in a fierce whisper before disappearing up the stairs with such gracefulness that none of the treads groaned out their usual squeaks. Isobel could see why the girl had become a sound technician.

In the kitchen, Isobel took the jug of sun tea that Elyse had set in the window that morning and poured it over ice. Her cousin appeared to be recovering from the wedding situation, as she and Lizzie had taken to calling what had happened in Boston. In the last two weeks, she'd started cooking classes, which meant that they hardly saw her. When Isobel had her heart broken the first time, her mother had told her the only way to mend it was to get on with life. Waiting around only made grief insufferable.

Isobel's heart had been broken so many times she needed only a day or so to get over rejection. Before meeting Tom, there had been no one serious. Nine months of stand-him-till-you're-bored-with-him, as Isobel liked to think of her one-plus-night stands. The stuff with Tom was Lizzie's fault. She and T. J. were the type of couple who made you want to get into a relationship—like watching a triathlon made you think you could do one. Lizzie and T. J. were fit and purposeful. Isobel had sworn off relationships after the dating horror show that had been her late teens and early twenties when people had still expected great things from her. She dated older men, established in their careers. More often than not their agents or handlers arranged it. She'd fallen hard for two or three of them, and then there were those awful months when she'd been spectacularly dumped by a man whom most of America was in love with.

And that had been the beginning of the end of everything in Isobel's life. His verdict that she wasn't good enough seemed to pervade casting directors' assessments of her acting and her potential to move from the small screen to the big screen. She stopped getting calls, stopped being asked to read scripts. All of it, in a matter of months, dried up. There had been precious little in the five years since that ended. Her last movie—a bit part in an indie she'd done in an attempt at being a grown-up—had been panned and then hadn't even been released in the theaters. One of those straight-to-DVD flicks. Not to mention that she'd stupidly agreed to a frontal nudity scene, which people used stills from for pornography sites. Her agent didn't speak to her for more than a year after that. He'd told her not to do it, warned her about the consequences. The first she'd heard from him since the indie flop had been when he'd called about the *Where Are They Now?* show.

Isobel finished her tea and put the glass in the sink. She listened to the strangers moving around in what she'd come to think of as her place. What would they think of this mess of a house? Looking around the kitchen, she tried to see it through their eyes. The floor, which she'd been admiring moments before, looked crafty instead of craftsman. The metal cupboards would be beautiful when they were actually refinished. She'd arranged with an auto detailer to powder coat the metal a beautiful off-white color with flecks of gold in it to draw out the colors of the floor. Right now, though, they were rusty and hung crooked so several didn't close. Benny's repairs appeared to have been made out of necessity and as cheaply as possible. There were holes in the plaster from when Elton had rewired. If it weren't for T. J.'s constantly watching Benny, they'd never have a hope of meeting the code requirements.

Looking again at the cupboards, the need to take action filled her with a restless energy. What could it hurt to begin? She found a drill motor charging in the corner and without thinking through the consequences or even making a plan, she began to unscrew the hinges on the cupboard doors. She started at the top, standing on the counter to reach the cupboards attached to the upper portion of the wall.

The dust on top of them was two inches thick. She supposed no one had been up here in years to see the tops of things. If she stood on her tiptoes, she could peek over the lip of the cupboards, which had been topped with a molding of sorts to make them appear more elegant. A few small boxes nestled behind the decorative frame of the cupboards and were covered with a layer of the greasy dust that coated the top of the molding. A grapevine-patterned border ran along the length of the wall between the ceiling and the cupboards. One of the seams had come unstuck and the corner flared out from the wall. Isobel stretched for it, grasping it between the tips of her fingers and pulling at it. The brittle glue on the back gave way easily. In less time than it had taken her to climb onto the counter, she'd pulled away an entire length of the hideous border.

Laughing, she spun on one foot and nearly lost her balance. From behind her she heard clapping and turned to see both her cousins standing near the back door. They'd just come from the hairdresser, and Elyse sported a pixie cut that emphasized the sweetness of her face. Before she could compliment her, Isobel flailed about and then grabbed hard onto the upper cabinet.

"Careful," Lizzie said, stepping forward.

She smiled at them, meaning to let them know it would all be fine, but instead, in the half second it took for her to regain her balance, the cabinet tore loose from the plaster wall and crashed down onto the counter. The momentum threw Isobel off balance and she fell from the counter, half landing on Lizzie, who had rushed forward to try to catch her. Elyse screamed and then the sound of shattering glass echoed throughout the kitchen.

"Are you hurt? Are you hurt?" Isobel asked Lizzie.

"I don't think so," she said, putting her hands down and struggling to stand up. "My leg."

Isobel held her breath, not wanting the worst to have happened. Lizzie stood, but carefully and without putting weight on her right leg.

"It'll be fine," Elyse said, tugging at the ends of her newly shortened hair. Her voice was low and calm. "Take a step. I'm sure it's fine. You didn't land on your knee."

Lizzie looked at both of them, her eyes wet. She took a step forward and then another. She walked across the room and then did a few jumping jacks. "It's fine," she said. "Fine, fine fine."

Elyse smiled and then looked up at the beaded curtain, which still rustled with movement. "Who are they?" she asked.

Jake stood in the entryway, his camera on his shoulder. Craig stood to his left, giving him hand signals about what to film and where to focus the lens. The girl Kitty had crept around to the glass windows and pulled the shades down. She stood almost behind the refrigerator so she'd be nearly invisible in any wide shots of the kitchen.

"Those are the people we're going to pretend not to see while they shoot a sizzle reel."

"Starting now?" Lizzie asked.

"Guess so," Isobel said, getting to her feet and surveying the damage. The cupboard itself had dented like an auto fender when it hit the ground. She cursed. The cupboards were impossible to replace—the manufacturer, St. Charles Steel, didn't even exist anymore. She kicked at the now warped metal and looked at the wall where they'd been attached. The plaster behind them had torn away in large chunks, revealing the lathe and through that the clapboard of the house. A dozen jelly jars were broken in bits across the tile floor. Isobel's sense of accomplishment at having started a project faded. Her face reddened as she surveyed the disaster. "Were these your grandmother's?"

Lizzie's blue eyes softened. "Doubt they hold any meaning. Granny liked to save everything—margarine tubs, aluminum foil, bread ties. We cleaned a lot of that stuff out when she died and left the practical stuff. Mom never got sentimental about things."

"I'll pay to fix it. All of it. I mean, I was going to anyway, but I can cover this and more," Isobel said, walking to the closet for the broom and dustpan. She knew her cousin was concerned about money, which was why Lizzie had agreed to the television show in the first place. Craig had offered to pay her an amount large enough to cover the cost of finally bringing the house fully up to code. There was the possibility of more money on top of that if a network picked up the show or even if Craig could find another investor or two to film a pilot.

Elyse stepped forward to hold the dustpan for Isobel. Her eyes flitted from the broken glass to the crew. "Surely this part isn't worth filming—who is ever interested in clean-up?"

"It'll take you guys a few days to get used to having us here," Craig said. "Until then we'll film most of what we see. You never know when we might need this footage."

Over the next week, while the crew filmed, Craig followed the three of them around asking a series of increasingly unrelated questions. They learned to ignore Jake and his camera as well as Kitty and her silent, stealthy way of slipping a wireless microphone on them or skittering around the house with the boom. In many ways, Kitty with her small frame and impossible thinness was the one most at home in Spite House. Isobel wished she had a clearer picture of what Craig wanted for his sizzle reel. There seemed to be as much footage shot of Lizzie as there was of Isobel, and yesterday the entire crew had followed Elyse to her cooking class. They'd wanted to come to the community center to film Lizzie and Elyse and the work they did with the girls there, but Rosa May had been adamant in her opposition. Isobel had wanted to try to explain that it could be a good fundraising opportunity for the school and for Rosa May's programs, but nobody asked her for advice or even her opinion.

Unlocking the back door, she stepped inside, not expecting anyone to be there. She wasn't supposed to be there, but after she'd dropped the cabinets off at the detailer's shop, she realized she'd left the hardware at the house. She intended to grab it and be back out the door in a matter of minutes, which was why she left the keys in the lock and the back door open. The shoddy patch job Benny had started on the plaster where the cabinets had fallen caught her eye. He seemed to be getting worse. Not that he was a problem that Lizzie would deal with. Her cousin was as sweet as pie, but terrible at conflict. She never should have hired him.

In many ways, Isobel was older than her cousins. While they'd spent their adolescence in school, she'd spent hers playing at being an adult. She wished other people knew this about her. Because she was the baby of her family, everyone treated her like a child—it had always been that way. Maybe for a brief moment when Lizzie first became part of their family there had been the possibility of Isobel's not being treated as fragile, but then Lizzie became a big sister and extended the same protective feeling toward Isobel that she had toward her younger siblings. She took up the plastic bag with the hardware and turned to the door, thinking that the way people treated her was as much her own fault as theirs. She smelled smoke. Benny stood in the doorway squinting at her through the hazy late afternoon light.

"Watcha doing here?" he asked, leaning against the doorway.

"I live here."

He dropped his cigarette on the threshold and twisted his foot to put out the few embers.

Isobel's eyes searched Benny's face for some sign of why he was acting strangely toward her. She'd seen him drunk before, but this appeared to be more than that. "Maybe you should head home for the day," she said.

"You shouldn't tell me what to do." He took a step toward her. "Besides, home is right there." He gestured outside the house to his RV, which Isobel took to mean the trailer that had become a near-permanent part of the lot next door to Spite House.

She couldn't help herself. The smart move would have been to keep her mouth shut. "That's illegal, you know. If Lizzie finds out and tells T. J., you'll have to leave."

He looked as if he hadn't heard her. The skin underneath his eyes was dried and wrinkled like tissue paper.

"I can do what I want. You know this place was supposed to be mine? I mean, Mellie offered to sell it to me
when Annie got married. Would've given it to me for a
song, too. Knew all the problems with the place. We all
thought a guy like that, a Northerner, wouldn't ever let
her come back to this place."

"They're coming back," Isobel said, uncertain of
what Lizzie's parents wanted with the house. It didn't
make sense, but then not much about Lizzie's family
had ever made sense to Isobel. She remembered her
father talking about how hard his little brother made
life. Of course, that had been before, when their own
lives seemed easier than they should be.

"We'll see about that," Benny said, giving a sort of
chuckle that turned into a raspy cough.

Isobel forgot her concerns about Benny and moved
toward him. "What do you mean?"

"People got other plans for this place, you know? I
don't want to see Lizzie waste her life waiting around in
Memphis with a guy like T. J. You know what he is?"

Isobel shook her head. She didn't want to interrupt
him, thinking Benny was on the verge of revealing the
truth about facts that Isobel hadn't previously realized
were lies.

"Nothing better than a meter maid. Going around
fining people for stuff that nobody but him gives a rat's

ass about. And I'm no racist, but them dating doesn't sit right with me. You know what I mean? I worry about that girl. She's more fragile than the rest of you." He fiddled with the brim of his hat and then seemed to see in her what others had not. "I mean, you're as fragile as a pit bull. Your daddy did something right."

"You shouldn't talk about people's fathers," she said. She had nothing to fear from Benny. He was a worthless drunk. Taking a step toward him, she inquired after his own children. If he wanted to bring up fathers, his own abilities were fair game.

Pulling the brim low over his eyes, he looked away from her. "My kids is fine. I do all right as their dad. I'm not perfect but I keep an eye on my daughter and kick my sons' behinds when they need it."

"But you don't see them that often? Do you?" She took another step toward him. "Who threw you out of the house this time? The mother of your daughter or the mother of your sons?"

Benny took his hat off and looked wildly around the kitchen. His eyes landed on the jagged hole in the plaster. "That's going to cost you extra and I think you ought to be nice to me or you'll find more surprises in this house when I'm done."

"More surprises?" She looked again at the shitty start he'd gotten on repairing the wall.

"I'm saying I like to take out my own kind of insurance." He swayed a bit and then put his hand back on the doorframe for support. "I gotta make sure Papa gets paid cuz I hear you three are about out of money."

"What are you talking about?" Isobel's mind worked to try to put together what Benny meant. He must have been doing more than drinking. Usually he was a comical drunk but at that moment, his words held an edge to them.

"I'm just saying that plaster might not have been damaged if that leak in the roof had been patched up."

She set the bag with the hardware on the table and fished around the piles of tools until she came up with a flashlight. Pulling a ladder over, she walked to the area where the cupboards had fallen. She'd been right about their being ruined. Her plan now was to install shelving on the wall instead of trying to match the lower cabinets. The walls were plaster and lathe, which essentially meant that the heavy plaster had been smeared on top of thin strips of wood. Benny had torn the jagged edges of the hole away and smoothed them in preparation for laying on new plaster. He should have fixed the broken pieces of wood, but instead, he'd nailed several paint stirrers to the exposed studs. She turned the flashlight on and shone it toward the top of the hole where the plaster had failed. Then she reached and felt carefully around the wood and remaining plaster. Bits of the material crumbled in her hand. The wood felt damp and cool. She pulled a chunk of plaster out and stood on her tiptoes to peer into the space until she traced the source of the water to the corner of the room where the windows met the wall.

"How long have you known that was there?"

Benny shrugged and the corners of the lips tugged upward into a smirk.

"What the hell?" She tore a chunk of the damp plaster from the wall and threw it at Benny. It hit him in the chest. He staggered backward as if he'd been hit by a rock. "You checked these windows out in February. That was your first job and you ignored the broken seal?" She threw another piece of the wall at him and he stumbled, falling down the porch steps and onto the gravel beside the entryway.

Isobel jumped from the counter, getting close to Benny. "You're fired."

He looked like a pill bug trying to right itself. Finally he rolled onto his stomach and then using the handrail pulled himself into a standing position. "You can't fire me."

"I can," Isobel said. "I did."

In her periphery, she saw Jake walking around the corner of the house, holding his camera down by his knees.

"You're not the boss," Benny said, taking one step toward her. "You're a little girl."

"Get out of here," Isobel said, her voice rising. "Give me your keys—to everything, the trailer, the house, all of it. I can't even let you drive home in this condition."

"What's going on?" Jake said.

"Nothing. We're fine."

"Are you sure?" Jake asked, bringing the camera to his shoulder. "I'm sorry, I've got to. He'll be pissed if I don't get any of it."

She ignored him and kept her eyes on Benny. The presence of the lens appeared to have a calming effect on him. He'd avoided the cameras when they were at the house and now that Jake's was on his shoulder and pointing in his direction, he couldn't get away fast enough.

"Give me the keys," she said, holding out her hand.

Benny turned his back to the camera and dug around in his pants pockets. "How am I going to get home?" he asked. "Ain't no bus runs along here."

"Walk," Isobel said. "You got any of your personal effects in the trailer?"

He nodded.

"I'll let you get them and put them in your truck. But you're not driving."

Jake pulled his phone out and began texting furiously. Before putting the camera back up, he explained to Isobel that he'd planned on filming some exterior shots—close-ups of the house's unique architectural details. "Mostly for my own reel," he said. "Craig doesn't care about that stuff. They're on their way. I'm really sorry about having to film this."

"You should apologize to Benny. He's the drunk one."

By the time Benny had emptied the trailer, Kitty and Craig had arrived and offered to get Benny home themselves. "We can do the exit interviews that way," Kitty had said to Craig.

"Good stuff," Craig had said to Isobel before getting inside the cab of the truck.

His voice chilled Isobel. She hadn't fired Benny for the show, and yet objectively, it created the drama that had been missing the last few days. She shook her head, trying to figure out her own motives.

Jake and Kitty followed them in the SUV and in a moment Isobel was alone again in the house. The whole exchange had taken less than an hour. The sun sat in nearly the same place it had been when she'd come home. She stepped up onto the back stairs and took her keys out of the door. She still had to take the hardware to get painted. But she felt protective of Spite House and didn't want to leave it alone.

Instead, she stood in the kitchen and looked at the torn-up wall and thought about Elyse, with her broken heart, and Lizzie with her broken leg. She supposed both were doing what Benny had been doing to Spite House. They were working on fixing the outward appearance of something without first finding all the damage that had been done.

Summer 2001: Old Silver Beach

At sixteen, the Triplins were oblivious to the world outside themselves in a way that was abhorrent in anyone but teenage girls and saucy sitcom sidekicks. To make matters worse, Isobel and her cousins had been adolescents before terrorist attacks and the recession became the bulk of news headlines. That summer the news had been filled with old men flying balloons around the world, a missing Washington intern, and sharks. All issues of little consequence, especially given what would come after Labor Day that year. Isobel wouldn't have taken notice of any of this news, except that every other day someone at the beach would think they'd spotted a fin and scream at everyone to get out of the water. The lifeguards would take up the false alarm and whistle until a whole shivering mass of wet bodies stood at the shoreline, craning their necks trying to get a look at what could possibly be a shark. So far, in her time at the beach, this crying wolf business had happened half a dozen times.

As always, Isobel and her family had been the first to arrive at the Cape, but that particular year, her brothers hadn't come. Joel was studying in Amsterdam and Carl hadn't wanted to leave his girlfriend. Her mother and father typically arranged their schedules so they could spend most of the summer at the Cape. This was because for the whole of the eight years she'd been working on *Wait for It,* her family hadn't lived together. Her mother lived with her in Los Angeles and her father and brothers lived in Sacramento. They spent most weekends together and any stretch of time when the set was closed—like during holidays and the beginning of summer. Isobel hadn't ever been lonely at her grandparents' house, but she'd also never been there without her brothers. Complaining about her boredom elicited little sympathy from her parents. "You've got to learn to live without an audience," her father had said.

After the first week, which had been among the slowest of her life, she convinced Elyse to drive up to the Cape on the weekends and arranged to fly Lizzie out early since her cousin was on a different school schedule than her siblings. Several years earlier when the depth of her soccer talent had become evident, one of the private schools in Memphis had snapped her up. As a result, she was always on breaks at a different time than her family.

So it was that the three of them were at the beach for the first real shark sighting. It had come on a Sunday near the end of May when the weather was warm enough for tourists and weekenders to fill the beaches with their blankets and coolers. The Triplins had been sunbathing and because it was unusually hot, they'd also been taking periodic plunges into the bay— strategically staged in front of the lifeguard. Isobel remembered toying with the idea of faking a cramp so the boy wonder with his chiseled chest would have to save her. They'd laughed about it but agreed that if anyone could fake needing to be saved, it would be Isobel. When the piercing cry of "shark" echoed over the water, they'd been directly in the line of sight of the lifeguard. It shocked Isobel to hear such a high-pitched scream from the boy. First of all, he looked like a weightlifter and second, the other shark alarms had been made by beachgoers. Usually a mother in one of those suits with a skirt, wearing a floppy hat, would run into the shallow water, snatch up her toddler and scream to the people around her about seeing a shark. Then, eventually, the guards, blowing their whistles in a way that always made Isobel think of sex, would herd everyone out.

"He's serious," Lizzie said, tugging on Isobel's shoulder.

"Don't worry about it," she said, diving under the water to pull at Elyse's ankles.

Elyse refused to get her hair wet. She fended off Isobel's attempt to dunk her and explained the panic to Lizzie. "They've been doing this all week. It's like that wolf thing."

"Except that in the end of that story there really was a wolf," Lizzie said. She linked arms with them and half pulled and walked them to shore. Isobel would have continued to object, but looking up at the shoreline, she saw that they were among the last out of the water. It had never cleared so quickly before. Also, instead of searching the horizon and the endless stretch of water, people were pointing and murmuring to one another. Excited voices occasionally rose to a near shout.

"I saw it."

"I think it swam by me."

Despite her natural disdain for adults and their concerns, Isobel felt herself get caught up in the panicky buzz that surged through the crowd. She shaded her eyes against the sun and searched for the telltale fin of a shark.

"This is exactly like *Jaws*," Elyse said. Later that summer, when they found the book on their grandparents' bookshelf, they read it aloud to each other, giggling over the author's description of a woman swimming naked. When they got to the horrible parts where people were killed, they stopped and talked through the what-might-have-beens in that dramatic and self-involved way only teenagers can do without the practicalities of life slapping sense into them.

The fin, when she saw it, broke the surface of the water like a knife sliding into soft butter. The ripples came after it had come up. She saw it before anyone else, but she couldn't bring herself to point at it, to scream out, as another woman did seconds later. The beach erupted into chaos then, with mothers grabbing their children and the lifeguards on their bullhorns telling people the beach would be closed for the rest of the day.

Lizzie had started a conversation with a teenage boy standing next to her. He talked on and on about all that he knew about sharks, explaining why he knew, without a doubt, that the fin they'd seen belonged to a great white. He was nobody any of the cousins would have given notice to before. Except for his height, he didn't look like he'd hit puberty. His chest was concave and he hunched his shoulders, which were covered with pus-filled acne. Despite his appearance, his deep voice and the confidence with which he spoke to Lizzie had drawn eavesdroppers—Isobel among them.

"If you do see a shark in the water, you can't out swim him. You have to face him. I've read of men in shipwrecks who punched the sharks in the nose and that was enough to convince them you were a predator. So that's what I'd do. You can also grab him in the gills—that's like our eyes. It's where the soft tissue is."

"Can you dig your nails into its eyes?" Isobel asked.

"I don't think so," the boy said, his voice thick with superior knowledge.

At being so dismissed, Isobel's face turned red and she stepped behind Lizzie, muttering under her breath to Elyse, who stood next to her, about the asshole, while a small portion of the crowd stepped closer and nodded. Isobel was glad when Lizzie disagreed. Her cousin shook her head at him as if he were confused. "No, no, no. Seems like the best thing to do is stay out of the water. I don't think I'll ever win a fight with a shark."

"It's not a fight, it's survival," the boy said, staring at Lizzie as if he didn't quite understand what she was saying. It might have been her accent, which in times of stress became thick and heavy. Or it might have been that Lizzie had a distinctive view of the world. Isobel didn't notice such differences anymore.

On the walk back to the house, they talked in low whispers about the shark. Isobel was more angry at the dismissiveness of the boy than fearful of the shark. The shades on the house were drawn, which she might have noticed and thought strange, but they were too intent on the drama of what had happened at the beach. Their grandfather's truck was gone. Her grandfather liked to spend his afternoons at the American Legion, while their grandmother browsed the antique stores in town. Because Isobel's brothers hadn't come that year, the Triplins had taken over the sleeping porch, which usually became home base for whoever the oldest cousins were.

They went in the side entrance, still talking quietly, and flopped down on their cots. Isobel reached into her bag and pulled out several fashion magazines she'd purchased over the preceding weeks. The others threw their own reading material onto the pile and before long, they were mindlessly looking at photos and reading lists of tips and tricks. Elyse paged through a tabloid, asking Isobel what was true and what wasn't. Lizzie, who would be the last of them to lose her virginity, made faces at *Cosmo* as she read it.

"I'm not allowed to get this," she whispered, covering up the word "orgasm" on a page. "Mom says it's pornography."

"Nah, it's the stuff you need to know that moms will never mention."

Lizzie continued to read the article, the whole time a blush of red creeping up from her neck to her face.

Elyse peered over her shoulder. "Do you know what my mom said about blow jobs?"

Isobel had looked up then, aware of loud stomping on the stairs. She'd also wanted to know what Elyse's mom thought because she seemed too square to even know what a BJ was.

"She says that men—"

"You lazy piece of shit." Isobel's mother's voice cut through what Elyse had been about to say.

They froze. And then looked around to see if they were being yelled at. Lizzie flung the magazine onto the floor, where it lay open to a picture of a woman wearing a man's white collared shirt straddling a chair.

"What the duck," Elyse said. It was a holdover from the year they'd discovered swear words. Their parents had all made them stop using them and to thwart the system, they'd started saying "What the duck" as often as possible to irritate their parents. "Duck" had become an inside joke among the Triplins.

"What are you doing, Nora?" Isobel's father said. "What's all this about?"

Isobel's eyes grew wide. She'd never heard her parents fight. She'd actually rarely seen them together in the last few years. At first they'd all tried living in an apartment in Hollywood during filming, but her brothers hadn't wanted to leave their schools. Instead, their father had stayed with the boys and for the months that they filmed, Elyse's mother lived with her in a one-bedroom apartment that was near the set.

Before she could process the sound of her parents fighting, she heard a commotion—sounding like something had been thrown down the stairs.

"We should go," Elyse said in a low voice. "They don't know we're here. We were supposed to be out until dinner."

Isobel wanted to leave. She knew she should leave, but she couldn't make herself move from the cot. If they'd been a little older with more insight into the adult world, they would have made their presence known by dropping a book or faking a loud conversation. Elyse pulled at Isobel's arm. Lizzie opened the side porch door, which made an awful squeaking sound.

"Shh, they'll hear us," Elyse said.

"What do we do?" Isobel asked, looking at the door and back at the house where her parents' fighting had dropped low enough that they couldn't hear them.

"Try not to listen," Elyse said, throwing her a pillow to put over her ears.

There were more loud thumps and then it was her father's voice, as angry as she'd ever heard it, that boomed around the house. "What did you expect me to say? That I'm glad for you? That I want you to sleep with other people?"

The fight continued with each of them lobbing sentences at each other as if it were a tennis match. "It's like we aren't even married," her mother said.

"I feel married. Or at least I did until you told me about the men you slept with."

"I thought we could get a clean start. That's what you said this summer would be about. Isobel's old enough to live on her own now and she'd be fine in the apartment by herself."

"She's sixteen."

"She's old for her age and she's got a good head on her shoulders."

"How do I know that? I haven't spent any time with her over the last few years. It's been the two of you and it turns out you've been down in L.A. fucking strangers."

Her parents had argued their way to the parlor, which was where the side porch connected to the main house. They were no longer yelling, but Isobel could hear them as if they spoke directly to her. She'd long since dropped the pillows on the cot and although neither of her cousins would meet her gaze, she knew from their posture that they'd also heard the fight between her parents. Elyse had moved to the door as if she couldn't bear to miss any word, even one spoken under Isobel's mother's breath. Lizzie stared out the window, her shoulder blades drawn back toward each other as if she were trying to get them to touch.

Her mother's voice lost its edge. "I wish that sex had never gotten mixed up in marriage. It would be so much better if they had nothing to do with each other. You're a great dad and good partner and that ought to be enough—"

"Stop making bullshit excuses, Nora. Stop it. You can tell yourself whatever you want, but you can't tell me this. When you let me, I was a good lover. Sex and marriage? That's the package—there's no pulling them apart."

Isobel had lost her virginity earlier that year. The kid who played her younger sister had a brother who sometimes visited the set. He was a regular kid. His parents thought he might be a hockey star for a while, but then he never got good enough so they left Canada and put all their eggs into their daughter's basket, which, judging by the success of Isobel's fake kid sister, was probably a smart move. Anyhow, she'd seen him around for years and then last year he'd shown up with a mustache and a guitar and Isobel had let him get her drunk on wine coolers in her trailer.

She wasn't sure it counted as sex. They'd gotten undressed and he'd put his dick in her. Her mind was screaming, *I'm having sex, I'm having sex,* but part of her was nervous about the fact that he wasn't wearing a condom. When she asked him if he had protection, and that was the only word she could find to describe what she wanted to say to him, he pulled out and masturbated until he came on her breasts and stomach.

As she listened to her parents fight, the images from that almost sex night kept flashing in her head, only in her mind she kept replacing her mother with herself. It made her want to throw up to think of her parents having sex. To think of her mother having sex with someone else made her want to take out her eyes and stuff them in her ears. Instead, she took all the pillows from the cots and crawled underneath her cot. "Make it stop," she repeated a dozen times. Lizzie joined her and after a long while, Elyse left her post at the side door and lay down on top of the cot they were under. She leaned her head over the side to speak to them.

"It doesn't look good," Elyse said. "I think your mom's going to leave."

"And go where? Home? How do you know that?"

Elyse looked away from Isobel. The blood was rushing to her head, giving her face an odd purple coloring. "I heard your mom on the phone last weekend when I was down here. She talked to somebody she called 'honey boo' and then hung up and then called some airline to confirm her flight from here to Las Vegas."

"How could you not say anything?" Isobel asked. She punched the underside of the cot.

"I didn't understand what I was hearing, but now." Elyse stopped speaking and then after a moment of silence, pulled her head back up on top of the cot. "I know it looks bad. It's going to be bad but you'll get through it."

They heard a car pull into the gravel drive and honk.

"Tell her goodbye for me," Isobel's mother said. She opened the front door.

Isobel scrambled over Lizzie and burst out of the side porch and into the parlor. She raced into the living room in time to see her mother close the door. Her father stood a ways from the door, wearing only his swimming trunks and his glasses. His shoulders sagged in a way that she'd never noticed before. "Tell her yourself," she said, opening the door and stepping onto the front porch. The driver wrestled her mother's suitcases into the back of the cab while she sat sedately in the backseat, her attention focused on sorting through her purse.

Isobel strode to the cab and pounded on the window. Her mother glanced up and mouthed, "I don't have time for this."

The cabbie told her to stop banging on his car and shut the trunk. He got into the driver's side door and spoke with Isobel's mother before putting the car into drive and stepping on the gas pedal. Only when the car was in motion did her mother roll down the window. She held out an envelope addressed to Isobel, who took it and ripped it into several pieces. She took a few steps after the car and then stopped.

Her mother sighed and, leaning out the window, yelled as the car turned out of the driveway, "When you're older, you'll understand what I'm doing. Moms are people too."

As old as Isobel got, she never understood her mother's decision to leave. That day, after the sound of the cab's engine blended into the noise of the main street, she sat down in the gravel, unable to make herself return to the house. Her father, similarly broken, stayed on the porch crying. Isobel wished she could cry, but the emotion inside of her refused to break the surface. Instead she spoke about the shark's fin. Her words carried over the empty yard and bounced off the trees that lined the property. Around her, she felt Lizzie and Elyse picking up pieces of the envelope she'd torn and scattered. Their bodies moving close to hers, but leaving enough space so that she didn't feel the need to run.

She didn't know how long she sat in the gravel. When she was done talking about the shark, she'd started piling up the stones—seeing how many bits of rock she could stack on top of one another before they fell over. Her father stopped crying and went inside the house. From behind her she felt her cousins approach, their tread soft in the gravel. They reached down in a way that felt choreographed and linked their arms through hers, lifting her in one motion from the ground. For a moment she felt weightless. Then her feet touched the ground and several of the rock towers fell over. Those that didn't topple she kicked at and then smoothed her toe over the gravel until all the signs of a disturbance were leveled.

"We're going down to the beach," Lizzie said.

"Thought you should come with us," Elyse added.

For the first time Isobel could remember, the parking lot at the beach was empty. Large handwritten signs explained that the area had been closed due to shark sightings. There were a handful of other people on the beach—most of them had binoculars and were scanning the water for signs of the shark. Every ten minutes or so, the lifeguards played a prerecorded message reminding people to stay out of the water. The cousins laid out their towels and settled in. They exchanged little conversation—passing sun block when asked or offering the headphones when a favorite song played. The sun began to set and Isobel sat up watching its slow descent. The beach emptied, with the last lifeguard telling them to keep out of the water before he packed up and left.

When they were alone on the beach, Lizzie put down the book she'd been reading. "Feel like talking?"

"We could go for a swim," Elyse said. "I always feel better when I'm weightless—like all the stuff I'm worried about drifts off and leaves me alone."

As an answer, Isobel stood and took off the hoodie she'd been wearing over her suit and walked toward the water. Her cousins followed. They knew, without speaking of it, that they would be safe in the water—that after what had happened back at the house, there could be no more tragedy in their life. In the water, Isobel floated on her back and talked at the stars about her mother, about what she'd seen over the last few years and about what it meant now that she was gone. Her cousins listened and whatever she said, they agreed with her.

October 2012: Memphis

"I've never understood Columbus Day," Isobel said, staring at the enormous stack of pancakes in the middle of the table. For once everyone had the day off and Elyse had insisted on starting the day with a proper feast. "What exactly are we celebrating? It's not like he really discovered America. I mean, the people who were here, they knew it existed, right?"

T. J. nodded. "It's no stranger than Labor Day. If you ask me, people need a day off from work every now and then. Makes the job a little sweeter. Without good ol' Columbus and his three ships, we'd be staring at a long stretch of uninterrupted work days."

"Gift horse, mouth," Elyse said, setting the last of her cooking mess in the sink.

"I can't eat another bite," Lizzie said, pushing her plate away.

The half-finished kitchen made Isobel feel like she had an itch she couldn't scratch. In the last few weeks, she and T. J. had inspected the house from top to bottom looking for weaknesses that Benny had overlooked or covered up. The production crew had gathered enough material for the sizzle reel and retreated to the warmth of Los Angeles.

Elyse took an envelope from her pocket and slid it over to Lizzie. "There's nearly a thousand for the cookbooks," she said, gesturing to the empty shelves on the baker's rack. "The library is going to have me do some demonstrations next weekend with the waffle iron and talk about a few other historic ingredients."

"Good for you," Isobel said, marveling at how much growth her cousin had shown in the last few weeks. She wasn't sure what Landon had said to her, but whatever it was had given her the closure she'd been looking for.

"Maybe you should think about starting that ice cream and pie shop," Lizzie said, pocketing the envelope.

"How about you?" Isobel asked, looking at the dark circles under Lizzie's eyes. "How are you?" She and Elyse had expressed concern about Lizzie to each other in the weeks since Benny's firing and the discovery of the damage he'd done to the house. Lizzie had grown increasingly erratic in her behavior. She blamed it on the impending arrival of her parents, whom she refused to speak to on the phone, and on worries about money.

Despite this undercurrent of tumult, none of them spoke directly about what Benny had done, how Isobel had fired him, or about Lizzie's obvious distress. It was one of the benefits of being around people you'd known your whole life. With her cousins, she didn't need to provide context or background for her actions. They understood the unspoken and were able to act without being asked, like trapeze artists. The moment one of them went sailing into the open abyss, the other two were present with either outstretched arms or a safety net. Isobel wasn't sure which one Lizzie needed— maybe both.

"She's fine," T. J. said. He took Lizzie's hand and kissed the back of it.

"Ready?" Isobel asked T. J.

Today they were crawling underneath the house to inspect the floor joists and the plumbing although, since neither of them knew much about plumbing, she didn't know what they'd be looking for. If she didn't feel so damn guilty about firing Benny, she'd let T. J. crawl under the house himself and she'd spend the day putting the cabinets back on and installing the shelving above the sink.

He nodded. "You probably want to put on long sleeves and thicker pants. I'm not sure what's down there. At the very least ants, at the very worst raw sewage."

Like many houses in Memphis, Spite House didn't have a basement. Instead it sat on a raised cement foundation with a crawl space underneath. Isobel adjusted her headlamp and watched T. J. shimmy his way into the narrow space. They'd left Lizzie and Elyse painting the second floor of the house, which felt safe now that they'd been over the roof to make sure there weren't any more unrepaired leaks. "Do you think Benny even went down here?" she asked.

"Hard to say. I do know you all were out of town when the plumbing repair was done, so it seems like we should check the work."

"I guess so," Isobel said. The dirt felt cold and for the first time in her life, she realized why people had root cellars. She let T. J. get ahead of her and looked up at the subfloor, trying to guess what part of the house they were in. The entry to the crawl space was on the back end of the house, underneath the large windows. Her line of sight was interrupted only by a few cement footings and the distance the light from her headlamp would travel. T. J. had crawled off toward what Isobel guessed was the kitchen area. She moved to where the house narrowed, inspecting the space where Elton and Benny had found the hidden room.

"Where are we at with the judge?" she asked, breathing in the musky air.

Although she hadn't talked to him directly about the issues that had arisen with the occupancy permit, Lizzie had told them that an investment group headed by the city's former mayor had been interested in developing the empty property next door. Once T. J. had been removed as their inspector because of his relationship with Lizzie, they had an old friend who worked in code enforcement take over and he made it his business to remove any obstacle they might have—including Spite House.

"He's backed off. Judge Hootley never could stand Mayor Tortinger. So that helped you guys." T. J.'s voice echoed as if they were in a tunnel. "I told Lizzie that her family might not have to worry about it this year, but that at some point when the financial incentives were high enough, they'd have to fight to keep the place. They should sell it now and get out before that happens."

"I doubt they ever would," Isobel said, listening to the echo of her own voice.

"Damn it," T. J. said. "Damn it."

"Something bad?" she asked, trying to back out of the narrow passageway. "Something expensive?"

"Those shoddy plumbers Benny hired cut into the floor supports to run the new pipe."

Her heart sank at the thought of the time and money it would take to add additional joists to the floor. "Does the pipe look good at least?"

"I'm afraid I'm going to have to tear up your beautiful kitchen tile," T. J. said. He fished around in the toolbox he'd pushed through the crawl space and then hammered a nail up through the floor. He crawled back toward the entrance. "You coming?"

"I'm going to keep looking," she said. "Don't do anything to that floor until I get out of here."

He grunted and shimmied his way out of the crawl space. Isobel started to follow him but instead found herself crawling along the southern exterior wall toward the front of the house. Her headlamp was less effective in this portion of the crawl space because of the adjacent building that blocked any light from filtering in through the small access gaps. Her father had insisted that his children create structurally correct buildings from their Legos or Lincoln Logs. How mystified other children had been watching her snap together floor joists and footings. Sometimes these buildings sat for months on their kitchen table, a visual reminder of the permanence of strong foundations. And then her mother, with a carelessness they never expected, would sweep the houses, apartments, skyscrapers, and log cabins into a large plastic storage bin.

The floor beneath the stairwell sagged and her head scraped against the unexpected change in elevation. She flattened herself to the floor and then rolled onto her back to inspect the subflooring. Above her, she heard the doorbell and then T. J.'s heavy step as he walked from the kitchen to the front of the house. She couldn't hear the exchange of voices, but wondered, as dust floated down, the specks illuminated and made into spots of brilliance in the glare of her headlamp, who it could be. What was it they said? That dust was mostly dead skin. She pushed against the warped floorboards. There was almost no give—as if whatever heavy load had been pressing on the boards all these years remained. Puzzling over what it could be, she became aware of a stench and the feeling of something wet against her back. Slowly, she rolled back onto her stomach and pulled up onto her hands and knees, backing away from the spot where she'd been lying. At the edge of where her light reached, she glimpsed a bit of movement and leaned forward to make it out. Maggots crawled over the remains of a dead rat.

She screamed.

Above her, feet pounded on the boards at the same time that she scrambled backward as fast as she could move on her hands and knees. Coming to the exit of the space, she clawed at her shirt and pulled it over her head, afraid to even look at the wet spot on the back of the shirt. Instead she threw it aside and crawled over to a patch of grass, rubbing her back against it as if she were a dog trying to scratch an itch. "Get it off, get it off, get it off," she said, pounding her fists against the ground and fighting the urge to throw up.

"What happened?" T. J. asked, standing above her.

"Are you okay?" Tom asked, crouching beside her. "Are you hurt?"

"Dead rat," she gasped, realizing as the feeling of wanting to retch passed that she wore only her bra and a pair of jeans. She sat up and crossed her arms over her chest.

"I got off work early and wanted to see if you were free for a late lunch," Tom said, taking off his hoodie and passing it to her. T. J. pretended to be interested in the view from the backyard.

She nodded, trying to think of anything other than the rat.

"We're about done," T. J. said. "I've got to find a way to sister the two joints that the plumbers cut into—"

"I can get my dad to do it when he comes out for Thanksgiving," Isobel said. She knew that Lizzie felt strange about T. J.'s putting too much into Spite

House—partly because he worked for the same unit that had been giving them such a hard time and partly because he and Lizzie hadn't worked out whether their relationship had a future.

As if reading their minds, Lizzie stepped onto the porch and asked what all the screaming had been about. Elyse showed up a few seconds later, a paint brush still in hand. "Are you okay? We heard you screaming, and I thought you'd been stabbed."

"I can't even talk about it," Isobel said. "You'll have to get T. J. to explain it to you. I'm taking a break—but first a long hot shower."

Tom's face reddened at the mention of her bathing. They'd taken the physical part of their relationship slow. It wasn't like he hadn't seen her with her shirt off, but they hadn't yet slept together, and Isobel wasn't sure they would. She'd felt over the last few weeks that he was withholding something from her. "Want some help around here?" he asked T. J.

"I'll only be a few minutes," Isobel said, walking into the house. Behind her everyone started to discuss the issue with the flooring, each of them assuring the others that tearing up the kitchen floor to get to the subfloor would be the last option. She walked by the stairwell, running her hand along the enclosed space and considering how she could open it without doing too much damage to the wall. There didn't appear to be an obvious point of entry. It would be another problem for her to solve.

After her shower, she picked up the pile of clothing she'd dropped on the floor, which included Tom's sweatshirt. Thinking it might be contaminated by the rat guts she'd had on her back, she carried it downstairs to the washing machine, emptying the pockets of everything out of habit. She pulled out a matchbox car and two ticket stubs from the local movie theater. Glancing at them as she started the washer, she paused. They were from an earlier showing that day. She was sure he'd said he'd be busy with work most of the day.

"You about ready?" he called from the bottom of the stairs.

Not sure what to do, Isobel dropped the ticket stubs and the car into the washing machine and closed the lid. Whatever it was he was keeping from her would come out eventually. That was about the only lesson being in Hollywood had taught her.

"What exactly are you looking for?" Elyse asked, following Isobel as she moved the electronic stud finder along the base of the stairwell.

"I need an opening," she said. "But it has to be between the studs or I'll end up making everything worse. It's what I do."

"You have to stop feeling bad," Elyse said. She rapped her knuckles against the wall. "Isn't this how people used to do it? Listen for the sound to change?"

"That's for secret passageways," Isobel said. "You know, as if you were Nancy Drew."

"I am Nancy. Didn't you hear about my work with the clock tower?" Elyse asked, holding her hand up as if she were peering through a magnifying glass. In the last few weeks, Elyse had regained some of the weight she'd lost during the Landon fiasco. The pounds looked good on her, as did her hair, now that it had grown out a little.

"This is exactly the sort of house Nancy would wander into."

"We've even got our own mystery," Elyse said.

"That we do," Isobel said, taking a pencil from her pocket and marking a small "x" on the wall. Unlike the rest of the walls, which were horizontally laid poplar, the stairwell had been skim coated and covered in ornate wallpaper. Initially, Isobel had hoped to enter the space beneath the stairs through the kitchen, but she'd had to rule it out because it was where the HVAC had run the vents for the air conditioning. The green and gold wallpaper would be impossible to replicate, but as beautiful as it was, it did show its age, with a few seams split and the corner near the far wall peeling.

"Have I told you my theory on that yet?"

Isobel stopped and then restarted her scan for the next stud. "What theory?"

"About Benny?"

"I don't want to talk about Benny."

Elyse leaned in and lowered her voice. "Not even about him being Lizzie's dad?"

Isobel dropped the stud finder. "No."

"I'm not sure, sure, but it makes more sense than anything else. Think about it."

"No," she said again, leaning against the wall and then sliding down to the floor. "Talk me through it."

While Elyse explained her theory, Isobel half listened to her and half thought about all of her interactions with Benny—trying to figure out if he'd ever dropped any hints of his own. Elyse's hypothesis was based on three points. The first that he knew Lizzie's mom when she got pregnant, the second that Lizzie's mom had stayed in touch with Benny and had in fact suggested him to renovate the house, even though he was terrible. The final point had to do with Benny's hands—Elyse felt they were almost exactly the same as Lizzie's. There were other reasons too, but most of those relied on Elyse's interpretation of the behavior of Benny toward Lizzie. "He treats her differently than you and me," she said. "You know, like he worries about her more, thinks she needs help. And why else would he go to all the trouble with the house? He's desperate to stay in Lizzie's life."

"Or he was desperate to figure out a way to keep getting a paycheck," Isobel said.

"I'm right," Elyse said.

Isobel banged her head against the wall. It returned a reverberation, which at first she didn't consider. Her mind filled with the possible ramifications of Benny being Lizzie's father. She couldn't see any upside to it. Benny had six other children by three different women. He didn't see any of them often, he drank too much, and he was bad at his job. There was nothing of a father in him. "I don't know," she said, banging her head again—her subconscious telling her there was something wrong with the wall.

"I'm sure," Elyse said. "I just don't know what to do about it."

"Nothing." Isobel knelt and faced the wall, pushing against the lower portion where her head had rested. In that particular spot it felt more like wood than plaster.

"We can't do nothing."

Not knowing what to say, Isobel concentrated on the wall. Elyse sounded like she was talking about more than Lizzie's situation. Her words had echoes of all that had happened that year in the house. "Do you see this?" she asked, putting her hands on the wall and pressing so that the area where she pushed bowed in.

"Weird," Elyse said, pushing with her. "Let me try something."

Placing her fingers on it, as she would on a Ouija board, Elyse pushed firmly in each direction. When she pushed to the left, the wall slid open and a faint musty smell entered the hallway. They sat back and looked at the opening, which was about the size of a dog door.

"We need a light," Isobel said.

Without a word, Elyse hurried down the hall and returned a few moments later with Isobel's headlight and a flashlight. "What a strange house this is," she said, turning on her flashlight and directing it inside the opening. "You seen this before?"

"Never," Isobel said, leaning her head inside the space. The interior didn't look much different from other areas she'd seen under stairs. Some were enclosed and some open. This particular space had an unfinished quality—subflooring and studs behind the plaster. She crawled partway into the space, wondering what it could have been that warped the floor.

"Are you sure that's safe?" Elyse asked, trying to shine her flashlight around Isobel's body. "I think I see stuff back in the corner."

Isobel crawled completely inside the space. The rear portion of the secret room was stacked nearly to the ceiling with boxes. She looked up, trying to gauge the distance from the floor to the top of the stairs. It was tall enough for her to stand, although she had to be careful because of the uneven spacing of the subfloor. She realized that from underneath the house, the stacks of boxes that nearly filled the space had fooled her into thinking the area had finished flooring. The boxes were wooden, and tufts of straw-like material poked out of the sides and tops.

"Should we open one?" Elyse asked, having joined Isobel in the small space.

"Maybe we should wait for Lizzie," Isobel said even as she reached for the nearest box. The top had been nailed shut and there were no markings on the side of the container.

"Let's at least take it out into the light," Elyse said.

Isobel bent to lift the box and then called her cousin over to help. It was heavy enough that they ended up sliding it out of the secret doorway instead of carrying it. Despite all the movement, the box gave no indication of its contents. In the comparative brightness of the hallway, the box looked smaller and older than it had in the stairwell.

"We ought to wait," Isobel said, running her fingernail along the top edge of the box, checking to see if any portion of it was loose.

Elyse took a photo of the box next to the opening and sent it to Lizzie. "Let's see what she says."

They stared at the box for a few moments. "You really think Benny's her father?" Isobel asked when the silence between them had become oppressive.

"It makes as much sense as anything else."

"But why wouldn't her mom have told her? He's not dangerous or absent. I'm not sure the secrecy makes any sense if he's her dad."

"But he's a disappointment. Think about it. After all these years of not knowing, it would be such a let-down to find out your father was a drunk with scores of illegitimate children. And besides, you know how religious her parents are. What's she going to say to the younger kids?"

"I'm not convinced," Isobel said. "Are you going to tell her your theory?"

"Don't know yet."

"I wouldn't. Not without being sure."

Elyse reached out and pushed at the box with her toe. "Wanna shake it? See if we can figure out what's inside?"

They put their ears to the box and wiggled it—tipping it one way and then the other. Up close, the box smelled like musty books and beeswax. Isobel thought that Elyse was wrong about Benny, but she didn't know what her cousin knew. Elyse had always been better at listening to other people's conversations, especially adult conversations, and who knows what she'd heard over the years that made her believe that Benny could be Lizzie's father.

"We should ask Benny. If he didn't sleep with Lizzie's mom, then he can't be her father."

"Are you going to ask him?" Elyse asked.

"We could ask her mother," Isobel said, trying to think of the last time she'd spoken to Aunt Annie.

"I think we should tell her." Elyse paused to slide her phone out of her pocket and then continued. "Otherwise it'll seem like we're going behind her back."

"Are you still pissed about something?" Isobel had learned through the years that Elyse's resentments and annoyances surfaced on her face the way gold settled to the bottom of the pan.

Her phone buzzed back immediately with a text message. "Lizzie says we should open it. She can't leave practice for another hour." Elyse tried to pry off the lid with her fingers and then slid her car key into a small opening and tried to use it as leverage.

"I'll get a crowbar," Isobel said, heading toward the kitchen, where they'd let the tools pile up in the last few weeks. She didn't find a crowbar, but she did find a large hammer with an extended claw on the back of its head.

"No, I've almost got this," Elyse said.

In the two months since the wedding, Elyse had worked through much of her obsession. Isobel wasn't sure if it was the frank talk she'd had with Landon or if she was seeing a therapist in secret. Lizzie thought that something about being in the house had helped her to realize that for a life to be good, it didn't have to be big. They hadn't addressed it directly with Elyse for the same reason you don't talk to a man crossing a tightrope. When she was on the other side of processing the drama of Landon and Daphne, she'd bring it up and all of them could laugh about how sneaky Lizzie and Isobel had been. They'd stolen her phone, sent messages from her, and then kidnapped her. All in the name of helping her save face.

When she returned, Elyse was sheepishly trying to fish the remains of her car key, house key, and work key out of the box. "Damn it, damn it, damn it," she said, not making eye contact.

"You should've stopped when you broke the first one," Isobel said, trying not to laugh, but failing.

"Don't even say it," Elyse said, falling into laughter with Isobel. The prospect of opening the box had made them giddy.

Crouching down, Isobel slipped the claw end of the hammer into the top edge of the box where they'd found a small space between the top of the box and the lid. She put one foot on the box and leaned all her weight on the hammer. The nails groaned as if they were being tortured, a few of them letting out squeals of protest. The lid inched up. Isobel changed positions and tried from another corner of the box. On the third try, the nails gave way entirely with a suddenness that sent Isobel sprawling backward.

Elyse scrambled to the box and pulled out the straw-like strips that served as packing material. She pulled out several wooden boxes imprinted with dark writing. Each of them took one and fiddled with them until the tops slid away. "What is it?" she asked, holding up a bottle for Elyse's inspection. "Whiskey?"

They puzzled over the labels on the bottles, each of them using their phones to try to figure out exactly what they'd found. "Jack Daniel's I've heard of," Isobel said, running her finger over the label. "But who the hell is Geo A. Dickel? And what is sour mash whiskey?"

It wasn't until Lizzie arrived home a few hours later with T. J. in tow that they fully uncovered the mystery of the liquor. It turned out George Dickel was a lesser-known maker of fine Tennessee whiskey. The four of them sat around the kitchen table staring at the bottle, trying to decide whether they should drink it. They'd gone through the other boxes and determined that whatever it was they'd found, there were at least a hundred bottles of the stuff—all of it from 1908. Lizzie's best guess was that her grandfather had stored the liquor away when Tennessee stopped making its own liquor in advance of the national prohibition and then hidden it in the house as he built it.

The question they asked themselves over and over as the night unfolded was what the bottles would be worth. T. J. thought they were mostly worthless and that they'd be lucky to get $50 a bottle from the few collectors who were interested in history. Elyse felt the value was higher—pointing out that the value of wine increased with age. In the end, they'd gotten out the handful of jelly jars that hadn't broken when the cabinet fell and poured themselves shots of the whiskey.

Isobel leaned over and smelled her glass. It had the scent of burned wood and maple syrup. She mostly drank wine and was unprepared for the burn that jumped from her stomach to her throat after she'd swallowed it. Only Elyse and T. J. took the shots in stride. Lizzie, who almost never drank, doubled over coughing after the first shot and then sipped at her second shot the rest of the night. After a moment the burning subsided, replaced by the faint aftertaste of brown sugar and nuts. They drank another and then again, toasting one another and figuring that, at the least, Lizzie could make a couple thousand off the stash of whiskey.

About the time that Isobel began to feel unsteady on her feet, her phone rang. It took her a moment to recognize the area code as being from California and before she answered, she hushed everyone. It was true what they said, if you wanted a thing too much, it hid from you, and the moment you stopped wanting it, the thing that you wanted most showed up. Craig's voice on the other end of the line sounded like he was across the ocean instead of across the country.

"I've got good news—two networks interested in seeing a pilot and enough investors to fund the thing."

With her entire body warmed from the inside out, Isobel lost all apprehension. She screamed in happiness and before Craig understood what had happened, he'd been put on speakerphone in the middle of the table.

"Tell them," Isobel said.

"Are you there?" Craig asked. "Have we been cut off?"

"No, no. We're all here. I want you to tell them."

All around her, the people she loved most in the world raised their glasses of hundred-year-old whiskey and toasted the possibility that everything would work out in the end.

November 2012: Memphis

"**A**re you sure you aren't bothered by the cameras?" Isobel asked Tom. He hadn't even blinked twice the first time she showed up at the home improvement store trailed by Jake and the rest of the crew, which had grown to nearly a dozen people this time around. But now they were on a date—or what passed for a date on reality television.

"What cameras?" Tom asked, holding her purse while she slid into the green booth.

"Don't talk about the cameras," Kitty said. The sound girl had indeed been promoted to field producer for the pilot, which they'd sold to the investors and the studio as *Southern Bel*. Of course the fact that no one had ever shortened Isobel's name to Bel didn't concern Craig. "It's a concept," he'd said to her. "Nothing's set in stone." He had however insisted that everyone call her Bel, which made for lots of stuttering as the cousins and Tom got used to the forced nickname.

Isobel sat down. "Is this a local place?" she asked, looking around the restaurant, which was in the only part of Memphis that reminded Isobel of the West Coast. Tom took his seat—or rather he expanded into the space, looking at home in the restaurant as he did everywhere.

"You come here a lot?" she asked.

"Enough," he said, handing her a greasy plastic-coated menu. She didn't understand how he could be so comfortable in his own skin. Lizzie thought it might be because he spent his weekends on stage with that band of his, but Elyse said it was because his parents were still together.

"Why the band?" she asked. The point of this outing had been to establish that they were dating—for the show. Craig had talked to her about making sure the conversation covered their backgrounds because it would make it easier to set Tom up as a character.

"Youngest child," he said, shrugging.

"Me, too," she said, raising her diet soda in a mock toast to an accomplishment neither one of them had any say in. "What does that mean? We're immature brats who'll fight over who gets the most attention?"

"Nah," he said. "Or rather only if we're ever on stage together—there'd be a fight."

"I'd win," Isobel said, wondering what sort of band he had. Lizzie told her that in Memphis music flowed out of the Mississippi and into everyone's veins: having a band was like saying you restored old cars. It was what people did in their spare time. Still, she wasn't convinced it was a hobby until Tom got out of his car to pick her up for their date. Instead of wearing a T-shirt or other merchandise advertising his band, he had on a short-sleeved button-down that was tight in a way that indicated vanity about his looks. The restaurant was a local burger chain—known for its buttered buns and cluttered décor. They encouraged people to write on the walls, and at the booth where they sat, thousands of people had autographed the plaster or scrawled bits of wisdom. They took turns reading them to each other while they waited for their food.

"For a good time call your vibrator," she said.

"Here's one. 'Be careful, I bite.'"

"Mrs. Looper is a pooper."

He laughed the loudest at that. "That's something Bobby would write."

"Bobby?"

Tom looked away from her, and then the waitress arrived with their food. He showed her how to put the toothpick in her straw and launch it at the ceiling where thousands of others had landed, their cellophane flags making the tiled ceiling look like a map of places people had been.

"How does a thing like that start?"

He reached across the table and held her hand. "How does anything start?"

She lowered her eyes and then took a bite of the burger. What was between them felt different from most of the other dates she'd been on. She didn't know if it was because he was different or because of who she allowed herself to be in Memphis. For one thing, she'd never once sucked in her stomach when she saw him. In getting to know him at the home improvement store, there'd always been a context for their conversations. She'd ask him about the grit on sandpaper or the best glue for pipes and then if they ran out of things to talk about, she could bring up insulation or light fixtures. Mostly they hadn't run out of conversation.

She tried to picture him in his other life—performing on stage. Not that she knew much about it. He had the sort of face that would always look younger than he was—at least unless he lost his hair. What beautiful hair he had, a sandy blond color and always somehow looking as if he were two weeks overdue for a cut. He reached for his soda, and she scooted forward in her seat so that their legs touched. His feet tapped out a rhythm that she felt under the table as his knees moved up and down to the song in his head.

"No, really. Tell me about your band?" It felt artificial to ask him, but Craig had wanted to establish that theirs was a new relationship, so he'd told them to go over stuff and pretend like it was a first date, even though it wasn't. Tom had agreed without really agreeing.

"You know, I sing and stuff," he said and then pushed aside his empty burger basket and leaned across the table, drawing her into a kiss. It felt more private than it ought to because her hair created a curtain around them. He smelled like lemons.

"Oh," she said when he pulled back. Two of the cameramen and Kitty with her damn mic had moved in so close that Tom accidentally elbowed one of them in the back when he slid back to his seat.

"I like you," he said.

It made her want to kiss him again. Instead, she looked around the restaurant to see what sort of interest their display had drawn. A few tables from their booth, several college-age students had their heads together whispering. They looked up at their table and then returned to a heated discussion. Of course they'd drawn attention. Isobel told people she hated to be stared at, but it wasn't true. The cameras made it more obvious that she was someone other than an ordinary person. "I think I've been recognized," she said, discreetly pointing out the table.

Tom nodded. "Part of the job, huh?"

"Kind of hard not to be, given all of this," she indicated the crew without actually pointing them out.

"Can we go out after this? There's a—"

"Excuse me." They were interrupted by one of the girls from the other table.

"Of course," Isobel said, turning toward her, ready to sign whatever it was she wanted, and also to talk a bit about what it had been like to be on the show. Girls this age typically wanted to talk about how they'd been awkward and how much they'd loved seeing her transform on the show. This girl was pretty though, and Isobel couldn't imagine her ever going through an awkward stage.

"No, no," the girl blushed and tugged at the hem of her shirt, which had the image of a nut silkscreened on it. "I'm sorry—I was trying to—it's just that I was there last night and I—"

Tom took the sharpie the girl had in her outstretched hand. "You want me to sign the shirt?"

The girl nodded. Isobel eyed the logo that distorted itself over the girl's large breasts. *Fat Squirrels.* She leaned forward. "It's easier to sign on the back," Tom said, putting his hand on the girl's waist and nudging her slightly so that she turned around. "Mind your hair."

The girl gathered her long black hair in her hand and then giggled as Tom touched the pen to her shirt and scrawled out his name. Across the room, her friends hooted at her. When he was done, he touched the girl's shoulder and thanked her for coming to the show. "I haven't missed one," she said and bounded back to her table.

"I guess you're the famous one." Isobel fumbled with her purse, wanting to get enough cash out to pay for their date. It seemed important that she remain in control. She dropped two twenties on the table and bolted, moving so fast that the crew didn't realize she was leaving until she'd stepped out the front door and onto the sidewalk.

In the time it took her to draw two deep breaths, Tom was out on the sidewalk with her. "Hey, hey," he said.

"Who are you?" she asked.

"Can we ditch them?" he asked, taking her elbow and steering her toward his car. On the ride over, Jake and Kitty had been in the backseat, filming their pre-date chatter, which had mostly concerned the work they needed to do to finish the kitchen.

Isobel hesitated. She should say yes and jump in the car with Tom, but it would be foolish to piss off Craig and the crew for a few moments of private conversation. She dug her heels into the ground. "I can't. I—"

"Really?" he crossed his arms.

"Another time."

The skin around his eyes and his mouth tightened. "I don't want to talk about it in front of the cameras. I like you and anything I say about the band will make it seem like I don't like you and you've got a dozen reasons not to like me. Most of which you don't even know yet."

"Like what?" she asked, afraid of what answers he might give. And yet she wanted to know who Bobby was and why he was often vague about where he was during their time apart.

He looked at the door to the restaurant.

"This isn't how I wanted to do this." He ran his fingers through his hair, pulling on the ends. "I have a kid. I'm a recovering alcoholic. I knew who you were the moment you first wandered into the store and I pretended I didn't because I wanted you to think more of me."

The door opened and the crew stepped out into the street. Kitty missed the step and stumbled, one of her shoes sliding off her foot and clattering into

430 • COURTNEY MILLER SANTO

the street. Why on earth was that girl wearing heels? She looked like a toddler with lipstick. Isobel looked at Kitty, trying to figure out what else was different about her. She felt the heat of Tom's body next to hers. Isobel thought about the matchbox car she'd found in his sweatshirt and the movie tickets. Part of her had thought it was another woman, another date, but she hadn't asked him. Now she wanted to ask him about his kid, but she knew that anything said with the crew around would be put on film and used when the moment was right. A good editor could do wonders with scenes. What had happened in the restaurant could be made funny or romantic. They could make Tom look like a dick or a nice guy. It depended on which way their story went. Isobel wished she could see the future, wished she could know how their story would turn out. She grabbed his hand and squeezed.

"Sorry," she said to Jake, who she knew was giving her the stink eye behind the camera lens. She still needed him on her side with the show. As much as she trusted Jake, she'd come to loathe Craig.

She let Tom open her car door for her.

He slid into the driver's seat and took several deep breaths before starting the car. "Isobel—I mean Bel," he said. "It'll be fine. Just fine."

Behind her, Jake and another crew member entered the car, adjusting their equipment to make the transition appear seamless. Tom settled himself in the driver's seat and turned on the car. Then, because she wanted to let Tom know that she understood what he was trying to say, she put her hand on his thigh and squeezed. "I think you'll like my dad," she said, raising her voice so it would be clearly heard over the car's engine and the shuffling of feet and bodies. "He's sort of a jack of all trades and way back when, before he had any of us children or got married or got divorced, he played keyboards in his college band."

"So long as he doesn't play the accordion, we'll get along fine," Tom said, taking up her hand and massaging the back of it as they drove.

Attention, she thought, leaning her head against the window. It felt like a force that needed a formula. If Newton had been a youngest child instead of an oldest, surely he'd have discovered the law of attention, which identified the amount of attention needed as inversely related to one's capacity to feel loved. It became more apparent every day that this particular television show was a bad idea. In fact, the whole idea of her trying to remain an actress was probably a bad idea. But having those cameras around closed up the vacuous hole inside her that craved attention. And yet she wasn't

432 • COURTNEY MILLER SANTO

an extrovert. The paradox of Isobel was that while she preferred to be in the corner hiding from people, whenever she found herself there, she got mad because nobody was paying her any attention.

"You should be talking," Jake said from the backseat.

Kitty murmured agreement and shifted through a notebook she'd been carrying around. "Talk about Thanksgiving," she said. "We don't have anything on that yet."

"Thanksgiving it is," Tom said.

Isobel felt the attention on her as they talked, and the heat of the camera acted faster than all the shots of whiskey they'd drunk when they found the stash to ease her mind about all she didn't know of her own future.

In preparation for Isobel's father's coming, Craig had asked to talk to each of the cousins about their fathers. As the crew had filmed them over the last week, a story slowly emerged. It was strange to think of reality shows as having writers, but they did. Someone back in California, a woman named Beverly, looked at the footage they'd shot and read through the production notes. It was her job to try to make a story out of the raw material they sent. She'd decided, according to Craig, that the arc should focus on the visit of Isobel's father.

The day before her father arrived, the production crew transformed the front closet into a sort of private confessional. Craig followed Isobel around the house, giving her the highlights of what Beverly thought should happen.

"We should start with a scene of you embracing on the porch."

"He's not going to call me Bel or really do anything you tell him to do," she said to Craig. "I want you to know that right off."

Craig crossed his arms when she protested. He listened and then continued giving her notes, which included the fact that they weren't finding her relationship with Tom believable. "We need to understand why the two of you are together. Find a way to have him save a cat or whatever it is that would make him likable."

He finished with Isobel and went in search of her cousins, presumably to give them their stories as determined by the all-knowing Beverly. Jake pulled her aside and said he had an idea he wanted to talk over with her outside of work. It rattled her because she didn't know how to take it. At first she was afraid he was hitting on her, but then he handed her his business card—one that wasn't for Craig's company but that read *Jake Left Productions*. She agreed to coffee after they were done filming the pilot.

Before beginning the confessionals, Craig made what amounted to a speech. "Reality is a tricky business. Or rather, capturing reality is a tricky business. I want each of you to be as honest as possible, but make sure that you talk to the camera. Don't talk to Jake—he doesn't care, don't talk to Kitty, even though she'll be asking the questions, and don't think too much, just talk."

Isobel avoided looking at her cousins. She knew that what Craig was saying felt sleazy and managed, but she also knew it was true. "I don't know if this is a long-term project for us," Lizzie said.

Craig waved her concern away, already processing his next thoughts. "We're going to pretend like we've already got money in the bank on this project. That's how much I believe in it. If you say something I can't use in the pilot, I'll save it and use it in the second or even, hell, tenth, episode."

Crossing her arms, Isobel sat down on the chair they'd dragged into the hall closet. The battery pack for the microphone dug into her back, and she shifted until she was comfortable. It was good to remember that all of this, even what she said during the time they were getting ready to tape, could be used in the show. Her words rang back in her ears. She should find a way to explain that to Elyse and Lizzie, who were talking in low voices in the hallway while Kitty and Jake finished setting up.

Kitty checked the lighting and adjusted the glare around Isobel's face. The room felt overheated, and the seat, because of its metal frame, was uncomfortably warm. The first few questions were about Isobel's family. She walked them through the overall happiness of her family and tried to skirt the issue of her mother's having abandoned the family for a semiprofessional surfboarder she'd met at an audition Isobel had gone on. Kitty pushed her about her mother, asking how it had felt to have her father become the primary parent during the last years she worked on the television show. Taken one after another, the questions and her answers felt banal, but in her mind, she pictured the way Craig would find an old clip of her from *Wait for It* looking sad and then they'd find some Facebook photo of her mother and Chip. Or even just Chip. And over all of these images would be Isobel's voice flatly discussing what it had been like without her mother in her life. "In the end I didn't miss her," she said. "That's the kind of guy my dad is. Capable of being two parents if needed—you know like those emperor penguins who sit on the egg when the mother goes away."

Isobel was so wrapped up in thinking about her mother that she didn't register the change in topic as it was asked. It wasn't until she saw Kitty's body, which had been relaxed and fluid as she held the boom mic, tighten that she realized Craig had taken over asking the questions and had moved her into dangerous territory.

"Did you guys view Benny as a father figure?"

"A father figure? Benny?"

Craig stared at Isobel and then raised two fingers, motioning for her to continue speaking.

"We're grown women. I'm not sure we're looking for fathers."

Craig's lips tightened into a thin line. He crossed and uncrossed his legs and seemed to read over several of his questions before selecting the next one. "Did Benny get fired because it would save you money?"

"No," Isobel said. Craig's head tilted in a way that indicated he needed her to incorporate the question into her answer. "I fired Benny because he'd become a liability. His work had become dangerous. The question of money didn't enter into it—although I'm sure it'll help not to have to pay a drunk to take naps in his RV."

She smiled at Craig, working out what it was that he'd been after. She figured he was trying to find a way to make Benny sympathetic.

"I think we've got what we need," Kitty said after a few wrapping-up questions. She turned and invited Lizzie to sit where Isobel had been, hurrying her cousin into position. The speed with which they moved meant that Isobel wouldn't be able to warn Lizzie to stay away from any questions they asked about her father. Lizzie didn't know that they knew about her stepfather not being her real father. That had been such a huge mistake on her part, to tell Craig that in the first place.

They didn't ask Lizzie directly about her father. They followed the same line of questioning they had with Isobel, asking if Benny had become like a father to the women. Lizzie was stiff and awkward answering the questions. She had a look on her face as if she'd shown up at the right place but the wrong time. Isobel couldn't put her finger on what was wrong with the situation. She felt relief when they all got through their interviews without incident, although she couldn't shake the heaviness that had settled on her shoulders as she watched Lizzie in her interview.

Isobel's father stood out in a crowd. Not because of how he looked, which was exactly ordinary, but because of the way he held himself. Faced with uncomfortable situations (and waiting on the curb for his daughter to pick him up fell squarely into the category of awkward), he stood as he had in military college. It looked as though he were trying to get his shoulder blades to touch each other—his rigidness mediated only by the way the wind tousled his hair. Since her mother had left, her father had never figured out how to get a haircut when he needed one.

Rolling down the passenger window, Isobel honked, waved, and called out, but he only acknowledged her when she pulled the car up directly in front of him. "Such fuss," he said, tossing his carry-on bag into the backseat. "I told you I could take a cab."

"Memphis isn't a town you take a cab in," she said, leaning over the seat to hug him.

"It's been too long," he said. "I'm used to seeing you for monthly Sunday dinners"

"I know," she said, trying once again to find a reasonable explanation for her decision to abandon L.A. for the South. Coming up blank, she offered what she had at the beginning. "Lizzie needs us."

"I wish you were as close with your brothers as you are with your cousins. They miss you."

It wasn't that Isobel didn't miss her brothers, it was that their lives mystified her. With full-time jobs and families, their worlds revolved around commitments she couldn't understand. Often when she was with them, she felt as if they spoke a foreign language.

"Wait till you see the house." Isobel reached over and tugged at her father's seatbelt to remind him to use it.

"I'm more interested in you."

"Don't say it, Dad."

He rubbed his hands on his jeans, as if wiping them off. "I can't help myself. You have so much more talent than you know and you're wasting it. No, that's not right, squandering."

"It's not a waste of anything," she said, putting her blinker on after she'd already exited the interstate. "Lizzie needed the money for the house and, frankly, I needed the exposure."

"That's what I'm talking about. You don't need exposure, you should get out of the television business. Try your hand at one of the million other things you're good at."

"Like what, Dad?"

He looked out his window as Spite House came into view. "What a house. I've always said anything that makes you look twice is worth twice as much."

She looked, trying to see it through his eyes. They'd managed to make the place beautiful with the work they'd been doing. Lovely curtains hung on all of the balconies and the small but beautiful door had been painted a dark green. Jake, followed by Kitty, stepped onto the front porch. "You ready?" she asked.

They'd had to coax him into being on camera. Isobel would've been happy to leave him out of it, but Craig was intent on making the point that after all that had happened in Isobel's life, she was ultimately her father's daughter. Part of the compromise to get him to do the show had been to agree to film his arrival at the house, not at the airport. Being made a fuss over in public would have been too much for her father.

Stepping out of the car, he turned to Isobel. "So, let me get this straight, we're having Thanksgiving today, even though it isn't for two more days."

"Right, Daddy. They need to let the crew go home to their own celebrations."

Neither one of them were mic'd yet, so Isobel didn't worry about their conversation as they walked up the set of concrete stairs. Her father had only a duffle bag for a carry-on, and he handled it as if he were a college kid unconcerned about its contents.

"Are we doing it over again on Thursday?"

"Nah, probably leftovers. I think Lizzie and Elyse are eating with T. J.'s family. Rosa May invited us too, but selfishly I want you all to myself."

"You girls need to get married, start families of your own," her father said.

"It isn't like that, not for any of us except Lizzie and I don't think—" Isobel stopped speaking when she saw the overhead mic stretch out over their heads. She wrapped her arm around her father in a sideways hug and laughed. He stiffened next to her and turned his head, as if he couldn't figure out where to focus his attention.

"Act like we're not here," Jake said from behind the camera.

"Maybe talk about how the house looks the same or different. Or Isobel—has she changed since you saw her last?"

The silence thickened around them and then her father cleared his throat. "It looks like you've got a rotted soffit here."

Isobel blinked back tears. Her father's fallback had always been to talk about the flaws he could fix. "Oh, Daddy, you have no idea."

The crew filmed them replacing the rotten board on the underside of the porch roof for about thirty minutes. Lizzie joined them as they were finishing up. "They're making Elyse nervous," she said. "I think she wants them out of the kitchen until the food's done."

Lizzie looked up to where Isobel's father stood on a ladder. "How you doing, Uncle Drew? Did you see the mess your daughter made of my house?"

"I see it now," he said, screwing in the plywood he'd cut to cover the hole.

"Not my fault," Isobel said, taking the drill motor from him so he could climb down the ladder. "It was all that Benny's fault."

Kitty stepped onto the porch. "What's this about Benny?" Her voice was too high to be casual, and Isobel looked at her carefully.

"Nothing," Isobel said.

"We should get you all set up for the dinner," she said, handing out the wireless mics they'd wear for the rest of the night and explaining what they should talk about at dinner and that they should turn their mics off only if they were using the bathroom. "I mean actually peeing and stuff. If you go in there to tweeze your eyebrows, leave it on."

"This is weird," Isobel's father said.

Kitty patted his arm, getting closer than was necessary. "You'll forget you're wearing it in no time."

"Don't," Isobel said. "I mean you might, but don't forget you're wearing it."

Kitty unfolded a piece of paper and glanced at it. "Production notes," she said, turning to go into the house. She stopped and looked at them over her shoulder. "You know with your dad here, it might be a good time for the three of you to talk about fathers, you know—especially considering the situation with you, Lizzie. It must be hard to be the only one who doesn't know her dad."

"What is she talking about?" Lizzie asked as Kitty disappeared into the house. "How does she know about my dad? That wasn't part of anything I ever said to her."

Isobel's face reddened as she considered the slip she'd made. "I might have accidentally mentioned it," she said, knowing how Lizzie felt. There were parts of Isobel's own life that she had no intention of living in front of the camera.

Elyse stepped onto the porch. "It'll be ready in about thirty minutes—are Tom and T. J. still coming?"

No one answered her. Isobel's father hugged her. "I see they've got a microphone on you as well."

"We can't talk about it," Isobel said. Lizzie turned away from them and walked inside the house. "I mean the crew, the stuff they do to us."

"Is she mad?" Elyse asked, untying her apron and setting it on the ladder.

"I'm going to go get washed up," Isobel's father said, following Lizzie.

Isobel climbed the ladder and sat a few steps up from the bottom rung. She stretched her legs out. "You ever hear that saying about poking a sleeping bear?"

Elyse nodded. "You shouldn't."

"Right. But the thing is, I think I did."

"So, tell it to go back to sleep," Elyse settled herself on the last rung and looked up at Isobel. "Or shoot it with a tranquilizer gun."

"I wish." The moment Kitty had walked away, Isobel had started going through all the possible outcomes. The best one involved the fact that they knew nothing and nothing happened. The worst was a scene where their Thanksgiving dinner devolved into an episode of Maury Povich with a number of men taking DNA tests to prove they were or weren't Lizzie's father.

Rubbing her temples, Elyse sighed. "I can't talk in code forever. What are talking about? They're going to find out anyway."

"Lizzie's father," Isobel said, half expecting Kitty to appear and confirm that they were in fact listening to every breath. Instead, Craig's car pulled up to the curb, and he stepped out carrying an enormous yellow and orange centerpiece. They watched him struggle with it, walking as slowly as he could, feeling with his foot for the steps because he couldn't see them.

"So what if they do know? Isn't it time everything came out into the open? What's the worst that could happen? You had to know this would happen."

Her cousin had spoken too quickly not to be trying to cover up something. "What did you do?"

"The rolls will burn," Elyse said, standing, grabbing her apron, and retying it around her.

Craig called out for one of them to hold the door. Isobel ignored him and followed Elyse, yelling at her to explain what she meant. She chased her cousin down the narrow hallway and into the kitchen. Jake sat at the table, his camera at his feet. As he pulled apart one of Elyse's rolls, hot steam floated into the air.

"Let it go," Elyse said, taking the pan of rolls from the stovetop and moving them to the counter. Jake dropped his roll and picked up his camera.

"Did you tell them about your theory?" Isobel asked.

"What if I did? Isn't that what we should do? Isn't that what you did for me?" Elyse lifted the foil from the turkey and crumpled it into a ball. Juice from the bird dripped down her sleeve.

"You're not Lizzie," Isobel said. "The whole situation is entirely different. I thought you'd have learned your lesson with Landon."

"What lesson is that? How to be happy and fulfilled without a man? I know you could teach a seminar in that one." Elyse threw the foil ball at Isobel, striking her in the shoulder. Melted butter splattered onto her blouse.

"Come off it. You know that the whole point of that was to prevent you from making a fool of yourself. You can't change people. He'd already chosen and it wasn't you."

Elyse picked up the carving knife.

"I thought we were going to let Daddy do that," she said.

"I never agreed to that. You just assumed it," Elyse said, waving the knife at Isobel. "This is exactly like you. You've never been able to see outside of yourself." She jabbed the knife into the bird so that it stuck straight up, like a flagpole. "The thing with your mother messed you up in ways that you can't even see."

"My mother has nothing to do with this," Isobel said. "This is about Lizzie and this absurd notion you have about Benny."

From behind them, Lizzie spoke. "What about Benny? What about me?"

They turned quickly. Lizzie stood next to Isobel's father in front of the beaded curtain. In the corner of the room, Kitty had her head bent toward Craig—the ostentatious centerpiece at their feet. Their posture made Isobel's stomach turn. There was something in the way they both checked their watches that told her there would be so much more to this fight.

"Why are you arguing?" Lizzie asked, taking a step toward them. "We don't fight."

"Should you be filming this?" Isobel heard her father ask Jake, who'd positioned himself next to Elyse's elbow. The kitchen felt like a sauna—the windows steamed over and dripping with condensation.

"Maybe we should fight," Elyse said.

"But we don't," Lizzie said. "That's why I love you. Everyone else I know goes at it with each other. My parents, my siblings, my teammates. But we don't. We can't start now."

"We're too old for this," Isobel said.

"For what?" Elyse asked. "Pretending that we're not grown-ups with grown-up problems."

"I don't think we're pretending," Isobel said, considering all the ways in which she had been playacting since coming to live in Memphis.

"That's all you know how to do," Elyse said.

"Stop it, stop it, stop it," Lizzie said. "Just tell me what this is about."

Elyse took a deep breath and looked at Isobel before speaking in a rush of words. "Look, I know you will think this is crazy, but I've thought for a long time now that Benny is the most likely candidate to be your dad, and I think it would be a shame to waste the opportunity to find out. I mean as long as we've known you, all you've ever wanted to know is who your dad was and you always said it didn't matter who he was or if he wanted to be your father, you needed to know for your own sake. And it's not that I believe in fate or God or whatever, but it's as likely that he is your dad as not. It's like Occam's razor. The simplest answer is the right answer. And Benny. He's the simple answer."

"I don't understand," Lizzie said.

"You should tell her that you shared this little insight of yours with Kitty and Craig," Isobel said, knowing even as she spoke that what chance she'd had at getting this television show was slipping away. It had never been her they'd been interested in. Lizzie with her near Olympic pedigree and complicated family would be the star.

Lizzie sat down on the floor and drew her knees up to her chest.

"I must insist you stop filming," Isobel's father said. Out of the corner of her eye, she saw him step in front of Jake. Kitty moved forward and began to argue about their right to be there. Isobel sat next to Lizzie on the floor and after a moment of awkwardness in which Elyse looked at the back door for more than a few seconds, she took off her mic and sat down with them.

"I'm sorry," she said, laying her head on Lizzie's shoulder. "I'm sorry. I wanted to help like you'd helped me. It was hard—the thing with Landon, but it was right. I kept telling myself I was making the hard decision."

"Stop talking," Lizzie said. "Is it true? Can it be true?"

Isobel started to explain why she thought it was all a bunch of bunk when her father knelt down beside them. He turned his body away from Isobel and spoke directly to Lizzie. "Sweetie," he said, taking her hand. "Have you talked to your parents about this?"

Lizzie nodded at him. Elyse tried to explain the years of asking, the phone calls, their absence and how in the end her mother simply would not tell her a single truth about her father. He put his hand on her cousin's head. "I asked Lizzie. I need Lizzie to tell me."

Watching them, a warmth flooded Isobel. Her father had a limitless capacity for love. He radiated it in a way that enveloped all of them in the room. From the periphery of her vision, Isobel saw Kitty stumble toward them as if Craig had pushed her. "I need you to put your microphones back on," she said slowly without looking at them.

Isobel stepped out of the circle, caught Kitty by the arm and pulled her into the narrow hallway. "We're done here," she said. "You can come back tomorrow. Or not." Kitty needed little prodding and in a moment she was out the door muttering about how they'd work around this hitch.

Jake had followed them and he stood for a minute on the porch looking as if he had much to say to Isobel. Instead, he leaned in and apologized. "I still want to talk to you," he said. "But not about this—or what they want to do with Lizzie."

"What do they want with Lizzie?" Isobel's skin felt light as it tightened around her. Jake shook his head. "It doesn't matter now anyway."

"That's enough," Craig said, cutting off their conversation. "I've had enough of this nonsense. All of you signed a contract that gives us every right to be here, to have you cooperate."

"Not now," Isobel said, backing away from him.

He stalked her like prey, continuing to talk about obligations and burning bridges. She walked around the ladder and he walked under it, trying to cut her off. "That's bad luck," she said over his threats.

Craig looked up and then leveled his eyes at her. "You make your own luck, and mine is going to be made on this show. Or at least on Lizzie's show."

"That wasn't the agreement," Isobel said.

"It's your own fault. We tried to get you to talk about your mom, but you said she was off limits. Of course, that didn't stop us from calling her up and trying to convince her to fly out and surprise you for Thanksgiving. Turns out she doesn't want to see you—especially if your father is around. That's one messed-up family."

"You shouldn't have done that," Isobel said. She hadn't talked to her mother in three years. The thought that Craig had called and wondering what lies he'd told made her stomach clench in sharp pain.

"There's so much I shouldn't have done. But I did it. I'm doing it." Craig's eyes kept glancing at the street. Isobel followed his gaze, trying to anticipate what would happen next. He'd made himself at home under the ladder, appearing to relish the danger of taunting luck.

"Just shut up, Craig. Shut up and get the hell out of here." Isobel stepped away from him and craned her head down the street. She saw Jake's car make a left onto Tennessee Avenue, and then she saw a flash of purple coming up Beale Street.

Craig began laughing, and not because he was uncomfortable or nervous. He laughed like a man who'd won. There was something wrong with him. She watched the purple bus move down the narrow road and slow to a stop in front of Spite House. In large gold letters on the side of the vehicle were the words *Who's Your Daddy? Mobile DNA Testing.*

"That's too far," Isobel said to him. "Way too far."

Craig smirked at her. "Do you know who the test audience wanted to see more of?"

"I don't care," Isobel said, her hands shaking with anger.

"It wasn't you. They're tired of you. It seems people think of you as an annoying neighborhood kid who never leaves home. You're not pretty enough for television and not talented enough for the movies, and if there's one truth we learned from this experience, it's that you're not interesting enough for reality."

Without considering what she was doing, Isobel stepped forward and unlocked the safety hinges on the ladder and then kicked at it with her feet so that in one loud, quick movement, Craig and the ladder fell in a heap onto the floor of the porch.

"That's what I think of you," she said. "Sue me, sue Lizzie, do whatever it is you do, but get the hell out of here." She locked the front door behind her and pulled the shades. Methodically, she walked around every inch of Spite House and closed it off to the outside world. She found her father, Elyse, and Lizzie in the cupola. From the looks on their faces, she could tell that they'd watched the entire scene unfold. Lizzie had her knees drawn up to her face and refused to make eye contact. The purple bus was still parked in front of their house. Craig stood in front of it gesticulating wildly, a telephone to his ear and in conversation with the driver of the vehicle.

"I think we're trapped for a while," Elyse said. "It's a good thing there's plenty of food. I've called Tom and T. J. and told them that dinner's off."

"Oh," Isobel said, realizing how much more of the day they had left. It felt like an entire season had passed already.

"We've been waiting for you," Isobel's father said and patted the seat next to him.

"Should we be up here?" Isobel asked, still shaking. She felt exposed on the roof, as if they could see inside and still hear what was being said.

"I think we're safe," Elyse said. "I had a whole conversation with Kitty the other day where she told me to stay the hell out of here because, try as they might, they couldn't make it work for filming, for sound, for shit. That's what she said."

Isobel's father put his arm around her. "If you're strong enough, Lizzie, I've got a story you might be interested in hearing."

Lizzie looked at him and sighed.

"I'm not supposed to know this," Isobel's father said, "but I do and once I tell you, it can't be undone."

Elyse leaned in. "I knew someone had to know."

Isobel stayed with her head on her father's shoulder. Her mind raced with a thousand questions and for once they were all about her own life. She'd stopped caring about Lizzie and her problems. She wanted to know about her father. How could he be such a good man? Why hadn't he gotten married again? Why had her mother left?

"Lizzie," Isobel's father said.

Her cousin sat up and blew her nose on the edge of her shirt. "I'm ready," she said, reaching out a hand for Elyse and a hand for Isobel.

"I don't know all the details. You'll have to go to your parents for that, and they may tell you or they may not. I can't say." He stopped talking. Isobel watched his face. It had become still, as it did when he was trying to figure out a particularly difficult repair. "Your father is your father. I mean he's not only your stepfather, he's also your biological father."

"Impossible," Lizzie said. "They didn't even know each other and he would have been"—her voice trailed off as she did the math—"sixteen, no, fifteen when my Mom got pregnant."

Isobel looked at her father over the silence. He shrugged and smiled as if to apologize for having kept such secrets for so many years. She wondered what secrets they would keep from their own children and whether any of the cousins would make mistakes big enough to change a life. She moved away from him and toward her cousin, who'd drawn up her knees again and started rocking back and forth like a child on the verge of action.

"You'll have to tell her a little more," Elyse said. "It's not enough to know for sure that you're right."

"Do you understand why I'm telling you?" Isobel's father asked.

She wasn't sure she did, but she nodded, as did Elyse and Lizzie.

"Your life is not your own," Elyse said, "and what is it they say about telling out of turn. I can't believe I was so stupid about this whole mess. Lizzie, I'm so sorry."

Lizzie looked up. "What else?"

Isobel's father told them what he knew. When Lizzie's mother was twenty-four, she'd taken a job working at a law firm in Boston. He wasn't sure how she'd come by the job, only that it had something to do with one of the lawyers in the firm being from Memphis. Each time he offered a new part of the story, he made Lizzie promise to check with her parents. He kept telling her that they'd have the full story and he was bound to mess up some detail. That same year she was working in Boston, Lizzie's father got a job at a deli in the building where her mother worked. "I can't tell you what happened between them, who knew what or when," Isobel's father said. "I just know after it was all over, my baby brother asked me if I could keep a secret and told me he'd met a girl from Memphis and fallen in love."

"In love," Lizzie echoed, as if it were a password she had to remember.

"And what?" Isobel asked her father. "You just remembered that conversation years later when he said he was marrying Lizzie's mother and decided she was the girl from Memphis?"

"Did you ask Uncle Jim about it?" Elyse asked. She'd scooted to the very edge of the window seat and looked as if she might fall off. "I mean, do you know for sure?"

Isobel's father sighed. "Real early on, that first summer you came to Boston, I asked him, and he said you were his. Since then, well, it's gotten to be a thing we can't talk about."

"That's it," Lizzie said, standing up. "That's the truth then."

"What are you going to do?" Elyse asked.

Lizzie rubbed her eyes. "I'm going to eat that turkey you made and give thanks. And then after I've had enough time to digest dinner and all of this, then I'll decide what to do."

To her surprise, food sounded good to Isobel, too. "I'm starving," she said, recognizing the feeling she normally killed with a cup of coffee or a stick of gum, "and I'm not going to stop eating until my pants are too tight to sit comfortably."

The week after Thanksgiving passed in a blur. It surprised Isobel that instead of dwelling on Craig and the potential for disaster, her thoughts most often turned to Tom. She couldn't figure out where they stood. She introduced him to her father the few times they went to his store to get supplies, but they hadn't been alone since their disastrous pretend date. Isobel and her father worked their way through the list of repairs that T. J. said needed to be done for them to get their final occupancy certificate for the house. Lizzie refused to talk about her father. She'd drawn a red circle around December 21 on the kitchen calendar, which everyone assumed was the day her family was coming home from Russia, but no one dared ask her about it.

"We're in the eye of the storm," Elyse had said when Isobel tried to talk to her about Lizzie's non-reaction to the news she'd waited her whole life to hear.

"But is it normal?" Isobel had asked.

"There's no normal," Elyse said. "The thing you want is healthy."

"Fine, then is it healthy?"

"Hell no. But what's she going to do? Write a letter? Have it out with them on e-mail or on the phone? She's doing the only thing she can do."

"Wait?" Isobel said.

"Wait," Elyse said.

These conversations and others emotionally paralyzed Isobel so that instead of dealing with the problem of Tom, or Craig, or Lizzie, she turned to her longest-standing impasse—her father. While under the house sistering the joints that Benny had weakened, she asked about all the stuff she hadn't had the courage to before. Seeing Lizzie act as if she were the living dead scared Isobel into getting over her own fear with her father.

She remembered part of a poem one of her stylists had taped to the mirror. It was one of those addresses to young people. At the time she hadn't thought much of it, except for one line that sometimes appeared in her mind as if someone had whispered it into her ear. *"What you fear will not go away: it will take you into/ yourself and bless you and keep you."*

"What happened?" she asked her father—or rather his feet as that was all she could see of him in the crawl space.

"With your mother?"

She liked that he knew what she was asking about. It made her feel like she had someone on her side, like her cousins. Their shorthand way of speaking with one another gave her a feeling of protection.

"If you ever get serious about anyone, it would be good to remember that it is impossible to live separately and try to stay married." He shimmied forward on his stomach and then rolled onto his back. "Pass me the level."

She rolled onto her side to reach the pile of tools they'd dragged into the small space and sifted through it until she found what he needed. "Seems obvious. But why did you? I was making enough money that we all could have lived together, especially when the boys were out of the house."

"It wasn't about the money." He marked the beams with a pencil and then passed the level back to her. "I kept thinking you'd give it up. That your mother would see the foolishness of it all and come back home. Instead, that world and, honey, forgive me for saying this because I know it is important to you, but that world isn't real. Your mom forgot that."

As they busied themselves with the work of attaching the new support beam, their conversation dwindled to requests and directions. Isobel's mother had remained in Hollywood. The first relationship hadn't lasted and neither had the ones after that. She took up Pilates and looked younger than she ever had when Isobel had still considered her to be a mother. She dated a rich man long enough to convince him to invest in a Pilates studio located between a casting agency and a Starbucks. It did well. The first year Nora's Pilates was open, the "N" fell off the sign. Her mother never replaced it. Sometimes in a casting call Isobel would find herself in a conversation with another twenty-something actress who extolled the virtues of Ora and her method for removing stubborn fat deposits and it wouldn't be until after the conversation was over that Isobel would realize that they'd been talking about her mother.

Her father interrupted her thoughts. "Have you seen this?"

She crawled around the tool pile so she could look over his shoulder. On the old beam, someone had carved a lotus blossom and underneath it were the initials R + M. She ran her fingers over the scarred wood. "Must be Lizzie's grandparents. Melanie and Roger."

"I thought he built the house before he met her," Isobel's father said. "There's another one on this beam—you have to look in the same spot, by the joist."

Isobel found eight carvings—all similar but with slight variations caused by the wood or the knife used. "Maybe he did it afterward, when he worked on the house."

"That's what was missing between your mom and me," her father said, running his fingers across the carving on his beam. Isobel had moved toward the front of the house and she wasn't sure she'd heard him correctly. She held her breath waiting for him to elaborate.

"You want a relationship to last? That person has to be in your thoughts even when they're not around. All that business about absence making the heart grow fonder. It's a good test. If you don't miss a person when they're gone, don't marry them."

"It's not that simple," Isobel said, thinking of her own relationships.

"Sure it is," her father said. "You know I told your brothers this before—explained to them that what they were looking for in a partner was exactly that. Sure you want to be compatible and sure you want to want the same things, but honestly, it's a good test. It should be the only test. Think of Roger down here working on the house and his wife above him, making dinner or cleaning. He missed her so much and she was right upstairs. That's what you want: someone who'll carve your initials into floor joists."

"And you never felt that for mom?" Isobel asked.

"She never felt that for me. And the hard part is I always knew it. I just didn't think she'd leave me."

"It's getting cold," Isobel said. She pulled a tarp over the tool pile and army-crawled to the exit. Her father followed. Although she hadn't spoken it, what she'd wanted to tell her father was that her mother had left all of them. It wasn't just him she didn't love enough.

"What are your plans?" her father asked, dusting off his jeans.

"Plans?" Isobel couldn't figure out what part of her life he was talking about.

"I mean for when Lizzie's parents come home in a few weeks." He brought his arm around her.

"I thought I'd do Christmas with the brothers and then head back to Los Angeles. The house will be mine again in January once the renter moves out."

"It'll be nice to have you closer." Her father looked as if he might say more, but instead he tousled her hair and they let themselves into the kitchen and warmed up with coffee even though it was late afternoon. Elyse joined them and then, after the sun had nearly dropped into the horizon, Lizzie appeared, covered in grass and mud from her soccer practice.

"We should go out," Elyse said. "Why waste a good caffeine buzz?"

"Too much trouble," Lizzie said. "I'd have to shower."

"Doesn't Tom have a show tonight?" Elyse asked.

Isobel nodded and cut her eyes at her father. She'd planned to take him and show off her boyfriend, but their conversation underneath the house had exhausted her. It had her second-guessing everything with Tom. Did she miss him when he was gone? Did he miss her? Were relationships even possible? "He's at Minglewood."

Her father brightened at the mention of Tom. "I'd like that. I still feel cheated that I didn't get to have fake Thanksgiving with him."

Isobel wasn't sure she wanted them to get to know each other—the act implied more intimacy than she felt with Tom. "I didn't think you'd want to go," she said. "It'll be young people. I mean kids, really still in college."

Somehow it was decided that everyone would go. T. J. arrived and they all squeezed into his Suburban, arriving at Minglewood early enough that Isobel and her father had time to chat with Tom before a crowd formed. Her father asked him about his guitar, and the two spoke as if they'd always known each other. Watching them, Isobel felt her heart expand in her chest—there was something in the way Tom looked at her father that conveyed respect and interest. Although Isobel didn't like to admit it, she'd been thrown by what Tom had said about being a dad. She didn't care that he was recovering. You couldn't shoulder a purse in Hollywood without bumping into someone who was in a twelve-step program.

"Do you like him?" her father asked.

The room had filled and had that overheated atmosphere that happened when crowds gathered in the winter. When he was performing, Tom looked taller and wider. He filled the vast expanse of the stage in a way that he didn't in everyday life. His voice wasn't perfect—or rather it didn't have that too-perfect trained quality that too many alt indie singers had. His voice reminded her mostly of Memphis, which is to say it had grit to it and the sort of quality that came with knowing people didn't like you but that was okay. Isobel had yet to meet a Memphian who didn't tell her what was wrong with their city, but they said it the way her grandmother used to tell people to stay out of the kitchen if they couldn't stand the heat.

"What's not to like?" she said. Even as she answered her father, she was trying to put Tom to the test he'd told her earlier. She tried to think about a time when he hadn't been in her life. What it had been like the last few weeks with the distance between them.

"He seems to have all the qualities," her father said.

"He's got a kid," Isobel said.

"That's tough. You have to see what kind of father he is and then you have to know enough about yourself to know whether you can handle being the other mother."

"It's too much to think about," Isobel said, turning her eyes away from the stage and watching Lizzie and T. J. together. He had his hand in her back pocket. That was a new habit, one that had come out of the news about Lizzie's father. She looked contented if not happy and after a moment, Lizzie put her head on T. J.'s shoulder.

"I think they'll make it," she said.

Her father nodded. "She'll need him and you guys too."

There was something wistful about his voice. "You aren't staying?"

"I don't think I should," he said. "You know how sibling relationships are. I'm not sure mine and Jim's can stand the strain of this. If I were here when she tells them she knows, I'd have to take sides and I don't want to do that."

"Have you told him that she knows?"

Her father looked away from her.

"Dad."

"I had to, honey. He's my brother, and the only way they'll solve this is by walking into it with some preparation."

"You shouldn't have done that," she said, knowing without having spoken to Lizzie about it that her cousin needed the element of surprise to get the truth out of her parents. "They aren't going to tell her what really happened."

"Do you think they even know?" her father asked. "That's the myth—that adults understand or can explain themselves. We can't, you know. Nobody can."

Isobel shook her head. She didn't want to fight with her father. Out of the corner of her eye, she saw Elyse leaning over the bar. In a flash, she considered all that had happened to them this year, and knew what her father said was true. She also knew they were now adults in every sense of the word.

"Wanna dance?" her father asked.

"Nobody dances," she said.

"No matter." He took her hand and found enough of a four-four tempo in Tom's song about a smoky bar to start waltzing. She remembered dancing with him like this as a child at someone's wedding. It was a surprise talent that her father, who never wore a suit, should be so light on his feet. He'd taught her at a young age that everyone could dance if they had a strong partner to follow. He whirled her around the back of the crowd and people gladly made room for them.

The music changed without Isobel's realizing it, and in a moment Tom had transformed himself into Elvis and was singing "Until It's Time For You To Go." Her father smiled and with just a twitch of his arm telegraphed his intention to spin her out. Isobel relaxed her body and followed her father's lead. As the song ended with Tom singing about staying, her father dipped her, and the crowd, not sure why the song had changed or who Isobel and her father were, broke into the sort of applause audiences reserve for magicians. Isobel felt as if a trick had been played on her and that because of it, her whole world was about to shift.

December 2012: Memphis

Contrary to T. J.'s assurances that he'd handpicked a colleague who would pass them, the code inspector looked nitpicky. He fussed with his tie as he walked through the house—clipping and unclipping his tie tack and reaching down to dust off his shoes and his pant legs after walking through each of the rooms. Isobel kept as close to the man's elbow as he allowed, which gave her the occasional opportunity to read from his clipboard.

"How's it look?" Elyse mouthed when they entered the kitchen.

Isobel gave her a quick thumbs-up. They'd been through the house from top to bottom and she felt as if they were almost finished. He had the option of checking the crawl space, but it wasn't mandatory. Isobel guessed that what T. J. had meant when he said this particular man was easy was that he didn't like to get dirty, which meant he didn't go above and beyond. Her father's rule had been to never wear a shirt that wasn't already stained when he went to a job. This man took the opposite approach. He'd been impressed with their electrical box—by how ordered it had been. Isobel silently thanked Elton for the extra work he'd put in. From the pocket of her voluminous skirt, her phone rang. She glanced at the inspector, who appeared to be looking at the view of the Mississippi. Sliding the phone out, she glanced at it and then without realizing it, she answered it quickly—afraid as she was when fishing that at any moment the fish could jump the line.

"You there?" Jake's voice boomed over the line. He sounded like her grandfather—a man who never believed that mobile phones were the same as landlines—talking in a way that sounded like shouting.

"I'm here, I'm here," she said quietly so as not to draw the attention of the inspector. She turned her back to him and saw out of the corner of her eye that Elyse was motioning her to put the phone down.

"Can you meet?" he asked.

"You're here?" she asked. "Why are you here?"

"I'll explain it later. I'm on my way over."

He hung up the phone without any sort of leave-taking. She turned back to the code inspector to see him handing Elyse a pink copy of the inspection. Nodding to him, Elyse handed him a plastic-wrapped plate of cookies. When he had stepped out the door and into the yard, her cousin raised the paper in the air and hollered. "Spite House is legit," she said.

Isobel wrapped her in a hug in the bright kitchen. "Where's Lizzie?"

"Sleeping," Elyse said, raising her hand to stop Isobel from protesting before she could even start. "Don't. Her parents come tomorrow and it's like I said, she's saving up her energy for the tail end of the storm."

"You know, we might be her only family after tomorrow." Isobel thought about all the damage that could be done when Lizzie confronted her parents about their years' long deception. "It's illegal what they did, isn't it?"

"They're long past the statute of limitations," Elyse said.

"She asked you to—what—mediate?"

"I don't really want to be there, but—" Elyse didn't finish because, as Isobel knew, it was what they both knew. She'd thought Lizzie would want T. J. there too, but somehow he'd escaped the event. Isobel figured it was precisely because he and Lizzie were serious that he wouldn't be there. Whatever happened tomorrow would taint their relationship, and if he were there and things got ugly, he might never repair the relationship with Lizzie's parents.

"I'm going to leave this in front of her door. That way when she does wake up, she'll have the right sort of start to her day."

Isobel made a cup of tea. Instead of sitting at the table, she stood on the lotus flower in the center of the room, tracing the mosaic with her toe. The kitchen had turned out beautifully—of course, the privacy scrims she and her father had installed on his last day there had cost her the last of her savings, but it didn't matter. It was, if there were such a thing, a perfect space. The sheer window coverings cut the glare of the windows, but not the transparency, so light streamed in and the river was still visible.

She'd never been able to watch herself perform without feeling a sharp pain in her chest at all the imperfections captured and preserved on film—or as was more likely now—in digital form. The kitchen felt different. There were minor imperfections, but they lent character to the space. If it had been flawless, it would have been sterile. She rubbed with her toe at a line of grout that rose above the tile line.

Finishing her tea, she walked to the front of the house to look for Jake's car. Meeting him on the porch felt preferable to letting him into the house—not that he'd done anything specifically wrong except work for Craig, but the whole crew felt tainted to Isobel. What they'd been planning, that surprise DNA test, was abhorrent in the same way children's beauty pageants were. She pulled a sweater from the front closet and slid her feet into the boot slippers she kept there. Upstairs, she heard Lizzie turning on the shower and the high notes of an excited conversation with Elyse.

Jake had shaved his beard. She blinked a few times to try to reconcile the man in front of her with the man she'd last seen. He grabbed her in a bear hug that lifted her off the ground. "You look worried," he said. "Don't be. I've got a plan for you and me. It's a good one too."

Without realizing what she intended to do, Isobel reached her hand out and touched his bare chin. "I don't get it, why shave in the winter when you need the extra fur."

"It was all for a bet. Now that it's over I can go back to my real face," Jake said. "Are you going to invite me inside? Like you said, I'd need fur to stay out here."

"As long as you're not packing," she said, opening the door and following him down the hallway.

"You mean equipment? I've got nothing but a pen on me." He whistled when he saw the kitchen. "Damn. You did fine work here. I didn't think these cabinets would work, but with this countertop and the back-splash. Beautiful."

He continued to run his hands along the work she and her father had done in the last weeks while she made more tea. It pleased her to hear someone else praise the space. Lizzie had been too dead-eyed to notice, and Elyse had been full of complaints about the logic of the layout, wanting to move dishes and appliances around until it was suitable for her approach to cooking. "It makes me wish I could stay," she said, realizing only as she said it that it was true.

"Why don't you?" Jake asked, bending over to look at the finished floor, which they'd sealed to prevent discoloration. "I've always loved the lotus. You know what they say about it?"

She shook her head, the thought ringing in her ears that she wanted to stay, not just in the house, but also in Memphis, and especially with Tom.

"It's the only flower that blooms in shit."

"Mud," Lizzie said from the doorway. Elyse stood behind her. "It was my grandfather who made the mosaic. One of the things I found in the boxes of Grandma Mellie's stuff was an envelope stuffed with doodles of the flower next to snatches of my grand-father's writing. I guess it was what he was good at. Thriving in difficult locations."

"You look good," Isobel said, thinking that for the first time in weeks her cousin's eyes didn't appear cloudy. She started to explain to her cousins why Jake was there, but realized as she spoke that she didn't really know. "Why are you here?" she asked.

"I've got a proposition for you," Jake said, gesturing to the table. "But first I have to plead mea culpa." He explained that after the disaster of their fake Thanksgiving, he'd gone back to his workspace in Atlanta and looked over the footage that he'd shot. What he found most interesting in the hours and hours of recordings were the parts where Isobel was working on the house. He took a sip of his tea and turned to her, "You come alive in those shots and, frankly, in all the others you look like someone pretending to be you. That's why reality shows with actors are difficult: they often don't know how to be themselves in front of the camera."

"Ouch," Isobel said.

Elyse laid a hand on hers. "It's not just actresses. There's quite a few people out there pretending to be someone they're not."

Jake had taken these bits of footage with her fixing or explaining what she was fixing and arranged them together in his own version of a sizzle reel and sent it to a production company he'd worked for in the past. "The guy loved it. They do a ton of stuff for those fix-it and home and garden networks. I mean he's practically ready to sign you for a full order without even seeing a first episode."

Around her, the cousins talked to Jake about the possibilities this show offered. The sound of their voices was like the chatter of squirrels. The noise surrounded Isobel and took the air out of the room. It could be everything that she wanted, but it could also be a trap. "What about Craig and that whole mess?" she asked.

"He's done with you," Jake said. "It's a good thing too—his production company is having problems—ones bigger than your deciding not to work with him."

"He won't make a fuss about the footage?"

"I already paid him off," Jake said.

Isobel leaned away from him. "That's not your concern. You shouldn't have, and I'm sure I can repay you for your trouble."

"No, no. It's not like that. He was ready to trash it all and I offered to buy it, to see what I could do with it. I told him I was ready to move out from behind the camera, do a little producing work on the side." He dug through his pockets. "In all my excitement, I forgot this." He held out a piece of paper.

Isobel took it and examined the waiver, which absolved her and the cousins of any debt owed to Craig and turned over the footage to Jake.

"He didn't give you this out of the goodness of his heart," she said.

Jake looked away from them. "Look, I feel like I owe the three of you something. I should have stopped the paternity nonsense when Kitty brought it up. It's not even compelling television. But I was pissed at him and thought I'd let him dig his own grave without considering how it would damage you guys."

"It's okay," Lizzie said. "I think it's all going to work out in the end."

Isobel narrowed her eyes at Jake. The way he'd spoken quickly and then changed the subject made her suspect he was holding something back. "You had leverage, didn't you?"

Jake raised his hands, palms up. "I can't say. It's all part of the deal."

Elyse cleared her throat. "It was Kitty, wasn't it? She and Craig in a compromising situation?"

"I didn't tell you anything," Jake said. "But I've always been friendly with Mrs. Craig."

"I never liked Kitty," Lizzie said. "Something about the way she was different with you depending on who you were."

Isobel wondered if she could be something other than a failed actress. She'd gotten good at rejection, at making up excuses for why she'd failed—she wasn't right for the part, her hair was the wrong color, she was too short, too tall, too skinny, too fat. It seemed like she needed a Goldilocks job—one where she could finally be right. Of course she didn't know enough about this new job to know what that might be. "I'm not sure I understand what I'd be doing," she said.

"You'd be the host, you know, talk to the camera, chat with the homeowners and then get in there and make a plan for fixing their house. Easy stuff. Shoot three episodes in each town, you're on the road a couple months out of the year and then off for the rest. Heck, you can pretty much live anywhere you want, as long as it has an airport."

Isobel nodded, realizing after he'd given her this last bit of information that she wasn't ready to leave Memphis. "What's it called?"

Jake rubbed his hands together as if he'd been waiting for the questions. "*Bad House.*"

Lizzie laughed. "I get it," she said. "That's good."

"Why not *House Whisperer*?" Elyse asked.

"*Houses Gone Wild,*" Isobel said, allowing herself to get caught up in the celebratory mood that surrounded

her. It was good news and she ought to take it at face
value.

The arrangement had been that the Triplins would
be out of the house when Lizzie's family came home.
Isobel imagined that her cousin hadn't wanted to confront her parents with her siblings present, but Lizzie
didn't share much of her plan with them. They sat
on the second-floor balcony of a bar that jutted out
over the river—or where the river would have if they
hadn't been in drought conditions.

"It looks so different," Elyse said, leaning over the
balcony and staring at the river rocks below them.

"It smells," Isobel said, bringing her nose to her
wrist to alleviate the drying-out smell that surrounded
them. She looked at her phone to check the time and
then back out at the river. Without water covering the
flood field, Arkansas didn't loom as close. There were
large irregular patches of sand that made Isobel think
of the beach.

Elyse followed her gaze. "It's more dangerous
now."

"What?" Lizzie asked, drinking the last of her
wine.

"The river. When it's flooded, all the treacherous
spots get covered up and buried in water. But now

everything's exposed. A couple of kids drowned last month—they were fishing with their dad and got out to play on the sandbar, only it isn't like regular sand. The water is still running underneath it so when you put any weight on it, you sink."

"I thought quicksand was a myth," Isobel said. "The stuff of Saturday morning cartoons and melodramas."

"It's the real deal," Elyse said. "Rosa May knew the boys who drowned."

Lizzie's phone buzzed. She looked down at it and then called the waiter over and asked for another glass of wine.

"Are you sure?" Isobel asked. She hadn't seen her cousin drink since they'd found the whiskey.

"I'm sure," Lizzie said, gulping down the wine as soon as the waiter brought it over.

"It takes a while to work," Isobel said. If she were her cousin, she wasn't sure there would be enough wine in the world to take the edge off the conversation she needed to have.

"Is your—" Isobel didn't know how to refer to Lizzie's father. "—Uncle Jim going back to his firm?"

"Pretty sure. The guy who owns the place is Mormon," Lizzie said. "They look out for each other.

Elyse stopped Lizzie from ordering a third glass of wine. "So does family."

"That's it," Lizzie said, responding to the buzz of her phone. "They're home, the kids are out at the movies."

"So we're up?" Elyse asked, taking Lizzie's keys from her purse. "I'll drive."

"We could have walked," Isobel said as they piled into the car. "Drive around the block a couple of times," she said to Elyse.

"No," Lizzie said. "The faster I get this over with, the better."

Elyse idled the engine in front of Spite House. In the few hours they'd been gone, it already looked different to Isobel. Lizzie's younger brothers had scattered their toys on the second floor balcony and her sisters had pulled up all the blinds in the cupola. Lizzie reached across the seat and turned the engine off.

"Ready?" Isobel asked.

In answer, Lizzie opened the car door and glided up the walkway with a fluidity that told Isobel the alcohol had finally started to work on her cousin.

"She's drunk," Elyse said.

"My guess is that what is waiting for her inside the house will sober her up fast."

"It'd be better if she weren't," Elyse said as they got out of the car. "I think she needs to hear, really hear what her parents have to say, and you know how a little bit of alcohol can make it all feel unreal."

Elyse followed Lizzie up the sidewalk and Isobel trailed them. "I don't think she could do this if she weren't."

They stood in front of the door and for the first time since she'd arrived at Spite House nearly a year earlier, Isobel stretched out her hand and knocked. In a similar gesture, Elyse reached forward and pushed the doorbell.

"That's probably overkill," Lizzie said. She offered a strangled laugh and leaned against the doorframe. The sounds of someone fumbling with the lock made everyone straighten. Elyse pulled up the neckline of her shirt, Lizzie pulled her hair out of its ponytail, and Isobel stopped biting her thumbnail. They'd never locked the door in the daytime and it made opening the door take a thousand times longer.

"Girls," Aunt Annie said, stepping out of the house and drawing them into an embrace. The openness of the gesture confused Isobel, as did her aunt's appearance. She hadn't seen her in person in several years, but the image in the Christmas cards over the years had been one of a comfortably plump woman with shoulder-length hair dyed several shades too dark to cover the gray. The woman wrapping them in hugs bore only the slightest resemblance to those photos. She'd let her hair go gray and it was cut in a chin-length bob that didn't look so much chic as severe. Her skin, although tan, had a yellowish cast and was loose with a crepey texture that Isobel associated with the elderly. She'd lost enough weight that she was thinner than any of the Triplins.

"You look—" Isobel searched for the right word.

"Terrible," her aunt finished.

"Oh, don't say that," Elyse said. "Skinnier is always better."

"If you'd had the year I've had, I'm not sure you'd say that. I had so many problems that I feel like my body has been to war the past year. Really too much to go into and now is not the time."

Lizzie found her voice. "Are you well now?"

"I'm fine, I'm fine. Let me just say that you shouldn't drink tap water in Russia," Aunt Annie said, ushering them through the doorway and down the hall. "I made cookies."

Isobel cleared her throat and exchanged glances with Elyse as they entered the kitchen. "I'm not sure today is the best day for cookies." Earlier, they'd agreed that their job was to stand as witnesses for Lizzie. To be the people she could dissect the conversation with afterward. Elyse had explained the concept of an advocate in health care to them at the bar. When people were under stress, they weren't able to process information in the same way. As Isobel understood Elyse's explication, advocates came along to doctor's appointments and listened to what was said, occasionally asking questions to clarify information or to support the needs of the patient. Over drinks, Elyse had asked Lizzie a series of questions about what outcome she wanted from the confrontation with her parents. They'd promised to keep quiet unless they felt that Lizzie needed help.

"We might as well talk over food," Aunt Annie said, practically pushing them into the kitchen and into chairs around the table.

"Where's Jim?" Lizzie asked, casting her eyes around the space as if there were a crowd of people.

Lizzie's mother passed around cookies. "I can't believe what wonders you all have done with the house."

"Mom, I asked where Jim was."

Aunt Annie sighed. "Just give me a minute. I haven't seen you in three years and I want to pretend for a minute that we're going to be okay. Your father will be here soon. I wanted to talk to you first."

"Is it true?" Lizzie asked.

"Let me explain." Aunt Annie took a cookie and nervously broke it into increasingly smaller pieces until it was a pile of crumbs. She licked her finger and dipped it into the crumbs and then brought her finger to her mouth, licking off the cookie fragments.

"Explain what?" Lizzie slapped her hand on the table. "How you lied? How you managed to sleep with a teenager? Why you married him after so many years apart?"

"If you want to know, you have to listen."

Elyse reached out and laid a hand on Lizzie's arm. "She's right. Let her get it all out." Isobel made noises of agreement although she had no idea what course of action would be best. If it were her mother, she'd probably throttle her and ask questions later. Wasn't that a useless thought? Her own mother hadn't ever bothered to explain her behavior.

Lizzie nodded, although to Isobel the savage way in which she inclined her head seemed to convey "fuck off" more than it did her cousin's willingness to let her mother speak. Aunt Annie pushed the crumbs away from her. "Nothing tastes the same."

"Go on," Elyse said, and Isobel admired the way her cousin was able to change the tone of her voice to one that encouraged without intruding. Without intending to, Isobel took one of the cookies and ate it. She wondered what a witness was supposed to do, what she could do. Her only expertise was in observing others. In learning how people's faces looked when they experienced different emotions. It didn't seem that she was born knowing how to mimic emotion like so many of the other actresses she knew. That Hollywood man, the one she'd fallen too far in love with, was the one who'd taught her the trick of face watching. After it was over and done with, she'd decided that he was a cipher— that he had never felt a real emotion in his life, but had learned his whole life to fake it, which was why he was such a good actor. Isobel watched her Aunt Annie, paying attention to the way her body shifted, the way she was unable to settle into one position. Occasionally she turned her gaze on Lizzie to see if she'd softened her posture or opened her face. She did this as Aunt Annie explained the past.

"This place was different when I was growing up. Grandma Mellie was angry. She'd been angry her whole life—trying to make up for the mistake she made in marrying my father. I know I should have told you about that before too, but now that you know what sort of house I grew up in and what people knew about us, you can understand why I kept Jim from you. It wasn't the sort of place you wanted to be. I'd made plans my whole life to get out, but then life came and I didn't leave. I got a job clerking down at the courthouse and it was a good job. The sort where I'd meet the kind of men who had the ability to get me out of that house with my mother. I know you don't want to hear this part, but I think it is important. You need to know how sheltered I was, how, when I decided to go to Boston with Mr. Lauderbach, I might have been twenty-four, but I felt like I was just out of high school.

"Lauderbach was a young attorney and he ended up marrying a girl he'd met in college whose father owned a small practice in Boston. They specialized in probate. He'd told me to write him if I ever wanted to leave Memphis. And I did.

"He wrote back to me to ask if I wanted to spend the summer as a nanny. His wife had just had her second child and needed help looking after the two-year-old. Something had gone wrong with the birth and she'd need to be in recovery all summer. I didn't even tell my mother I was leaving. I wrote him back that I'd be on the next bus up there and to let me know the exact address. He was nice. I think he'd wanted a Southerner to lessen how foreign everything was up there. He had me cook for him too. Nothing special, but cornbread to go with dinner or pimento cheese sandwiches. I taught his wife how to do that when she was feeling better at the end of the summer.

"They were good to me. I had Sundays and Mondays off and mostly I spent them walking around the city. Some people thought I was crazy because it was so hot that summer, but you know how after you live in Memphis, nothing seems hot. I met your father when I was walking around. I'd broken the heel off my wedge and he rescued me. Took me to a shoe shop in the building where he worked. He told me he was in college and I said that I was also, too afraid to admit the truth. After that, we met on my days off and talked about everything except ourselves—I mean the part about who we were and where we were from. I guess now that it was because we were both lying that we didn't talk about it. At the time it felt romantic, like we had so much in common that we didn't need to discuss the boring stuff. It also felt impermanent, meaning I knew it wouldn't last and that I could be my true self with him and also the person I wanted to be."

Aunt Annie swallowed hard at this point in the story. Isobel watched her trying to work up to the part about getting pregnant. She appeared to make peace with the idea and her face softened. She finally settled into one pose, with one leg drawn up underneath her, her elbows on the table, and her head resting on her palms. Glancing at Lizzie, she saw that the story was having the opposite effect. If possible, she looked stiffer and angrier—her hands balled into fists that swung back and forth hitting her own legs.

Lizzie curled up her lips. "So you didn't know. That's the reason for all this deception? That you didn't know how old he was?"

"She didn't say that," Elyse said in her measured voice.

Aunt Annie smiled. "It's okay. She's jumping ahead a bit in the story. No, I did know, or rather I found out and I told myself it didn't matter. The relationship had become physical by then and like I'd said before, I wasn't about to let go of spending time with someone who I trusted enough to be my true self. The summer ended and I went home, not expecting to hear from Jim again, but for the first time in my life making real plans to leave Memphis, to leave my mother. I'd planned to go to New York and get hired by one of those prestigious nanny services and then make enough money to go to night school to become an accountant.

"Of course, none of that happened. I got home and several weeks later I realized I was pregnant. I didn't tell your father. I went back to work at the courthouse and Grandma Mellie took care of you. It turned out she was a terrific grandmother. In all the ways she'd failed me as a mother, she succeeded with you. After your father graduated from college, he tracked me down, but I was dating someone—a man I thought I'd end up marrying—and I didn't ever call your father back. He tried again a few years later, this time showing up at Spite House and having coffee with Mellie until you

returned home from school and I returned from work.
I was engaged at the time to the other man, but the
moment I saw your father and you sitting together, I
knew I'd have to marry him."

"That doesn't explain why you lied to me all these
years about who my father was."

Isobel watched as her aunt got wordlessly up from
the table and called up the stairs to her husband. "This
is the part I need your father to explain to you." She
settled herself back at the table and they waited. She
looked at the floor. "It's such a pretty tile. I wonder
why my mother ever covered it up."

Lizzie's father entered the kitchen with red eyes and
a handkerchief clutched in his hand. Isobel remembered Uncle Jim as having laughing eyes, the sort of
crinkled, good-natured look that made you want to tell
the man a joke to see him laugh. She'd never seen him
as old, but in the kitchen, with his back hunched, he
might as well have been seventy as fifty. Annie looked
more alive than he did at that moment. He exchanged
a wordless look with her that appeared to convey the
entirety of the conversation they'd had with their
daughter.

Lizzie stood. "Whatever you have to say, I'm not
sure it'll be worth my time."

"Let him say it," Elyse said. "He's your father."

"What is it they say about the sins of the fathers?" he asked. "I didn't want them to be yours. At the time it felt like nothing to keep it from you. I thought we could have the best of both worlds—that I could be your stepfather and never have to worry about your real father because I was that too. And I loved your mother so much that I couldn't see making her less in your eyes. Anyway, we figured that to tell you and to admit to those around us what had happened would change how everyone looked at you."

"Not just me," Lizzie said. "You—both of you would be exposed."

He hung his head and scuffed at the floor with the toe of his shoe. "We've tried to make it up, be the sort of people who make the world a better place."

"You did that out of guilt. All of it—joining that church, serving the mission, all your good deeds weren't done out of goodness, but out of obligation," Lizzie took a step toward her mother. "Did you think you were forgiven when they dunked you under the water?"

"Lizzie, it wasn't like that," her mother said. "How could any of it be like that? It was the best we could do at the time."

"And when I asked, kept asking, why didn't you find a way to tell me?"

Lizzie's father coughed. "You were right. It was more about us than about you. But once we'd made the decision, there never seemed to be a way out of it."

"I saw what my mother went through having married her uncle, and I didn't want to be that person known for the one sin I'd committed at the very beginning of my being an adult. My mother only got over it when I had you. With you, she was someone other than a sinner, a freak, and I wanted that. I kept telling myself that if we waited until you had your own family, it wouldn't matter."

"But I needed a father," Lizzie said. She was inches from her mother's face. "I needed a dad more than you needed to forget what you'd done."

"I'm here," Lizzie's father said. "I've been here ever since I knew you existed. Can't that be enough?"

"You want too much from us," Lizzie's mother said.

Lizzie drew back her hand and slapped her mother across the face. The echo of the sound silenced the entire house. Her father stepped in between them. "We were wrong," he said. "We're probably still doing it all wrong."

"I want you to have the house." Her mother rubbed at her cheek, where an imprint of Lizzie's hand had started to form. "After Drew called us to let us know what had happened, I realized that this house no longer belonged to me. I called a few people and found a nice place to rent starting next month out east with a big yard for the kids and closer to your father's work."

"I did all of this for you," Lizzie said.

"I know." Jim ran his hands along the countertop. "You thought you needed to make up for something. I can't even imagine for what—"

"For failing," Lizzie said.

"Oh, honey," Lizzie's mom reached out and wrapped her arms around her daughter. Isobel didn't even realize she was crying until Elyse handed her a napkin. "You're the best of us. Even in failure you can't lose."

"I don't want the house," Lizzie said between sobs. She pushed her mother away. "I want a normal family."

"Then sell it," her father said. "Use the money and start over. Make the family you want."

Isobel moved to her cousin's side. Elyse joined her, patting her back and making soothing noises over Lizzie's sobbing. "If you two want to fix this, you're going to have to come clean to everyone. Own up to what you've done then and now."

Her father nodded. "I'm not afraid anymore."

Lizzie's mother stood up. "I'm putting the house in your name. When we move into the new house next month, it'll be yours to do with what you want."

Isobel sent Elyse to the car with Lizzie and then she hugged her aunt and uncle. "There's no way to fix this right now. You need time. And you have to know that if she doesn't want to fix this with you, then that has to be okay."

"Someone should tell your mother the same thing," Aunt Annie said.

New Year's Eve was unusually warm. Isobel shucked off her jacket and stretched out on the blanket they'd laid on the bluff in the backyard of Spite House. Tom hooked his leg over hers and touched his head to hers. Behind them, she listened to the noises of Lizzie's younger siblings as they ran through the house, gathering stray belongings in anticipation of the move to their larger and more suburban home the next day. Elyse stepped out of the kitchen and walked over to them.

"Ollie, ollie oxen free," she said before joining them on the blanket.

"Are we base?" Tom asked. "I don't know, but I'm tired of running."

"She coming out?" Isobel asked.

"I think so," Elyse grabbed for Isobel's mink muff and shoved her hands in it. "T. J. told me he was going to pop the question out here."

"Is she going to be okay?" Isobel asked.

Tom pulled Isobel on top of him and put his hands in her back pockets. "I think she'll be fine. You girls are like those weighted punching bags—always bouncing back up."

"I wouldn't say that," Elyse said—ducking a mock punch from Tom.

"That's true enough," Tom said, and said more, but Isobel didn't hear any of it over the fireworks that lit up the sky.

Lizzie stepped outside. "Hurry up," she called to those still inside the house.

Isobel watched the explosions, thinking how much they all had to look forward to. Elyse would leave tomorrow for Boston. Her father had recently retired and had pushed her to come home. If she had to guess, she thought that he'd help her find what she wanted. She might have to put in a few more years tending bar, but she'd find her way to her dream. Isobel and Tom were flying to Missouri the next week to start filming an episode of her new show. The homeowners lived in a converted grain silo and had a list of repairs taller than the structure itself. And Lizzie. She looked behind her. Right then, T. J. was kneeling down asking her to marry him.

Behind them, Rosa May and her family clapped. The joy on their faces was brighter than the explosions of light in the sky. Aunt Annie and Uncle Jim stood back a ways, smiling but careful not to get too close. There was no way to fix everything, but they'd started and the love that existed between them gave Isobel hope. In her mind's eye, Isobel saw a long and happy life for her cousin. One where she coached teams to victory and had the children she needed to heal the damage done by her family.

She looked then at the house—with its imposing wall of glass and saw the best of themselves reflected in it. Despite everything, Spite House had saved them all.

Acknowledgments

Spite House—with its narrow façade and breathtaking view—has been in my imagination as long as I can remember. About ten years ago, I used it as the setting for the first story I wrote after deciding to stop talking about writing and write. And although that story lost its luster quickly, the house remained a glimmering Valhalla and my fingers itched to find the characters who could call Spite House home. Although this book didn't come as easy as the first, in the end I got it right thanks to the people in my life.

Carrie Feron is a brilliant editor. She trusts the writing process enough to ask questions instead of giving answers. Because of her experience and exceptional intuition, those questions were always exactly what I needed to get me to the point where

I could make the story in my head match the one on the page.

I feel so lucky to have landed at William Morrow. They believe in authors like children believe in the Tooth Fairy. Thank you to my tremendous publicity team (Ben Bruton is a genius); and a special thanks to Tessa Woodward, who has moved on to better and brighter, but left me with Nicole Fischer, who knows the answers to questions I forget to ask.

There are not words enough to express my gratitude that Alexandra Machinist exists in the world and is excellent in all the ways I will never be. Your world is beautiful and strange, and I'm glad you are so skilled at being in it. And if there's someone I want to grow up to be, it is Stephanie Koven. Thank you.

Deepest thanks to Leslie Graff, Patti Meredith, David Williams, and Lindsey George, who read a very early draft of this novel and helped me to find ways to make it better. My writing group remains ever stalwart and ever needed.

Finally, thank you to my husband, who tells me every day that I'm his favorite person in the world. He is more than that to me. He is my only person in this world. And to my children, who in the end everything is for.

HARPER LUXE

THE NEW LUXURY IN READING

We hope you enjoyed reading
our new, comfortable print size and found it
an experience you would like to repeat.

Well — you're in luck!

HarperLuxe offers the finest in fiction and
nonfiction books in this same larger print size and
paperback format. Light and easy to read, HarperLuxe
paperbacks are for book lovers who want to see
what they are reading without the strain.

For a full listing of titles and
new releases to come, please visit our website:

www.HarperLuxe.com